HARKAITZ CANO

TWIST

Translated from Basque by Amaia Gabantxo

archipelago books

5|18

Title: Twist / by Harkaitz Cano ; translated from Basque by Amaia Gabantxo.
Description: First Archipelago Books edition. | New York : Archipelago Books, 2018.
Identifiers: LCCN 2017055991| ISBN 9780914671831 (pbk.)
Subjects: LCSH: Basques--Fiction. | Friendship--Fiction. | GSAFD: Political fiction
Classification: LCC PH5339.C36 T9513 2018 | DDC 899/.923--dc23
LC record available at https://lccn.loc.gov/2017055991

Archipelago Books
232 Third Street, Suite A111
Brooklyn, NY 11215
www.archipelagobooks.org

Distributed by Penguin Random House
www.penguinrandomhouse.com

Cover Art: *Female Artiste*, Joseph Beuys, 1950/1951

This book was made possible by the New York State Council on the Arts
with the support of Governor Andrew M. Cuomo
and the New York State Legislature.

Archipelago Books also gratefully acknowledges the generous support of
the Etxepare Basque Institute, the Lannan Foundation,
the National Endowment for the Arts,
and the New York City Department of Cultural Affairs.

PRINTED IN THE UNITED STATES OF AMERICA

TWIST

Death keeps me awake.
　　　　　　　—Joseph Beuys

CAMBALACHE, 1983

IT'S NIGHT OUTSIDE, or at least it ought to be.

In the bowels of the earth it's always night; the mole's hour in the mole's dominion. Do underground dwellers care about daylight? Not much. You've been one with the earth for a while, and at first you thought it best not to move at all. Aren't your bowels and the earth's one and the same? A telluric voice speaks: abandon your bones now and forever, who the hell cares. Aren't bones drumsticks for percussionists, flutes for flutists? Are you really that attached to those humeri, those tibiae, which at this point would hardly even rattle a kettledrum? Is there anything better than a cozy lie-down? Thousands of worried insomniacs would agree: the best hours are the hours of sleep. But all these years of stillness cannot possibly be good. You'd like to dance with those stiffened extremities, awaken the tips of your fingers and toes. "If only I could free my fingers from their restraints and click them together again!" You feel that instead of plumping your cheeks, the cement dentists use for their prostheses cakes your face; besides, it's hard to open your eyes, "the guy who embalmed me wasn't exactly a pro," and a white dust drier than the soil itself has taken over a section of your brain: memory loss, magnesium, limescale.

How long does it take for a body to decompose? Six, eight, ten years? Forensic anthropologists say it depends on humidity. Wanna try? Kill a cat and leave it on a chilly window ledge, see what happens.

Can't remember a thing. Your head is so white, as if they'd whitewashed you into a tabula rasa. But the brainwashing has not been thoroughly successful. There is a tiny light at the end of the tunnel; take that ignited thread between your fingers and pull at the yarn one tug at a time, careful not to break that tenuous thread, so fine and brittle. You remember a little something, yes: you are capable of building sentences, linking words. You are syntax. Pure grammar. An amalgam of words without identity. You will soon recover your memory. This is only a big bout of amnesia, you must have hit your head, surely, rouse yourself, shake off the listless drone of the newly awake, the savage pain of a tequila hangover, tequila or whatever it was, that distilled poison you used to drink twenty-odd years ago. No, you know it already: this won't be easy, it'll be nothing like getting up from a meadow, brushing off blades of grass and whistling "Xarmengarria zira" down the winding path.

It is going to be quite difficult to get out.

What is out there? Is anyone waiting for you? Sprigs of lavender, tubby pine trees, heather everywhere, baby fig trees too young to bear fruit, trees beaten down by the merciless sun and curled into themselves right next to the cromlechs, as if regretful of their own birth, trees punished to provide their own shade; barren berryless bushes, brambles, a eucalyptus perhaps, fir trees. And the rest, a desert. By the sea, the earth smells stronger. It's sweltering and the lack of drinking water weighs more heavily on the tongue than the consolation the sea breeze seagulls bring. Patchworks of tar on a provincial road. The scent of fennel and sage sprouting on the roadside; sand and aniseed. Rosemary needles are there too, ready to prickle the fingers of those who approach. Although it doesn't come from the sea, the air is in turmoil – a south wind instead of the northern *tramontana* – and blows the dust upward. Look at the insomniac lizards, so still, stuck to the rocks like fridge magnets: hands up. This is not too different from the Mexican desert. Although the heat isn't quite as scorching here, of course. The cacti are not so prominent either, they are smaller and more scarce.

Mexico? Tequila? Why the sudden mention of things on the other side of the ocean, *güerito? No mames, guey*! You've never been to Latin America, and never will! Memory's traffic signals, no doubt. This narrator is looking for himself: a clue that will reveal whether I should address you formally or informally. I've been such a bastard to you. I wasn't always good to you; you would hate me if you were alive. Reader, pay attention to even the most random details my mind leaves for you. The shattered remains of a broken bottle, the smell of last night's burnt wood in the air, soothing hippie songs strummed on an old guitar in bygone scout camps, brotherhood songs, *"zergaitik galdu itxaropena berriz ikusteko, zergaitik galdu itxaropena berriz ikusteko,"* people celebrating impossible future encounters; they're so short-lived and dim ever so quickly, those eternal two-weeks-of-summer friendships. Go, go on: long tall green blades of grass, rare shiny-leaf mint, the smell of alcohol or tar, something not quite as obvious as petrol, not as profoundly nausea inducing. A polluted sea is more bearable than the smell of diesel on the road. The wind blows the dust upward again, there is no one there. That's it, that's it: you were wearing a Mexico World Cup T-shirt. That's what it was! You've never been to Mexico, but you were wearing a Mexico World Cup T-shirt and in handcuffs, your feet dragging, your ankles bound together (bound together again? Yes: bound once, twice, three times, bound four times, tightly bound, very bound, bound in such a way that your ankles still hurt twenty years later, bound in such a way that if you told anyone what happened to you, they would feel the tight bind in their ankles too). As they dragged you through the brambles maybe you thought of the advantages of peyote. *If I were on a roller-coaster ride, or on an acid trip, if only all this were a lie!* No, I don't think so...It doesn't look like you were alive when they brought you here. Or maybe you were? Did they shoot you in the head right here? Were you dead when they brought you, a corpse already, eyelids closed? Those who brought you here, then, did they no longer need the handcuffs? Let's imagine that it was so, that it happened like that: that they brought you here without handcuffs. Or maybe they brought you alive but wearing blindfolds, mouth gags, wrists bound together with torn-up sheets. Your executioners were cruel and intelligent. To take cruelty beyond a certain point, to give the screw another turn, requires intelligence; and whether we like it or not that's a fact the Devil knows only too well.

Can we hear the waves of the sea from here? No. The sea is pretty close, but not close enough; the Mediterranean Sea is a quiet receptacle today. Don't fool yourselves: the sea is a hallucination, nothing else, for the dead.

Brambles and a clearing. And more brambles that have nothing better to do than bore us and test our patience. There is sand in the clearing and this encourages one to entertain the fantasy of walking barefoot, however soon thereafter stones appear, gravel and not-quite gravel, tiny and not-quite-so-tiny rocks. At the point where the path fades. These are not bushes like ours in the Cantabrian shores – they're sparser, their green not as lush; a green dusted with a matte white sheen like the opposite of mint leaves; *there*, *there*, and *there*, dry upright brambles like whips, old boundary walls made of flat piled-up stones; the men arrive sure-footed, their eagerness for a swift finish hiding their nerves. Maybe one of them is familiar with the place. He carried out a dirty job here before. What dirty job, impossible to know. Alone or with someone's help. Are we far from the road? One kilometer away? A kilometer and a half? Just half a kilometer? There is no need to go so far either, three steps off the road take you far away from people's usual paths and habits. Most often two steps are enough to remove oneself from the more commonly traveled road. One single step suffices to fall off a cliff.

Because it's nighttime. It ought to be nighttime and it is. The road is not a main road. *This motherfucker doesn't deserve that we hide him well, someone thinks. Mangy dog, we should hang you from a streetlight as a warning to others like you, we should leave you on the roadside like a rat, burst belly up, just like you did with Trota, we should run you into a ditch and explode you; hopefully some carsick German tourists will find you with flies around your mouth.*

But the question here is not what you deserve.

This has nothing to do with what you deserve, *but with what they want to hide.* A good airtight alibi, the certainty that no one can be touched, that they're safe, even twenty years down the line, their hands and their records clean. Safe. While they prescribe law and punishment and memory. *We went too far.* They went too far and they still haven't come back. Too far. Where?

Here.

Maybe they came here by car, maybe they carried you on their shoulders; bitter paradox, to think of those mendacious souls carrying you on their shoulders, *bidean anaia erortzen bazaik, lepoan hartu ta segi aurrera, tralala,* like in the song. But who is mendacious, who does mendacity belong to? You might understand them, you should understand them, be able to inhabit their skin.

If you were in their skin, you would be the same, the same as them and their circumstances. "I am I and my circumstance; if I do not save it, I do not save myself." The second part of that sentence by the famous philosopher is often forgotten, who knows why. But no one inhabits anyone else's skin anymore, do they? It's hard enough to withstand our own skin, why would we think of inhabiting another's. The difference is that now you're in your own bones, and not in your own skin.

The trunk opens with a bang. Could be a van. An eighties van, an Ebro with a dodgy suspension and, due to its worn-out rubber, squeaky and ineffective windshield wipers that set your teeth on edge. The vehicle staggers where dust meets sand. The corpse in the trunk moves; under the flashlight, a lifeless head with a deep cut above the eyebrow. Soon they cover you with a maroon blanket, a second skin.

"Yes, I realize that perfectly. I am resisting temptation for now and addressing you directly, I don't know why, it's what comes naturally to me when I speak to the dead."

The dead; they are many and always grateful for a bit of entertainment.

Here. These are the eighties. In the Spanish State, two out of every ten people of working age are unemployed, according to official data of course; the Swedish tennis player Björn Borg retires this year, Martina Navratilova wins Flushing Meadows; at the Vostok base in Antarctica temperatures reach below negative

128° Fahrenheit, the lowest ever recorded on earth; it's been six years since Elvis Presley's death, that's someone else who ought to wake up one day; in the Bellvitge Hospital, in Barcelona, they perform the first-ever liver transplant in the Spanish State, it's not all slaughter when scalpel slices skin; on March 8, and coinciding with International Women's Day, Ronald Reagan declares the Soviet Union "an evil empire"; on September 1 Soviet hunter planes shoot down a South Korean commercial flight due to an unfortunate mistake, and unfortunately 269 unfortunate souls die. It is the year of Tennessee Williams's death, Desire is the name of a neighborhood in New Orleans. Some have actually made up for their ancestors' bad actions; rather late, it's true, but something is better than nothing – don't lose hope, contemporary witches, burning already thanks to the New Inquisition: resist! Today is May 9 and John Paul II, the pope who kneels down and kisses the ground wherever he goes, the same one who was almost killed by the Turkish hit man Mehmet Ali Agca on the KGB and the Bulgarian Secret Service's orders two years ago, pardoned Galileo Galilei; things in palazzis, as you know, move piano-piano, but eventually *lontano. Aspaldian espero zaitudalako ez nago sekula bakarrik,* I've been waiting for you for so long I'm never alone: could be a line by Galileo, but it is also the title of Arantxa Urretabizkaia's book, published that year; Margaret Thatcher wins the election in Great Britain, and, man, was it a home run; six years have passed since they last used the guillotine on someone, and only two since the Élysée Palace abolished the guillotine (*la mort de la mort*), even though sixty-two percent of the French were against it, even though sixty-one percent of French people disagreed with François Mitterrand celebrating his victory by releasing five thousand prisoners, even though and despite the fact that, therefore and otherwise, politicians are still leaders and charisma is more powerful than surveys.

In this year, 1983, Michael Jackson's extremely successful *Thriller* album comes out; also Imanol's *Iratze okre geldiak*; Anjel Lertxundi publishes *Hamaseigarrena, Aidanez*, Madonna sings "Holiday" flashing her belly button; the actor Christopher Reeve films the third Superman movie: this time he will turn evil and, later on, of course, return to being good again; a year ago Felipe González reached power under the motto "Por el Cambio" (For Change), and he said only one word in the campaign advert: "Adelante" (Onward). Three years ago now Sandinistas assassinated Somoza, Nicaragua's exiled dictator; it happened on Avenida Francisco Franco, in Asunción, Paraguay: the body was burned to a cinder, but the engine of his Mercedes car kept running, "You can always trust a German car."

The RDA is not a joke or a theme park, it'll be six years before the Berlin Wall falls, only one before the disciplined and hormone-pumped Romanian athletes win a bucketful of medals at the Olympic Games in Los Angeles, and the same again before we meet Carl Lewis, "the Son of the Wind." The franchise business, and the security guards that come with it, have not yet arrived; the only security guards we know come in armored cars and ooze a certain film noir glamour, and not the sadness of the *mileurista* wages twenty-five years hence. Children know pizza only from movies; photocopies are an almost unthinkable luxury, it's not so easy to copy things and multiply them, not easy, not so easy at all, they still use duplicators, and the toxins in the ink are more intense; we write using typewriters, and when we do so we put carbon paper under every sheet, to keep thin carbon copies of the most important documents, damn carbon paper, blessed carbon paper; even though he has already written it, we still haven't read Borges's assertion that mirrors and copulation are abominable, or Benedetti's that the original sin isn't that grave, but photocopies are; wooden windows reign, we still don't know PVC or double glazing, titanium is science fiction, in the popular mind, stainless steel is still the most prestigious alloy, in the ovens of foundries they use asbestos as if it were cake mix; you have to stick your finger in a hole to dial a phone number, the most sophisticated computer in most houses is a calculator that extracts square roots; *marketing* is too modern a word, shop windows are but dark soviet warehouses in which stock piles up, you need to cross the *muga* and enter French territory to see a proper shop window, a luminous, elegant display case, tastefully arranged, like in Galeries Lafayette and others like it (don't forget your passport); on the French Basque Country, on the other side, supermarkets look like jewelers to us, because Europe still bleeds bile through its frontiers and barbed-wire fences. Because contraband is still something more than a scream against all sides, it's still an existing occupation, and carries the risk of imprisonment.

The men who have brought you to this place so close to the Mediterranean and private hunting lodges haven't suffered the demand, necessity, and mandate of English-language academies in order to get a job. Their lack of knowledge is such they don't even know what *X marks the spot* means, they don't subtitle movies in our – our? – country, instead, we have a magnificent army of erasers – they call them dubbing actors – who will vanquish anyone's words with their fairground-charlatan voices; policemen educated on the language of metal in gray academies would find it difficult to imagine the myriad colors in shop windows and the gigantic suburban malls of the nineties; the railway gauge is different here and, even though the belief is widespread, it's a lie that the Caudillo, dead eight years ago now, decided it, although it was obviously to his advantage. Why? So that in case of war foreign trains full of foreign weapons and foreign preserves with foreign labels and foreign ideas and foreign Dannon yogurts from those bright-lit supermarkets that look like jewelers don't reach the heart of his sweet little dictatorship beyond the French frontier. Those rushing men who kick up sand with their boots are the obedient servants of an outmoded institution in an outmoded country, musketeers of a state that in two years will join

NATO, in three will enter the European Union; they wanted to be swordsmen but they were born too late, such a pity, *quel dommage*; they work night shifts, twelve hours, sometimes they go too far, it's understandable – they should tie a fishing line to a thumb to reel themselves in, to not veer too far. They come from a dictatorship and its rules. Rules or entrails, one and the same. They are going to bury him. In the hole. *There, there*, and *there*. Only they know where. In the entrails of the earth.

"They look pitiful, we can't leave them like that: make them disappear."

"The fewer people who know about this, the better."

Even brambles have eyes. Three people can keep a secret if two of them are dead. But let's not lose track. Where were we?

Here. *X marks the spot.* They start to dig as if searching for treasure. No, I lie, they start to dig as if they know they *won't* find any treasure. There are two of them, maybe three. They're dressed normally – *plainclothes* – and it's not easy to discern who ranks higher. The man who seems to be in charge does nothing but bark orders. They do what they do without thinking much about what they're doing. Mechanically, but with the added stress of the shiver that might run up your spine when a dead man stares at the back of your neck. It's the fear. It's the rush. It's the unease. The eyes of a corpse on the back of your neck. Even if the dead is well and truly dead, even if he is covered by a maroon blanket like a second skin, even if you can't see his eyes. Even if they can't see your eyes. There is no moon, thank God. It's a balmy night, you can hear crickets and cicadas when the sound of shovels stops, when they stop digging into that neutral, cracked earth, covered in dust and dryness. They are armed Adams: apparently Adam was the first to dig holes in his garden, that's why they say that if a shovel can be said to be a weapon, Adam perhaps was the first armed man. The fact is, there is no great difference between a gardener and a grave digger: both are Adam's successors, both are armed beings. The obedient man's back starts to get sweaty as he digs and digs, as he figures out the center of something every time the metallic tip pierces the earth, strike with thy rod as you pray to thy God: *let there please not be rocks just here, for goodness' sake*. But, who is he praying to? To the night, he keeps praying to the night and to nocturnal beings.

It's cold, their teeth are sweating.

The steam comes in and out of their mouths quickly. White in the night. Threads in the dark. Smoke in the shadows.

It's a starry night, but they are not looking for stars.

The first job is to dig the hole. An appropriate hole. One that can *host*. One in which you fit to lie down to sleep. Or with bent knees, no need to overdo it. Besides, dusk shrinks us all somewhat, we are all one centimeter shorter at night, when we go to bed. Let the humility that night awards us help us make a smaller grave, so that the holes are lesser. And it is night, it ought to be night. A quick calculation, "We'd better not fall short, keep digging." Now the obedient minions feel the weight of senseless work: "This motherfucker is making us sweat more than that fatso Mariluz." A harlot known by all, apparently, that Mariluz. And the younger of the obedient men, Hernández, even though he doesn't know her, laughs shamelessly so the others won't think him queer. Adam's heir starts off letting out a few loud cackles to make sure no one takes him for a faggot, who knows what crime he'll end up committing. And there, right there, goes Hernández's gardening vocation, if our armed friend ever had one.

Do ghosts prefer southerly winds? Are Mediterranean ghosts calmer? They say that in Northern Europe ghosts are loud, horrifying, that their shrieks are more out of tune because of the cold. With Northern ghosts – Irish, Estonian, German, it's easy to imagine them coming at you with a knife and no explanation. Mediterranean ghosts, however, are not as gloomy, it's impossible to take them too seriously; even when they kill you, they do it in an incompetent way; Don Juan Tenorio and others like him are laughable, buffoonish, and sometimes it's their own comedic candor that makes them all the more fearful; we'd risk our necks to bet that they'd rather dance to a tambourine than use a knife; Mediterranean ghosts sound like they'd be fun to have a few glasses of wine with. "Ghosts fervid for Frescuelo and María." Is there a really frightening and serious ghost in Spanish literature? And in the Basque Country? Who are they? What are Basque ghosts like?

Here?

"The hole is ready, boss."

"Keep digging."

Twentieth century. Look. Halogen? What is that? Window light is either blue or yellowish, and lightbulbs burn out and you replace them and that's that. How many elevatorless homes. Or rather, how many houses with narrow, single-door elevators. And our mother's fears every time we climbed one: don't get too close, she'd say, someone down the street had his arm amputated because it got trapped in the door as the elevator ascended. You can lose a hand, it might go too far and you may never get it back. Pedestrian area? What is that? Twentieth century. It trapped us, it did, the century, like mousetraps snare rodents: alive and inescapably. And just like the mouse in the mousetrap watches time pass, so we watch the twenty-first century, while the trap keeps us stuck in the twentieth. And it's going to take a while.

Cambalache, siglo veinte.

"Keep digging."

"But, isn't this enough?"

"Keep digging, damn it! It needs to fit two!"

Did they bring you wrapped in a brown blanket by any chance? It's a maroonish color, there's no doubt about it. Your blood coagulated such a long time ago, not a drop flows from you, other than the liquid that oozes from a solid, curdled scar. Like San Gennaro's effigy in Naples, another Mediterranean saint or ghost, he cries tears of blood every so often too, that's what devout Neapolitan Catholics claim at least. But no crimson tears emanate from your body. You don't have a drop of life left in you. You are not there anymore. Not there. And neither *there*, nor *there*, nor *there*. Your family, however, would like to know where you are. *X marks the spot*. Many years will pass before they do, and your relatives will age as every wrinkle in their faces marks their anguish and their unknowing. The smell of fennel and heather and lavender shall remain, the tourists and the main roads will come closer, and the roads will get wider, and urban areas will sprawl, and there'll be roundabouts. What were capillary veins are now main arteries and easy to prick: some say that roads are a means of getting the organs to communicate, something we didn't have in the eighties... In the eighties the bull's tail and the bull's liver and the bull's stomach and the bull's heart and the bull's eyes and the bull's intestines only communicated through zigzagging capillaries, circulation was bad; each organ, each population, functioned independently; cars: two-tone Deux Chevaux (black and dark red) and (white) SEAT 600 and (cider-bottle colored) Minis and Citroën Dyan 6. In the eighties in radio programs the morning hosts greeted their listeners differently: "Sunny day all over the bull's hide today, *queridos* listeners." The *queridos y queridas* shtick came much later: back then *la querida* was someone bourgeois adulterers would install in an apartment.

Cambalache, siglo veinte.

As the years pass, nights will not be quite as dark anymore, in the nineties here and there you'll see fluorescent lights in industrial naves of varying degrees of sophistication; judges and democratic forensic experts will turn up with their just-washed faces to dig you out of the grave with great technique and sumptuous professionalism, with Virginia instead of dark tobacco cigarettes in their pockets, or maybe not even that, just the tyranny of nicotine patches. "We know how to do this, don't get in the way and let the professionals do their work." They know how to pour salt on your wound with latex gloves. It is even possible that some of them are the same ghosts who buried you back in the day, *volver, volver, y las nieves del tiempo blanquearon mi sien*, that tango about returning "with the snow of time on your temples" (yours don't need whitening, seeing as how they're full of limescale). But let's not get ahead of the wheel of time, *oh what will be, will be*, it will be years before any of that, none of us is as pompous a narrator as to claim omniscience, or absolute ownership of that wheel.

For the time being AIDS is a new thing in Europe, in the United States they have started to whisper about it, and this year the European Parliament Commission formulated the first vague demand for research into the subject. When he bends down, one of the obedient men pricks a finger with a rosemary bush, he hasn't been tested. We are in the twentieth century, stuck in the mousetrap with our vigilant mouse eyes; we live in the eighties, who hasn't lost a friend to heroin; perhaps a few years from now the HIV virus will catch up with the obedient man, on his free night, after a sad fuck in a roadside brothel on the way to Miranda de Ebro, with a heroin addict prostitute born in Chueca – who knows, maybe it was Mariluz, oh light of my life! – he will die in eighteen months, suddenly, as if hit by lightning, with wrists like narrow emaciated chicken claws, "Hell, it's so seldom I get it into a hot, wet pussy, no fucking way I'm covering my cock." We wouldn't like to be in his skin. He wouldn't want to be either, if he knew every nook and cranny of it, but sometimes it is good for survival to put a second skin on your cock, just like it is also beneficial to protect our bodies with borrowed skin to avoid a descent into madness.

Who would want to be in their own skin if they knew themselves inside out, down to the last corner?

But this is something only an omniscient narrator can know and do, and who wants to inhabit the skin of such a know-it-all? To each his own. It's not good to know everything either.

Vargas and Hernández open the door of the car, van, vehicle, and unfold the blanket without even thinking that that big item of bed linen they're unfolding could very well be the bull's hide, *queridos* listeners. *Bueno, bonito, barato, Paisa.* Good, beautiful, cheap. There are still few immigrants selling wares out of their blankets in Spain, the North Africans and Sub-Saharans prefer France; to tell the truth, the Basque language still hasn't come up with the neologism *etorkin* to refer to the few immigrants who do sell watches and trinkets; we think they are a minority, that they are exotic, we are so naïve, singing songs like "Ze hurrun dago Kamerun," Cameroon is so far away, and so far away too is the need to retell experiences in real time. Although during the floods of '83 and due to the bursting riverbanks many births come early, the true wave, the African wave, is still to arrive: no one has heard the words *patera* or *cayuco* in relation to dinghies overflowing with immigrants. The enemy is at home and, in summer, it is still the gypsies who sell watermelons by the roadsides. Moroccans criss-cross the bull's hide in endless lines during the summer vacations, stopping in *Hispania Una, Grande y Libre* (Franco dixit) just long enough to pee and tiptoe around, as uninterested in the harsh surface of Castilla as the wheels of their old Citroën, Peugeot, or Renault with tottering piles of junk on their roof racks are in the asphalt. "Who are these people, Mom?" "Moroccans." "Where are they going?" "Home." "What are the Moroccans carrying on top of their cars?" "Televisions, rugs, radios, furniture, blankets."

"No, the blanket must disappear too. We can't leave anything behind. Not even the smallest thing."

When they throw your corpse in the pit, your bones crack, collecting earth, dust, sand.

That's when the second vehicle arrives. The driver is not as dexterous: unconcerned about avoiding the brambles, he drives straight through them to reach the hole lit up by the headlights of the first vehicle. The headlights illuminate a rustic swimming pool filled with roots, a little earthly orifice. An empty swimming pool soaked in a cone of spilling yellow light. A tomb, quite a regular one, all things considered, and since digging at night can be complicated. The trapezium is not so crude after all. "Fantastic, fantastic. You've done a great job, guys."

"Big enough for two!"

But, here is the first surprise, just like the femme fatale who must always appear at minute twelve of every Hollywood film, just like the blond chick the script – or the scriptwriter's lack of talent – always demands.

They bring another one in the second vehicle. You feel it as if you were in his skin. He was your friend. Your closest, a brother.

He is on his knees, his eyes covered with scraps of cloth. The first bullet wasn't enough. I'll tell you about the second one quickly, it's too painful. All right, let's pretend I already did.

They'll bury you together, both of you now free of flesh and pain. Soon your bodies will be but ciphered bones. No messages arrive from your undecipherable corpses. You can't say, for example: "It was kind of you to dig so deep, even though this insistence in reaching the crux of the question was purely a selfish impulse; it was so kind of you to bury my friend with me, together forever in an embrace of bones, always close, always brothers, thank you so much, we will never be able to repay, to settle, to cancel this debt. What you've done to us you won't be able to repay, settle, or cancel either: let's say on a Sunday afternoon, when you least expect it, when soccer-fueled radio screams recall other screams. We are at peace. The families – yours and ours – will have to fight the ghosts." The future will have to fight the ghosts. They'll bring dozens of Argentinean psychoanalysts by boat, *Cambalache, siglo veinte, vibrante, bárbaro*, they'll have to fight the silence and the ghosts, vibrant, barbarian, twentieth-century tango-singing ghosts. Your sons and daughters will have to fight the ghosts. Fuck the future and the people of the future, the fucking future, have a blast and break a leg. *Break a leg,* modern policemen will learn to say in English-language academies like Home English. *Mucha mierda*, yes, that's what actors say, *mucha mierda*. Lots of shit. On so many other occasions, some things are much easier said in another language, in another language *y a mí como si te meten un yunque por el culo*, etc. Yeah, shove an anvil up your ass, see if I care, Mariluz. What did you leave us? "What do you mean what did we leave you? You inherited our ghosts. Is that not enough, ingrates?" You can pretend that everything is as it ever was, you can swap neighborhoods, housemates, partners, emotional support and drainage, even cities, but old ghosts will appear when you expect them the least.

"You deserved it, you chose your own fate."

"Live with that, fucker."

"Live with that here."

"Amen."

But the job isn't done. We don't know whose idea the quicklime was. Vargas, Hernández, they call each other by their last names, even though the lieutenant colonel has expressly forbidden them from doing so. Leaves no trace, it's clean, burns through everything. Not even dogs would be able to find them.

Not even dogs.

Afterward the dust and the years can do what needs doing. A blank slate.

"Soto, you don't know what you're going to become yet, do you? Want me to tell you? I don't think you'll like it. Oh yeah, you do? Okay, Soto, you asked for it. Initially and like all martyrs you'll become adrenaline for the people. And later, like all martyrs, you'll become anesthesia for the people. Mentioning formaldehyde is perhaps too cruel, and anyway, in a few short years they'll put the word *people* itself in formaldehyde. Why do I say that? Because the word *people* will lose its meaning, my dear friend, *cher ami, querido amigo*. They'll treat it like an ugly tubercle, yes, don't look so surprised, don't look at me that way... I shouldn't explain too many things to you at once, right? I should shut up... People – I'll use that word for now – get used to things. As I was saying, like all martyrs, at the beginning you'll be the people's adrenaline, and later you'll become the anesthesia of that ugly tubercle called *people*. Adrenaline in the first instance, a symbol of injustice, because you'll be the common thread of many outbursts. Because weddings bring weddings, and funerals, more funerals. Later on, anesthesia, because too many people for too many years will find too many things on your skin. Adrenaline and anesthesia, maybe both at the same time. When people are short of strength, they'll dip their heads into your unknown grave, into your pond, and they'll swim in that bath, that pool of hatred and fervor of yours. 'Well, yes, what our boys did wasn't good, but look at what they did to Soto and Zeberio... have you forgotten? Didn't you love them?' People won't forget, and people won't forgive."

The first door slams shut, then the passenger's. Slam. They switch their flashlights off before getting into the cars. The second car and the obedient men inside of it, both in their behavior and their demeanor, are but a shadow of the first. Everything we do has been done by somebody else before. Wherever you go, someone has been there before.

The obedient men are silent inside the cars. Windows closed, deaf to the crickets and the cicadas. Someone starts to get nervous. Silence is a rat that gnaws at our conscience.

"Christ, someone put the radio on! This is like a funeral!"

Or: "Cigarette, anyone?" Back then people had no qualms about smoking inside cars. Twentieth century, *siglo veinte, cambalache*. That mousetrap. None of them smokes, but they're in no position to reject the cigarettes offered to them, given that they come from Vargas, Hernández, and many others, obedient men here to bury two dead. Three fireflies and smoke, car windows closed. Each engrossed in his thoughts. All dying to wash their hands. Random Freudian thoughts leaping from the transcendental to the quotidian: they are human, of course they are human, too human, they have just left death behind, and one of the policemen's brains demands a glass of Anís del Mono aniseed liquor and a bar of Lagarto soap (lizard, *lagarto*); another counts how many days since he got laid, since he rammed it into something warm (*sin meterla en caliente*); the third one contemplates his son's fever and the slim chances of his wife being awake upon his return, and whether she'd get angry if he woke her and took her from behind, to feel in his skin again, fuck her with her clothes on, push her panties aside and feel the friction of cotton on his cock. Will they wash their hands at the station, or each in his own home? Will they all wash them twice? Take turns? Will they sniff their fingers before they place their hands under the tap? Will they know that they need to sing "Happy Birthday" three times as they wash to get rid of all the bacteria?

"Una mano lava otra mano, dos manos lavan la cara." One hand washes the other; two hands wash the face.

"Los uniformes de diario no se llevan a casa, se lavan en el cuartel, ¿no conoce las reglas?" Regular uniforms are never taken home, they're washed in the station, don't you know the rules?

But they're all in civilian clothes. *De paisano.*

– 32 –

The first car goes away. The second car goes away. Let's envision the following: one of the obedient men, twelve years later, on holiday in Nerja, in the South, in a house with whitewashed walls. The sun burns the whitewash, and the obedient man goes momentarily blind while the comforting thrust of a gulp of brandy like molten lead tells him, never convincingly enough:

"You did what you had to do."

The whitewashed wall will tell him:

"You did what you had to do."

The torturer soon will have domestic concerns of a different ilk: his son's joblessness, his wife's diabetes, a tumor, alternate ways of looking at death, another prism.

"*Order, arms!*"

"*Due obedience. These aren't people, they're scum; diligence, execution, a job like any other, a clean fight against the riffraff.*"

"*Yes, commander.*"

"*Attention!*"

"They look pitiful, we can't leave them like that: make them disappear."

Here.

Thankfully nobody wants this buried treasure. Even those who buried it would have difficulty finding it again. With the rains and the dust of more than twenty years, even the brambles have changed place, *allez hop!* The lion draws circles and leaps, docile, when told to, then takes a few steps to return to the same position. Brambles leap in the same way given enough time, just like desert dunes at night. Fennel, lavender, and rosemary, yes, they're still there. The heather and the sticky sap of pines. Plants are wise, wiser than humans, or at least more patient. Which is not very difficult, really. Some fallen branches imitate the tracks of an anarchic train in an abandoned station. It's the first thing you see. Dry branches that look like the skull of some animal on a circle of stones. Your skull. The first thing you notice when you wipe the dust from your eyes is some femurs and hip bones covered in lime. You have to make a supreme effort not to assume that they belong to a calf. You find it hard to stand up, it's difficult when you don't have heels: the bones are not where they should be, and the wind whistles through your gaps. Since this white doesn't look like the usual bone white, you decide to rearrange them on the ground before you leave, and to blow on them one by one to clean them, blowing away the lime, blowing away the ants that tickle your arms. You recognize a femur, but you're not very good at anatomy and, although you place the tibiae, you have a feeling a rib is missing... Is there maybe a child in Nerja who is using your rib to rattle on his toy drum, pump-a-rum? One rib short, oh well. No big deal: you take one of the spare ones from the other side and reestablish balance, symmetry, which, on the other hand, is not really so important. A dog approaches. It looks at you, dribbling. You throw the spare rib at it: delighted, the dog catches it and scampers away to bury it in some secret place. You smile for the first time.

Deliver thy bone unto the world.

Despite these shortcomings, it seems to you that the lungs could survive inside the rib cage without falling to the ground. You crack your fingers until you produce a god-awful snap – "that's a good start: I've only just stretched out and my first wish has come true" – and put them all back in place. You start to walk, self-sculptor, dragging your feet, trying to imprint yourself with a semblance of what you once were.

The little bones in your hands were in good shape, it wasn't necessary to rearrange the puzzle, thankfully. You take the skull in your hands. It's not even that heavy. "Eyeless skull, do you look anything like me? Something smells rotten: don't worry, heaven will direct it." The Danish ghosts are very far away, like the holed cheeses of Denmark; oh, hang on, those are Swiss. Neutral cheeses with neutral holes.

Are you there?

Are you far?

Are you in the bones?

It's not the same to be in the bones as to be *pure* bone.

You're in your bones again. In your skin. *I wish I had a comb at hand.* You can't help that absurd, frivolous thought.

Perhaps because you're looking for a comb, unconsciously you look at the pit, and what do you see? Certainly not a comb; a broken mirror, a skull that is not yours burned by the quicklime, a jaw that looks dislocated, blackened teeth, a lot of bones out of place, which unlike you are asleep and lifeless. You touch him hoping for a sign, you caress his jaw hoping for a sign: a Braille of life.

"Won't you come with me, Zeberio? Come out, my man! Wake up and let's get going!"

You grab him by the shoulders, wanting to wake him from his long sleep, but his clavicle breaks in two when you shake him, fragile as a thrush's skeleton. When you try to link the joints back, an apple of plaster disintegrates in each one of your hands. You blow the dust away. You understand. He's not coming. He's given up. He doesn't feel like living, taking revenge, laughing. You don't even try to change your friend's mind. Respect is owed to the dead who want to remain dead. Dead and asleep.

You sigh. Life is a solitary job. Death too, apparently.

You leave your friend behind and walk toward the turnoff, missing more than just a rib. Every now and then you look back. You'd like your friend to come with you, but he's not following.

Zeberio is staying in the pit forever: silent Zeberio, discreet Zeberio, crazy Zeberio, brother Zeberio.

It's night outside, or at least it ought to be. You leave behind a sign that says VALLE DE LA ESCOMBRERA 10 KM and stand next to another one that reads LA APARECIDA 4 KM; more than stand, you hang in there, with scarce hope that someone, unafraid of hitchhikers, might stop for you. Who knows, maybe a German family, a group of young hippies in a Volkswagen van packed to the rafters, driven by a hashish-loving woman with long hair and small but beautiful breasts. "Don't they say it's free to ask? Are there any hippies left after all this time? We should be in Europe by now, with all our rights and duties, right?" A shiver runs down your spine: what if you meet up with the people from then, Hernández, Vargas, those armed Adams without gardening vocations? No, some things only happen once in life, once in death. The Devil's rows are not that crooked. It'd be such bad luck to bump into those obedient people after more than twenty years... No, you don't think they'll come back this way. The murderer doesn't return to the scene of the crime. Because they lose the courage they had for an instant. Perhaps because they can't conceive that they once possessed such courage.

Isn't it beautiful to be alive?

But you're not alive exactly: you're dead and awake. It's not the same. You hunger to see how things have changed, you want to see the world the way it is now, different. You want to bump into your friends, all aged. To laugh at their contradictions. It's beautiful to be alive, of course it is, even if only to see how everything's changed and gone to shit, it's beautiful to return to life. Why shouldn't the dead enjoy that privilege? It's not fair.

Certainly, this has nothing to do with what we deserve... You're a bit naïve for a spirit from the beyond. And a bit of naïveté is not too bad, not even for ghosts. It passes with time.

You manage to get rid of the last bit of insulating tape on your mouth. You're thirsty. You could kiss anything, any cold metal, anything but silver, a piece of cloth, only to make sure that your lips are still in place.

You feel dampness in your mouth. "Good. This is me, here are my crooked teeth."

In the far distance you can see the lights of a Shell gas station next to a hostel: Hostel Europa. *Bad sign*, you think, *businesses are always named after what they don't have: Eden Inn, Paradise Supermarket... Hostel Europa? Excusatio non petita... Therefore, we are not in Europe, it's just a nominal matter. Maybe those dubbing actors with fairground-charlatan voices have killed Europe.* Disappointing, particularly for European humanists, if they weren't all dead. Given a choice, you prefer the gas station to the hostel. Shell. You get out of one clam and into another. From pit to pit and then repeat. Along the way you leave a trail that looks like a line of chalk but is quicklime. Like a wolf does with urine, you mark your territory. You trace the lines and the limits of the playing field. An improvised soccer field on the beach. With quicklime. Before, only the quicklime was quick. Now you are too. Quickened. More or less. Dead but alive.

You've a wound, red, on your eyebrow. You take a drop of blood to your lips. You smile. It's a miracle: the Neapolitan Saint Gennaro cries again. The scent of rosemary tickles your nostrils with warm licks. You've returned to yourself, although you don't quite dare to check your pulse, and, rather than turn your thoughts to yourself, you prefer to sharpen your ears, trying to discern the rumor of waves.

Can't discern anything.

Maybe one or two kilometers ahead, who knows. Valle de la Escombrera. La Aparecida. Waves. Waves. Shock waves. It's too soon to give up, you've only started.

No comb then. No sign of your thick glasses. But you see well all the same. Better than ever. And simultaneous to your surprise, you spontaneously decide to smooth down your hair with your hand in a gesture of happy vanity, and consider that courteousness and vanity are not – not at all – the most insignificant features of the living. But an intermittent absence diffuses the presence of your body, and you're not sure if what your fingers touched are your old locks of hair, or just the warm Cartagena air.

There is no doubt: you're in your skin again. And no one is going to deny that. Just like night ought to be night, just like the sea ought to be covered in blue, you ought to be in your skin.

FIRST DIFFUSIONS

IDOIA ERRO HAS BEEN at the receiving end of many jokes because of her green Mini Cooper, which has helped her develop great reflexes: "Your car is civil-guard green"; "Laugh on, but they never stop me"; "it's just like a box of After Eights"; "I don't like minty men." She is good at verbal ping-pong, she wouldn't have otherwise risen through the ranks so quickly to become editor in chief of the culture section of the *Egin* newspaper. That is precisely the newspaper Diego Lazkano carries, folded, on his lap. It reads REAGAN RELAUNCHES HIS PROPAGANDA OFFENSIVE AGAINST THE USSR, although the main front-page photograph is of one of a considerable-sized demonstration against the destruction of local businesses that took place in front of the church of Ororeta.

"Nervous?"

"Just a bit."

They stopped dating three months ago and Diego, due perhaps to the sizzle of attraction abandoned lovers sometimes retain, finds Idoia more beautiful than ever. She wears a pixie cut but not like those women who, wanting to be free of the tyranny of looking after their tresses, find vindication in the pragmatic kind of freedom short hair provides; hers is a far more sophisticated look: a curl fixed upward, hair cut short with great styling, shorn selectively by expert scissors. Diego remembers how, when Idoia used to sit on his lap, he'd grab her hair to gently pull her head sideways and kiss her neck. Although it's short now, there's still enough to justify that same gesture. He's succumbing to the persistent fantasy of ex-lovers, of course. How to control an intermittent passion that seeks to reignite a past that reason froze and stored away? *Don't go there, Diego*, he tells himself. But it's impossible. And the truth is that, yes, Diego used to pull Idoia's hair to kiss her, but only because she'd done it to him first. He must confess. Idoia taught him everything he knows about women, and now that the lesson is over, she has left him alone to test his knowledge on others; "there, love, that's enough." Because Idoia didn't want a stable relationship, Diego has the painful sensation of having been thrown not just off the bed, but overboard. Besides, Idoia is two years older than him, which seems an insurmountable distance when you've just turned nineteen. It's not always the case but, in being with her again this time, he relives the pain of the breakup. The thought that he'll no longer be able to sleep with Idoia in her pixie cut makes him feel something that is not quite a lover's sadness but, rather, the sadness of a sentimental collector.

"When does it start?"

"In Basque at eight p.m., and in Spanish at ten p.m."

"*Baizea!* Two shows in one day? You're all crazy, Diego."

Baizea, how he loves the way she says *yeah right*, the way she speaks, in and out of bed. Around the time he started sleeping with Idoia, he was stunned by the controlled violence of her sex: how she'd give in to her own excitement and give herself over completely – he wasn't sure to whom – and ride along as she grabbed his hair as if he were a horse; and how he too dared take firm hold of her hair for the first time and contemplate her neck before biting it; because, no matter what they say, it isn't all sweetness and caresses in bed, not everything needs to be tender, although it's important to keep a watchful eye on every gesture that departs from tenderness. Never before has he seen the earrings she is wearing on those tiny lobes he wants to bite. Stabbed by the vision of the ear wires, he feels a prick of jealousy in some indeterminate place between his lungs and his stomach. *Doesn't she wear the ones I gave her anymore?*

Diego forces himself to remember the hateful pact he and Idoia made together – "we can be friends, right?" – and to dispel the weakness that threatens to betray him, he pushes a tape into the cassette player. As if the silence inside the car were to blame. Idoia clears her throat above the crackle of the beginning of the tape.

"Your article on Dario Fo..."

"Yes?"

"It's not going to come out next week, we're short of space and would need to cut it down too much. Is that all right?"

"I'm in no hurry."

No hurry, none whatsoever. How could he. In that relationship, Diego Lazkano was never "Sitting Bull," but rather "He Who Waits." Her meetings went on, there were always last-minute changes, unexpected events. Such was the life of the editor in chief of a newspaper's culture section. More responsibility, more work hours, and a symbolic raise. In any case, Lazkano accepts, almost happily, that to wait for someone you love is part of the deal, convinced that the experience of absence underscores presence in a way that enhances the time spent together, making it glow and exist more intensely. In love, and not only in love, we must learn to enjoy the time prior to the preamble. Perhaps life is not much more than that, in the end: a series of preambles that lead nowhere. A series of moments prior to the preambles. A building of shambolic architecture. No matter how much we scratch the itch, there is never enough relief.

Lazkano recognizes Silvio Rodríguez's voice, although he's not familiar with the song.

"Silvio?"

Idoia nods. Then shifts gears and goes quiet, looking out the window; she is not uncomfortable but realizes a moment of discomfort is in the cards. What do you call that moment when, just before feeling uncomfortable, when you know you're going to be uncomfortable? So many words need to be invented still.

"*¿Te molesta mi amor?*" asks Silvio. Does my love bother you?

It's not a Silvio Rodríguez tape, but a mixed tape of love songs someone has made especially for her. Next comes the Scorpions' "No One Like You."

"They're selected songs," Idoia says.

Selected songs, of course. Selected by whom – better not to ask. The same guy who got her the earrings recorded the mixed tape, no doubt. Although Idoia is really into art, she's not very good with music. Lazkano feels that this anonymous guy keeps throwing darts at that indeterminate space between his lungs and his stomach; he can't help glancing at the glove department. In the Afga-branded orange case of the cassette – the only one among the road maps – he sees some unknown person's clumsy handwriting; it's a man's hand, no doubt. Lazkano feels helpless. *It used to be me who made her mixed tapes.* And as a matter of fact he too has just bought the Scorpions' *Blackout* LP, and the last time he played it he actually thought that Idoia would enjoy listening to "No One Like You" in her Mini. But it's too late now: he's been replaced. Someone got ahead of him, not just as a lover, but also as a purveyor of music. Diego realizes – the pathways of the mind are incomprehensible – that the second fact hurts as much as, if not more than, the first.

"Good luck."

She says "good luck," but what Lazkano hears is that other line: "We can be friends, right?"

"Aren't you coming to the show?"

"I have to go back to work, maybe this weekend…"

"Call me, I'll leave tickets for you under your name."

Diego swallows his pride and adds: "I'll leave two tickets."

Idoia nods and Diego closes the Mini's door on the boulevard, in front of the traffic lights by the Barandiaran Café. He feels as if someone had sucked the life force out of him. Lacking the strength to ask for a pick-me-up at the café, he walks past the Pequeño Casino and heads toward the Antzoki Zaharra Theater. Gloria shouts at him:

"Where on earth have you been, you? No, don't tell me: I'd rather not know… You're all going to end up in jail… You're the only one who's not dressed yet…"

The protagonist, Ana Etxarri, deep in her voice exercises, approaches Lazkano mimicking a duck, with her fingers splayed in front of her mouth, as if to say "ignore her big mouth, it's opening night and she's nervous." Tonight Kepa Zeberio will be in charge of the lights.

Xabier Soto is there too, visibly excited. One of his librettos is getting staged for the first time.

"I was beginning to think we were going to have to replace you, *primo*…"

No more substitutions, please. I just have a small role in this one but only I can play it.

They don't have any understudies, of course. When one of the actors gets sick, someone else in the company plays the part.

And anyone could play Diego Lazkano's part actually, as he only has three or four lines.

He realizes the seriousness of his father's issues when he has to go to pick him up at the post office. He rings him in tears: "I came to the wrong place, Diego," and Diego finds his father's words hard to comprehend, why wouldn't he just, after having gone to the wrong place, reroute and go home on his own. Even the reason for the call itself, "I came to the wrong place," "Come pick me up, I'm at the post office," is foreboding – his father never calls him – and he wonders if perhaps he's had an accident he's ashamed to mention over the phone.

It's raining buckets and instead of in the street, he finds his father standing next to the security guard. From the distance, his father's profile looks pathetic and defeated.

The security guard hands over his father, as if he'd been in custody.

"Is this your father? I think he got disoriented."

Lazkano nods and father and son walk away, son holding father gently by the elbow in the rain. *Disoriented, what do you know about that, it's not like security guards are the most* oriented *people in the world*, Diego tells himself.

"What happened, *aita*?"

His father shows him the books: they have library stickers and have gone through many hands. They're bestsellers, good for passing the time; Lazkano doesn't have the will to register any of the titles, it's been many years since he followed the whims of general readers, it depresses him to see the shit people read.

"I wanted to return them to the library. Today was the last day, you see? I can't keep these books for a day longer."

He speaks as if it were a matter of life or death, stressed out of all proportion, as if that last day were Judgment Day. And, besides, his habit of going to the library…it's not like they are exactly short of money. There are too many things about his father that he still doesn't understand, things he gave up hope of understanding a long time ago.

"And why didn't you return them? Should we go together now?"

If Diego thought the old man couldn't crumble any further, he was mistaken. His browbeaten look makes him lose three inches in height. Something or someone is shrinking his father. With eyes full of tears, powerless even to feel shame, he tells him:

"I went to the wrong place, I got confused, Diego. I got in line at the post office, waited until I reached the counter, and got it into my head that I had to post these books."

They're about twenty steps away from the post office, closer to the back gate of the Buen Pastor Cathedral than the post office itself, and unable to fit under one umbrella, they each offer one arm to the deluge that is falling from the sky. The main post office building in Donostia and the building that hosts the Koldo

Mitxelena Library look the same from the outside. The mirage of symmetry. Anyone could get confused.

"You were absentminded, that's all. Let's drop the books off now, stop worrying."

"You don't understand, Diego: I was *convinced* that the books were parcels that I needed to post. I waited my turn for half an hour...the post office employee looked completely puzzled. Do you know what that means?"

Lazkano had always heard – and this is something that makes him feel guilty – that in cases of mental illness, the family usually spots the signs before the sick person; what's more, even when the sick person notices something, he tends to dismiss the first few symptoms and minimize their importance, and it's the people around him who worry and urge him to go to the doctor. It isn't common for the sick person to detect his own illness, because mental illness almost always brings self-delusion with it. This wasn't the case with Gabriel Lazkano and, for Diego, this was clear evidence of the scant attention everyone at home paid the old man. Simultaneously, and rather frightened, he tried to assess how much and in what ways awareness of his illness would affect his father's life. How long since neuronal synapses began to disconnect? Had they detected the illness sooner, would he have had a better chance of delaying its progression with the help of medication? There was no way of knowing. For the next three or four weeks, Lazkano canceled all his commitments – he was launching his latest book, which was apparently going to surpass the success of his previous ones – and together with his mother and sister, took his father from test to test, from hospital to hospital.

The first diagnoses coincided in saying that the analyses didn't show anything out of the ordinary. But they were cautious all the same: "The brain is still the great unknown." After these positive messages, he received his mother's call.

She didn't call him in tears but, rather, after having cried. She pointlessly tried to hide it from him. Lazkano's job required that he observe the human condition, instincts, yearnings, impulses, and construct coherent fiction based on such observations; details are his life, it's the only ability he has that he can be proud of. And so he immediately noticed his mother's unease.

"Your father has started to say strange things."

Earlier than they thought, without warning, and while all scans and MRIs showed nothing conclusive, they entered the uninhibited phase. He's well for long stretches, and then starts saying the first thing that pops to his head. Or maybe it's not exactly like that, Lazkano thinks, maybe rather than saying the first thing that comes to mind, what he's doing is saying things that were kept in the back rooms of his mind for a long time; strange opinions, revelations and reproaches that seem too well chosen, things that happened a long time ago that he kept from his family, things whose veracity or falseness were hard to establish.

"When is Angeles coming?"

"Angeles?"

"Maybe I didn't tell you...remember the time I went to Amsterdam? I met the love of my life there: she lived in Eivissa, I should visit her, it's been so long. I bet the weather is wonderful in Eivissa right now, unlike this depressing drizzle."

When Josune, Diego's sister, asked him to stop talking nonsense, Gabriel Lazkano took the photograph of a young woman out of his wallet. As he threw it on the table like a *mus* player who shows a winning hand, their mother started wailing and crying.

Diego tries to remember when was it that *aita* had gone to Amsterdam for work. It'd been at least fifteen years: he took a course on natural pest control and "sustainable" methods of insect elimination. There was a word he would jokingly use quite often around the house in that time: *ecopoison*.

"You're not sick...you're going crazy."

Soto is angry with Gloria. He thinks the director is too soft. She's not sufficiently engaged. "Art, art... nonsense; there are terrible things happening out there, *primo*, and Gloria doesn't want to know." She seldom joins them in demonstrations. And there are plenty springing up at the moment: she didn't go with them to the march against the Lemóniz nuclear station, or to the gathering in Bilbao in support of some abortion practitioners sentenced to six years in prison. "She lives in her own fucking Tower of Babel, bourgeois daughter of the bourgeois," he tells Lazkano, admonishingly. "Or what's worse: an aristocrat at heart; because the bourgeois might do things badly, but at least they try to do something." Today the director told them off again for going to "those meetings." It's up to you whether you go or not, but you'd better come to rehearsal on time, do you hear?" "Who does she think she is, *primo*? Our mother? Miss Maria Pilar?"

"You're going to end badly."

"Don't expect me to come to get you out of jail."

"Like we've money to pay an attorney."

She unleashed all that at them, and Soto was incensed. He took the libretto and threw it in her face, while he shouted that if she kept disrespecting him, she would have to count him out. "Are you coming, *primo*?"

But Lazkano knew it was just a tantrum. Zeberio picked up the libretto leaves strewn all over the floor. Lazkano placed the scenes in order again, all of them, one by one, even though Soto hadn't numbered them.

Despite the fact that Lazkano only speaks a few lines in the play, he practically knows the whole thing by heart.

Shortly after Gabriel let his tongue loose, he and his wife started sleeping in separate beds. And, finally, the diagnosis arrived. The confirmation came from Santos Herguera, an old family friend. For a long while now, he'd been chief of the Division of Cognitive and Memory Disorders in a hospital in Dallas, and they took advantage of his summer holiday in Donostia to pay him what in other circumstances would have been a first visit.

The least of it is putting a label on it. It's some kind of dementia, not Alzheimer's. He showed them color diagrams of his brain, sophisticated tests they don't understand at all.

"And they haven't been able to tell you anything? I can't believe it."

It's unfathomable that in the twenty-first century *American* doctors have to come to reveal things to us; unforgivable, according to Diego. There was no miracle cure that would stop the disaster: there were mental and physical exercises, strict controls, pills of every color; the family was going to have to keep a very watchful eye on him to make sure he took them all.

"Look after your father, but take a break from looking after him every now and then too, take time to look after yourselves."

None of it stopped old man Lazkano from speaking about Eivissa, or addressing his wife with the name of the mysterious Angeles. Always mixed in with some fruity sexual fantasies that Diego cringed hearing out of his father's mouth: "When will you let me come all over your tits, Angelines?" Sentences which, once the initial shock and scandal wore off, the family processed and accepted with complete normalcy, and drove Diego to understand the depths of his father's proclivities. A true writer must learn to extract some learning from even the most adverse set of circumstances. And Diego was sure of his vocation, even if he hadn't always been, even if he'd had to slam shut a lot of the rooms in his mind in order to ascertain his vocation.

No: his life hadn't been easy either.

Diego's father sometimes embraced his wife passionately, but her embrace wasn't really what he sought, rather, he sought the memory of that woman called Angeles. He couldn't understand why she rejected his kisses. Only when he was asleep did his wife plant a butterfly kiss on him. Only then did he seem like her old husband, her Gabriel.

Diego and his sister tried to find traces of the woman called Angeles. A phone number, her complete name, her family names. Begging for discretion, they showed her photograph to his father's closest friends. But no one knew anything. He hid his secret very well, somewhere.

After a series of ups and downs, after six months, his mood changed. "I'm sick, right?" he'd ask suddenly, and then spend hours not saying anything, with a lost look in his eyes.

They institutionalized him when he refused to eat and go to

the bathroom. Barely a month later, when it seemed that the strict hospital discipline and routines had had a stabilizing effect on his situation, Gabriel Lazkano disappeared.

He left a note, an astonishing feat for someone in his state: "Begoña, Josune, Diego, I love you but I have to live my life now." The names of his wife and children impeccably written in capital letters, the ghost of Angeles nowhere to be seen. Neurologists and psychiatrists didn't know what to think. "It's strange," they said, and Diego began to feel bored with the narrowness of their linguistic register: *strange* is not a scientific word in the slightest.

Neither the police nor the family ever heard from Gabriel Lazkano again.

It'd be cruel to say so, but to think it is human: although for several weeks Diego Lazkano and his family lived through many sleepless nights and sighed many hopeless sighs, waiting for a call that never arrived, their father's disappearance also had the inadmissible inverse effect of bringing them peace.

Many years had passed since Soto and Zeberio disappeared: strangely enough, Lazkano didn't initially associate his father's disappearance with the disappearance of his two friends. It didn't cross his mind to think that, although very differently, his father, like Soto and Zeberio, was also "disappeared." Disappeared, disappeared, disappeared... disappearance is the axis of his life, an eddy that pulls him who knows where.

For the first two years after their father's disappearance, Diego and Josune visited the morgue together several times, taking turns. After eight years the official declaration of his death arrived and, with it, a sort of suspended stillness: a precarious, nameless stillness, a nuanced quietude that reverberated in their chests.

Lazkano continued to write; Josune, teaching dance. Their mother gathered the pieces and reassembled the puzzle of her life, substituting the missing pieces with the fabric of oblivion and fantasy.

"Do you think they do this in every theater in the world, Gloria? This only happens here because this country is ridiculous! A show in Basque at eight p.m. and another at ten p.m. with the same actors, acting out the same parts in the same play, but in Spanish this time. It's schizophrenic... we waste our talent, Gloria, how can we do a good job this way... it's impossible!"

Soto is indignant. The play left people indifferent and he blames their lukewarm reception to the need to work in both languages simultaneously.

"If we don't do it this way, it's not profitable."

"Yeah right, c'mon, Gloria..."

"Should we break up the company? Function at an amateur level? Perform only in sports centers and schools?"

"As if we didn't perform in sports centers and schools already..."

"The Vulpes that you talk so often about...don't they play in even dingier places?"

"But they're punks!"

"So are we then."

"You? You, the barefoot countess, a punk?"

"I'm sorry but things are what they are."

The argument wasn't new, but it came up again after the ten o'clock show, because Lazkano inadvertently said one of his lines in Basque during the Spanish performance. Lazkano was completely dejected, although the others tried to rest importance to his mistake.

"The audience didn't even notice, Diego: you have to realize that they only come to see it once, and avant-garde pieces often mix languages, I'm sure they found a reason for your speaking in Basque..."

Soto didn't miss a beat:

"Avant-garde? Are you trying to insult me, Gloria? Are you?"

It's hopeless to try to cheer Diego up. Today Lazkano wants to be alone and doesn't join the others in the celebration. To make matters worse, he still hasn't heard from Idoia: she didn't show up to see the play over the weekend, and the last time he called her he didn't get through because apparently she was "in a meeting."

The morning after his mental lapse he buys the newspaper and glances at the contents of the culture section, curious about what might be to blame for the new delay in the publication of his article on Dario Fo. He opens the newspaper impatiently end sees that there's a full-page article written in Spanish substituting his piece: SILVIO RODRÍGUEZ, LA PLUMA Y LA TROVA. Quill and song, indeed – everything is falling into place. He scrunches up the newspaper until it's completely wrecked and throws it into the trash can next to the newspaper kiosk, to the seller's astonishment. He regrets his childishness as soon as he's done it and buys another copy of the newspaper in another kiosk on his way home. He hasn't set foot in the university for weeks, but he doesn't care. Sociology can go fuck itself. Exams are a long way away. He opens the newspaper's culture section again and checks the by line of the article on Silvio Rodríguez: Mikel Remiro. He finds the article quite underwhelming, inconsequential, and filled with pompous, overwritten clichés and enough adjectives to make anyone puke. Silvio Rodríguez, Scorpions… maybe this Remiro dude knows a thing or two about music, but as a writer, he's pathetic. Diego tries to face the truth: Idoia left him for a third-rate writer; who knows, maybe that secret relationship had something to do with her throwing him overboard so happily. No, Idoia didn't play by the rules. Just as the suicidal impulse living inside his head was contemplating different ways of ending his life – poison, hara-kiri, death leap – his phone rang. It was Ana, the protagonist of the play. She was calling to ask how he's doing and to see if they can meet up for a coffee.

The great Ana Etxarri, the most beautiful Ana with the loveliest smile. One of those gorgeous women men stop paying attention to because they seem unreachable. Of course they could meet up for coffee. In fact, he needs that coffee above everything else if he's going to gather the wherewithal to continue taking part in the play. Next week they have six shows booked in Bilbao, and while pondering multiple methods of suicide, one thousand times he decides and one thousand times he postpones the decision to quit and ask Gloria to replace him.

Ana is so different from Diego. A woman of clear vocation who, since starting drama school, has thought of nothing else. She attends every workshop: mime, voice, kataki, eastern dances, fencing...if one amongst them is to become a great actor, they all agree, it will be Ana Etxarri. That's why Gloria has chosen her as the lead.

"Do you remember the course we did with Roulant?"

Lazkano makes effeminate hand movements as he mouths an answer. It wasn't difficult to imitate Professor Roulant, who had come from Lyon to teach an intensive weekend course.

"The fundamental lesson, *c'est ça*: 'It's a matter of making a drawing with gesture, and then filling in the drawing with words. From that moment, movement and text go together, hand in hand. To remember the gesture is to remember the words.' But I'm incapable."

"You have to make an effort."

"Making an effort is hard."

"You're not wrong about that."

Lazkano made an effort, but didn't succeed. He felt increasingly uncomfortable on stage, and that would be his last collaboration with Gloria's company. He decided to abandon that vocation and focus on his studies. Besides, as Diego liked to say since he began waking up next to Ana: two actors in one house would be too much.

Diego Lazkano was happy. Thanks to Ana. Thanks to the shiny puddles of her green eyes. And that black hair shaped like a sickle, framing the white arc of her face. Thanks to the books they buy for each other, because they both want to read. Every time Ana rehearses a new play, Diego reads with her and then attends premieres with great satisfaction and without nerves, enjoying the radiance of his woman on the stage. In the same way they try to make things different each time they speak to each other, they vary things when they touch each other: one caresses the other's face after peeling an orange with his fingers. It doesn't matter if his fingers are cold between her legs, and later against his nose, cold and smelling of orange. It's all Diego needs.

They are one of those couples people envy when they see them walk down the street; so attuned to each other they even smile in the same way: they're like loving siblings, and should disguise their happiness to dampen the disgust they induce in jealous pedestrians. They've infected each other not only with their gestures, but also with each other's reasons to be happy; everything is times two, really: every reason belongs to both of them while, before, each had carried their own. Especially memorable was the day when they arranged their LP collections together in alphabetical order on the same shelves. "A union stronger than marriage," they tell each other after aligning their Patti LaBelle and Mikel Laboa, Echo & the Bunnymen and Errobi LPs side by side.

A private sphere, something intimate, something that's only mine? Of course I have that, thinks Diego. The closeness of his dear friends Soto and Zeberio is something the couple enjoys, but the political militancy, the meetings and talks they organize in their house, the screams and running escapes from the police in demonstrations is something that belongs only to Diego. Ana has her own private sphere too. What is it? Diego isn't sure. It belongs only to her. It's something he doesn't pay special attention to, he prefers to hold on to their shared way of manifesting their happiness.

When they start living together they compete to see who can do the dishes first, who can make the bed first. The object of the game is to surprise the other, and see their smile when they realize that the job they were about to do has been completed by the other; and to make love then. Unmaking the bed that has just been made.

To be crazy in love, to brush your teeth before eating. And then instead of eating make love using every single finger and licking everything.

They make coffee at night and their nails are black with coffee grounds. Who knows what corners of their bodies those fingers will imprint with the scent of coffee.

"Where were you?"

"At Soto and Zeberio's."

"Conspiring?"

"Listening to music..."

He has it all: friendship, love. The love of his friends and the friendship of his love.

With sundown, the smell of coffee has substituted the embolus of the smell of oranges, but it's still there in the back-ground like a continuous hum, the sweet shrill of orange peel echoing against the exciting bitterness of caffeine.

To keep mixing things up, Diego bites Ana's neck the way Idoia had taught him; her belt falls off, mother-of-pearl buttons hit the ground, nails caress lips, a finger penetrates a furrow; they want to perfume, bend, smell, kiss, slurp each other. The tips of Ana's fingers touch Diego's erection too soon, she didn't expect to find it so close to his belt. She caresses it with her fingers first and her nails next. They smile: keep it different, until the end of the day, until the end of all days, backs turned to the evidence that says there will be an end of days.

And then fuck those backs and fuck that evidence.

The theater group had started to slowly fragment and languish. TV steals up many of the contenders in the acting profession: some decide to become news anchors, others do dubbing courses and decide to exploit their voices for a living; an intelligent choice, perhaps, since the voice is the last bastion of youth and age takes longer to show there. An actor knows that great talent is required in order to age in the world of entertainment. Not all of us are Orson Welles.

Either that, or gain some weight and become a director. Go from being a chess piece to a chess player. This is the pathway Gloria chooses at the beginning. She continues to obstinately produce low-budget plays while she studies fine arts in Bilbao, sticking to her absurd fixation of not turning up to premieres – some kind of superstition. While the premiere is taking place she hunkers down in the Boulevard's cocktail bar, drinking gin and tonics, pretending to the barman and to herself that she isn't nervous at all, lighting one cigarette with the previous one's butt, until the clock warns her that the play at the Antzoki Zaharra is about to end. Then she asks for the check and returns to the theater. She likes to sneak out and then sneak back in the same way; she's always very on top of her actors during rehearsals, so she allows herself this little desertion. The first time it worked out very well and she's repeated the ritual since: stealthily returning to the theater when the play is about to end, she likes to breathe in the tension in the stalls, to sense the laughter or the silence inside the theater as she crosses the foyer and the empty bar.

Only then she asks her colleagues: "How is it going?" Although it's a useless question because by then Gloria perfectly knows how everything is going, failure or success are palpable in the air and on the faces of her actors; if they managed to move the audience, if the audience laughed when they were supposed to laugh, if they held their breath when they were supposed to do so. Then comes the applause, the invitation to join the actors on the stage, the bunches of flowers, the love, the kisses, the thankyous, the achievement is all yours, the actors', thank you so much, thank you from my heart, I love you too.

"Actors are whiny little spoiled children, Lazkano: every now and then the horses need to be rubbed down." *The horses need to be rubbed down*, quite the way of putting it.

And who rubs down the horse breaker, Gloria? Lazkano is speechless when Gloria announces that she'll be giving up on theater as soon as she finishes her fine arts degree. While Zeberio was putting away the lights, Soto and Lazkano found her sitting, looking dejected.

"I'm not as strong as I thought I was, this job requires courage of steel… it's not for me."

Something she overheard by chance in the bar Paco Bueno truncated Gloria's indestructible spirit. She'd taken a trivial comment voiced by someone in a dive bar and turned it into a tremendous tragedy. It can't even be said to have been a commentary. In truth, they're just two words.

"It can't have been that bad."

"Someone asked 'what did you think?' and his friend answered 'so-so.' *So-so?*"

Lazkano can't believe it. Proud Gloria, who looks down equally on good and bad reviews, saying things like "they haven't understood shit; these idiots don't even know who David Mamet is"; unbreakable, omniscient Gloria, so sure of herself and every step she takes, is about to give up because of such a stupid comment?

"That's not so bad, is it?"

"It's the worst thing anyone can say about something you've created, Lazkano."

"First off: you don't know who was talking, and whether they know anything about the theater," Soto says, trying to encourage her too. "Second: don't we belong to the Handke School? We don't give two hoots about the public."

"You're not going to persuade me, Soto… I give up."

"You have to keep going," insists Diego softly. "You'll see it differently tomorrow."

But this doesn't happen. That was the last play Gloria directed. Just like that, she abandoned the theater to become immersed in the world of art. She gave it all up and moved to Barcelona.

Those two beloved friends, Soto and Zeberio, in any case, weren't they elevated to that category by virtue of their death and his guilt? Rather than the best friends of his life, weren't they, increasingly so, the best friends of his death, the best friends of his future death awaiting him patiently on the other side? His beloved friends' torture and disappearance joined ranks with his own father's vanishing. Just when Soto and Zeberio's disappearance had started to diffuse a little – just a little – in his memory, the responsibility Lazkano feels for all the disappeared, rather than shrinking, increases and becomes more piercing. His father's disappearance only makes Soto and Zeberio reappear before Lazkano's eyes, they reemerge in his memory, their absence becoming more pressing by the day. Their profiles redefine themselves, newly distinct, as if he'd been looking at long-lost photographs. "There are three of us and we've all disappeared; there's no hope for the first two, there may be some for the third."

But for the third one too, for old Gabriel Lazkano, hope was decreasing by the day. If he didn't reappear by the second week, according to statistics – and statistics are a courtesy of the police – it was unlikely he'd be found alive. Initially he thought about them as "his three disappeared," but after a while it was "his three dead." That's when a kind of fisherman's widow's obsession took hold; after the temporary declaration of "legal absence," he understood the unbearable unease felt when the sea doesn't return the bodies of seamen. He understood. He needed a body. He needed one of them at least to be present as a corpse, for his bones to confirm the end of his story. A body would mean that he was somewhere, in some specific place, that his story ended there, and that sense of placement would mark a sense of an ending. A place offered repose not only to the dead, but also to their families and friends.

Without a place there was no repose, or at least it was more difficult to find it. Cemeteries fence off death, without graveyards death could be anywhere, and families would lose the ground beneath their feet and go mad. Think of that. Times three.

"The sink is clogged, *seme*, can you come over?"

His mother's call departed from her usual requests, it had echoes of that other SOS, "I came to the wrong place, Diego." As soon as he arrived home, his suspicions were confirmed.

After working the plunger hard for a while and using a fair amount of force, he managed to free up the pipe. The culprit appeared to be quite a large clump of white hair. He stared at his mother to check if the hair was hers. She hadn't combed it yet, she must have cut that thick lock that very morning. The scissors were still on the table.

"What did you do, *ama*?"

"I felt so lonely. I wanted you to come over."

The wages of despair, Lazkano suddenly understood: not having the energy to even pretend. Cutting your own hair, clogging your own sink with it to then call your son so he'll come to see you.

The disappeared, Lazkano wondered, *could it be that they cause in the not-disappeared something like a desire to disappear too?* Perhaps because of the blow they've suffered, their usual structures, schedules, and behaviors disappear too. It's not just that they don't have the strength to recover the life they had before the disappearance of the person they loved, it's that by erasing themselves too, by changing their behaviors and state of mind somewhat, they feel closer to those who are no longer there: "Before you disappeared I lived happily, now I must live with sadness; before you disappeared I used to eat out on Sundays, now I must eat at home; before you disappeared we used to spend our holidays in the mountains, now I should spend them by the sea." It's an unconscious, absurd behavior that separates us from our old routines, as if, in abandoning them, in removing ourselves from our habitual spaces and placing ourselves somewhere else, we could somehow bring our disappeared back.

Lazkano was at a loss. Pink rubber gloves on and withered

– 67 –

white lock in hand, not knowing what to do with it at all – throw it in the trash, down the toilet, or hand it over to her. Locks of hair are used to conjure spells, as tokens of love. What do you do with a lock of your own mother's hair?

It was true, maybe Diego's mother didn't know it but she had decided to disappear; to do so, instead of jumping headfirst into a river, she'd try throwing herself down the sink drain bit by bit, starting with the easiest bit first, a lock of her hair.

"We'll meet down there, down the gutter, in the bottom of the sea, deep in the well."

Diego Lazkano remembers the first time he heard the acronym AK-47. The first time he heard the initials of the FMLN, the Salvadoran guerrillas. The first time he heard the words *sleeper cell* and *embryonic cell*. It all happened the same day, with Zeberio and Soto, while the latter removed a Victor Jara LP and replaced it with one by the Doors on the record player. "Don't torture me with that music," Zeberio snapped. Because Zeberio liked Victor Jara; he liked singers whose songs he could understand. So, nothing in English, of course. No American music, of course. "Don't torture me with that music," his hair stands on end when he remembers it, he remembers it as if it'd happened that very morning, when, in fact, twenty-five years have passed. He remembers as if it'd happened the day before, that fun afternoon he had, that exchange between Soto and Zeberio while Soto blew on the needle of the record player to get rid of the accumulated dust after having given them a lesson on the Rumasa pyramid scheme and the Iran-Iraq war; three friends who hadn't yet gone underground, in the same house, unafraid, with their futures wide open, as open as the horizon. Soto and Zeberio, dramatist and lighting designer respectively, were, like Idoia, older than Diego. He would almost always keep silent, admiring both of them unconditionally, with a passion that was as repressed as it was devoted.

The newspaper spoke about the Farabundo Martí National Liberation Front, the FMLN guerrillas, peasants, pupils, even bishops that were *disappearing* in El Salvador. It wasn't the only place. It was happening in Guatemala too. In Chile. Uruguay. And many other places.

"They abandon bodies in ditches. Look at this: the head of a peasant left in the playground of the school for his children to see."

"Terrifying."

"It's not like the FMLN are angels, exactly: they use AK-47s, they finance their missions through murder and kidnapping – but their violence is child's play compared to the extreme-right militias of El Salvador."

"And you know who's training those militias, right, Soto?"

"Yeah, I know, don't start with all that again: the Americans, who else. Bell Helicopters, M16 rifles… I know, I know, but if you think I'm gonna stop playing the Doors and put Victor Jara back on because of that, you can dream on."

Diego Lazkano continued reading the paper: seventy-five thousand dead in El Salvador alone; that's half of Donostia, he thought, and considered that what was going on in the Basque Country was really nothing; luckily, they'd never suffer or cause such rivers of blood as the ones experienced by the tiny Latin American country. Seventy-five thousand dead, a million refugees, another million left homeless. Those were enormous numbers, and the small numbers associated with theirs turned their conflict into a shrug-worthy matter. It was all a matter of scale, of perspective and numbers, that's what Soto said – and Zeberio didn't argue against him. The use of violence was measured with different parameters in that house; it wasn't questioned, it was all part of the logic of the dynamics of war, all militants and leaders accepted a certain level of cruelty, they didn't think of particular consequences, but of symbols: it was the symbols that were "removed," and no one's head would ever be left in the playground of a school where their kids went to learn. Diego Lazkano thought like this for years, and although the way he saw violence changed with time, he thought that cruelty and numeric comparisons with El Salvador were probably always present in the minds of the leaders of the ETA, whom he imagined hiding in farms in the agricultural depths of France. His biggest mistake was perhaps to assume that something like a bearable number of deaths could ever exist; a Latin American jungle got stuck in their heads and they got lost in it; hell, they even came to think that jungle was the Basque Country. And it wasn't. Even if every mental lucubration could easily turn into a forest or a jungle.

Diego Lazkano remembers the first time he heard the expression *sleeper cell*, and how attractive and soothing those two words seemed, because he believed in the revolutionary potential of the people in hiding, asleep somewhere, because he couldn't imagine that a "sleeper cell" could do anything that bad, really; and, as a matter of fact, it couldn't, unless it stopped being a "sleeper," and in that case it could do anything – good or bad. But for as long as the cell continued to sleep, so did many dreams. That's how Lazkano saw it, so naïve and so young still. It didn't cross his mind to think about nightmares when the man who led their group turned up in their house.

He was a redhead, with freckles all over his face. Back then he had seemed very old, but he couldn't have been older than forty.

The beardless Lazkano, on the other hand, must have looked too young to the Redhead, and he paired him with Zeberio in hopes of turning them into a "sleeper cell," while he suggested he had "some other duties" in mind for Soto. And just like that, the pair linked forever by death could have been Lazkano and Zeberio, or perhaps in this case, Zeberio and Lazkano, the other way around. However, when they were about to leave the house and the Redhead handed over the car keys to Lazkano, things changed forever.

"I...I don't have a driver's license."

Diego was so ashamed he barely whispered the words. The Redhead stared at him in astonishment and then turned to Soto and Zeberio with a doubtful look that seemed to say: "What sort of people are you bringing along? Couldn't you have said something sooner? We won't get anywhere like this. With people who can't drive, what commando, what sleeper cell, or what kind of bullshit do you think we can organize here?"

Finally, the Redhead took pity on young Lazkano and, avoiding his head, threw the keys at Soto.

"You take care of it then, Soto."

"*You*, come with me...We need people who're not on file."

Lazkano doesn't have a name: the Redhead calls him *You*.

Lazkano remembered the staircase as if he'd walked down it the previous day: how he took the steps one by one, with their ledges curved slightly to the left, following the redheaded leader, feeling useless, disabled by his inability to drive. Wasn't it a fact that Idoia had driven him everywhere in her Mini? And now he couldn't even do that, because Ana didn't have a driver's license either.

And there Diego went down the staircase next to the Redhead, with a Salvadoran jungle imprinted in his mind, "we need people who're not on file," oblivious to the fact that he's leaving behind a certain death; incognizant of the fact that being competent and useful doesn't always lead to salvation, that sometimes ignorance can save you; unaware of the fact that the gods haven't abandoned him in the slightest, rather, they've chosen him, while he wonders, all along, what could possibly turn out to be his mission.

Lazkano didn't initially understand Gloria's desertion, what led her to Barcelona and the art world; probably because back then he still hadn't published anything. Now that he's become a novelist, however, he understands her motivation perfectly: the assessment "so-so" is the kiss of death.

Some of the theater friends who collaborated with Diego and Gloria tried their luck in cinema. Not very many good films were made in that brief period of resurgence, but at least there were more than in the following years. The expected renaissance didn't take place. That was an isolated spring, the promise of a summer that never came, accompanied by the cruelty and deception of all false springs. Even Ana, that different sort of love that came without shadows, against all prognoses, left the theater and found a civil servant post in Donostia's municipal library. Sara Fernandez was the only one who persevered and found success and, twenty years later, still garnered respect and admiration in the theaters of Bilbao, Madrid, and Barcelona. Madrid beckoned, she went, and, after a time, was wise enough to return – not like others, with her tail between her legs, but before being changed and sidelined by that cliquey provincial world. Every time she went to Barcelona on tour, Sara would call Gloria; on this occasion, because so many years had passed and because Diego was also visiting, the three got together around a table in Sa Cantina.

"And what happened to our great white hope?"

"La Bella Ines? She left the theater a long time ago. She hasn't been seen again since *The Mousetrap*. I hear she works in a highway tollbooth."

"Not bad, she went from one trap into another."

"You're still the same bastard you always were, Diego," Gloria threw in, taking pity on their absent friend.

Sara hadn't lost a speck of her energy. She followed a strict diet and never touched alcohol. Diego and Gloria polished off the whole bottle of Chablis.

"We should do something together."

"I completely agree, Sara. Right now: let's have dinner. What do you think, fish or meat, Lazkano?"

"No, Gloria, seriously: let's adapt one of Lazkano's novels and have you direct it ..."

"You are forgetting two tiny details: I no longer direct, and Diego hates the theater."

"I don't understand, Gloria, you must know so many people here in Barcelona, why don't you go to the theater more often?"

"I haven't set foot in a playhouse in twenty-five years."

"I don't believe you."

"Believe me."

"Tell me the truth, Sara: don't you feel like you've seen everything already?"

"No, Diego, not at all."

"You must be very special then. I thought that theater actors and directors never attended their colleagues' plays unless they were completely certain that what they were about to watch was much worse than what they usually did. Only then do they go. For artists, protecting their own ego is more important than keeping up to date with things."

"That's pretty miserable, Diego. Is that how novelists work?"

"More or less, yeah."

"I was going to leave you both a couple of tickets for the play this weekend."

"Don't take it the wrong way, Sara, I love you to bits but I'm not going to go."

"And you, Lazkano?"

"To be honest, theater and I...what can I say, I developed a dislike for it. I suffer too much: for the audiences, for the actors... and for myself above all, I'm not going to lie. The mere fact of having to make the people on your same row of poorly attached stalls stand up, far from instilling a sense of camaraderie, makes me feel like a passive member of a collective I don't belong to. It's been a long time since I've gone to the theater or to any demonstration – for the same reasons."

"Oh well. For me, there's still nothing like it... when the lights are switched off and I hear someone walk onto the stage in the dark, and I hear the cracking of the boards, and I feel like I don't know what's about to happen, and I hear steps on the dais before the play starts, I get goose bumps. And, it goes without saying, when it's me who walks on those boards... it's like walking toward a precipice in the dark."

"Lucky you, you never fell off it."

"You're mistaken: I've fallen off more than once. That's the best part. The risk of the fall, and the certainty that you'll have the chance to fall again."

Lazkano believed that those months of his early militancy and his life with Ana, until Soto and Zeberio disappeared, were the best ones of his life. But perhaps he placed too much value on friendship. The truth about friends is something else. Something coarser. Friendships have an expiration date. Just like there's a word assigned to girlfriends of the past, to the exes that were and are now crossed off the list, why shouldn't there be a word to designate those who were our friends for a while but no longer are? Don't we all have ex-friends? Those who are no longer our friends, do they have to become our enemies? Not quite. The opposite of friendship is not enmity, but indifference, abandonment, inertia, apathy. The main reasons why friendships are lost are not betrayal or sudden ideological divergence, but the unavoidable entropic motion of life. Friends use one another because it's too hard to overcome the insecurity and the mutations of adolescence in solitude; because it's not easy to create a band on your own, someone has to play bass and percussion, which no one ever wants to do; because we need someone's protection; because student housing is too expensive and parents breathe easier if they know their children don't live alone; because even though we deliberately forget, there are always practical motivations behind our actions, and in this way and bit by bit we create what for a time seem like unbreakable bonds; because in drunkenness and in sports, loneliness is too sad when you're twenty years old, and because a shared taste in beer and music translates into enough affinity to talk into the night; and because a line from a song – *ezin zaitut begira, gehiegi da Pakean utzi arte* – is enough then. But then couples happen, so longed for at one point, only to then become strange elements that rub against friendships, organic shrapnel that change the power dynamics among groups of friends, "don't think about it, what had to happen happened," and from that point on, who knows when or why, everything starts to dissipate: after meeting up twice a week you start meeting every other week, until you realize you find hanging out boring and annoying, and phone calls start to replace meeting up, and during phone calls you keep from talking about the things you want to talk about when you meet face-to-face, and then the day to meet face-to-face turns into a burden and something that's further and further away, and when you finally meet face-to-face you don't know how to talk and only manage a bunch of superficial topics, and in the end you only hear news of your friends from other friends. You get news of the illnesses of parents, the births of children, invitations to weddings, and that's all. You fake happiness. You see them at funerals. You don't feel their sorrow but pretend that you do.

What you don't tell friends increases, as does what they don't tell you. And your malicious tendency to judge them grows, even though you are only aware of stray fragments of their lives. You fill in the voids with mistaken assumptions, justifying or censoring your friends' attitudes almost always inaccurately, getting further and further from their truth and yours: because staying close to one's own maliciousness is no way of approaching someone else's truth. You once inhabited the same skin, yes, but the desire to do so has slipped away.

Most of one's time goes toward directing and organizing the enterprise that is domestic life; you often see parents who, forgetting the essence of parenthood, train their children for the future, holding incomprehensible conversations with them as if they were conducting business, fearing that one day those children, those monsters, those angels, those saviors and destroyers, might be in charge of their own lives. And despite that, they overprotect them, betting everything on those little arrows directed at their future; and that leaves no room for friendship, there is no time and, when there is, time is limited and the encounter brief, an obligation really – "I have fifteen minutes" – and the coffee needs to be downed in one gulp.

It's possible and, more than possible, very probable, that those who were once friends become acquaintances, that one day their attitudes and expressions begin to feel remote, that you stop understanding their humor, that you can't discern a joke that covers up a deeper pain or a cry for help. Yes, it happens. Friends become acquaintances and, given enough time, acquaintances become strangers, the key to their time and trust is lost. At that point, you're forced to admit the painful truth: perhaps you never were very good friends after all. Beer and music kept you close, brothers in arms.

Every now and then new friends may appear, usually related to your work, most of them linked to new preoccupations and interests, often too stemming from family connections; but that sense of an eternal blood covenant is a thing of the past: the promise of loyalty chiseled into a sculpture made out of the mud of friendship, the promise implicitly forged through shared, healthy, rivalry-free laughter. And there's no one to blame: the only guilty party is you.

Why not admit that friendship is similar to those absent minded love relationships between teenagers: an accumulation of apparently inexhaustible power, a magnetic bond that seems unbreakable, when the truth is that it's something that by its very nature is circumstantial and perishable. There are exceptions, of course. Charming bars that age along with their clientele. Friends who, against all prognoses, and without needing to meet every week, manage to maintain a level of complicity decade after decade, either because they are too generous or because they're unselfconscious; or, alternatively, because they are true gardeners who, out of that old patch of friendship, tenderness grows and genuine smiles blossom. There are those too, who share an illness or a serious condition with the same passion with which some people embrace a lover; there are those who, when not in agreement, maintain heated discussions; there are friendships that are like a couple's relationship, or are even better than a couple's relationship; or, furthermore, that are like relationships between lovers and even better than relationships between lovers; who hide nothing from one another and, if they do, don't do it out of malice or self-interest.

So many things can be shared with a friend: a bad habit, a weakness, a sorrow, a secret. And then there are relationships like the one Lazkano maintains with Gloria, which are worth their weight in gold; no matter how long since they last spoke, it always feels like they've just been talking the day before, there are never any false starts, they can pick up the thread of their conversation anywhere. But these are exceptions, and the majority of people go through life without friendships like these. So Lazkano should be happy. And perhaps he's mistaken in thinking that if Soto and Zeberio had remained alive, his relationship with them would have been just as stimulating as his relationship with Gloria. It's impossible to compete with dead friends, they're invincible, so you idealize them in irrational ways. It's more likely that Soto and Zeberio too would have become acquaintances, and later strangers, erased by the unavoidable erosion of life. Like going from being a stranger to being an acquaintance and then a friend, but doing the process in reverse, eventually becoming diffuse.

He could imagine Zeberio, for example, as the father of three or four kids, checking to see if they're asleep through the crack in the door, picking up and washing his teenagers' dirty sneakers, taking them fishing, teaching them to bait the fishing hook, to build a radio with paper clips, razor blades, and a bit of wire attached to a chunk of wood. He could imagine Soto as the president of Basque PEN, giving lectures everywhere, indefatigable in his defense of the rights of Kurdish journalists, writers, and translators, going here and there, a nomadic bird without ties of any kind, being always first to arrive in places where injustice is most flagrantly present. Each would have his life, they would see little of each other, he only needed to think of his old friends, Sara Fernandez, La Bella Ines, and so many others…Maybe Soto and Lazkano would only hear about each other through the press: "Will you look at that, indefatigable Soto has written another play"; "Ha! Lazkano has just published another one of his unbearable, obsessive, unraveling novels." They would become each other's spam.

"But, what's *spam*, Diego? Explain it to us, we've no idea."

He'd have to explain so many things to Soto and Zeberio if they were resurrected.

Why? Why the hell did things have to be that way? The lives denied to Soto and Zeberio had in turn wrecked and consumed Lazkano's life too. Or was it the other way around?

If they hadn't been murdered, they would have disappeared from his life all the same: during his worst sleepless nights, Diego comes to almost accept this fact. But they were killed, and this anchored them to his living mind; not to just any kind of limbo, but to his mind. The limbo of his mind. And now he can't get them out.

He remembers how deeply Zeberio blushed, down to the roots of his hairy beard, the day he introduced Ines to him, how his eyes lit up and smiled. Zeberio wasn't one to show his emotions, and when Lazkano left to make some coffee in the kitchen he was on his own with the girl and quite lost. He soon found an excuse to go to the kitchen: "Lazkano, this girl is an actress, right?" Diego answered that she was: "Haven't you ever done the lights for her?" he teased, in an uncharacteristically cheeky tone. But Zeberio was too frazzled to notice: "What's she doing here?" Lazkano informed him that she wanted to meet Soto and that's why he'd invited her over, that he'd be over as soon as the coffee was done, not to worry, that he knew how talkative she was and he would not leave him alone with her for long.

"Does anybody know where Soto is?"

Zeberio was so transparent, Lazkano immediately noticed the disappointment in his face, almost heard him berating himself for entertaining the thought that he might have a chance with the girl.

He had no idea where Soto the nutcase was. *Nutcase, clown*, that's what they called each other. Lazkano sighed, the coffee started to burble to the top of the Italian percolator.

"We'll have to deal with her ourselves."

La Bella Ines was a walking radio. They called her *la bella* not because of how attractive she was, but because of how firmly she believed in her beauty. She seemed quite asexual, although her rather generous breasts dispelled such doubts. Lazkano was surprised that such an androgynous, skinny girl was to Zeberio's taste; he was surprised and delighted, because Zeberio the silent mountain man and Ines the bony chatterbox would make quite the interesting couple.

While they drank coffee listening to the Joy Division album Diego had put on, Lazkano found himself discovering a Zeberio he'd never met before. It was no exaggeration to say that there was an element of fascination going on in there, because, just like

Soto would have preached if he'd been with them, *fascinus* were Roman amulets to ward against the evil eye that were shaped like erect penises.

Ines had only performed in three plays, but she was the host of a music program on the newly created Basque TV (everybody looks more fleshy on television, and it's true she was photogenic), and around that time she was often in the papers because she'd been the lead of a mediocre movie premiered during the San Sebastian Film Festival. Back then, everybody thought she was an actress of great promise.

"Have you seen the last Costa-Gavras? Unbelievable. I really recommend it. They say it's political cinema, as if movie making isn't a political act in itself, right? I watched it last night in Pequeño Casino, how I love that cinema... it's charming, isn't it? So much more than the others, Savoy or Miramar, or Amaya... right? Which ones do you like? Cinemas in San Sebastian are *out of this world...*"

Lazkano remained silent because when it came to that girl and all those questions she answered herself, it was impossible to know if she expected a response or just a nod. He remained silent also because he expected another *right?* that didn't arrive on this occasion (he'd counted twenty once, in one of her soliloquies).

Lazkano observed Zeberio, not daring to say anything. It was then perhaps that Diego first became conscious of his behavior. He was able to speak naturally to Soto and Zeberio, whom he admired so much; why not, he wasn't so different from his idols and, depending on the subject and the context, he could be as good as, or better than, them. In Soto and Zeberio's presence, Lazkano would always speak last, stay in the shadows; he was always the third to offer an opinion, and if they didn't ask for it, he'd just say nothing.

"I like the Astoria," said Zeberio finally, sounding like he'd had to go a long way to fetch those words.

"The Astoria is okay, but the movies they play are not so good."

Lazkano would never forget the look on Zeberio's face at that moment: dejected, disappointed. He'd had to make a supreme effort to utter the words "I like the Astoria," and La Bella Ines, oblivious, had thoroughly dismissed his opinion.

Maybe we all live lives that aren't our own. We're hooked on otherness, forever chasing the next fix.

Or maybe this life we call our own really is ours, but only relatively, because we've built it on memories and shaped it through imitation, following a game of mirrors; this life we call our own is referential, perhaps one hundred percent so, an accumulation of borrowed desires: not only the inevitable mélange of the people we admired as children, the people who educated us, the film stars we emulated (those too, of course), but also, why not, the accumulation of the desires of those we admired and imitated, those who educated us; as if we knew what moved them, what they really desired, as if *they* had ever known what they truly desired; a confused amalgamation of *presumed* desires by those we admire and imitate, therefore, that moves us further and further away from our true abilities and settles on preestablished outlines, powerless to burst through those steel frames imposed on us. As if we really know the desires, behaviors, and motivations of those we imitate. We've believed those borrowed identities, and borrowed new identities against the pretend capital of those borrowed identities; and that's what we refer to as the *self*, although it's nothing but false financial engineering applied to feelings, a thorough lie: a borrowed identity that borrows a new identity without any savings or starting capital. Left to our own devices, deep inside, we've no idea what we truly desire; we've never asked ourselves.

When did this start? Was it always so? Are the family values and the power of religious and sexual iconographies that have been pressed upon us through every pore solely to blame for our detachment from ourselves and our true vocations? Can we be authentic without feeling ridiculous and remain within societal bounds? Are being authentic and being oneself the same thing? Is there a way to escape all this? No, there isn't. Not at least without casting off all lines, without cutting free from our environment.

Diego Lazkano wanted to believe that there was a way of going back to the root, to the authentic impulses of the self; that it was possible to apply a corrective quotient to the standard identity imposed on all of us, and that for that purpose, it would be interesting to analyze the things that repulse us, dig deeper into them; force ourselves to visit the places that disgust us and meet with people who repel us; because in that way our real identity would emerge: digging into that hatred and disgust, to our surprise, we may sometimes hit on something stimulating and attractive. And that would change our way of looking at the world and its inhabitants. It was easier to say all this than it was to actually do it, though.

This affected everyone, for sure. But in Lazkano's case it weighed more heavily because he was conscious of the issue of borrowed identity, which for most is an unconscious fact. Diego fed off two shadows, they were his sustenance, he let those two shadows settle in his head. Soto and Zeberio, Zeberio and Soto, that feeling of living for them had been inside him for years; as if it were his responsibility to live the lives they hadn't lived or as if it were even possible to live three lives at the same time.

Quite a few years passed before Diego saw Ines again. With time, the people who used to appear in newspapers no longer did, and those no one would have ever dreamed would be in print start to show up. Something like that happened with Diego and Ines when the former started to be a regular presence in the press thanks to the success of his novels; Ines, on the other hand, disappeared completely. They crossed paths at a very boring party during a film festival that Diego only attended because he had to. Two long decades and a lot of alcohol had taken their toll on Ines' body, and he almost didn't recognize her.

"What a boring party, right? You remember me, right?"

The voice, the peculiar lilt of the repeat, acted like a switch.

He almost put his foot in it ("La Bella Ines!") but luckily he was able to hold back.

"Ines!"

It wasn't even eleven o'clock yet and she was already swaying on her high heels. The teeth were her own, although it looked like they'd moved around a little. He had to admit that the pounds she'd piled on didn't do her much harm: she had lost the androgynous appearance of yore. Her body was equal to her bosoms now.

She placed her hand on his shoulder, glass and all, and Diego panicked, thinking that she'd spill her drink on him.

"Lazkano, Lazkano...how we've aged!"

Especially you, thought Diego in a burst of vanity, steeling himself against unsolicited opinions.

"You know the nickname we had for you in the theater group, right?"

His fortress was at risk. The poor woman they called La Bella was in possession of a secret weapon that could hurt him.

"The Little Prince."

"The Little Prince?"

"I don't believe it...no one's told you until now?"

He had to lie: "Yes, of course, but I'd forgotten."

"You were so blond, with those curls, you looked like a prince, a child, and those big gray eyes of yours...And always so elegant, with your shirt tucked inside your trousers, wearing the clothes your mommy bought for you, right? Oh, those were the days!" Lazkano bit his lips to swallow his pride.

"It doesn't look like Ken Loach is coming tonight. Why don't you and I go to some quieter place? My house is not far from here..."

He remembered Zeberio just then. How much he liked Ines – "I like the Astoria" – and how they'd disappeared him from the face of the earth before he could see through any of his dreams or fantasies. Yes, he would sleep with Ines no matter what. He owed it to Zeberio.

"You're nervous, right?"

Nervousness masked a lack of appetite. The smell of incense and the elephant-print foulards hanging from the windows in lieu of curtains weren't helping either.

"Let me help you."

He kissed Ines, paying untold attention to her teeth, which looked like they were about to fall out, like domino pieces, one after the other. He felt the woman's rough fingers grabbing hold of his penis. *Ora et labora. If I were my cock*, thought Lazkano, *I'd run like hell from these claws*. But Diego wasn't his cock and she had her own plans, as he'd soon discover.

"You like it, right?"

Not much, he told himself. Things that we think but won't say. Even less he liked her calling him "Little Prince" over and over as she rode him; the sentence "I want your milk, Little Prince" didn't exactly rank high among the phrases that turned Diego on. Maybe it did among Zeberio's? He doubted it. He felt obliged to remember him while he lay naked with Ines: "Is it you fucking her, Kepa? Or is it me in your place, in your honor, doing what you weren't able to do to show you that I love you?"

What memory of Kepa had Ines retained from that day when they had coffee together? Why didn't he just ask her that? Why didn't they try to reconstruct those moments together, sharing their contradictions – "No, it wasn't like that: we drank coffee in the kitchen, not in the living room; and no, it wasn't Joy Division, it was New Order" – and trying to throw light on the tricks memory had played on them? Instead of doing that, Lazkano tried to bring to fruition an old fantasy of Zeberio's among elephant-print foulards and incense smells, in the pits of decadence, in a completely nonsensical way.

Ines tied a knot in the condom and stared at the semen floating there, as if she were expecting to see fish in an aquarium.

There might have been one last chance to do something with a modicum of sense: he should have stayed for breakfast and asked Ines about Zeberio. Ask her what she felt when she heard the news about his disappearance. If something had stirred inside. But no, Diego didn't have the strength to stay. He abandoned La Bella Ines to her sleep and had difficulty finding the door, hidden behind a blue uniform that hung from a hook: it was a man's uniform, a highway tollbooth one. Diego decided it was better not to think about the owner of that uniform at all.

That's the best part. The risk of the fall, and the certainty that you'll have the chance to fall again.

They're Fabian and Fabian. They call each other Fabian from under their respective hoods. They are like a comedy act.

"*¿Te gusta el teatro, verdad?* You like the theater, right? Fabian likes it too…he's so into theater, you know. He used to love the stage, but had to give it up because he wasn't making enough to live on. Now he doles out the parts. *Se encarga del reparto.*"

"Get it? Do you know what he means when he says I dole out the parts? *Soy yo quien reparte.*"

The two men wearing hoods show Diego a bunch of photographs.

"Do you know this one?"

They've tied him to a chair and, with each question, give the legs of the chair a kick, making it stumble but not badly enough to fall over. It's enough, however, to make the person on the chair feel dizzier and dizzier.

"And this other one?"

Diego doesn't recognize anyone in the photographs and tells the truth: he has no idea. But every time he says so, one of them punches him in the stomach, while the other pinches him softly on the back in a very disturbing way while holding the back of the chair.

He is feeling so unwell that he hopes, from the bottom of his heart, to see someone he knows in that pile of photographs. *Let someone turn up, I'll tell you that yes, I do know him: but please let someone I know turn up, for the love of God.*

At last, one: he's not a fellow commando, nor anyone from the militant group, but a junkie from Herrera, a loser they all know, so desperate to shoot up he once held up an espadrille shop. Diego thought his time had come.

"This one, yes, I know him."

Not one, but two punches to the stomach this time and, more surprisingly, the man who's been pinching him softly on the back smacks the back of his head hard.

"Are you pulling our leg? Everybody knows that guy."

Only then Diego begins to understand the mechanics of torture: the interrogation is completely illogical, the whole objective is for the tortured never to know what the next move is, the next reaction might be. In this way they erase your identity, they set your nerves on edge, leave you completely disoriented and terrified; and then, when you're completely in their hands and at their mercy, confessing becomes your only option, the only means by which you may not lose your mind. You see no way out other than giving your friends up and, even though you hate yourself, that deformed self that you hate right then is so deranged and unmoored that you hate him as if he were someone else. Someone who's intimately linked to you, but is not you.

They put needles under his nails.

"Should we apply the Boger swing to him, Fabian?"

"A foreign technique? No, not the Boger swing…"

Lazkano has no idea what the Boger swing might be. Blood is pouring out from under his nails. They play Rocío Jurado singing "Como una ola" in full volume on the cassette player.

Like a wave.

"Don't torture me with that music."

Fabian starts singing:

"Fui tan feliz en tus brazos, fui tan feliz en tu puerto…"

I was so happy in your arms, I was so happy in your port…

"He's so theatrical, isn't he?"

They place a piece of metal between his teeth and lips and slap him on the face. When he spits on the floor he sees it's a coin with Franco's head on it, *"Sentí en mis labios tus labios de amapola, como una ola."*

I felt your poppy-soft lips on my lips, like a wave.

Do not let me go, thinks Lazkano, *if I must continue being a rag doll I will, but I'd rather be in your hands, with my wrists bound together; don't reward me by removing the handcuffs, keep squeezing me like a lemon after I tell you everything I know, until there's nothing left of me, I beg of you. Destroy me. I deserve it.*

They force him to lie facedown and put one of the chair legs on the back of his knee. They perforate and burn the soles of his feet. When they crush his little toe with a pair of pliers, he waits no more. He lets it out. There was no need to apply the Boger swing. *Apply or perform*? Who knows.

"Moulinaou Street," he says.

"Dónde hostias. Where the fuck is that?"

"In Angelu."

In his naïveté, Lazkano thinks they'll get him out of that basement and into the police station. But the truth is that they are not in a cell in a police station, but somewhere else. He should have realized it, but he's too out of it to notice details, to inflict the measure of time and space on those senseless events. It's a big farmhouse, set apart, far away from noises: car noises or any other kind. The building seems to sit on top of a hill. Only the sound of birds outside, birds singing without a worry in the world. When they climb the stairs he sees a big window and it seems to him that, as they approach it, the two men, Fabian and Fabian, who drag him off, arms bound, clasping his elbows tight, lessen the pressure, as if in getting close to the window they were giving him the option to kill himself, which is what he thinks: *Throw yourself out the window and redeem your betrayal, if you have the balls.* Yes, it's an invitation, he won't be a rag doll anymore, he won't be a traitor anymore, one leap and he'll never have to look at himself in the mirror again, the window is open, he can hear the birds singing to him, "Jump, Diego, c'mon, don't be a coward, the birds are asking you to do it, show now the bravery you didn't show before. Fly."

And he does.

His two keepers let him go – he knows they were inviting him to do it, there is no doubt now – he rests a shoulder on the frame and jumps out the window with his eyes closed. He falls onto some ferns, and soon sees Fabian and Fabian laughing by the window: he fell only about a meter and a half. "What, you thought the torture was over? No way! Your pathetic suicide attempt was part of the game, it was just the last turn of the screw to totally wreck your identity." The last one? Surely not...*the show must go on!*

"See, Fabian?"

"I didn't think he'd dare. Anyway, he didn't shout anything when he jumped...I was expecting a "Gora Euskadi Askatuta," freedom for the Basque Country, or something like that."

Fat Fabian reaches out to Tall Fabian, who is apparently so fond of the theater, and hands over three brown one hundred peseta bills for the bet they'd made. They both come out through the window, which can't be more than two meters high. The two hooded men help him stand up and Lazkano, humiliated, decides he won't look at them again. Then, as if they'd decided that their captive had seen too much, they cover his eyes with a black, opaque eye mask, before they force him to climb into the trunk of the car. He spends the rest of the evening there. They don't move the car. When they take him out and bring him back to the same cell, he notices that it's colder outside.

He thinks he hears the echo of Soto and Zeberio's screams through the corridors.

"Do you recognize your friends' screams?"

They caught them. On Moulinaou Street. In Angelu.

It's them, there's no doubt. He's especially shocked by Zeberio's deep voice, so accustomed he was to his silence and discretion. His howls are anything but discreet.

Finally, they let Diego leave. Look at it this way: sometimes setting you free when others are still imprisoned is a form of revenge.

"You haven't been very helpful, but it's all right. Since you've belonged to a theater group and my friend Fabian here loves showbiz, we're gonna let you go."

Diego is about to say that, truly, he hates the theater, that it's Soto who loves it, but he doesn't do that. He doesn't say a word. Not this time.

"But before anything else, we're going to do you a favor."

Fabian takes out his switchblade.

Idoia's call caught Lazkano by surprise. He hadn't heard from her at all since he'd moved from Angelu to Lille, and from Lille to Donostia. Only sporadically he'd get indirect news about Ana: she had two kids and still worked at the library, although she was in the administration now. She was one of the bosses. She lived in Larratxo, a neighborhood of Donostia, and he never saw her in the city, although he remembered the shiny puddles of her green eyes and her perfect twenty-year-old body every morning. He still loved her, the way only a flawless happiness one has run away from can be loved.

"I'd like to interview you..."

How things change, comrade: Idoia had left *Egin*, the leftist Basque newspaper and now worked in the Bilbao offices of *El Mundo*, a right-leaning Spanish newspaper.

Instead of one of the cafés from their second life – when they decided they'd stop sleeping together – they chose a café from their first life, one they used to frequent as a couple. After the interview, they happily stay on to have a beer in the Barandiaran. They've plenty to tell each other. Idoia's mom has cancer, life has begun to show them that it's time to turn the corner.

Cruel irony: Diego confesses that his mom has cancer too;

they diagnosed her two months ago. His father disappeared and was never seen again, dementia. Shocked by the news and the connection spontaneously reawakened between them, Idoia can't suppress a sincere *"baizea*, it's not true, is it?" that transports Diego to a different era. She always had a beautiful voice, although she was deaf to his calls to join the theater group. They order another beer and continue talking about the stage and the malignancy of the tumors and their chances of remission, the benefits of a change of diet, the evils of red meat and other matters. They are thoroughly informed on the subject. Idoia more than Diego, which doesn't bode well for Idoia's mom, Diego decides. The more you know, the more serious the illness.

Idoia hasn't changed at all in these years, at least not as much as I have, and that doesn't bode well for me either, Diego then tells himself.

"I didn't know this sickness was so related to numbers. Everything is about 'rates.'"

"Numbers soothe people."

"I don't know if they soothe people, but they soothe doctors for sure."

The ailments of parents. A signal: in a few short years they'll become our ailments. It's about time they told each other what they kept to themselves in the past, without shame or remorse. "I was so hurt by your indifference, you were so insensitive when you delayed the publication of my article on Dario Fo." He should tell her: "I loved biting your neck, your way of suggesting we should fuck; how you'd wait for me in bed, naked, smiling, how you'd caress and scratch the wall with your eyes closed as you straddled my face tempting my mouth with your slit; I regret not waking next to you more often. But we said no remorse." No tricks either, no suggestions that they *could* have something together. No regrets and no false hopes.

"Are you still with Remiro?"

Mikel Remiro. Silvio Rodríguez, *la pluma y la trova*. Quill and song.

Idoia opens the palm of her hand as if to signal five, and displays her wedding band with a look of resignation. That, at least, is what Diego sees.

She tells him that they don't have children: they tried, but she never got pregnant. "It's Mikel, he can't." They're considering adoption now. China, Ukraine, Morocco. Diego has a dentist's appointment at five p.m., but he doesn't mention it. He doesn't even call to cancel the appointment. It's raining outside, it's cozy inside, but the café is filled to the brim, they feel observed, the atmosphere is not precisely conducive to discretion, everyone can see them. This would be the moment to say goodbye and wish each other the best and wish the worst for their respective mothers' rhizomatic creatures. But they don't want to. Even though they should start talking about things that can't be talked about in order to keep talking, that's not something they want either. They've already deconstructed their old friends' CVs, as well as the first divorces and separations among them – special emphasis on that point: "So many of us fail at it" – and the name and clientele changes of the bars of the good old days; they even go through a quick assessment of current politics, a subject they never touched *in the good old days*. They are back at the beginning.

"Soto and Zeberio – that was so hard."

"It has been hard, it's still hard," he corrects himself in his mind. He thinks it, but doesn't say it.

Diego would like to say many things to his friend from a bygone time ("I am weakened, we are both weak," things that we say when we feel weak), but he knows that more intimate circumstances are required to talk about certain intimate matters, and that only far from the world, on a white bed in a white room, with white sheets and their two naked bodies, only there would he be able to tell her most of the things he's got in mind. He'd like to ask her many questions and for her to ask him just as many. And answer them one by one openly, caressing each other's backs vertebra by vertebra, as if counting the rings of a felled tree, staring at each other every now and then, spying on each other to establish how much they've aged, and, afterward, as a form of psychotherapy, tell each other some too-painful things, having chosen to repress others that might hurt even more.

The conversation takes place in Lazkano's house: Diego lying on top of Idoia, his increasingly engorged penis quiet on the furrow of her butt, and the girl with both hands folded under her chin, her auburn-dyed hair cascading down her back in a long ponytail, nothing to do with her *garçon* hair days, both looking out the window instead of looking into each other's eyes. Both naked in a room where everything is white. Both lamenting the miserable world out there without much conviction.

He'd like to tell her, and he does: "I discovered ways and pleasures that I never knew with you." He'd like to tell her, and he does: "You left me only good memories." He'd like to tell her, and he does: "I owe you the feeling of not having wasted my youth in vain." He'd like to tell her, and he does: "There is such a thing as dysfunctional desire, a construction of desire that helps us function, and you've collaborated in the construction of my dysfunctional desire. You are important to me, even though I have hardly seen you in these past few years. Or maybe that dysfunctional desire of mine is what's important."

He'd like to tell her some things, and he does, but at one point the thought crosses his mind that many of them he should say to Ana, instead of Idoia.

"I'm not saying anything new, but, if we were transparent, if our thoughts were in plain sight, we'd all be in hell and be happily ashamed...or shamefully happy, I'm not sure," Idoia says. "Happy criminals," she adds then.

"It's almost like *you* are the writer," Diego says. She's still very good at verbal ping-pong.

Maybe she still doesn't like minty men, Diego's eyes well up, and his tears move Idoia to tears. How time wrecks us. *Does my love bother you?*

"I want to be your purveyor of songs again."

They should have parted as friends at the Barandiaran Café, avoid the conversations and secrets shared in bed; soon, on the table they vacated, young horny couples would sit and not feel obsolete while talking about love... They should have parted as friends, but they weren't friends: they'd been lovers, they'd stopped hearing from one another, their parents were sick, they'd had coffee, avoided certain subjects and tentatively approached others, they'd whispered some things into each other's ears and clumsily undressed one another; and realized, as soon as they walked out into the damp night, that the rain had aged less than them, and that they had no intention of returning to their previous lives.

They were too tired to resist the temptation of staying in bed, naked, on top of one another, giving in to desire.

Before long, Idoia had gathered her belongings and moved to Diego's. At the beginning, Lazkano thought she'd brought an astonishingly small amount of luggage along. With time, he understood that she'd left everything to her husband, that she felt guilty at having abandoned him and that, as some sort of compensation, she had left him in a state of pretend widowhood. "I'll no longer be with you, but all the things we shared will stay with you, the objects and memories, the things we bought together and separately, the practical and symbolic purchases, I leave them all here; you decide what to do with them." It wasn't just her attempt at minimizing frictions after the emotional breakup of their long-standing coexistence; it was also her way of giving herself completely to Diego, or at least that's what he thought, because if their love didn't survive, Idoia would be left with nothing; and the fact that she wanted to share his material life too, his pots and pans and his sheets, the blankets on his sofa and the chairs on his balcony, his nail clippers and hair dryer – isn't that commitment? He understood it all as a sign of her unconditional love: "I believe in this relationship with every fiber of my being, you're the gamble of my life, I do not contemplate the possibility of the crumbling of our love, I don't have a plan B."

And things went well for the first few months, Idoia grew used to her new habitat, to Diego's ungodly hours – he always wrote at night – and the incomprehensible neurosis that led him to lock up his writing desk and his study, to that insane secrecy that she found initially interesting, later ridiculous, and finally exasperating, to his unpredictable mood swings, to his warped reasons not to have children ("my genes are too defective, it's time to put an end to this genealogical tree").

Diego revealed every detail of something he'd never confessed to anyone before, surprising even himself as the words came out of his mouth in front of Idoia: how and where those marks on his skin came to be – "But before anything else, we're going to do you a favor" – after he confessed that Soto and Zeberio were on Moulinaou Street – "where the fuck is that?" "In Angelu" – and how it was then, only then, when he'd said all he could say, once the torturers knew what they wanted to know, once he'd tried to kill himself, it was then and not before that they branded him with those letters that would remind him not of the police, but of the name his own comrades would give him: they didn't spell out that Diego was a terrorist, a kidnapper, or an assassin, they weren't the GAL death squad's initials or his captors' signature, no; what they wrote on his skin was nothing but the truth. Under torture, yes, but, all the same, he'd given up two of his comrades who'd been forced to go into hiding after holding up a bank with toy guns (the real ones didn't arrive in time), two puppies who were too young for crime and repentance; even though they were older than him, they were still too sleepy, their "sleeper cell" not fully formed yet.

If they had captured Soto instead, would he have given up Zeberio and Lazkano? He would never know.

"Not with a *b*, you ignoramus! It's written with a *v*! *¡Es con uve!*"

When he heard them say it, he couldn't imagine what they

were doing on his back, still hurting too much from the needles they'd stuck under his nails and on the soles of his feet, because apparently no traces are left on the soles of feet; we've inherited, from our primate cousins, the ability to walk on thorns and keep going. And that travesty on Lazkano's back. Did one of them really think it was written with a *b*? It was possible, although in that moment he thought it was a calculated strategy, repeated over and over with the object of blasting his morale. And it worked, of course it worked. The pain of not being able to guess what Fabian and Fabian were tattooing on his back was no lesser pain than the one caused by the stabs into his feet and under his nails: "What are they doing? What are they writing with a *b* instead of a *v*?"

"*Qué más dará.* Who cares, let's leave it as is, with a *b*."

Here's a hitherto unexplored classification that pushes beyond the typical good cop, bad cop dichotomy: educated cop, uneducated cop.

So he carried that silent brand with him, which he'd so often contemplated in the mirror, which he never dared show anyone, which was too distressing to show in court (and what was the point, anyway, they always said wounds like those were self-inflicted, plenty of judgments established that).

That word. *Chibato.* Snitch. Misspelled with a *b* instead of a *v*. Because it was true. Even though it happened under torture, he'd given his two friends up – "Moulinaou Street, in Angelu."

Because he should have been there instead of one of his friends. Because he didn't have a driver's license. Because not having one changed what was supposed to have been his first mission, which would have led him to suffer a degree of torture far worse than the one he'd experienced, and would have ultimately killed him.

What he obviously never told Idoia was what he did when they let him go free. How he went to Angelu and found the house on Moulinaou Street where Soto and Zeberio hid half empty; how worried the owners of the house were about them; how the Redhead watched mistrustfully from a nearby bistro without coming anywhere near him and, how, remembering Soto's paranoia, when he was left alone in it, he searched his room from top to bottom and found Faulkner's *As I Lay Dying* and a salmon-pink folder, and inside all of Soto's typewritten manuscripts, hidden under a blanket with the winter bedding, invisible to everyone, on the highest part of the wardrobe.

And Idoia, even though there was barely a trace of the letters branded on Diego's back anymore, still saw them, she saw that *chibato*, and she saw the snitch too. She began to regret having fallen into Diego's arms so easily, although she realized she had no right to think like that, that Diego wasn't guilty, that it was hard enough for him and he was tormented enough as it was, that he'd paid the price for his sin a thousand times over with the accumulated insomnia of all those years, while the men who tortured him walked the streets freely, probably not too far from there, not having lost any stripes and having probably earned a medal or two for their inestimable service to the motherland.

Things were getting worse for Idoia at work. She complained a lot, especially since they started asking her for radio collaborations. "Comprehensive journalism." They were exploiting workers without any qualms.

"What do the regulations say? Surely what they're asking of you is not legal…"

If only it were so easy, Idoia tells herself. In truth, they hardly saw each other: by the time she arrived home, Diego was already under lock and key in his study, writing. She ate dinner alone. By the time he went to bed it was six or seven in the morning. They'd barely spend an hour together in bed before Idoia would get up to catch the bus and go to work. In circumstances such as these, their sexual relationship could only be somnambulist. They only had weekends together, and even then indifference reigned: by midday Diego would push away the copy of *El Mundo* and start reading *Berria*, old *Egin's* new incarnation, displaying his scorn for the newspaper Idoia worked for quite blatantly. While Diego prepared coffee and grapefruit juice – his usual breakfast – Idoia ate a light meal. They couldn't even share that. Theirs was a perpetual jet lag reaching from opposite directions.

"I'm thinking of leaving the newspaper."

"You could…money is not a problem right now."

"I won't leave until I have something else lined up."

"I could get you work as a reader if you want…is that something that might interest you?"

"As a reader?"

"Fede always needs readers at the publisher's…they don't last long, you know how grumpy he is. But you could give it a go…"

"Would I need to write reports?"

"Not exactly. His eyesight is failing and he needs someone to read out loud to him. I think that with your voice…"

Fede Epelde, Diego's editor. A sybaritic, grumbling sixty-something. No, thanks. She'd rather stay where she was than go and work for him.

Not many months after Idoia substituted a dead relationship for a stimulating one, the new one started to decline. She left her husband without a second thought, it came easily, which would seem to indicate that she'd been ready to take the leap for a while. But that didn't at all guarantee the solidity or longevity of the new relationship. Truth be told, the spark died down pretty quickly. Diego was jealous to the core. He detected potential rivals in all Idoia's interviewees. They were mostly second- and third-rate politicians, people who bored Idoia to death, but Diego, always on the threshold of paranoia, sensed that interviewees went into full peacock display at the expense of the interviewer. Things got worse when the newspaper strengthened its culture section and Idoia, her hopes somewhat renewed, started interviewing dancers, actors, and writers every now and then. According to Diego, they were all mediocre, secondhand artists, parasites who lived off public subsidies without ever lifting a finger. That's why she was surprised that when she interviewed Txema Santamaria, Diego had nothing but sweet praise for him.

"That's a really interesting guy. Compared to all the other good-for-nothings...he's got a very good head on him."

Idoia was surprised because by that point they never agreed on anything and, for once, she thought the same. To her, Santamaria had always seemed a seducer through and through, someone with very clear ideas, a hyperconscious photographer who knew that what he did was only for a minority; a hipster committed to the olden ways who developed his Ilford films at home in a darkroom and wouldn't print many copies of each negative, someone who was always in search of new horizons, who was so different from all the other photographers she'd met at the newspapers.

Lazkano's comment surprised Idoia more so when she realized that Txema was a dear friend of Lazkano, even though they hadn't seen much of each other in the past few years; that his first book's author photograph, "the best portrait anyone has ever taken of me," was Txema's work. Idoia could only agree, the photo was gorgeous, all chiaroscuros, the kind you never tire of looking at. He showed her the portraits he'd taken of the members of the theater group: Zeberio with a stage light's lead wrapped around his neck as if it were a scarf, Soto dressed as Groucho Marx, Gloria, baton in her hand, indulging her director's role, Diego sitting with his arms around Ana's and Sara's shoulders. All of them smiling.

"Ana...you two made a good couple."

She meant it, but said it intending to hurt him. Diego welled up. "Yes, I remember her every morning, I abandoned her; I too know how to disappear from someone's life without warning." He thinks it, but he doesn't say it.

"And this one?"

"We used to call her La Bella Ines, don't you remember her? She used to join us in every demonstration..."

"The same girl who was in Agatha Christie's *The Mousetrap*?"

"The very same one."

"She's so young here...I wouldn't have recognized her."

"And the photographer, Txema, of course. We could have him over for dinner sometime, if you'd like."

Idoia agreed at the beginning, but tried to dissuade Diego after a while. She didn't want to have Txema over for dinner, she liked him too much, he might become the escape point from the routine that bound her to Diego – that photographer was a lover and she knew she could easily jump into his arms, he was more than "a really interesting guy." Obviously, she didn't say any of this to Diego.

"We've both been in a bad mood lately, let's give it some time."

"What?"

Idoia was beginning to get tired of having to repeat everything twice. "What?" "How?" It was never enough to say things once, Diego was always lost in his thoughts; when a couple started with that kind of stuff – *what, how, say that again* – it was a sign that things were coming to an end. But the end can last a long time. Even a whole lifetime, in some cases. Mostly because Idoia didn't want to admit that moving in with Lazkano, betting on him, putting all her chips on one number, had been a great mistake.

"What?"

"I'm saying it's not the best time to invite anyone over. Maybe he didn't like the interview. We spent two hours in his studio, I've had to edit the content a lot…I might be uncomfortable."

"Nonsense. I'm sure he's going to find it so funny that you and I are together."

And Diego, stubborn: "I'm going to call him." And he does. "Don't do it, Diego, don't you realize? You're letting the wolf into your house; you gave your friends up once, under torture, and now you're giving yourself up, you'll regret it, don't encourage your old friend: he's much more interesting than you." She thinks it, but she doesn't say it.

They decide to eat out. It's a weekday. Txema is opening an exhibition in Donostia and is going to spend the week there; and yes, he found it funny that Diego and Idoia are together. Txema liked, no, *loved* her interview in the newspaper – things people say out of politeness (or not) – "I was about to call you to congratulate you." They go through two bottles of expensive wine, laugh nonstop, Diego and Txema, Txema and Diego. Having them both in front of her, it's obvious to her who is more original, more anarchic, more passionate, who believes more in what he's doing. *What are you doing, Idoia? Are you about to make the same mistake? Don't you recall that you spent your chance to start over a year ago?*

Apart from that comparison from which Lazkano comes out the loser, Idoia detects other alarming signals. Even though Diego addresses Txema with sincere admiration ("a true photographer in this world of fake artists"), the admiration isn't mutual. When Txema finally stops going on about the photographs he takes in abandoned quarries and houses and – with forced politeness – asks him, "What about you, what do you have in mind? Will there be a new novel this year?" Idoia clearly notices that he's not really paying attention, that he's completely indifferent to Diego's verbal diarrhea, and that nothing is more pathetic than realizing a friend you admire looks down on you with feigned deference. Actually, something is: not noticing that your friend looks down on you while your wife does.

As they order desserts, and Diego gets tipsier – he's the heavier drinker of the three and the one compulsively topping off their glasses – Txema's eyes turn more and more blatantly toward Idoia, he stares into her eyes for longer – "what are you doing with this milquetoast?" – maybe because he has perceived the woman's desolation: Idoia has sent him imperceptible signals that he's been able to pick up; the tiredness, the tiredness again, a leaden counterweight that makes truth rise. She doesn't have the strength to pretend, just like, later, when Diego gets up to pay, complaining about the waiters' slowness, she doesn't have the strength to push Txema's hand away when he takes the opportunity to grab her arm.

"I'm at the Hotel Orly, call me."

"Will you look at me with those same eyes after you've come?"

Txema doesn't answer the question. Instead, he dives into Idoia's thighs, and she feels him write, with the tip of his tongue, every truth and every lie they could tell each other. And it occurs to her that words are unnecessary, that they are all useless, whether they are written in a newspaper or in a book, whether she's written them or Diego has, that the only thing that matters is the tip of that pleasurable tongue, which, if it weren't for the feel of Txema's warm hands on her thighs, she could mistake for the wet beak of a little bird. Idoia bends until her knees touch the mattress; like a trap opening up, she lifts her waist and arches her back and feels Txema's teeth retract, although in that moment a little bite would do nothing but increase her bliss, so possessed she feels by the desire to explode. Panting, she throws a cascade of sheets on the floor, kicks the air, and, pushing the blankets away, peels the mattress, leaving it naked, clean. When her breathing subsides, she starts sucking her lover's cock.

"Will you look at me with those same eyes after you've come?"

"Are you as daring as I think you are, my filly? As self-destructive?" Txema caresses Idoia's beautiful mane while trying to find some white hairs, and finds three or four; Idoia's tresses make him think about the way the horsehair in an overused cello bow breaks up; now Txema is a blind mother looking for lice in her child's head, "Let's see if I can find more out-of-tune strings among these fine hairs"; all in vain, his sense of touch is not that refined. *These imperfect details that reveal aspects of our aging and decrepitude . . . these details always turn me on so much*, thinks Txema, *because they make that moment of ecstasy-that's-not-so-different-from-others more real*. But it might be better to stop feeling for white hairs, because when you find one you find another and so on and so forth.

Dawn comes silently into the room, apart from a few random smacking sounds, the smack of saliva, the smack of tongues and lips that softly meet and pull apart. Idoia thinks that life escapes while she holds the man's cock tight between her legs; she doesn't want to come, not yet, she doesn't want to leave this world, the world of pleasure.

"Will you look at me with those same eyes after you've come?"

The blinds are not fooling anyone, dawn is breaking, soon they'll come to clean the room, cart and all; Idoia looks at the bedside table: there it is, they forgot to hang the DO NOT DISTURB sign from the door – in five languages, no less, although Basque is not one of them, of course: the whole world is foreign to us – and all they need now is for someone to knock on the door and come in. That fear adds a slight delay to Idoia's next round of sighs.

"Txema," she murmurs twice, and those four syllables are open containers, overflowing bowls that spill over. "It excites me to hear you say my name," he'd confessed earlier. And Idoia thinks that his wife must not say his name when they make love, that her way of doing it must feel anonymous and that's why he prefers her in bed. People come and go along the corridors; wheeled suitcases, ping, the elevator's bell. They go up, they go down, they come in, they come out. It's the drywall, everything filters through, even people's coughs. Txema hasn't come yet and Idoia takes his glistening shaft in her mouth again, pushes his thighs apart while placing her clitoris in Txema's direct line of vision. He doesn't dare ask if she likes to swallow cum, or if she only does it to pleasure him (it gives him pleasure, it's true, and each time Idoia's throat pulsates differently), or if it really gives her pleasure to finish like that. He doesn't ask her what differences, what nuances, she detects in alternate sperms, if there are any, doesn't she sometimes think that, after swallowing sperm, fertilized tadpoles, twin frogs, could appear in her vomit? He might ask her after two, three, or four dates, as a joke. There may not be as many dates. There haven't been many before now.

Last night they watched a pornographic movie together in their hotel room. Txema wants his next exhibition to be a pornographic series. "I'm researching on the Internet, have you ever looked for pornography?" Idoia confesses that she never has, and suddenly feels like a nun. "You should try someday, amateur porno is a world unto itself: it never ends."

But theirs will, their world will end.

She doesn't swallow his cum today, and she washes the mess off her hand by rubbing it against her thigh, kisses Txema, and walks to the window. She opens the double curtains, the black ones first, a transparent set afterward, as if the play, the show, is about to start; but something else needs opening first: the blinds, halfway up. Her pupils panic when they absorb a beam of light that looks to have been washed through with chlorine. It could be arm wrestling or a sword fight: who will avoid looking at the clock the longest? Who will hold out for longer the need-curiosity-desire-want to check out the time? Isn't the question in both of their heads? Aren't they both trying to guess it by the light flooding in from the street?

Who is weaker?

What does weakness have to do with being realistic?

Who will be first to allow the world outside to enter their kingdom of sex and pleasure, ruining the vibe with the wrong turn of phrase?

Who will need the least time to slip right back into the daily routine of work?

Who will be first in thinking up practical questions, coming up with alibis, realizing that we're not immortal but we are immoral? Who will be first to modulate their voice with deliberate inflexions?

Who will leave the hotel room first, even when they are still inside it?

Idoia stands in front of the mirror so that, instead of one, two people will be candidates for the sad little title of Most Miserable and Cowardly Person in the World Today. "Why do I punish myself continuously?"

When Txema comes out of the bathroom, the swords in his eyes are still high up, looking straight ahead.

Idoia is by the window. She lights up a Marlboro. An arrow of smoke stabs her breast, she scratches between her legs, right there where the semen is drying, relieving her itch in a slightly masculine way. Txema likes that gesture. He should tell her. She's got quite a bushy bush, earlier he'd found a black, very black, hair trapped between his teeth. *I love these moments with her, I wouldn't like to lose them. I should tell her*, thinks Txema.

He thinks it, but doesn't say. "Later, after two or three dates."

"Looks promising."

He's talking about the weather. The light, however (the light, too, unfortunately), that cascade of light that looks like it's been washed with chlorine and disinfected, filtered through the carpet dust and the hotel's air conditioning, that light can seem sad on occasion.

Txema puts his pants on, Idoia too. No underwear: just jeans on skin. She kisses Txema on the lips and, playful, sticks her used thong down the waist of his pants, as a stimulus for his worn-out balls, which have retreated into their sack. A souvenir devoid of nostalgia.

"Don't forget me, okay?"

But, in the way she's looking at him, Txema reads something else: "Don't even dream of hurting me, okay?"

But Idoia still loves Diego a bit, she likes the way he is at home, she lives comfortably and easily with Diego, despite every "what?" and "how?" Besides, he is in a very good mood, it looks like things are going well with his latest book, although Idoia still has no idea what it's about. And even though Txema tells her "I want to photograph you naked," and Idoia replies "don't even think about it," "don't use cheap tricks with me" or "*baizea*, don't tell me this cheap trick works with the others," and Txema retorts "what others?" Despite all that, even though it feels like he turns her skin inside out and makes her feel things she hasn't felt for a long time, she decides to be honest, because she knows that she's just a plaything to Txema, that he receives a lot of phone calls he never answers, and that his face shows her, when he turns the cell phone off without answering, that the calls come from women, and not just one woman – his wife. And since she has decided to be honest, because she can't stand leading a double or a secret life, she confesses everything to Diego, her foolishness, that she slept with Txema, his friend, "a true photographer in this world of fake artists." And Diego goes quiet and a bit pale, says "thanks for telling me the truth" while swallowing all his pride, and disappears for the night, leaving her alone in a house that no longer feels her own.

After a sleepless night, the phone rings. The call is from the hospital. Idoia's mother died.

White roses on a black coffin, and suddenly we are surprised: obvious beauty reawakens us briefly at unexpected moments. A call from Mikel *la pluma y la trova*, quill and song: "It's so nice of you to call me," Idoia says, and she really means it; "how are you?" and she, instead of telling him how she is, tells him that her mother "was very sick, she died like a little bird," and he replies "call if you need anything." Her ex-husband comes to the funeral, and to the burial too. Her colleagues from the newspaper offer their condolences: Roger, Victor, the intern Pilar. She is grateful. Very grateful. Diego doesn't hold her hand until they start to lower the black box. He does it softly, and Idoia squeezes his fingers.

"There is no sex life in the grave." She thinks it, but she doesn't say it.

It's only with dusk that Idoia realizes that Diego was wearing the suit that he always wore to his book launches to her mother's funeral. She's not sure what that means.

Perhaps it's not the right moment, but she doesn't know what else to say:

"I've been so crazy, I can't even think of seeing him again. I would understand if you...however..."

"No. I want you to stay. I love you."

He says it almost in tears. "Not as much as I loved Ana, but I love you." He thinks it, but he doesn't say it.

"Would you forgive me if I did something like that to you?" Diego asks her.

Idoia is too tired to lie. Tiredness has always been very relevant to their relationship. Now too.

"I don't know. I don't know if I'd forgive you."

"I understand."

"With time, we forget everything."

Diego doesn't say anything. Only to himself: "Yes, we forget everything, like my father did."

Idoia kisses him, undresses him as if he were a child, and then starts to undress herself. Diego is not playing along, so Idoia caresses his spine vertebra by vertebra, as if counting the rings of a felled tree, until she reaches the place where that now-erased word used to be: *chibato*. They haven't made love for a long time. Idoia wonders if Diego masturbated often in that time. Seeing how quickly his penis becomes erect, it would seem not. And she finds that hypothetical fast flattering.

He mounts her from behind, on all fours, without reciprocal caresses, and pulls his member out at the last moment and comes all over her back like a porn star, vigorously. She senses as much aggression and ire as pleasure in Diego.

They both know they don't have a future together.

LEGIS SILVA – THE LAW OF THE JUNGLE

SOMETIMES, THE ENGINEER FORCES HIMSELF to remember the day they kidnapped him. It seems very far away, but he knows he mustn't forget:

"When I get out of here they'll ask me all the time, and I'll have to give them every single detail. The air was cold, I'd just had a shave and put on that Williams lotion my wife found too strong. They grabbed me from behind, I felt an arm, one above mine and another around my neck. I quickly realized that the hands belonged to two different people. There must have been a third one driving, that's usually the case. They told me they were the ETA and that they were kidnapping me, to keep calm, that nothing bad would happen if I obeyed. 'Nothing bad is going to happen to you...' They covered my head with a black hood; although, to be honest, they were the ones wearing hoods. What they put on my head was more like a black sack that smelled of dust and apples, without any holes for the mouth or eyes, I can't say more than that; who knows what the original use of that rough sack might have been, who knows what attic it must have been kept in, if it might have covered someone else's head previously. How many sacks like this one do armed organizations require for this type of endeavor? Ramming a head into a black sack, is there a more perverse gesture a torturer can inflict on his victim? 'You are a victim, therefore you must put the black sack on your head.' I could hardly breathe inside the car, inside the black sack, but I fell asleep very quickly, I'm sure they gave me something, either they injected it or they made me smell it, who knows. I didn't feel any pricks on my body, only an intense smell, like the smell of farm tools piled up in a farm's attic."

He's going to tell it just so. And then he'll tell how he woke up in the *zulo*. A hole, a square igloo, a mousetrap that looked like an irregular room in a mental asylum: with tiny holes, perforations that allowed the air to run through, although just barely, and a trapdoor that linked him to the outside world, the world beyond the doghouse that was his habitat.

And then the ants. "There were hundreds, they came out of the holes and crawled up my arms," he'll say, in a way that many would find hard to believe.

They weren't carrying weapons. At least they never showed them to him, although maybe they kept them well hidden; they knew that it would never cross the kidnapping victim's mind to confront them, to try to run away.

How do you pass the time when you've been buried alive?

It's imperative to establish discipline. Make some decisions. Schedule your time. He asked them for a watch, and they gave him an old Casio wristwatch, the kind you get from duck shoot-ing galleries at carnivals.

That's what he told his kidnapper. "It looks like a prize from a shoot-a-duck range." And he'd swear the kidnapper smiled, even though he couldn't see his face. The engineer would have never thought he'd utter such words in a hole in the ground: *shoot-a-duck*.

It's important to know what time it is, how many days he's spent there, exactly.

He does his exercises before breakfast. Squats, crunches. Fifty of each. He could do more, and he did do them, filled with ire and impotence, during the first few days, but it wasn't a good idea: with all that sweat, the walls got coated in condensation and the air turned unbreathable for the rest of the day; inside the hole things have their own measure, which is absolutely not the same as the measure of things outside, it's another, new, a com-pletely different one. Condensation must be considered. After that, breakfast arrives: he eats it slowly, paying close attention. When they bring him cracker bread, before spreading the but-ter on it he feels its hard, harsh surface with his fingertips, he caresses that cracker bread with a surface like sandpaper; after the first few weeks, he realizes that the most alarming aspect of being kidnapped is the loss of his senses: how continuously seeing and hearing the same things – in other words, practically nothing – dulls his senses, especially touch and sight. It's different with hearing: the opposite happens, it sharpens, to the point that one can even detect strange sound waves and murmurs.

At the beginning he couldn't hear anything. But it's impossible not to hear anything at all. His own heartbeat, for example, his bowel movements, the smacking of his tongue, the gnashing of his teeth, his breathing rhythms. Every now and then he snapped his fingers, right hand and left hand, to ensure that his body maintained its usual ability to make noises. That he was still *himself*. And then, of course, there were the noises from the outside. The ones he thought he heard during the long hours he spent on his own, without perceiving a single sound or signal from his keepers.

As if he were a fox, his hearing sharpened with the passing of time. He thought he heard the faraway sound of water sliding down pipes, something like the sounds refrigerators make in the middle of the night. But the place he was in wasn't a house. However, the sounds that made him think of irregular liquid releases didn't stop at night, and he started to wonder if maybe, rather than discharges, rather than something liquid, those sounds were human voices. Human voices traversing the pipes. They didn't speak of serious things: they were lively voices, in happy conversation, people chitchatting. They weren't his keepers' voices, it's unlikely that they were, and there was no way of understanding what they were saying. It sounded as if someone, somewhere, perhaps in the middle of a silent forest, had left a radio on. His senses continued to sharpen, and he started to distinguish a word here and there, although admittedly this may have been a trick his imagination played on him. The voices carried a lot of rhythm and enthusiasm, it must surely have been the retransmission of a soccer game. Yes, he had no doubt about it. Those sounds in the distance were soccer sounds. Then, he started distinguishing the names of players: Sarabia, Gajate, López de Ufarte...A derby? But that soccer game was endless. That retransmission was much longer than the regulatory ninety minutes. Besides, and most surprisingly, even though the commentators spoke so effusively, they never called a goal. The game was never-ending and the result a perpetual no-score draw.

It was enough to go crazy. "Those voices down the pipes, that radio, they're only in my imagination," he told himself. He decided not to pay any further attention to those sounds.

Then the ants started to appear. Ants in every corner, biting into the wettest regions of his body.

One of his keepers placed a melon slice in a corner of the room, to attract them. It worked at the beginning, although it was quite nasty to see all those ants working diligently, covering the entire white surface of the melon's skin. But even that wasn't enough, soon the unwelcome guests started crawling up his ankles.

"These ants...can't you do anything about them?" he asked his keeper. "At this rate, they're going to eat me alive."

He said they'd try, and that he was sorry. Not about dragging him into that hole, but about the fact that there were ants in the *zulo*.

So he started killing them himself: the keeper helped him too. Afterward they swept them with a broom, but they started coming through the holes in the walls again, through the cracks, through everything.

He read the papers every morning, although the pages with news of his kidnapping were cut out. As the weeks passed, however, the newspapers appeared practically whole, untouched by scissors: everything has a sell-by date. They didn't mention the kidnapping anymore. They'd forgotten.

He woke up with a fever one day. He didn't think it was very high, but he was incapable of quantifying it. He couldn't finish his exercise routine. It was one of those slightly sweet fevers, the kind that overcomes you after sitting in full sun for too long a time. He found it nice, even. It was a change, and he'd had very few changes since arriving. It was a way of remembering, for a moment, the feel of sunshine, which he missed so much. The fever reminded him of his honeymoon in the Dominican Republic.

The mediator, Agirre Sesma, goes over the calculations that, from train to train, he's already made a thousand times in his mind. The kidnapping victim has been kept from his home for forty-seven days, his wife hasn't slept at all for the same amount of nights, worried sick about her husband's health. The kidnapping victim's wife says that health is very valuable, and that life is valuable too – life is especially valuable – and she appears willing to pay whatever they ask. That's what she told Murillo, the family attorney; the mediation chain is long because even though there's always a middle, it isn't always the same person who is "in the middle" of one or the other party. This is the key to this undertaking – it'd be too much to call it an art: the responsibility and hard work are dissolved bit by bit, from hand to hand. There is something noble about the endeavor, of course: mediators do their work voluntarily, with the altruistic intention of mitigating distress, or at least avoiding its spread over time.

As he spoke to the family attorney, the children sat around the table without saying a word. Apparently, they weren't in complete agreement with their mother, who'd seen her husband for the last time forty-seven days ago. What they had in mind, of course, was the fact that a large chunk of money was going to be deducted from their inheritance, shrinking a part of their future wealth – they could keep the meanness from their mouths, but it was firmly settled in their eyes, in an almost obscene way, or at least so Murillo said to the mediator: "They deserve having it all taken from them, every last cent, they're living off their father." It didn't sound like Murillo held his client's children in great esteem, because at the highest peak of his outburst he came to suggest, in front of the mediator, that the businessman's money would be better spent on bomb-making materials, that *that* was a better fate for it than his children's pilfering. "C'mon now, don't say that," Agirre Sesma said. And Murillo: "Give them a couple of months, they'll melt the steel and turn it into something else." The family attorney and the mediator understood each other well. The truth was, po-tah-to potato, the mediator was an attorney too, and Murillo had acted as a mediator on other cases, although he had a very different point of view about doing the work for free. "If I don't get paid, I'm collaborating with a terrorist group. If I get paid" – he always said – "I'm working. You should get paid too, Sesma."

So, he's got carte blanche. They are willing to pay the seven hundred million pesetas they are asking for, no counteroffer; that's what the family attorney told the mediator. To put special emphasis on the installments. He could take half the payment along, in a suitcase, and if he could manage to persuade them to receive the other half in three installments, there'd be no problem. And that if it was two instead of three installments, or just the one, they'd still manage, but that it would be easier for them if they could split it in three.

That is why the mediator, having left Montparnasse Station in Paris, on his way to the Tenth Arrondissement, dying to get to Brussels as soon as possible, makes calculations and ponders the rash promise of the previous day:

"I'll do everything I can."

It isn't the most difficult negotiation he's had to deal with, not by a stretch, or at least that's what he foresees. He's more worried about other things: on the one hand, the suspicion that he might be followed by the secret services; on the other, the responsibility of the money he's carrying in that suitcase.

Near Gare du Nord, he walks into the hotel he has reserved for three nights. He collects his key, goes up to the room, showers, takes the suitcase and goes to the underground garage. Just like they had promised, the car that's going to take him to Brussels awaits.

"Are you Agirre Sesma?" asks a red-haired man with a face full of freckles.

He nods, and the man sitting in the car alone opens the passenger's door from the inside.

The driver only addresses him again when he realizes that the mediator is nervously watching the road signs:

"The meeting won't take place in Brussels, but in Strasbourg. For security reasons. We've changed it at the last minute," he says in Basque. And as for the Redhead, who's no spring chicken precisely, the mediator Agirre Sesma wonders whether he's just a chauffeur or if he's something more. It's quite an irritating matter that concerns all clandestine activists: *With military guys, at least, one look at their stripes and you know their rank . . . but, with these guys?* He addresses him respectfully, just in case. The mediator offers a cigarette to the driver; he doesn't accept, says he smokes dark tobacco but doesn't like smoking while he's driving. *What a weird guy*, decides Agirre Sesma the mediator, looking down on his companion's bohemian look and inclinations.

By the time they enter the garage of a mansion on the outskirts of Strasbourg, it's been night for a while. "Wait here," the Redhead demands, and shortly after, a swarthy man with a bushy mustache arrives. He offers his hand while looking at the suitcase. He shakes Agirre Sesma's hand forcefully and, even though it might be strange to say so about a look, he also looks at the suitcase forcefully. The calculations he's made flood the mind of the mediator, and he sees different calculations in the eyes of the other man. Guessing the calculations of the person one is negotiating with is also part of a mediator's job. "This job of yours is a bit like a card game, don't you think? There must be some fun to it…how do you do it?" a kidnapping victim's family attorney once teased him. "Don't ask me how we do it, we do it and that's that; besides, it's not a *job*, we don't charge a cent," was the mediator's cutting reply.

"Murillo does."

"I am not Murillo."

But he wasn't wrong: although the correct word was *excitement*, not fun.

They take him through to the living room. Whose home might this be? Who lent it to them? Do they live in it? Is their job just to negotiate the ransom and decide where to hide it? Do they really believe in freedom and socialism for the people? How many years are they willing to sacrifice? A whole lifetime? A whole life negotiating and carrying briefcases from one place to another, involved in clandestine arms trafficking with Lebanon, cherishing and trying out the product with professional zeal? No, he doesn't think so. According to the mediator's calculations – and assuming they were well organized – these must be white-collar criminals, not too different from Wall Street accountants. Another type of mediators, in the end, just like Agirre Sesma, whose job is to get the money and administer it to get the most profit out of it. There must be others in charge of buying and selling weapons and, of course, others whose job is to use them.

The house is really old: at least the room where they sit him down is. The décor is excessively ornate and baroque, the multiple flower prints make it difficult to affix an immobile, die-cast profile to his interlocutor and memorize it.

"Did you have a good trip?"

The mediator decides to refer only to the journey to Paris:

"I like to travel by train."

"Yes: it's a bit long from Hendaia, but there's nothing like train journeys. Should we have some dinner? The lamb is excellent around here."

What is this, a restaurant? Just then the Redhead appears with a tray of roast lamb. He smells garlic, bay leaf, and mint. Chauffeur and chef. The bohemian, the Redhead, takes care of logistics – the mediator makes a mental note. He is not hungry, or, rather, he didn't think he was hungry until now, but as soon as he sees the lamb, all crispy on top, he remembers that it's been hours since he ate, and his appetite stirs up.

They bring wine too. The mediator drinks little.

"Jauregizar is fine: we give him all the tablets he asks for. We have also determined the day of his release, as long as we reach an agreement, of course."

That's the moment he was waiting for. According to his calculations, it's time to act:

"As you must know, things are complicated in the steel industry: only last year they had to get rid of seventy workers."

"*They had to get rid of*? More like *they fired them*. And, according to our information, it was seventy-two. If they sent you over to haggle, I'm afraid you wasted your trip…"

"We just want this nightmare to be over as soon as possible."

"We all agree on that."

"There are three hundred and fifty million in the suitcase. The family hasn't been able to put any more together without raising suspicion. Everything they had in private safe-deposit boxes and everything they could gather from trusted friends in the banking world is there."

"Undeclared money I see . . . very cautious family . . . but this is only half."

"I'm not going to beat around the bush: the family can pay up to five hundred. After Jauregizar is freed, we could make three payments of fifty each, just as you said."

"We'd be two hundred short."

"You'd ruin them. You can't pressure them like that."

"Let's do this: in eight months' time, you and I are going to meet in Geneva. You'll bring me two hundred, in one lot. And with that, we're even."

"I'd have to ask them."

"C'mon, c'mon . . . I know you've got leeway for that and more. What kind of a mediator would you be, otherwise?"

He could have just said yes. What did he care? Hadn't he managed to get the deal he'd promised the family? An even cheaper one, in fact? He remembered the heirs, those parasites that lived off their parents. He insists, however:

"I should make a phone call."

"No phone calls. Our next appointment is in Lac Léman. Geneva."

"In that case I can't guarantee – "

"In that case I won't give the order to free Jauregizar tomorrow morning. We know everything about the liquidity of Jauregizar Steelworks, my friend. This is a good deal. And you know it, Luis." The chauffeur, the waiter, the bohemian Redhead emerges out of nowhere, or maybe he actually never left; perhaps his pale, freckle-covered face, a redhead's face down to the last red eyelash, his almost transparent face, was hidden among the flowers of those over-ornate walls. We each have our own semblance, our own jungle. Come to think, the Redhead was the only one to refer to Agirre Sesma by his first name.

He brings a narrow of bottle of grape liqueur, *uxual*, right out of the freezer, and three little glasses.

"A deal is a deal," he says, and now, yes, of course, Luis Agirre Sesma sees, more clearly than ever, that the Redhead is the leader here. He imagines him hidden in a farm, collecting mint leaves and reading the financial papers. He's the big fish, why didn't he realize that before?

With a sigh, the mediator signals his agreement, a bit irritated by the thought that in calculating his calculations and his countercalculations versus the enemy's calculations, he didn't get it completely right.

I'm young, my blood runs too hot still, he admonishes himself.

They toast with the frozen little glasses without actually clinking the glass. But they come close. The mediator knocks his back in one gulp, without realizing that the two other men sitting at the table barely touch theirs.

Suddenly sleepy, his head lolls back and a fourth man – a little man wearing a hat who looks like a bellhop or an elf – comes running and catches his head with a pillow, as if it were a head that'd just been offed by a guillotine.

When the mediator opens his eyes, he's in Paris again, resting in his bed at the hotel in the Tenth Arrondissement, with all his clothes on, his black leather suitcase on the bedside table, and no one looking like an elf around him. He grabs the suitcase, lifts it. Empty, just as he thought. He goes out to the corridor and sees a copy of *Le Monde* on the floor: Margaret Thatcher and François Mitterrand smile and shake hands on the front cover. When he unfolds the paper, a train ticket to Hendaia falls out. On the other side of the window, Paris is deserted. Agirre Sesma has no doubt: it's either too early, or too late.

When he calls home, his wife, Emilia, gives him a message from Murillo, he needs to call him as soon as possible: another kidnapping. This time it's an engineer. It's not money they're after.

The kidnapping victim continues to complain about the ants. They multiply by the second and there's no way of knowing where they're coming from. He says they won't let him sleep. During the first week he was a model prisoner, he didn't complain about anything. It's Diego Lazkano's job to talk to him and tell him that everything is going to be all right. They have no intention of harming him. He tells him things like: "we're not going to hurt you," or "we won't do anything to you, don't worry." Although the kidnapping victim has a better way with words than he does, he does what he can and converses with him, that's precisely what he's there for, to tell the kidnapping victim that he can relax, that they're not going to kill him, that they won't hurt him, that they won't do *anything* to him, as if ripping a man from his everyday life and locking him in a hole is "not doing anything."

He collects the ants at the doorway with a broom, cleans the room well each time the kidnapping victim eats something, but they keep coming. And, what's worse, they're multiplying. He brings a mop, thinking that after sweeping, perhaps the toxic dampness of water mixed with bleach might keep them away. After he mops the outside, he hands over a damp cloth to the kidnapping victim.

"Dale una pasara con esto."

Give it a wipe with this. Many years later he will still remember, with shame, that he said *pasara* instead of *pasada*. "Dale una pasara con esto," *"emaiok pasara bat honekin,"* he'd thought it in Basque and expressed it in Spanish.

And the kidnapping victim cleans the *zulo* inside too, he scrubs it thoroughly with water and bleach, killing the ants that move around in long lines with fury, sure that they won't return. And those ones don't, but others do. Lazkano thinks that they look bigger than the previous ones, but it's quite certain that they're not: what's happening is that they're more visible now, because the floor is clean and shining, and because they're a bit obsessed and they fixate on the ants, they only have eyes for them. They mop, they clean, they kill armies of ants. All in vain. They keep coming in and out of the *zulo*, oblivious to all their efforts. Lazkano places a melon rind in a corner, to attract them. It works at the beginning, but the ants are too many and they seem to never give up.

In the end, in despair, he does what he should have done the first day. One night, when someone else is pulling his shift, he calls his father, whose business is precisely that; he feels doubly humiliated in having to ask his father how to deal with the ants; his father has spent most of his life destroying pests, but he doesn't know the first thing about it, not even the simplest tricks.

"You've ants at home? I'll come by tomorrow, don't worry."

How could he explain to his father that the ants are not in the apartment he shares with Ana, no, but in *a friend's house*, and that he doesn't want to do "anything traumatic," that bringing a fumigation team is too much, and isn't there a natural remedy, something that'll do the trick, maybe vinegar, something like that is what they need.

"Okay, so tell me where your friend lives and don't worry: I won't charge him at all."

He's about to hang up. How he'd like to say, "I can't take you to see those ants, *aita*," but he has to bite his tongue. Every father in the world is like that.

"What are they like?"

It hadn't even crossed his mind to think that there might be more than one kind of ant. But, of course, there are lots of different types of ants.

"Have you found the nest yet?"

So they have nests, ants do. Of course ants have nests.

"They're usually very persistent."

It takes him a while, but he offers him a remedy in the end: place a jar of honey somewhere out of the way. Observe what happens to locate the holes from which the ants emerge, and plug those holes with toothpaste. The ants inside the room will go to the honey, and, *in principle*, no more should come in...

"But if the nest in your friend's house is quite big, one of those bad holes, then the best solution is to fumigate."

One of the bad holes. Best to fumigate. Your friend's house. Quite a big nest.

"Thanks, *aita*."

"Will you call me to let me know if it worked?"

"As soon as I can."

And then he buys toothpaste, a jar of honey, observes the kidnapping victim's puzzled expression, with his arms and face covered in red ant bites, looking crazy. The ants no longer march across the floor, but keep safe on the walls.

"See? The ants don't know what's the floor and what's the wall," says the kidnap victim, "they can live without coming down to the floor."

"The two of us, you and I, we can tell the difference between floor and walls," the kidnapping victim seems to be telling him, trying to establish a bond between them, a bit of empathy, inviting him to join him in his fight against the ants. And, indeed, together they plug cracks and holes with toothpaste and it works, they never show up again. Not on the floor, and not on the walls that the ants confuse with the floor.

The kidnapping victim often wonders whether if it hadn't been for that issue with the ants, such a close relationship could have been established between Diego Lazkano and himself. He adopts him as a confidante; it is known that he doesn't speak at all with the guards from previous shifts, but that he starts chatting away as soon as Diego arrives; even though he is always covering his face with a black hood, they look into each other's eyes, so much so that Lazkano is pretty sure that the kidnapping victim could easily identify him in a lineup, he'd notice his gray eyes and that'd be that. *Maybe I should take my hood off, he'd thank me for it, this guy wouldn't give me up*, Lazkano thinks at one point, but he knows that rules are rules and that he shouldn't do such a thing.

And then the kidnap victim tells him details about his life: why he named his daughter the way he did, how his father used to send him to a hospital in Switzerland when he was young, to learn German; how his wife is a pharmacist.

"Any news?"

The kidnapping stretches on, and Lazkano doesn't know what to say anymore.

"Everything is going well," he tells him at the start, but later he starts to coldly state that there is "no news," because he doesn't think that hiding the truth can do him any favors.

The kidnapping victim, however, doesn't seem too anguished, it'd seem that he trusts him, that he's convinced that things are going to work out. He's not a businessman, his family doesn't have any money. He's an engineer. Once he dared ask what was it they wanted in exchange for his liberation. Lazkano didn't know what to answer. He is only a guard. "We need people who are not on file."

And then, that order from the Redhead:

"Your last shift, you need to be on the French side tomorrow, in Iparralde."

The man with the freckle-covered transparent face hands him an address. Angelu, Rue Moulinaou. That's it then, he has to go into hiding. That's it then, he'll have to kiss off the love of his life, Ana, without saying goodbye. That's it then, goodbye to the joint LP collection, resting on a single shelf in alphabetical order: Mikel

Laboa and Patti LaBelle, Echo & the Bunnymen and Errobi, "a union stronger than marriage." That's it then, goodbye to his *ama*'s sweet reprimands. That's it then, he'll never call his *aita* to ask him how to kill ants. How to kill cockroaches. Rats. He still has so much to learn from him.

"Where are we going to set him free?"

Silence is the answer; a resigned sigh from that redhead down to the last eyelash. A deep groan that seems to come from someplace other than his two nostrils. He waits and waits some more, but there is no answer. Finally Lazkano grabs the Redhead by the shoulders, recklessly: he should never do that with someone who outranks him and is older than him. He remembers the words *embryonic cell* or *sleeper cell* and suddenly realizes that, even though he wasn't aware of it until now, he is among those who've been awakened.

"We're going to let him go, right?"

In the silent house in Rue Moulinaou, in Angelu, he experiences his first day in hiding, the first day in which, as well as doing things outside the law, he lives completely hidden, awaiting orders. Remembering his parents, remembering Ana. And early in the morning he sees the picture of the dead kidnapping victim on the front cover of a newspaper he doesn't have the guts to open, in the kitchen, in that house in which everyone else is still asleep. *Aparece con un tiro en la nuca el ingeniero*...A bullet to the head, dead. The world, still as it is, becomes even slower, and the same thing happens to his heart; the windows are steamed up, not even a bird's feather moves in the Ecuadorian jungle he carries in his head. It's the hardest blow of his short life, a bomb that's blown to smithereens his idea of an "embryonic cell" or a "sleeper cell." It's as if they'd whisked away the ground beneath his feet. He didn't even say goodbye to the kidnapping victim (but how can you say goodbye to someone you've kidnapped and who, whether you know it or not, is headed for slaughter? How can you say goodbye to the kidnapping victim, when you haven't even said goodbye to your girlfriend, the love of your life?). He failed him, things weren't going well and he told him they were. If he'd known things were going to end up like this, he would have spoken to him differently, he would have taken the hood off from the start, fuck, what kind of a coward doesn't show his face; if he'd known things were going to end like this, he would have measured every word he uttered carefully, every word he shouldn't have said, including the laughable ones: "*dale una pasara con esto*." Wipe with this.

We killed ants together, he thinks. *He and I, we killed ants, and now he is dead. He spoke German, and now he's dead*, he thinks, absurdly, as if knowledge of the German language – any kind of knowledge – were an effective insurance against death.

Attorney Luis Agirre Sesma's offices were in a basement in San Marcial Street, a rather unpretentious place for someone of his standing, a man who'd worked in politics for thirty years, who knew the bitter side of a mediator's job firsthand. Under the staircase, one of the two sides was rented by a seamstress who did alterations; his was the other side. ADELA RETOUCHERIE, read the sign next door; and, below, an explanation between brackets: ARREGLOS. Just in case, it wouldn't be right to lose non-Francophile clientele for the sake of a display of distinction.

In that bilingual sign that displayed ambition and then retracted from it – *retoucherie, arreglos* – Diego Lazkano detected the perfect manifestation of Donostia's cosmo-hypocritical idiosyncrasy.

He rang the bell of the door without a sign, and waited for more than a minute and a half; too long, if you took into account the smallness of those basement spaces.

"I was waiting for you."

Agirre Sesma's eyes were kind and transparent, like a calm sea, the eyes of someone who'd lived and who'd seen a lot. It was not easy to figure out his age: somewhere between sixty and seventy years old, maybe. He was chubby, abundant in rolls of flesh that escaped from his suspenders, like sheets hung in an indoor patio. Agirre Sesma, with little hair left, had a round, symmetrical face; he was one of those men who, from the moment they are born, are difficult to imagine looking any other way, the kind who age very early and hang on to that same look for decades, until they die of a heart attack. His head was a little small proportionally speaking, taking into account that the bulk that expanded either side of his tie could host two men of Diego's size.

The basement was filled with papers, civil and canon-law code and jurisprudence books. The office was a bit soulless. As he walked along the corridor, he was surrounded on either side by books, piles of folders ,and towers made of magazines – *Punto y Hora, Cambio 16* – accumulated over the decades. They walked on very slowly, and when Diego noticed the broken hiss of the attorney's asthmatic breathing, he couldn't help feeling in his gut that he'd reached out to the wrong person, and the deep disappointment that came with it.

Wasted afternoon. I'll entertain the old man with a bit of conversation, and head back home.

Agirre Sesma collapsed behind a desk lit up by a table lamp, and invited Diego to sit on the armchair in front of him with a hand gesture.

"Before anything else: I don't want you to harbor any illusions. I haven't decided if I'll take the case yet."

Ha! Will you look at the old man! He hasn't even shaken my hand! He basically shares his offices with a retoucherie, *and intends to make me believe that his is a high-class attorney's office that chooses its clientele?* thought Lazkano. *What does he think, that I'm going to put this case in the hands of a dinosaur who could suffer a cardiopathy on the first round?* Because, besides intelligence and an encyclopedic ability, an attorney needed courage and energy, shrewdness, reflexes, cold blood, a firm hand, and thoroughly oxygenated rhetoric in order to get involved in proceedings with the Soto Zeberio case, which had been thrown out twice by the courts.

"I imagine that whoever sent you warned you that I retired from the courts a long time ago."

"He also told me that no one is better than you."

"I would need a lot of help... if we did manage to reopen the case, that is."

"I don't know how much you charge, but I'm not exactly swimming in money."

"No, money is important, but I wasn't talking about that. I was talking about bravery, about courageous people."

All right, it looks like we might understand each other after all, thinks Lazkano. *He knows that he's not up for much anymore.*

"Look, young man, I don't know if you've had any dealings with the law..."

"Let's say that I have firsthand experience with police stations..."

"Don't take this the wrong way, but police stations and prisons have nothing to do with the law."

"Really? I thought they arrested people in the name of the law. At least that's what they told me."

"My job is to put people in jail, or to get them out, and the method I use for that…"

"That method is the *law*, if I understand you correctly."

"It's one of the methods…not the only one, of course, but it's the best one I know, for sure. And, more than the method, what I know are its hidden nooks."

For a moment the snake hiss of his asthmatic breath takes over the office, as if his labored breathing and the hidden nooks of the law were one and the same.

"I know them better than anyone…Excuse my lack of modesty. Many people have avoided jail thanks to me. Even death, back in the day, more than once. I am proud of that."

All is forgiven, my man, of course it is. Bigheaded men like us understand each other well, Lazkano determines silently.

"With the Soto Zeberio case we're not going to get anyone out of jail. It's a different matter."

"Yes, I know it's a different matter. But it's possible that if we take things to the very end, more than one will have to see the sun through prison bars."

"That doesn't interest me."

Agirre Sesma smiles. Lazkano is puzzled by the attorney's last sentence.

"Did you say that doesn't interest you?"

"Not in the slightest."

"An attorney who is not interested in justice, interesting."

"*Justice*, that's a big word. Everyone has his own idea about it."

"They say that about asses too. We all have asses and the differences are massive."

"You have a funny way of speaking, young man. What do you do?"

"I leave crumbs on paths. He, he stops the birds from eating those crumbs, I fear." Things we think but we don't say.

"I'm a writer."

"Ah, a *creative*..."

"A creative," he says, like someone who realizes that an adult is suffering from the mental weakness that ails adolescents. Like saying "a romantic." Earlier he called him "young man," although Diego left forty behind quite a while ago. The attorney retakes the conversation.

"As you must know, justice is not something they teach in law school. The laws change, and justice changes. The laws that we inherited from the Romans try to extol the figure of the judge as an equidistant and just being, but that doesn't exist: no matter what TV series say, the law is an instrument of the executive powers..."

"Tell me the truth: do you think we stand a chance?"

"To reopen the case, or to, excuse my language, fuck over the guys who took part in the deaths of Soto and Zeberio."

"Both."

"Now, let me ask you a question. Be honest: what is more important for you? Your peace of mind, in other words, that thing you call justice ...? Or to find some scapegoats and make them pay a very high price for what they did?"

"You call them scapegoats, I call them guilty."

"You didn't answer."

Lazkano keeps quiet.

The attorney Agirre Sesma opens a drawer, takes a cigar out and brings it close to his ear, *rustle-rustle*, like a child who wants to hear the sea in a seashell. He lights it up slowly. Exhales the smoke ceremoniously. He takes great delight in smoking, the cigar's smoke takes a long time to leave his lips, as if its natural habitat was that mouth.

"Silence is not always the worst answer," resolves the attorney. "I'm going to take the case."

Agirre Sesma expects some reaction: a red carpet, applause, fireworks. But he doesn't get anything like that from Lazkano. All he hears is the roar of an engine outside. The rumble of city buses.

"But on one condition ..."

Enough, thinks Lazkano, *it's time to counterattack.*

"And what if I decide to look for another attorney. Maybe I don't think you're well suited for this ..."

"Whether I am well suited or not, you won't find anyone else who'll accept the case. Even less so, anyone who stands the smallest chance of winning the case. And, needless to say, as willing to shrink their honoraria. Don't fool yourself; the days of lost causes are long gone."

"So, what's the condition?"

"That you'll ask no questions. That you'll do what I say and how I say it."

"*I'll do what you say?*"

"I'll take care of the courts. But there will be a lot to do beyond that."

"Let's talk about money. How much?"

"I am an unusual attorney, your friend might have mentioned this: not a cent until the case is over. And then, we'll see."

"What will we have to see?"

Agirre Sesma's eyes crinkle with mischief and shrewdness all the way to the sparse hairs on his sides, drawing almost horizontal lines. He speaks, not without pomposity, from his refuge of smoke.

"Whether we manage to get *justice* or not."

Agirre Sesma doesn't usually attend the funerals of people he doesn't know. It is his opinion that they're always manipulated, be it by the left or the right, and he disagrees with building political capital out of the dead. But, on the other hand, what's the point of this butchery if not political returns? No, Agirre Sesma doesn't usually attend the funerals of people he doesn't know, but he makes an exception in this case. The engineer's case was particularly painful. At the beginning he thought it was a propaganda exercise, Tupamaro style: some newspapers complied with the demand to publish the kidnappers' statement on their front pages, even *El País* printed the whole text. Basque newspapers did too, and some Catalan ones. Not always on the front page, as they demanded . . . but the press was generous in this instance, and was willing to sacrifice freedom of expression to save a life, following the German Doctrine. It was all in vain.

They killed the engineer in cold blood all the same.

In the church, black ties and white shirts. Gray linen waistcoats. Long dark coats, down to the ankles, good for hiding guns. Agirre Sesma was astounded when the parliamentarian Murillo confessed that some colleagues from Congress habitually carried guns. Hair-raising. All those socialist politicians, each with his weapon. There was this feeling in the air that anything could happen, even a new attempt at a coup d'état, like the recent one on February 23, 1981.

In the church, the president of the Basque Autonomous Region, Lehendakari Carlos Garaikoetxea, and other chief executives from the Basque and Spanish governments, among them Minister Barrionuevo, freshly arrived, the previous day, for the funeral of national police guard Alfredo Trota, gunned down in front of his parents' glassware store. After what happened to the engineer they remained to pay respects and say farewell not to one, but to two victims, in the same trip. It's the last push the new Anti-Terrorist Law needed: astonishingly, from the opposition, Fraga and his right-wing parliamentary group have applauded Barrionuevo, a socialist minister. It's a detail that very evidently reveals the true dimension of the issue.

Murillo, an attorney and a member of Congress, tells Agirre Sesma that, in his opinion, ETA made a mistake: if they had offered a cease-fire just then, President Felipe González would have probably shelved the Anti-Terrorist Law. "Maybe he would have, maybe he wouldn't have." He thinks it, but he doesn't say it.

Agirre Sesma bumps into Javier Fontecha, recently named government delegate, even though he is younger than him; a man destined to occupy the highest ranks in politics. He's always thought that he's a sensible, mediocre man. He wouldn't be surprised if he got far.

"You had guts coming to the funeral," he provokes him, with cheap sarcasm.

"This is proving to be a very hard month, Fontecha."

"You didn't come to Trota's yesterday...there are classes, I see...first- and second-rate victims."

"I don't go to the funerals of people I don't know."

"Did you know the engineer?"

"His family."

"It's true then: I heard you were the mediator...but it didn't go so well this time."

"Every door was closed. It wasn't about money. There was no dialogue."

"You guys always get your chunk though..."

"We are not all like Murillo. I've never charged a cent, Fontecha. And don't even start again with the story of how we keep a chunk of the ransoms to finance our party..."

"I never said such a thing."

"Besides, who are you to question me? In France we have Mitterrand; in Portugal, Soares; in Greece, Papandreou's PASOK... all three socialist parties...you too could act differently, what else do you want to be in power for?"

Javier Fontecha sighs, but he doesn't answer. He's still young, although the dark leather of his overcoat and his tiredness and lack of sleep make him seem much, much older than his years.

ADELE RETOUCHERIE. ARREGLOS. They are in Agirre Sesma's bunker again.

"Why the sudden interest? Many, many years have passed."

"And just as many will pass again unless someone does something. The same thing that happened with the Civil War will happen: they'll open a small curtain, clap without enthusiasm, unveil a memorial, and when there's no one left to demand retribution or forgiveness, they'll say justice has been made."

"*Iustitia...ius sanguinis? Ius loci?* Justice, forgive my crassness, is the shaft of the cock: we don't suck our own because we can't bend that far. I thought this was clear from the last time."

Agirre Sesma had started to treat him with familiarity, but he doesn't dare do the same.

"They told me you love your profession. That you're passionate about it..."

"When I get down to work, my heart, I put it in a drawer. In my profession you need a second set of guts, and an enormous ability to swallow your own bile."

"For the love of God, then, why are you an attorney?"

"Certainly not for the love of God."

"I need help."

"And I need to know your real reasons, Lazkano *jauna.*"

"I told you..."

"The thirst for justice is never the real reason. People come to this office propelled by the desire for revenge, the love of money, the need to humiliate someone, by pride or by arrogance. But never because of a thirst for justice. If I don't know the real reason, it'll be hard to move forward... Forgive me, but my professional ethics demand that I ask you this."

But hasn't he already said that he would take the case? What was all that about now? Agirre Sesma senses Lazkano's confusion and charges on:

"What is it that hurts you? Where is the epicenter of all this? Where exactly is the compass's needle stuck?"

"If I tell you something that's hurting me, will we start working once and for all? Will that be reason enough?"

"What was your relationship with Soto and Zeberio? What is it that you owe them, why are you so bound to them still, so many years after their deaths? I want the truth."

This bastard is very good at grabbing the wren by its neck and strangling it until the oxygen stops going to its brain.

Lazkano has conflicting feelings, he feels a double stab. Soto and Zeberio. A double shudder.

"C'mon, I'm all ears. The truth is always the easiest thing."

"I don't think that's...I'm sorry, but truthfully, that's just my concern."

The shudder is a double one, indeed: on the one hand, he feels that the attorney's speech has wrecked his morale. On the other, for the first time, he feels he's found a shrewd, experienced man; what's more, a man who has the ability to use that shrewdness and experience. For the first time, he realizes that there's no doubt he's the attorney he needs. He knows where to dig.

"We're in a basement, dear friend. What these walls hear will remain within them. Take your time. Do you like cognac?"

"No, I don't, usually."

Agirre Sesma nods contentedly and fills a wide-bottomed, heavy glass with cognac. Then he places it very close to Lazkano, who takes it directly to his lips.

And as soon as he gulps it down, he bursts out:

"I gave them up…"

His voice quivers, betraying him again.

While Lazkano crumples and collapses, the attorney grows strong and imposing.

"They tortured you?"

Glugs of cognac pour into the bottom of the glass again. Into two glasses this time. Only the asthmatic hiss of breathing breaks the silence. Lazkano keeps drinking, and his eyes turn to the old framed laws on the walls. He can't read any of the headers, it's impossible.

The attorney switches off the only lamp on his desk. Treating the desk as a bar, he stretches his arms across, toward Lazkano, and places a hand on his shoulder, like a barman about to close for the night.

"Drink up."

Attorney Luis Agirre Sesma knows nothing about the journalist Julio Virado. It occurs to him he must be younger than him, and is curious enough to read some of his articles before the interview.

Emilia brings him the last few issues of *Cambio 16*. The attorney can confirm that Virado's pen is sharp, although he finds his articles and opinions suffer from excess padding. He is most amused by a sensationalistic report with the title *"El bosque vasco"* in which, in high literary style and with a lot of alliteration, he describes the Basque Country as a dense forest, a *foresta impenetrable* thickly layered with shameful interests, alliances, and acts of cowardice.

When Julio Virado is in front of him, he confirms that he's even younger than he'd imagined.

"What do you think about the arrest of attorney and parliamentarian Murillo following his role in negotiating ransoms with ETA?"

"Murillo has all my support. It's a travesty to punish processes of mediation that are carried out for humanitarian reasons. In cases of force majeure, and a kidnapping is such a case, criminal law allows us to pay ransoms and carry money across our borders."

"Even if that money is then used to buy weapons, and people are then killed with those weapons?"

"There is a conflict of forces majeures in that instance: but the urgency, the need to save the life of a person *now*, takes priority over a possible future terrorist attack, reprehensible as this may seem, because the first can be avoided and because the second is an abstraction. In the case of a kidnapping, the law must be placed in suspense; not only for the kidnapping victim and his family, but for the whole state."

"That's arguable, to the extent that it can hold a whole state at ransom at any given time..."

"That's what the German Doctrine dictates, and I adhere to that. We have to do everything possible to save whoever is at risk here and now. Afterward, we'll see."

"In Murillo's case, it's been harshly criticized that the attorney in question kept a percentage of the ransom after carrying out a process of mediation."

"This matter can be approached from different angles. I wouldn't do that, but Murillo's attitude seems thoroughly respectable to me...in his opinion, and given that his work as a mediator is linked to his profession, not to charge would be irregular, and not the opposite...He argues that were he to do it for free, that could arguably be construed as collaboration, which is defined by the law. I don't agree, but both attitudes are licit."

"What do you think about the projected reform to the criminal code?"

"I'm against it. They've requested the advice of Stampa Braun, and that's a fraud. What would you think if we asked Pope Wojtyla for advice on abortion law? The decision is made the moment an adviser is picked, not when the adviser offers his verdict. In any case, I think the priority is to establish a maximum period of pretrial detention as soon as possible."

"As you well know, some will perceive that as a weak and too lenient decision."

"We can't carry on the way we've been doing until now, keeping people awaiting trial indefinitely. It's strange, but while that's happening here, in Great Britain, Margaret Thatcher, who's never been accused of being weak or too lenient, has freed thousands of prisoners from British jails, under promise to remain in the country, after a commission revised their cases."

"Could you give us some more information regarding the rumor that more repentant prisoners are soon going to be freed?"

"First of all, I must tell you that I don't like that word at all. It's not accurate to talk about 'repentant prisoners.' That term was imported from Italy, and I don't think it's appropriate: we talk about reentry into society. And no, I can't give you any more information because this issue requires my utmost discretion."

Agirre Sesma found Julio Virado smart as a fox. He was also a deft manipulator, because even though he was quite faithful in his transcription of the interview, he exaggerated the weight of the words "repentant prisoners" in the highlights. There are ways and ways of bending journalism to benefit your interest. It wasn't Julio Virado who invented the phrase "doctrine of repentance," but from then on many news outlets echoed the terms "repentant" and "repentance." The process that had borne such great fruit up until then started to decline, and the pathways that attorney Agirre Sesma and his team had crafted for the rehabilitation of political prisoners became incredibly convoluted. Nobody wanted to be thought of as "repentant."

Before saying goodbye, Julio Virado shook his hand sportingly, and even handed over his business card. The detail grabbed Agirre Sesma's attention, because back then it was a usual gesture for attorneys, but not for journalists.

"I don't agree with you on practically anything, but it's been a pleasure," said the young journalist on his way out.

Frost has taken over the sidewalks, but Agirre Sesma keeps the heating off. He's not wearing a jacket, however, only a white shirt, a dirty tie, and suspenders. Diego Lazkano makes the mistake of giving him too many clues about what he's thinking: he steals several long glances at the heater.

"It's not what you think. I'm not a mean old man who hates wasting money on electricity. I like the cold. More than like it: I need it to feel alive."

"If you're hoping to get yourself some tuberculosis, that's not my problem."

"You're young, you don't understand."

"Yeah, the bars in my cradle block my view of the world..."

"I know that the ailments of age push people toward warmer climates, but that's not my case. It's cold that brings me the most pleasurable moment of the day…I cool myself under the shower with freezing water. It's the only way. You get goose bumps and those shivers return to the skin the smoothness it once possessed. It is, of course, an illusory sensation, but for an instant you think you recover the firmness of old times. After a certain age, nothing is real; there is only the sporadic memory of forgotten sensations, and not only when one wants them. I can see the impertinence in your eyes: sex? It's been a long time since I've known what it feels like. It's enough for me to feel goose bumps under the cold water tap. I wasn't really conscious of my face until I started to get chubby, you know? At one point you start gaining weight, your nostrils and your ears grow, and you're incapable of reading a book without seeing your nose…you know what that feels like? I don't wish it for you, putting all this weight on…your skin gets away from you, it emancipates from you, it becomes something else and takes on a life of its own, even though it never has the guts to completely leave your bones. In another time, I too aspired to elegance; these days, I'm content if I don't make people cringe."

He says all that without dramatizing, with a glint in his eye, Lazkano would say…even gleefully. It's not easy to distinguish his jokes from his serious comments. He grabs his hat and raincoat and points toward the exit.

"It's not all disadvantages. My office will never burn down because I left the heater on."

The *retoucherie* is closed.

"Did you ever bump into Adela? An extraordinary woman. She's always made more money than me."

Diego wants to show the attorney that he's good with jokes too.

"How can that be, when you both do the same job?"

"The same job?"

"You both mend things…"

Agirre Sesma gives him a knowing smile.

"That's the wisest thing you've said all evening. C'mon, buy me a beer?"

"So…are we going to work together then?"

"There's a lot to do. To start, the family."

"The family?"

"Are you in touch? Have you spoken to them?"

"No."

"Okay, that's the first thing then. We can't request that the case be reopened without the involvement of some family member."

He had no idea about what he might find in Zeberio's mom's house. He knew she'd become a widow a few years back, and he imagined her lifestyle, and her two daughters', was probably quite ordinary: each with her work and family, routine phone calls to tell one another that things were all right – "I'm managing" – and family visits once a week, plus mandatory birthday and Christmas celebrations, sweetened by the arrival of children and a commitment to the future, having parceled away the pain of the past for the sake of everyone's sanity. Many years had passed since they'd inflicted that wound that would never heal, if having your soul split in two can be called a wound. What happens to the wounds that haven't healed and you know for certain never will? What happens is that you learn to live with them, as if they were living entities. Because the pain of losing a son, that pain is equal to a whole living entity, a mini-being with tears, demands for attention, conjectures and superstitions, prayers not to be forgotten, approachments and distancings, a habit of disappearing for a while every now and then. A living entity who is dead, but awake. He had no idea what he might find in Zeberio's mom's house, but it wasn't difficult to imagine that he was going to find a house filled with images of her dead son, young forever. A whole house filled, everywhere, with Zeberio's childhood and first communion photographs. Flecks of fossilized joy disseminated along the shelves like sweet shrapnel shards. Those flecks of joy, could they be anything other than domestic stars in a constellation of pain? The photographs of the lost child, turned into pictures of a saint. On the way to Zeberio's mom's house, Diego tried to remember the more restricted but also more intense range of colors of photographs from the seventies and eighties: the bright reds and oranges from Agfa and Kodak prints; back then they developed them the proper way. Before the boom of pixels and screens everywhere, photographs used to belong, by right, to the realm of the fetish. He had no idea what he might find in Zeberio's mom's house, maybe an altar, the dead son's room left intact: a room that traveled back in time, with the same painted paper on the walls, faded fleur-de-lis patterns, Victor Jara LPs, books about the developing world and Marxism, a Che Guevara poster and another one of Pertur, the disappeared ETA leader, next to one another, ready to simultaneously break into song; hiking boots and multipocketed waistcoats, maybe – stuck to the wall with thumbtacks – some map of the world from back in the day before the dismemberment of the USSR and Yugoslavia, to remember that the world is the world and El Salvador is in El Salvador, and not in our heads; who knows, maybe Zeberio's shotgun, and, why not, a fishing rod behind the door.

He walked on, thinking about the house he might find; maybe he expected a house similar to his mother's, an ancestral family home organized around the stove, the radio, and the kitchen calendar, one offered by the Seaska shop or the Caja Laboral Bank; wide-bottomed TVs covered by crotchet mats; cathedral-like headboards, nostalgic *souvenirs*, cheap but brought from faraway places, a Lladró figurine or two, the rooms with bunk beds that brothers and sisters shared, where they fought, a still life hanging in the corridor, rather ugly rugs, maroon-colored encyclopedias on bookshelves made of dark wood; maybe a rocking chair, a survivor of the days when grandma lived at home; furniture that no one uses but everyone thinks it is a pity to throw out; a bedside table with a little lamp on either side of the bed, as established by the norms; maybe a sophisticated lamp, because for a while Zeberio's parents sold electric goods...maybe the sisters run the business still.

What right did he have to stir the matter of Soto and Zeberio, to ask their parents for a signature because there was enough evidence to warrant the opening of the case? Was it his place to get the ball rolling so that newspapers restarted their engines and flowed with new rivers of ink? Agirre Sesma had made it very clear that the family had to ask for it, that the family came first, that they deserved all their respect, and that they couldn't take a single step without earning their approval.

Two days earlier he had made an appointment with Xabier Soto's parents in a cafeteria. His *ama*'s words affected him deeply. "In the first few years, I liked seeing Xabier's friends. Talking to them about how far he might have gone, had his life not been cut short, what problems he might encounter, where he might live and what his job might be. It was his friends who kept him alive, and being with them was like being with Xabier. After a while I grew tired. Where was Xabier? He was dead. I could choose some of his friends and adjudicate their virtues and defects to our son. To continue the story when there was no story to continue. I could own their wins and their mistakes. But wasn't that a bit fake? To have a son and lose him is very tough: don't look for your son in his friends. Don't think that their wrinkles and their children and their white hairs are the wrinkles and the children and the white hairs of your lost son. If anywhere at all, your dead son is to be found in your way of speaking, your way of walking, or in your desperate way of looking at the world. And he is also in the strength with which you confront your desperate way of contemplating the future. That's how I see it, at least."

To hear her say that, while her husband clasped her hand. A tired husband, who was proud of his wife for having been able to face up to life. That strange kind of dignity that surrounds pain and envelops it. Xabier was the only son they had.

He wasn't going to find Zeberio's *ama* alone either. Her eldest daughter would be waiting for him; they'd spoken on the phone for quite a while, and she might have given some advance information to her *ama*; the hardest part of the job would be done by the time he arrived, they'd offer him coffee and pastries: hospitality above all.

He had no idea what he might find, but he definitely didn't find that. A modern, functional house, an active woman who looked after her grandchildren, corridors filled with toys and strollers; children's naïve drawings everywhere, disproportionately cute monsters; dolls that you wanted to touch, made of rubber and cloth; rhinoceroses and elephants in bright colors. And a detail that moved him to his core: a plaid blanket on top of a bed in one of the rooms. When he saw it he felt a knot in his throat, gripped by the memory of the day they got lost on the mountain: "Unbelievable, Zeberio. Really? What is this, your love nest? Is this where you bring your little nuns? You like sex in the wilderness, hey?"

Zeberio's *ama* paid him almost no attention. Her daughter, Kepa's sister, had inherited his same hard look, his air of distrust, the will to impose an agenda and not detour from it.

"We have half an hour."

That harshness shocked him a bit. Zeberio's *ama* didn't sit down with them; she was bathing her eldest granddaughter and only the sound of water splashing and the smell of soap signaled her presence in the house.

He found it hard to start, his body wanted to go off in tangents, meander around the compass's needle, share news and unravel the adventures of the past few years. It was difficult for him to start talking about her tortured brother just like that, while she held a baby girl enthusiastically sucking on a pacifier on her lap. He tried to do it softly, with the aid of clichés, the only thing that can help in such circumstances.

"I knew your brother well."

The woman's eyes sparkled momentarily.

"Lucky you, then, I wasn't so fortunate. I was thirteen when he disappeared, a child still."

A child still. She was talking about herself, but she could just as well be talking about her brother.

"He was a very cool guy. Very generous."

The woman nodded, an indifferent gesture. Even the baby in her lap was showing more interest, sucking on the pacifier with gusto. Lazkano continued talking:

"He didn't speak much, but if you caught him on the right day, or subject... Once we got lost hiking... weather was terrible and your brother... He had a refuge in the mountains, with blankets..."

"You want to reopen the case, isn't that right? I don't know if my mother is up to it... She's gone through that hell twice. To ask more of her at this stage..."

"There's new evidence. People who weren't willing to talk then want to talk now. We'd have the best attorney. It could establish a precedent for others, in the future. We wouldn't ask anything of you."

"In our case, not asking anything of us is already asking a lot, don't you think?"

Diego remembered something: *There's always another hill.*

"No doubt, Maite: the press will bother you again for a while, I can't deny –"

"Journalists keeping watch in the hallway, the phones ringing nonstop...we'd have to go to live in Switzerland...and, what, return when it's all over?"

Zeberio's sister smiled: a moment of tenderness, a feathery fleck of humor that was worth its weight in gold. Generous, reserved. Diego knew then she was exactly like her brother.

"If we're willing to run that risk, it's because we can see we stand a good chance; but it all depends on you."

She was silent for a while.

"Have you spoken to Xabi's parents?"

Xabi. That tendency to think of the other instead of ourselves. To think first of the pain of others rather than our own.

"They are in agreement."

She nodded, but not to say yes, just to signal she was thinking. The mother turned grandmother came into the living room with a little girl wrapped in a towel. She rotated the dimmer switch of the halogen lights and light flooded the room.

"You're practically in darkness."

Maite Zeberio spoke with determination:

"If they are in agreement, so are we."

Although he hates such celebrations, Diego Lazkano has no choice but to attend Agirre Sesma's birthday party. Thankfully no one knows him, and no one asks about his next book or how long it'd been since his last publication.

He can see the Kursaal cubes from the balcony. Moneo's

whitish prisms aren't lit up yet. The apartment's ceilings are high, and it feels like the home has always belonged to the same family. Bequeathed from grandparents to parents, and from parents to their children. Lazkano notices the spines of the oldest books. Nothing to do with what Agirre Sesma keeps in his attorney's office: Ludwig Feuerbach, Rosa Luxemburg, Antonio Gramsci, E. H. Carr, Leon Trotsky, Marta Harnecker... Engels and Marx occupy the same space as all the previous ones.

Agirre Sesma notices Lazkano looking at his books.

"I couldn't keep those in my office, they'd scare some of my clients off. Nowadays they'd think they're science fiction writers."

"An attorney of lost causes..."

"Let's say that I'm an attorney for causes that have been lost *in the short term*."

"The kind that are won in the long term."

"In 1977, for example, we worked toward the granting of a sort of unemployment subsidy for recently released prisoners, so that they wouldn't be condemned to stealing again; I'm talking about social prisoners, not political prisoners... Many thought it was an outrageous idea and it didn't move forward, but after seven years it did: in 1984 Congress approved it.

"Were you involved?"

"Well, we never quite sat on the mahogany chairs... But yes, we sometimes did the dirty work for the mahogany-seat-warmers... Those years were very intense: it's always more satisfying to create from nothing… You know that better than I do."

"You were a mediator too…"

"Murillo and I would take turns. It didn't always work… The engineer's case, especially, still haunts me."

The color drains from Diego's face. "We won't do anything to you, don't worry." *Dale una pasara con esto*. The man who spoke German. One of the bad holes. Best to fumigate. Quite a big nest. Killing ants. The engineer and him, hand in hand.

"You were the mediator?"

"Yes. Do you remember the case?"

Melon rind. Honey. Toothpaste. The ants don't know where the floor ends and the wall starts.

"Vaguely…"

"Back then people got really stuck in their position… When they were looking for money, like in Jauregizar's case, it was simple; however, when they were after propaganda… We all carry some thorn or other in our side, but… Who can I talk to about something like this?"

Lazkano tries to change the subject somewhat:

"For a while you defended people who had decided to take up arms."

"Because for a while we thought there were reasons to take them up."

"But you didn't…"

"I did my military service as a member of a surgical support team. All the blood I saw in those years sufficed for me…I was better suited for a different kind of fight."

"And better suited to stay in the shadows, right?" He thinks it, but he doesn't say it. Lazkano remembers an expression Soto coined: *penned struggle*. What did he mean by that, exactly? That the struggle needed to be led and authored by someone, written down, organized, or rather, that the struggle needed to be rich not as much with arms as with intellect? They were two very different things, could even be said to be unrelated. Typical Soto: even after all these years, his word games, his convoluted sentences, flooded Lazkano's mind.

Attorney Agirre Sesma changed the subject, the way he usually did when he sensed the possibility that someone might reject the logic of his discourse.

"Perhaps we should come to an equal position before we get into the thick of it, don't you think?"

The attorney stared at Lazkano, as if he were seeing a mirror reflection of himself at another time. *The risk of the fall, and the certainty that you'll have the chance to fall again.* Diego stepped away, recoiling at the attorney's attempt at inhabiting his skin, defending himself atavistically: "Don't involve me in your decline, don't hold on to me so we might both fall. We are two. We are not the same, we are not equals."

You are a toad, he thinks; attorney Agirre Sesma reminds him of an amphibian.

"Equal position? What do you mean?"

But he didn't find out. A girl wearing a black dress approached, her hair pinned up in multiple little plaits, turning her wrist as if she were twisting a light bulb to say hello.

"Look, this is my daughter: Cristina . . . Come, Cristina, I want to introduce you to a client."

"Happy birthday, *aita*."

She offers her dad a little gift adorned with a white ribbon, and kisses him and the man he's just introduced her to twice. The fragrant perfume the girl is wearing stirs something in Diego. The gift for her father wasn't wrapped in any shop, she's done it herself: it's tied in the exact same way as the ribbon that hugs her waist and hangs from the back of her dress in a long, slightly limp oval bow. A brooch in the shape of a horse on her chest, a horse that looks like it'd like to jump from one breast to the other. She's an apparition: she looks older from a distance, but becomes younger as she approaches them, revealing the truth of her age. Cristina, still on the other side of the abyss, still far away from decline and decadence. All of her is freshness, passion, smooth skin. The unforgivable youth that's unaware of its own insulting energy, that stirs in a savage man the need to grab her, although a civilized man never would, passions be damned, abysses be damned.

"Will you pay my father what he deserves, or will you do like the rest, give him a lot of work and paltry wages?"

"Cristina, please . . ."

"There aren't many like him, you should be proud of your father."

"And I am, don't think for a moment that I'm an ungrateful daughter. But these things have rather wrecked our family's finances. Has he told you how many times he's mortgaged this beautiful home? He survives thanks to a stipend I set up for him. Did he tell you?"

Even when she's ranting she's all joy and splendor. Agirre Sesma smiles nervously. From there on, Lazkano will secretly call him "the Toad." A young man, from the other side of the abyss, comes over and takes the girl's arm. Then the two of them walk away toward the epicenter of the party, following the call of youthful laughter. Lazkano observes the Toad. He seems a bit ashamed, uncomfortable.

"Don't pay any attention to my daughter. She loves to tease. Her mother was exactly the same, she teased me like that too. Emilia died two years ago, and..."

"I am so sorry."

"Come on, we are here to celebrate," he says, and drinks from his champagne flute without missing a beat, keeping his composure intact.

"Don't take this the wrong way, but I don't quite understand why you've invited me to your birthday party. It's not that I'm not honored, but..."

"We don't turn sixty every year. And I don't have so many

friends either...occupational hazard, as you might have guessed..."

"You could think the opposite too. I see a lot of people here. Did you work for all of them for free?"

"Working for free doesn't necessarily mean that people will thank you for it."

"That won't be my case."

"Too early to say. You've just told me you don't very well know what you're doing here, in the house of this old crow you've just met."

"Old crow is what you call yourself. I call you old Toad." He thinks it, but he doesn't say it.

"If it's easier for you, we can talk about the case: the witness you told me about, have you been with him? Is he willing to give evidence in court?"

"He says he won't...we need the right circumstances, he's too afraid. He says he knows the place, the location where they held us up."

"Could you make an appointment?"

"Any time. In your office?"

"Sounds good."

"Now, if you'll forgive me...I must go home."

"We all have our duties to fulfill. Homes to look after."

"You know that better than I do, sir," says Diego suddenly, looking at Cristina and raising his empty champagne flute.

"Please, don't *sir* me ... don't make me feel so old."

"Here's to a long life."

"Not too long if I have a say."

"Not even in good health?"

"When you're condemned to merely *contemplating* the flesh ..."

"You speak too much of the flesh for someone who claims to have forgotten all about sex."

"If you want to forget something, speaking about it is as good a method as never mentioning it. Write that down, you can use it in one of your novels."

Without reply, Diego heads toward the exit. The Toad's daughter seems to be enjoying her young man: carefree, champagne always close by, she lifts a hand to her mouth every now and then, when her laughter threatens to diminish her elegance. The horse is still on the same breast, up in the air, undecided about whether to jump across.

With a flick, Diego turns on the lights in the abyss of the staircase. He feels like he's been expelled from paradise. The lightbulb in the hallway is not bright enough for a building with such high ceilings.

Vargas's confession gave the case an important push. Not to mention, of course, the discovery of the bones. From one day to the next, the two disappeared boys were no longer disappeared. No one knew what to call them anymore.

Soto and Zeberio screamed again. Maybe they never stopped all these years. But now their screams were audible.

Diego Lazkano and Agirre Sesma accompanied Zeberio's sister and Soto's father to the mortuary in Cartagena. The forensic specialist warned them as soon as they went in:

"They're just bones, you won't be able to recognize them. We'll have to do DNA tests."

They insisted on seeing them. They said it wasn't possible.

"Nothing is impossible. Can I speak to your superior?"

The attorney talked to the forensic doctor's boss, and then with the boss's boss. And, later on, with the on-duty judge.

"We won't leave until we see the bodies."

Bodies, bones . . . It wasn't easy to hit on the right word. Agirre Sesma himself used different terms depending on who he was talking to.

At last, the attorney managed to get them permission.

"Go in two at a time, there isn't enough room for everyone."

Three went in: Zeberio's sister, Soto's father, and Agirre Sesma.

They swallowed hard and contemplated the remains. A man in a white coat stayed with them the whole time. What were they afraid of? Did they think they'd take the bones away?

Each body was on a stretcher. Zeberio's sister stared at one of them, silently. Soto's father stood in front of the other, covering his face with his hands, in silence too. They each chose their dead. Agirre Sesma didn't dare ask if they recognized them, or if they'd each chosen theirs instinctively. Some questions cannot be asked. Zeberio's sister hugged Soto's father then. They both stared at the same bones.

The man in the white coat started offering explanations.

"They buried them in quicklime. A hunter found them but since no one claimed the remains... they've been kept and labeled as John Does in the mortuary."

"All these years?"

The forensic specialist shrugged his shoulders without changing the expression on his face.

"How can you explain that a year after Soto and Zeberio's disappearance, these bodies emerged... and no one linked the two events?"

"We didn't have the computer systems we have nowadays back then," answered the forensic specialist. "Things weren't the same then."

Things weren't the same.

The bull's hide. *La piel de toro.* Capillary networks. Different train-track widths. Obedient men, fed through the roots by a dictatorship.

They took DNA samples. They left Cartagena and headed home, to unrest. VALLE DE LA ESCOMBRERA 10 KM. LA APARECIDA 4 KM. Soto's father drove. Next to him, Zeberio's sister. Behind, Diego Lazkano and Agirre Sesma. They all stayed quiet. The air freshener that hung from the rearview mirror exuded a pungent smell; white lettering on the little pine tree read "Arbre Magique."

Two weeks later the test results arrived. Positive. It was them. As if they hadn't known that already.

Newspapers and TV stations started to wake up from their lethargy. Overnight, everyone was concerned about the case. Horror, scandal. The remains showed clear signs of torture. The court case was going to be brought forward, it was clear.

Agirre Sesma did not take it well: "They're not doing it for us, but for them," he explained to Lazkano. "They don't want to give us enough time to prepare the case." What they don't want, at any rate, is for government delegate Javier Fontecha, Agirre Sesma's old acquaintance, to be splattered by any of it.

Vargas pointed the finger directly at Lieutenant Colonel Rodrigo Mesa.

"They look pitiful, we can't leave them like that: make them disappear."

It didn't escape anyone's notice that, back then, Rodrigo Mesa maintained a close relationship with Javier Fontecha. Several men under the lieutenant colonel's command were impeached, there were indications that new evidence pointed to Portugal, to Italian arms traffickers. The matter became more complex by the minute, and time was not on their side.

Lazkano found the door to the Toad's office open; a light was on at the end of the corridor filled with books, and he could hear a litany of voices at the end of the tunnel – the Toad, no doubt. Diego got frightened, thinking that the attorney had started talking to himself. Aranzadi case law books opened here and there, scattered documents, an increasingly intense musty smell, and, together with all that, something new: a fragrance that disguised the smell of sweat and Diego found familiar. To his surprise, Cristina was with the Toad, bent over a laptop computer, dog-eared law books, notebooks, and press cuttings, with her generous breasts swaying in a perfectly measured way under a low-cut red sweater, directly visible from Diego's privileged vantage point.

"Lazkano, I didn't expect you today...Sit, sit down here. We were about to finish..."

"I don't want to disturb you..."

"C'mon, we're almost done. Come and join us for dinner afterward! We just need to go through a few details."

"I didn't know that Cristina also..."

"It was my intention to hire an assistant, but since she studied law...Although, you know, by the second year she abandoned her father and her father's vocation."

"*Aita*, please."

"I gave her the role of defense attorney: we're rehearsing the trial step-by-step."

"So you're his assistant..."

"Who else could work the extra hours? If he's going to exploit someone, he might just as well keep it in the family."

The way they do with some girls, dark circles around her eyes imbued fresh-faced Cristina with the right dose of torment, taming her excessively youthful looks, changing a face that would otherwise be too childish, too soft, too devoid of personality. She smiled at Lazkano meaningfully, with her eyes the color of rum. She bent forward even more, placing herself farther from her father's eye line, her breasts and the brooch on her sweater in fuller view of Lazkano's eyes. That horse without a rider. A savage desire to tear her skirt off and throw himself at her overwhelmed him then. Something a civilized man would never do, passions be damned, abysses be damned.

"Rodrigo Mesa's confession, which he gave during the preliminary investigations, is unsigned. As far as he's concerned, the lack of a signature here is our biggest weakness."

"That's no problem: the judicial secretary publicly attested to Vargas's declarations. The confession is coherent and it coincides with what the other witnesses said, as well as with what Rodrigo Mesa said in his first declaration."

"It happens often: someone confesses something and then they retract. It was to be expected from people like Rodrigo Mesa and Vargas."

"This time they won't be able to retract so easily. Next question, Ms. Defense Attorney?"

"They'll request that the recordings be dismissed. 'Invalidity of secret recordings,' according to a March 3, 1996, sentence by the Supreme Court."

"Read it to me, please."

"'It is this court's decision to invalidate a recording of a group of four people carried out by one of them without the acquiescence of the rest.'"

"Yes, I remember that sentence. I don't see such a problem there: the court rejected the recording not so much because it was an attempt on the intimacy or the secrecy of the communications, since such a thing doesn't exist, but because..."

"A conversation obtained through such means is unacceptable in the midst of an ongoing criminal process, since it has no value as a confession by any of the participants, because it is provoked and not spontaneous, and therefore it lacks the guarantees established in our constitutional values."

"Bingo! But in our case it is not a *provoked confession*, but a recording in which the accused explains why he's changed his decision and, therefore, the judge will have to take it into account, whether he likes it or not. It's part of the process, or, rather, of an attempt to harm it. As a result, it's completely pertinent to the trial, to the extent that it's a test of the quality of the process itself."

"You seem very certain."

"Not really, not so certain... We'll have to look for decisions that support that thesis. They exist, but my memory is not what it used to be, Cris. Look it up, preferably by tomorrow."

Although he doesn't understand half of it, Diego witnesses it as if it were a tennis match. Pure delight. For a moment, that hard-fought *tie-break* manages to keep his mind away from the hesitant horse in Cristina's cleavage.

"We also have to take into account the quality of the recording, which is really bad. That's not something that's going to play in our favor to be honest..."

The Toad puffs up momentarily:

"You are mistaken again, precisely, Ms. Defense Attorney: they'll argue that the recording is a fake; but if it were a fake, the forgers would have taken the trouble of making a good-quality forgery, don't you think? Why forge something if the heart of the conversation is going to be barely understood, *ladies and gentlemen of the jury*? Besides, the recorded conversation is full of casual remarks that have nothing to do with the case. Hypothetically, it's possible to forge a recording such as this one, but you'd need a good collection of scriptwriters and an even better group of actors... And with regards to Vargas, if we know anything about him – and if you don't believe me, check the library of profiles they've drawn up for him – it's that he's a man without imagination. We'll force the psychologist who'll come over the first day to measure his mental abilities to ask him a question that makes that point clear. Take note: *trick question to reveal Vargas's lack of imagination.* Have you written it down? God, my stomach is rumbling. Can we go and have dinner now?"

"We still have to take up Rodrigo Mesa's declaration."

Cristina was playing five sets. *Deuce.* All her serves landed.

"When he declared, at the time of the initial investigation, he could hardly remember what he'd done on the night between October 15 and 16. In the previous trial, however, five years later, he recounted every single detail of what he did that night... the names of the cafés he went to, the family alibis... isn't that sudden resurrection of his memory a bit suspicious?"

"Not necessarily, *alabatxo*: what's my motto?"

"Let's submerge ourselves in subjectivity?"

"It's not enough to say it: let's put it into practice. Let's dive into it. Why did he keep quiet the first time? To protect someone, because he was hiding something. If he feigned amnesia the first time, the second time he lied barefacedly. Based on that change, we'll invalidate both declarations and demand a third, let's see what he says this time. Besides, at least one of the two accused maintains that he met up with them..."

"Pérez Gomera. Hernández, the other policeman on duty, says he doesn't remember anything from that night."

"Hernández is the gay guy, the one whose life they made impossible?"

"The very same."

"The media have punished him too much. We have to play Vargas's cards... we have to lean on him: his testimony is the most detailed and, therefore, the most potent. Vargas must be our main point of support."

"But he's an unstable person. He's been locked up in psychiatric hospitals twice. The first time, five weeks, and the second, two months. The defense attorney will play the mental-health card and cast doubt on his declarations."

"Vargas has been in psychiatric hospitals?" Lazkano intervenes.

"The second time was in a military hospital too. God knows what they did to him there."

"He's still sick. And not only mentally. He's quite old. They say he has lung cancer."

"He was in the military hospital when he retracted: he declared that they never held Soto and Zeberio in El Cerro..."

"But he'd said the opposite earlier...Besides, Lazkano himself can confirm that they were in El Cerro, can't he?"

Diego swallows hard. He remembers Fabian and Fabian. The Boger swing. That window. How he fell, pathetically, on the ferns. The policemen's laughter. "Who cares, let's leave it as is, with a *b*." He nods, and stares into Cristina's eyes for a bit longer than is prudent.

But Agirre Sesma didn't notice that look filled with innuendo and desire.

"Okay, let's see, yes: he justified his declaration before the investigating judge attributing it 'to feelings borne out of his situation, the loneliness and sense of abandonment felt by being imprisoned, and to the manipulation the judge exerted on him...' But you're still not paying attention, *let's submerge ourselves in subjectivity*: why did he feel alone and *abandoned*? Because he had carried out his part and Rodrigo Mesa hadn't, that's why Vargas felt alone and abandoned! Because they had betrayed him. If he had nothing to hide, if he hadn't done anything, or if he'd done what he did of his own volition, he wouldn't have felt in any way *abandoned*...don't you think?"

"I think you're falling short. We'll have to see what the judge thinks."

"What do you think, Lazkano?"

"I was thinking of Rodrigo Mesa...According to his statement, he'd never been to El Cerro, but here we can read that the first time they took him to El Cerro's palace he moved around there like he owned the place: without anyone's guidance, he found the rooms mentioned in the summary, the freight elevator, the gas stove...he found everything in a jiffy."

"You're right, Lazkano: his impulses, that need to show self-control, which is such a military trait, on the other hand, betrayed him...Beautiful paradox, don't you think? Even a child would have realized that it wasn't the first time he visited El Cerro."

"According to his statement, it was because he is a specialist in building structures. That he found everything through pure logic, in other words."

"He didn't even try to pretend. That shows he was involved..."

"It's getting late. The call to Cadena Ser radio in Cartagena... should we leave that for tomorrow?"

Now it was the Toad who wouldn't give up:

"Let's finish this: refresh my memory, what was it about?"

"It was February 20, 1984."

"Four months later, then."

"Yes."

"It doesn't really seem feasible that they'd keep Soto and Zeberio kidnapped in El Cerro for four months."

"No, it's not logical. Too dangerous, too long a time. Besides, this isn't Argentina, those clowns weren't prepared to torture anyone for a month...they didn't have the required infrastructure."

This isn't Argentina. This isn't Chile. Soto and Zeberio's voices again: *crazy, brother.*

"Apologies, Lazkano... I didn't mean to diminish the time of your arrest."

Cristina lifted her eyes from the pile of reports: she's surprised now. Is Lazkano earning points?

"Don't worry about me."

"Go on, Cristina."

"But, on the other hand, it's illogical that after taking such precautions to hide the corpses, when only four months had passed, they claimed the murders and revealed the exact place where they were buried, don't you think?"

"There's also the call to the newspaper *Egin* on October 25."

"A call from the Batallón Vasco Español, claiming that the bodies were on the road to Oursbelille, near Tarbes. But it wasn't true."

"It was a smoke screen."

"A very controlled blast of smoke in any case: too controlled. Whoever made that claim didn't know where the corpses were buried. Look at the map: Tarbes is northeast of Angelu, and the bodies appeared in the southwest, not to the north and not to the east, but the very opposite in both directions."

"What do you mean, that it was *too calculated* a mistake?"

"Yes, and another thing too: not all the men involved are going to be sitting in the defendant's chair."

"The ex-government delegate Fontecha, for example."

"And anyone above him."

"We knew that from the beginning."

"Fontecha's been accused."

"But not of the murders."

"*On verra...*Will you be able to live with that, Diego?"

What does he want him to say? Cristina notices Lazkano's nervousness, and retakes the conversation.

"I still don't understand the reason for their claim ... revealing the secret, was it a matter of collective arrogance? Or did someone take it upon himself to do it, without saying anything to his superiors?"

"Do you think that the call to Cartagena in January 1984 is something an individual did on his own? In an outburst? Without saying anything to anyone?"

"I'm thinking about Hernández ..."

"Because he's gay? You're prejudiced, *aita*."

"Maybe it was personal revenge, an accusation from someone with an interest in fishing in troubled waters, in getting someone high up arrested and rise in the ranks in the process."

"Do you think so?"

"We'll never know: but think, not all dogs are obedient lapdogs."

"Maybe you're right: it's possible that one of the collaborator civil guards in Cartagena would take credit for the kidnap and murder, to let it be known that the GAL hadn't disappeared, that, moreover, their actions would get harsher. In any case, the objective of that phone call was a clear sign of insubordination."

Among the brambles, reddish soil, and the remainder of a line that was once white. The once-white line met with another line to create a ninety-degree angle. The net and two metal posts that supported it have disappeared, but it's not difficult to guess that there was a tennis court there once, a long time ago. It's not to easy to establish, however, the way in and out of the court, because the pathways are completely overgrown at each of the cardinal points.

"Yes, this is the place."

The Toad puts an arm over his shoulders in a fatherly gesture.

"Do you want to go on?"

Lazkano nods, but that very real *flashback* into his past has affected him more than he thought it would.

He knows the place. El Cerro. They wouldn't set him free without having him listen to Soto and Zeberio's screams first.

"Do you recognize your friends' screams?"

They set him free, after humiliating him with the pretend suicide, after his confession. And being free would become unbearable.

"It smells exactly the same..."

After all that happened he got the hell out. His parents lent him money to go away, first to Paris and then to Lille. Before that, he visited Rue Moulinaou. He said goodbye to his friends from Angelu and confirmed their suspicions about Soto and Zeberio's disappearance. The fact that he didn't join the protests, demonstrations, or lobbying groups made people in the organization suspicious, but Lazkano had seen enough to know that he'd make his own way far from any organized structure. "Don't count on me." They called him a coward, a traitor. He already carried *chibato* on his back.

He still loved Ana, but after disappearing the way he did, he didn't even dare call her. He remembered her every day. And every day he remembered her in a different way, because remembering her differently was the way he had of holding on to her.

He spent three years in Lille. He attended university in the mornings and worked as a waiter in the evenings. He began to go out with a girl half seriously, but broke up when she started talking about returning to Ireland – she was from Donegal. He didn't want to have anything to do with places with ongoing armed struggles. Later, he started learning Russian: the girl from Kursk, Lena. A possible love. Lena's abandonment. She took a part of his past with her, and left him, in exchange, the ability to speak Russian quite decently. Diego came out the winner. Every now and then he worked for import-export businesses from Moscow and Kiev with offices in France.

The list of things that caused a knot in his throat that he

couldn't find a way to undo didn't grow too much in those years: Faulkner, the Doors, Victor Jara. Some promises: never to kill another ant, never to get a driver's license. An identity: a patchwork of people he once knew. A hidden vocation: being a writer, which he'd keep alive in memory of Soto.

"You died for me, you'll live through me."

"This is it then, this is where they held you." The Toad sighs. "And Soto and Zeberio too. You're going to have to testify."

"I'll do it."

"It'll be tough. They'll play hard. They'll have no compassion. They'll air all your dirty laundry. They'll investigate you inside and out. You and everyone around you."

"I don't give a fuck. I have nothing to hide."

"They'll say that you're an opportunist, that you're crazy, a terrorist, God knows what else. They'll ask why didn't you denounce them twenty years ago, that'll be one of their main arguments... how do you think we should explain that?"

"They found Soto and Zeberio buried in quicklime... and I didn't want to end up like that. Wouldn't you say that's quite a solid argument?"

Lazkano couldn't stop thinking about it: that Soto and Zeberio teamed up because he couldn't drive. And that even if it was through torture – this fact didn't console Lazkano – it was he who'd given them up. It should have been him instead of Soto. That's where his obsession of worrying about Soto more than

Zeberio came from; that, or maybe because he felt he and Soto were closer in personality.

The judge heard the two sides. They handed over all the documentation. They introduced the attorneys. Lazkano and the Toad were left alone: too many emotions in a short period of time.

"Did you notice the judge's smell?"

"His smell?"

"Yes. What do you think he smelled like?"

"Is this another of your *let's submerge ourselves in subjectivity* sort of tests?"

"Tell me: what kind of smell did you perceive in him? I noticed a long time ago that this judge has a peculiar smell."

"I don't know...perfumed?"

"Perfumed! C'mon, that's like saying that a color is colorful! I'll tell you: *silvae odorem leges sapiunt*...he smells like a forest..."

"A forest?"

"Yes! Like a young oak, like fennel, like dry leaves, like tall grass and moss. He doesn't smell like flowers, but like a forest."

"I didn't notice."

"Do you know what that means? That even though the object of regulation is to avoid the law of the jungle, the law itself is a kind of jungle: *legis silva*... The Jungle of the Law... We're about to enter a dense forest, a thick bramble patch. This is not an *hortus conclusus*..."

"That bullshit Latin of yours is pretty tiresome, Luis." Lately, Lazkano addresses him by his first name; the Toad and Diego have established quite a close friendship.

"Haven't you read old Horace? And you call yourself a writer? *Hortus conclusus*...enclosed garden...*Aranearum telis fas est leges comparare*...the law is comparable to a spiderweb: it only catches small insects."

Once again, Lazkano is not sure if he's serious or if he's pulling his leg.

The judge smelled like a forest, and more than twenty years ago, the jungles of El Salvador had entangled their minds. Were the two things related? Did it mean anything?

Back in the attorney's office. The last rehearsal before the big day.

"They won't admit to the torture easily..."

"What do you mean they won't?"

"Cris is right. Don't forget who these judges are: it'd be too much for them. The shots to the back of the head, they won't let those pass by. But torture, that's a different issue."

"But...the bodies were covered in bandages!"

"I know more than one defense attorney, Lazkano, who'd be cynical enough to use those bandages as evidence of the humanitarian character of the police. You've no idea who we're up against. They'll call a lot of witnesses, they'll bring specialists from abroad..."

"And the insulating tape on their mouths, that's evidence of humanitarian efforts too?"

"We can base our argument on that, but it won't be enough to prove torture in the eyes of these people. Perhaps we could argue the psychological suffering of being locked up for days, we don't know how many, not knowing where they were..."

"But they'll say that's part of the illegal arrest and kidnapping. *Non bis in idem.*"

"Forgive the bullshit Latin, Diego...but Cris is right."

"And the torn-out nails?"

"We'll have to await a more detailed report, it wouldn't be the first time they say that the nails came off the fingers *on their own.* The effect of quicklime, the soil...Given the way they buried them, they'll hold on to that."

"On their own? Please!"

"Calm yourself down, Lazkano. We'll request punishment for the torture too, but we must place our focus on the murders, we can't neglect the premeditation aspect: we'll highlight, above all, the fact that Zeberio was shot twice. We'll request the harshest punishment in the law for the murders. But I don't think we'll manage to add years to their sentences for affiliation to an armed group.

"Not that either? So the GAL never existed!" Lazkano shouts.

"They'll zigzag around the facts in order to weaken our arguments. I'd bet my own neck that they'll make up some little tale

– 195 –

of the *in dubio pro reo* kind. And, in any case, the absolute longest they'll spend in prison is thirty years, and some of them will carry out their sentences in military prisons. And then, we'll have to see, depending on the court we end up in, whether the robed *crow* we face there will put them through the third degree...there are a lot of pre-Constitution era dinosaurs in the courts, Diego...I don't want to give you false hope: if you're bent on seeing these people rot in jail, it's going to be better for you to forget about that possibility as soon as possible."

"Do you think they'll pardon them?"

"Maybe not immediately. They've learned about tempo by now, they're not stupid. They well know that they can't use adagio prestissimo. But a slow ad libitum, when things calm down a bit and the press starts looking elsewhere...Yes, unfortunately that's something that might happen...But they won't even need to; they can just falsify a medical report: you've no idea how often these tough military guys develop heart conditions after they've overexerted themselves in their duties! These people are owed a lot of favors, Diego, and they'll be paid generously for their silence when the focus of the stage lights is not on them anymore. They've been raised with military discipline, their honor code is cast iron. It's unlikely they'll say more than they've already said."

"And the politicians?"

"Politicians are more slippery. We can count ourselves lucky if we manage to tickle the throat of one of Fontecha's high-ranking bosses."

"I thought you were more ambitious."

"Ambition is a condition of youth, mine has shrunk to the same extent my prostate has swollen. It'll happen to you too. And then you'll remember good old dead Agirre Sesma, when the young bulls start to reproach your lack of ambition. Life is but a sigh...A concatenation of sighs that ends with the last breath. That's all."

"I noticed, Luis. I'm not that young myself."

Time to eat something. ADELA RETOUCHERIE. ARRE-GLOS. The street then. The light and the air.

The judges, the defense attorney, the prosecutors, the lawyers, the judicial secretary, the witnesses, the translators. They all gather, before the start of the hearing, in the same café near the federal court. Conscious of the possibility that they might spend the following night in prison, some of the accused arrive in the café very early in the morning: they are easily recognizable, as they obviously lack the habit of dressing too elegantly. Besides those who work in the courts, quite a few people who've nothing to do with the procedural world arrive too. Some regular *Madrileños* may feel lucky in that café, certain that no one is going to judge them: "I am not one of them, *I am free.*" They breakfast with the feeling that they don't owe anyone anything, that while everyone around them is waiting to be judged or to play an important role in declaring someone guilty, that's not their case. They equate not having to go to court with happiness, with relief, with a lack of duties and responsibilities. We all fool ourselves however we can.

Agirre Sesma had always compared the atmosphere in that café he knew so well with a sort of utopian space of *fair play*. Not everyone was the same there, but they all seemed the same. Everyone paid for their coffee. The game hadn't started yet.

Needless to say, Javier Fontecha and Rodrigo Mesa aren't there. They want to avoid the media at all costs. Maybe they went in the back door, like the ambulance that will bring Vargas in, even though the back door is accosted by journalists too. Agirre Sesma finds the atmosphere changed; it's been a long time since he's been there and he doesn't recognize most of the besuited individuals, although the judges give themselves away by the proximity of their bodyguards. He does recognize an attorney, someone a bit younger than him, who in the eighties used to always find himself in the same places Fontecha used to frequent. But the attorney doesn't recognize him, or maybe he's pretending to be distracted. Agirre Sesma has his daughter by his side; all the documentation is in a thick folder, and the day's script in a leather briefcase.

"Are you nervous, *aita*?"

"Lazkano should be here already."

Cristina leaves her laptop on a table and takes her cell phone out to try calling him again.

"He's not picking up."

"How strange," says Agirre Sesma. "He's called to declare as a witness today. How he was held in El Cerro. How he heard his friends' screams. Only he can state that. This is very strange."

It's eleven o'clock and they can't wait any more. Cristina and her father feel weighed down by intense disquiet. Later, when they learn of Lazkano's desertion, their disquiet will be overtaken by deep disappointment.

"Why didn't he come? He started all this."

"He must have gotten frightened. He must have his reasons," asserts Cristina, without much faith in what she's saying.

"We can't wait any longer," the attorney decides after a while, the broken hiss of his asthmatic breathing louder than ever.

They pay for their coffees and head toward the court's entrance. Cristina holds her father's index finger and they enter the forest on their own, without anyone's help.

THREAD OF THREADS

PEDRO VARGAS DOESN'T HAVE A PAIR of shorts to play tennis in. Rodrigo Mesa, however, does: whiter than white ones, just like his tennis shoes.

¡Va!"

When the ball hits the net's tape for the umpteenth time and falls by his boss's side, Vargas begins to think that even though he did it with the best of intentions, perhaps he shouldn't have raised the net this morning; Rodrigo Mesa often fails in his service, crashing the ball into the taut tape. It would have been better if he'd left it loose, just as it was.

"Second service!"

Bong-bong. One bounce, two bounces, ball up: pale yellow shines in the blue sky. Vargas moves forward from the back of the court. The boss's second serve is weak, he returns it easily, from quite far back, near the lateral line. Vargas likes to make his boss run every now and then although he knows that, ultimately, he has to let him win, and since his boss particularly enjoys seeing him show signs of frustration, sometimes he pretends to be angry, the way he's seen the tortured John McEnroe do on TV, even though it's Ivan Lendl who Vargas really likes. He's Czech, and he likes people of Slavic blood; cold people, even-tempered people who don't fly off the handle. Since he's already won a couple of games in this set, Vargas wants to send the ball out on purpose this time; but the ball, determined to fail, miraculously hits the baseline. The boss, unexpectedly, returns well, but his arm is perhaps too close to his body, and the ball goes sideways.

"The ball was in!" shouts Rodrigo Mesa, smiling, repeating a recurring joke in an advert for Bic shaving razors.

"Close, very close!" responds Vargas, giving his boss the answer he expects while caressing the sparse beard on his cheeks. In the advert, the umpire is referring to McEnroe's beard, and the tennis player doesn't react well to the comment.

"You cannot be serious!"

"No, your shave, Mr. McEnroe…it's very close."

"Should we leave it for today?"

Vargas is surprised: his boss doesn't usually like to leave things unfinished.

"Come over for a second."

Rodrigo Mesa is drying his wide brow and thinning hair with a towel. He offers it to Vargas afterward, which puts him on his guard, since it's the second unusual gesture from his boss. His superior's sweat repels him, but he doesn't dare refuse his offering and tries to pat the pearls of sweat on his temples with Rodrigo Mesa's damp towel as naturally as possible.

"Look, Vargas, they're wiping the floor with us, we can't go on like this. Don't you think?"

"No, sir."

"I've heard you were friends with Alfredo Trota."

"We did our military service together."

"We can't go on like this, hands tied, they have everything on their side... and if that wasn't enough, the refuge on the other side of the border. What are we, scarecrows? This has to end once and for all."

Vargas doesn't say anything.

"I've received instructions, from high up. They've green-lit us. Guarantees. *Guarantees*, Vargas. Do you realize what that means?"

Vargas nods, although he doesn't quite follow.

"The minister came to the last funeral. Do you know that members of his party are carrying guns? No one knows this, but it's true. They don't even trust their bodyguards! I saw it at the airport in Hondarribia. With my own eyes. The pilots lock their arms up while the plane is in the air, the law dictates that. I saw them collect their guns one by one before stepping off the plane. These socialists are not stupid, not at all!"

Vargas thinks to himself: "Weddings bring more weddings; and funerals, more funerals." He thinks it, but he doesn't say it.

Rodrigo Mesa keeps a tennis ball in his hands and, like someone asserting the power of *his* balls, he squeezes it and crushes it from the bottom until he deforms the hollow rubber sphere.

"Not everyone will be in the thick of it, but I want you inside. Only a selected few, the finest, like in a drugstore. *Como en botica.*"

Only a selected few, the finest, like in a drugstore? Vargas thinks that neither tennis nor refrains are his boss's strong point. He doesn't have time to think, however, that many of the evils of this world stem from a lack of command of language.

"If you're not sure, we never played this tennis game. And if you are sure…we didn't either…Do you understand?"

"Yes, boss."

"Can I count on you, then?"

Without releasing the ball, Rodrigo Mesa opens his hands like a man offering something, but the truth, as he stares hard into Vargas's eyes, is that he is in fact asking for something.

"Trota deserves that and more," he adds.

Emotional blackmail, comes to Vargas's mind. Having established a sweat pact instead of a blood pact now, he holds his boss's towel with both hands and returns it to him, bending his neck a little, which Rodrigo Mesa reads as a nod. Something is burning in Pedro Vargas's chest: hanging from his neck is a medallion of the Virgin of Vera Cruz; he forgot to take it off before the match and he knows his skin will itch afterward.

"We'll have to change doors and put locks in. We'll need chairs and tools, Vargas. Insulating tape, meters of rope."

"How many?"

"We can't run short," says Rodrigo Mesa.

Raise your glasses, here's a toast to exact and precise measurements! thinks Vargas, although he then replies all docile and helpful:

"I'll take care of it."

Shortly after, Virginia arrives with their little girls and kisses Rodrigo Mesa. "Are we interrupting anything?" Rodrigo Mesa says no, and caresses Sofía and Teresa: his two beloved daughters, what he loves most in this world. Vargas's wife will arrive later, with their only son, who, as well as being a bit older than Sofía and Teresa and being named after his father, seems to be destined to become, in time and to all appearances, his clone. Fortunately the boss's wife is a good cook, so they eat wonderfully; after their tennis matches they usually have a picnic right there; and the children play hide-and-seek, war games, cowboys and Indians, in the abandoned palazzo.

Innocent children's games, play cook, play shop.

"What would the gentleman like?" *¿Qué quiere el señor?*

"Milk." *Leche*.

"What kind of milk?" *¿Qué tipo de leche?*

"Butterfly milk." *Leche de mariposa.*

"I don't have any, sir." *No tengo, señor.*

"I do! I have butterfly milk." *Pues yo sí tengo leche de mariposa.*

And more games then: hide-and-seek, war games, cowboys and Indians, ghost hunting.

After running around, making noise, laughing, crying, and more running around, Rodrigo Mesa's daughters will use the white towel that was draped over the net; they'll tie it to the end of a stick to make a white flag and signal their surrender.

The day will surrender a bit later too. Orange rays of sun on the court's clay soil. Vargas will collect everything then, and make a mental note: they need to whitewash the lines of the court before the next match.

"Do you think it'll work?"

The palazzo is a bit abandoned, but it might work. It's spacious. Quite remote. There aren't many houses nearby, it's got protection and a perimeter fence. The streetlights, thanks to the town hall, are not very abundant, and that will make things easy. The few people who live there, in small, scattered apartment blocks, are mostly young families who can't afford to live in the city center. These are neat three- or four- floor apartment blocks, well built, good urban developments spaciously arranged; it's hard to imagine the building boom that will take place later, in the nineties. Surrounded by an old-fashioned garden and a tennis court riddled with puddles, the palazzo has lots of rooms, six or seven at least, he estimates at first glance. There may be more. And there must be a basement too, surely. There are cockroaches on the staircases, pigeons made neckless by the morning chill coo on the roof's eaves, paint peels off the walls, and everywhere but everywhere, chips of broken enamel. And dust, and spiderwebs.

"What's in the garage?"

"Not much now. The boys leave their motorbikes there sometimes."

Standing in front of the door, he pushes aside the heavy canvas that doubles as a curtain: cracked spark plugs in a wooden box. A green hose, punctured in all likelihood, the smell of oil and gas, a kayak tied to a red plastic buoy, a 1982 calendar from last year's World Cup. A Sanglas sidecar, an old Lambretta, an upside-down gas can, a Vaseline tube squeezed to extinction by buzzard claws.

"They bring dogs sometimes too."

"Dogs?"

"Yes, to train them."

"Well, they can't bring them anymore. No more dogs, no more motorbikes, no more tennis matches for a while. Is that clear?"

Fontecha is too young to be a government delegate, and he knows it. That's why he's despotic and arrogant. Because of that, and because he understands the post as a favor that they'll have to pay him for in the future, with even more succulent posts. It's as if his way of speaking makes him sound older, or twenty centimeters taller, or brings him within sight of the Devil's eyes. He fails in all three objectives.

"I'll tell the boys now, don't worry: lately, only Vargas and I come over."

They're still in the middle of the court, near the net. The

trace of lime on the soil has started to vanish and the net is loose, much lower in the middle than in the extremes. They go through the rooms. It smells musty, as if it's been raining on the carpet. It happens: sometimes the dampness outside manifests inside, and stains appear, revealing the true colors of the walls. There are some drips here and there, but the house is otherwise in pretty good shape. Not good enough to live in, obviously. The floorboards complain as they walk, the cork cracks. Yes to this, no to that, yes to this, no to that. "This, this, and this." All three without windows.

"I want a red mark on the door of each of these three rooms." In what used to be the kitchen, he turns a tap. Not a drop of water pours from it, unlike the roof.

"The water is off most of the time, but the plumbing works. If you want, we can turn the water on."

"Today if that's at all possible, Rodrigo."

"Leave it to me, I'll talk to Vargas."

"This Vargas guy... can we trust him?"

More than any loyal Christian, Don Pedro, my lord, thinks Rodrigo Mesa. But he says something else:

"Completely, sir."

"We must choose our men well, Rodrigo, this is a delicate matter."

"I understand, Fontecha. Here, I've made copies of the keys for you."

Rodrigo Mesa takes Sofia and Teresa to the reservoir, to go fishing.

"There used to be a village down there, once."

"Really?"

"And where are its inhabitants now?"

"They left their houses and went to live in other houses."

"And what did they do with their things?"

"They took them too."

"All of them?"

"All of them."

"And their dogs?"

"They took them too."

"And their cats?"

"Them too."

The two children remain pensive, staring into the water as if they can sense something in it. It looks like they can't think of anything other than the things one might take from a village that's about to be flooded.

"You can't see anything."

"It all happened a long time ago."

He bought new fishing lures, black-and-yellow ones, striped like bees. The girls have similar pajamas. Rodrigo Mesa's fish-hook collection is impressive. His daughters like to spend hours looking at them; his father keeps them in perfect order, the way a painter keeps colors on a palette. He dusts them with a brush.

He sometimes makes artificial flies himself, adding thread and feathers to the ones he buys in shops. "They look like earrings," Teresa remarked once. And she wasn't completely wrong: on one occasion he'd improvised a hook with an earring his wife no longer used. Fish like anything that shines.

"Careful, don't hurt yourselves, they're very sharp."

"Aren't you going to use a worm, dad?"

"No, we can fish without a worm too."

His daughters don't seem convinced. "And the fish will bite even if there's no bait on the hook? Impossible." They've seen too many cartoons, they find it hard to believe that you can fool a real fish with a plastic one, or with bits of colored metal that are not even shaped like fishes. They laugh, laugh in amazement. "Wow!" As their father shakes the fishing rod and they see how far the fishing line goes.

"Where is it? I can't see the line…"

"Some things can't be seen."

But now Sofia and Teresa have other things in mind. They leap and dance, holding each other by the hand.

"Can we put the radio on, dad?"

His daughters have absolutely no faith in their father's fishing. Rodrigo Mesa is not very good at saying no to his daughters either. They open the doors of the R18 and turn the radio on, searching for music.

"Hey! It took the bait!"

Sofia and Teresa seldom see their father look so happy. Which is reason enough to stop what they're doing. They help him reel in the line, although in truth, and because of its weight, he immediately realizes that the trout they caught is small, too small. He removes the hook from the poor fish, which flips and struggles for air while the girls shriek with excitement and fright. It's good for them to see fish outside the frying pan, that's what Rodrigo Mesa thinks, although his wife gets a bit upset if he guts them in front of the children. It's bigger than he thought, but he doesn't think it meets that required minimal measurement. He places the trout next to the pencil he uses to measure his catch.

"Almost, but not quite," he says.

He returns it to the water.

"Why did you let it go?"

"It's forbidden to catch such small fish. We have to let them grow. Otherwise, you get a fine."

"A fine? *You* can get them too?"

Rodrigo Mesa smiles. *Who guards the guard?* The question bounces around the corners of his mind.

"I can get them too, my love."

When they arrive home, Virginia tells him that Javier Fontecha called. He returns the call to confirm that it's true, that the Portugal thing is a go-ahead. That everything is going as planned. Exactly as planned. Shortly after, he receives the phone call he was waiting for. This time he picks up the phone. He always picks up when he's at home. They tell him the appointment time, in bad Spanish.

"No way: not in Portugal. Galicia is better."

He hears them argue at the other end of the line.

"All right, take note."

He writes their address down with a pencil, in the corner of an old day planner. "A fragment of Kosmos, the Russian satellite, could impact the earth today," the newspaper said, for a week. *It doesn't look like it hit us*, it occurs to him. The tip of the pencil breaks when he writes exerting too much pressure, so he asks one of his daughters to sharpen it again. She is delighted with the command and does it docilely. After five minutes she returns it to her father, sharp, but visibly shorter.

He'll have to remember to pick up a new one, because that was the pencil he used to measure the trout.

The meeting takes place in Redondela, in a field near the village, in the daytime. Rodrigo Mesa preferred not to meet in Portugal: given what they were going to pay them, the least they could do was cross the Minho to negotiate conditions. A Salazarista friend of Rodrigo Mesa's father put them in touch. He assures him that they can be trusted. People of scant words. Better that way.

He quickly rejects one of them: his skin is too dark. He is probably more effective in his work – he could easily imagine him in the Angolan War or in Cabo Verde, giving orders at the shooting range with a rifle slung over his shoulder, basically just another extremity – but his presence would be too noticeable. No. He'll have to make do with the other two. *Not the black one.* How could he say what he needed to say without appearing racist? Impossible. The other two don't look like the most discreet people in the world either and, even less so, in possession of the kind of self-control required to keep away from hard liquor for two weeks in a row. But things are what they are. Hopefully they'd do what they had to do well, and they wouldn't be too clear about what they were doing or who they were doing it for: that's what's important; although after a time of course the truth will come out and everyone will know. Submerged worlds tend to come to the surface, sooner or later. Although they try to behave with a certain deference, Rodrigo Mesa notices that they can hardly disguise their indifference. But they can't start looking for someone else now. Besides, what the hell, it's not like they had to perform open-heart surgery. It's not so complicated. Their task is of a different kind. *Let's hope they do it well.*

And the money is in the suitcase, they wanted it in French francs, God knows why. Their weapons will come from Italy; they'll tell them where to pick them up later on.

They want Beretta guns and Benelli semiautomatics. They are very demanding, these Portuguese guys.

"We'll have to see."

Since they don't know the language or the terrain, they'll need help, of course. Rodrigo Mesa will use some of his men as guides and as shields; he's weighing some ideas, although he hasn't made up his mind about anyone but Vargas. "Only a selected few, the finest, like in a drugstore. *Como en botica*." Pérez Gomera? Hernández? He's not so sure about this last one: he seems trustworthy, but too young. They'll join the Portuguese in the Beti-Jai Grill. But they have to know they can only give them coverage. If they get into trouble, then bye, they're on their own. The Spanish police cannot be mixed up in that.

"How will we know who they are?"

"They'll know who you are."

Rodrigo Mesa feels like the main character in a bad movie. He likes it. While thinking about movies he notices that the whiter of the two guys has quite a visible scar above his eyebrow. It's shaped like a second eyebrow, one without a single hair. Quite an evident physical marking, the kind you notice on first sight, something that sticks in your mind. But, after the look he got from the black guy, "You'd be too noticeable over there," he doesn't dare reject another one. He already knows they see him as "a fussy Spaniard." But they are the real fusspots: Beretta guns and Benelli semiautomatics – picky, are we? He'll have to tell his men to wear wigs and glasses. It'd be wise not to trust the professionalism of the Portuguese too much.

They don't trust Rodrigo Mesa either, it seems: they take their time to make sure they are not one cent short on the agreed price. They're not used to counting bills: they had to start over three times before they approved the wad. They are careless even in that.

Rodrigo Mesa walks away. He walks as if he were carrying something, although he should've felt relieved without the suitcase. He sits on the terrace of a bar to drink port under a silver sun. He watches the Portuguese climb into a beat-up Citroën Visa from there. He notes down the plate number, just in case. He orders a second glass of port, he deserves it.

"More than others, that's for sure," he tells himself, bitterly.

He takes a little sip, just enough to wet his lips.

"This one's for you, Trota."

You always have to toast someone. He couldn't think of anyone else. Even though he's never even seen Alfredo Trota.

The sun hides for a moment, one of those passing clouds. Obeying the superstition that states that it's bad luck to drink in the shade, Lieutenant Colonel Rodrigo Mesa waits until the sun comes out again to continue drinking.

The candidate arrives late because he's *the candidate*, and because we always expect a true candidate, like the brides dressed in white from way back, to make us wait. He's not just any candidate: he's the candidate to the presidency. Which is not just anything, because this turns him into a potential equation, a walking equation that computes the expectations of favors he might do for people in the future. That walking equation wearing shiny shoes might be a catalyst for the most magnanimous gestures, the most solemn words, once he reaches power – if he does reach power, which he just might. The candidate is a potential equation, true, but not a closed equation, he might be influenced by several factors: he hasn't fossilized yet, he's still somewhat flexible – only because he hasn't yet won – and people want to make use of the candidate's malleability to influence him, to make a good impression. He's very busy, so it's not a good idea to hog his attention or to be selfish and try to take advantage of brief lapses of his time to ask him for things; now is not the time for that, but it might be the time to put into practice the art of lightly planting the seedlings of those hypothetical future favors, through smiles, little taps on the back, emphatic nods, and other signs of unbreakable loyalty. "I'm with you, Presidente, for whatever you need, until the end, no matter what."

The candidate's charm resides in his ephemeral nature too: he's slippery, we know he doesn't have the time to attend to us, so he can't disappoint us. And we confuse that transitory impossibility of disappointment with infallibility – our greatest mistake.

The candidate arrives late, but he arrives, which is what matters. The candidate is here now, and as is to be expected he doesn't come alone, he brings along the people who organize his schedule, those in charge of communications, secretaries, and the other movers and shakers and advisers that make up his cohort; so many that it's hard sometimes to figure out who is leading. The candidate stretches his hand out to the party members that ask for it, although he doesn't know the names of most of them. He feels like a zookeeper feeding the flamingos. The candidate, putting his reflexes to the test, tries to grab and extract any virtue or extravagance that stands out from the whole from every place he finds himself in – he should be good at that. Thus, if he notices someone who is too young for politics, he grips their hand particularly hard, and tells them: "This is so good, I love it, the party needs young, committed people." He sees his followers as beggars, and himself as the one giving alms. Yes, he's conscious of it: he goes around giving blessings and ameliorating despair, so to speak. It's what people call *the erotics of power.*

After greeting a lot of people he doesn't know, he comes across someone familiar at last; he gives this one a powerful hug, as well as the de rigueur handshake and an exchange of pleasantries. Those who surround him will be able to interpret that, on a small scale, this is the *candidate's candidate*, the man that should be obeyed in the region. Every now and then they introduce him to someone new, to some local promise or some new member, an important professional or someone of renown in their sector. This kind of person, along with the handshake, gets a few words. Something like:

"I've heard great things about you."

On ninety percent of occasions, of course, the candidate hasn't heard anything, not good nor bad, about the person in question, but that's the least of it. The candidate knows that his handshake makes people trust him and that, beyond, makes them feel that he is with them, this is important; more so, considering that the person he's just been introduced to might be tomorrow's adversary or annihilator.

That, more or less, is what Fontecha remembered the day they introduced him to his party's candidate, who later on became president-elect. Fontecha had the dubious privilege of being one of those people the candidate addressed a few words to. The candidate knew nothing about him but despite that, and because he had to, because this life is nothing more than a succession of instants in which we're obliged to say what we must, he told him:

"I've heard great things about you."

Shortly thereafter, he was made a government delegate. But that happened many years ago, in another lifetime, and his political career never took off the way everyone expected. Fontecha's dream now was to become the man who says: "I've heard great things about you."

Lieutenant Colonel Rodrigo Mesa is usually in a hurry to remove his stripes. The uniform has always felt too stiff to him; Virginia once told him about starch, she irons it for him; it's not comfortable and he knows that that second skin is the first thing people notice about him – if not the only thing. That's what the uniform was invented for. To be seen from a distance, long before the person wearing it. Those colorful buttons on the chest, those little toys that some call medals and look so much like fishhooks. The higher he goes, the less he's obliged to wear the uniform, and that's his main motivation to keep going up in the ranks. He often thinks that he owes many of the habits of his profession to the uniform, and he has the feeling that when he takes it off he gets rid of those bad habits too: every evening when he gets home, he hopes to return to that happy and optimistic Rodrigo Mesa of his youth, and he's hoping he will, once he retires and is able to definitively remove that attire.

Stepping out of the uniform and getting a shave, those are the two main happinesses he allows his corrupt body: he thinks he recovers his nakedness and innocence when he removes that second skin. Getting a shave and the rub of the aftershave lotion on clean skin bring the ephemeral memory of the softness of his pink childish face, and with it a feeling of transitory rejuvenation.

Today's operation is special, however, and he has to enter the patrol with the stripes on, before he has a chance to shave. The judge who's just arrived from Madrid's High Court to direct the operation – "Direct? Ha! They wish!" – travels in the car next to his. It's the same one who once tried to link them to the GAL, funnily enough. It was a clean operation. Everything went well. The kidnappers offered no resistance, and one of them, the eldest, was recognized by Rodrigo Mesa.

That man has been sent to jail before. He spent at least six years behind bars, and he'll get twice as many this time. He got out of jail and immediately returned to life underground. As if he didn't know how to do anything else. In a remote corner of his mind where hatred and contempt have taken permanent hold, a spark of admiration for the accused suddenly flares up. His bosses can say what they want, but they cannot deny there was political motivation there: these aren't common criminals. Nothing like the playful contract killers who demand Beretta guns and Benelli semiautomatics. No, these are men of a different kind. And precisely because they are, the law applies to them differently. ZEN. Zona Especial Norte. Special Northern Zone. The plan initiated by that minister who looks like an owl was called that for a time. It's useless to deny it. That man, after some years getting a stripy tan, returned to the service of terrorists to take part in a kidnapping, be detained, and, loyally, hand over another ten years of his life to the cause. He had to accept that there were enemies and enemies, and Rodrigo Mesa acknowledged that this sewer rat had a well-developed sense of loyalty, that he was consequent with his ideals. He had no doubts about Vargas, but...who among the men under his command would preserve such loyalty and coherence after so many years? And, looking at it from another perspective: would he be loyal enough to have Fontecha's back and omit his name when, as it seemed, he was made to face a tribunal again?

Even faith is eroded by time.

In contrast with the two young kidnappers, who stare at the ground, the group leader looks into his eyes and lowers his chin, with a reverence that Rodrigo Mesa interprets as scorn. Reverence and contempt, both together. The sophistication of the gesture takes him by surprise and, although he tries to imitate him, he knows he's failed, that he only managed half the gesture, the reverential part, tainted with a trace of defeatist resignation perhaps. He feels that the accused has won this hand, and immediately after wonders which one of the two has aged more since the last time they saw each other. He'd rather draw no conclusions.

But these are nothing but fast sparks; everything is a momentary matter, that surge of unexpected admiration, the successive reverence and disdain. Soon, the kidnapped man's figure captures all his attention: his long beard, the too-large clothes that reveal the many kilos he lost while in captivity, the difficulty with which he opens his eyes, his extreme weakness, his inability to remain standing. Shivering under some blankets, the man seems sick, dying almost, as if he's just been rescued from the rubble of a collapsed building. *And they'll say* we *are the torturers*, thinks Lieutenant Colonel Rodrigo Mesa, and he returns to his role and his uniform, certain that the man will never recover from such a traumatic experience.

Rodrigo Mesa enters the damp *zulo*. Leftover food in the pans, gas canisters, milk in stainless steel canteen cups, a bag of rice, empty water bottles, old newspapers, a camera, blankets and a musty smell, a big, wide-bottomed pot filled with sand, which the kidnapped man must have used to do his business.

The judge and his assistants approach, to take notes and supervise the work of the crime scene investigators. The magistrate congratulates him and the lieutenant colonel perceives his usual, too-strong perfume. The gesture of reverence and scorn he received from the kidnapper before, now, at last, he's been able to return to the judge. It happens sometimes: we enact the correct gesture with the wrong person. Or maybe not: a gesture learned from the wrong person serves us to enact the appropriate gesture for the right person. Suddenly the patrol agents bring him a message: Virginia is calling. He's about to become a grandfather and both his wife and daughter are at the hospital.

They're having difficulties getting the baby out. They already knew his daughter had a small womb, but the baby's reluctance to get out must be strong; apparently the creature is not very inclined to leave the refuge. They have to provoke the birth. His adored daughter, Teresa, the youngest of the two, split in half; the thought of it gives him shudders and makes him proud at the same time. The process of her giving birth is more agonizing than what he'd gone through that morning. He would like to start imparting orders, but he can't do that here, despite still being in uniform; the colorful fishhooks on his chest are worth nothing. He has to share the wait with Virginia and with Teresa's dumb husband. Judging from the son-in-law's face, you'd think he'd been beaten up, *No one ever taught this one to behave like a man*, Rodrigo Mesa thinks. After two long hours, his daughter finally gives birth; an orange split in two, one of its halves with a vocation for endurance; the other, Teresa, you could say with a vocation for giving up. She really looks like someone who's just given birth, the baby sucked up a lot of her energy, she seems thin, more so when she tries to work out a smile, she's down to her very bones, with thin, disheveled hair; Rodrigo Mesa takes his fourth grandchild in his arms, a tiny baby that could be held with one hand, too blind still to be able to perceive the glint of the medals on his chest. After a lot of days, weeks, months, years, sometimes it happens that events concentrate in a single day, obstacles disappear, open-ended issues resolve; the world moves forward, unstoppable, complex, manifesting the obvious insignificance of our will and upending any plans we might ever make.

"It's a boy, Rodri," his wife says; and grandfather and grandson are, for a moment, two babies, each younger than the other.

How long has it been since his wife's called him Rodri?

"A boy, Rodri, like you wanted."

Even though it's a boy, he looks more like Teresa and not so much like the son-in-law. He must remain alert, in any case: you never know with people, they could stab you in the back and their faces change when you least expect it. He must remain watchful, in case he ends up looking too much like his dumb father.

They take the baby from his arms when he starts to cry; "it's because of the uniform," he apologizes, the fabric is so rough – Virginia told him about starch once. Then he remembers how that man cried when they freed him from his confinement, and is surprised to realize how little the kidnapped man's tears moved him, and how much his newborn grandchild's did.

Fontecha got home exhausted. Ever since he'd joined the domestic violence commission his sojourns to Gasteiz stretched for too long. Patricia was working on her laptop on the living room table, with a long-stemmed glass full of wine and three slices of just-toasted bread, each with a different cheese on.

"Work dinner, love?" Fontecha asked, with irony.

"Needs muse..."

He kissed her on the cheek and brought another wine glass from the kitchen.

"We've quite a complicated surgical procedure tomorrow. I was going through it."

"Let me guess: a valve replacement?"

"Yes, a complex one: we're going to stop the heart and lungs with the new machine. We'll be able to work more comfortably like that. Do you want to see the diagram?"

"Not with dinner, I'd rather not, thanks."

Patricia was passionate about her work. Like in all other aspects of her life, she was methodical, demanding, mindful of every detail in that area too. She liked things to go well and got very angry if they didn't go according to plan. She'd been experiencing a very happy interlude ever since they'd brought that new machine to the clinic, a professional joy that Fontecha didn't quite understand but found quite amusing all the same. He was always enthralled listening to her talk about how they used valves taken from pig hearts or about impossible alloys, although it was hard for him sometimes to follow her explanations. "We're going to stop the heart and lungs with the new machine to be able to work more comfortably." Were there really machines for that? Apparently, there were. Afterward a spark and everything just restarts. Fontecha wanted that to be possible in his work too: to stop for a moment his heart and lungs, not to have someone work on his entrails in the meantime, of course, but to be able to somehow take a rest. Afterward, a spark and he could continue working, with renewed strength, certain that his heart and lungs wouldn't fail him. It wouldn't be too bad either, let's not deny it, to be able to stop someone else's heart. He quickly drew up a long list of lowlifes whose valves he'd like to replace, lowlifes whose hearts he'd like to hold in his hands. Unlike his wife, Fontecha would get out of the operating theater leaving the patient's chest wide open.

"Not bad, this wine."

"Lately, and alluding to its beneficial effects on cardiovascular health, all my patients gift me bottles of wine," says Patricia with a smile.

Fontecha grabbed the bottle and put his reading glasses on to read the label: Château Latour, 1994. Grape modalities: Cabernet Sauvignon, Merlot, Petit Verdot, Cabernet Franc.

"How much would you say this bottle is worth?"

"A *mileurista*'s monthly wage. It's a Pauillac, from near Saint-Julien... Remember Antoinette and Philippe? They live not far from there."

Her mention of Antoinette and Philippe soured his drink. On one occasion they'd given him a young, low-quality wine to taste and, not knowing any better, he praised it. The three of them, Antoinette, Philippe, and Patricia, laughed at him. "The true wines are about to be served, reserve your praises for later," Philippe told him patronizingly, hoping to underline perhaps that putting up with jokes like that one was the price he had to pay to be accepted among his class. "You're not one of us, but we accept you...just know that the toll you'll have to pay for that is our petty-bourgeois disdain and giggles at the enormity of your unknowing. We'll teach you, but only slowly. We'll teach you, but we'll have fun in the process. Nothing comes free."

Nothing comes free.

The wages that supported the real expenditure in that household were Patricia's. The wine expert's vantage point was Patricia's. They were Patricia's too, although they were now "friends of the two of us," those yacht-owning summer friends who invited them to spend the Easter holidays in ostentatious castles in the Loire Valley. He was only a modest politician. A politician from the land of the barbarians, that's how they made him feel on the few occasions they visited Philippe and Antoinette. He felt so humiliated before them when his party, not knowing what to do with him, sent him to the European Parliament, and he had to confess to Philippe and Antoinette that, no, he didn't speak French or English. The French were true politicians, real statesman, French politics were top-notch politics, unlike what Fontecha and his party members were doing in Spain...On one occasion, Philippe gave him an article by Oriana Fallaci about Andreotti, as if that Frenchie boy could ever give him a lesson on politics – give *him* a lesson – when he'd suffered for years under the shadow cast by bodyguards, when *he*, the ex-government delegate, had breakfasted with news of a new assassination practically every morning in the tumultuous eighties. He still remembered Fallaci's article, the conclusion she'd drawn after meeting the head of the Italian state: "True power chokes you with silk ribbons, with charm and intelligence." Yes, that was the kind of sentence Patricia and her Frenchie friends liked. Philippe, Antoinette. A little wine and a cheese platter. But all of that was no impediment for Fontecha. Patricia was the love of his life, and he was willing to forgive everything, including the disdain and the giggles, even the pettiness, because he was completely convinced that she didn't mean to do it.

"You must've talked about the news in the papers, no? They've been ringing nonstop, up until ten p.m. I didn't pick up, of course. In the end, I decided to disconnect the phone. It's so funny…"

Fontecha knew full well what his wife was talking about. She found it *funny*? He refilled his glass of wine far beyond what was recommendable, and forgetting the restraint of Antoinette and Philippe, knocked back the cardiovascular health benefits of the Château Latour in one behind Patricia's back, knowing that she wouldn't take her eyes off the screen: valves, pigs, inert lungs and a paralyzed heart.

Seeing that Fontecha wasn't saying anything, Patricia retook the conversation. She still seemed amused:

"You'll have to clarify to the journalists that I am not exactly a cardiologist, but a *cardiovascular surgeon* . . . if this is how rigorous they are with all their news . . ."

Fontecha felt too tired, and a little disappointed. There was no cure for his tiredness, but he hadn't been carrying disappointment before crossing his front door, and this hurt him more. Even though he knew he would regret it as soon as he said it, he couldn't help it:

"Is it really *so* funny?"

Fontecha tried hard to smile while he formulated the question, but he knew he failed in the attempt, because of his wounded pride. Patricia took her eyes off the screen for the first time.

"You can't seriously be considering it, Javier . . ."

"Of course, it wasn't my intention, but . . ."

"Have you forgotten what we agreed?"

"No, but things have changed . . ."

"They'll destroy you, Javier. The candidate was chosen a long time ago, you know that well . . ."

"The party asked me to . . . I've received very important phone calls, from people you can't even imagine."

"That little Judas Fuchs who called you so that *you'd* ask to convene an extraordinary congress? You all came out for him like little lambs . . . *He* will be the candidate . . . Do you seriously doubt that?"

Patricia was right. Patricia was right about everything she

said. And everything she was reproaching him for now, they'd talked about multiple times after dinner, with disdain, laughing, underscoring how far they were from those miserly party intrigues, shielding themselves – through laughter – from those repugnant beings who'd stab each other in the back for a speck of power, casting protective spells that'd stop them from ever being tempted to engage in those fratricidal battles that brought out the worst inhumanity. Patricia was right, but that didn't make Fontecha feel calmer, not at all.

"Nothing's been decided yet."

Patricia stood up from her chair.

"You are *thinking about it*! Have you been brainwashed, or what? How long have you known? Why didn't you mention it to me before?"

"As I said, nothing's been decided yet."

"But you're *thinking about it . . .*"

"Yes, I'm thinking about it. What's so bad about thinking about it?"

"Everything, if you know from the beginning that what you're thinking leads nowhere."

"It might be an opportunity. The last one."

"They've given you a pick and a shovel so that you can dig your own grave . . . Fuchs will be the candidate, you know that better than anyone."

Perhaps because she understood that she'd been too harsh,

Patricia got close to him to whisper in a low voice, certain that physical contact would soften the cruel truth of her words. She brought her hand toward him, not to caress his neck lovingly, not to pat his shoulder patronizingly. She placed her hand somewhere in the middle. Lovingly. Patronizingly. Certain that the love he felt for her would tilt the balance toward perceiving the gesture as loving.

"Darling, don't you realize?"

"I've always supported you. I've always encouraged you in your career."

"I know, darling."

"And you, why don't you?"

"Let me be clear: the decision is yours. I will be by your side, you know that. But I don't think it's a good idea."

"Why?"

"Because you'd be throwing yourself to the wolves, and, I'm sorry, but you are not one of them. I wouldn't be with you if you were."

"But I used to be..."

"You, a wolf?"

"What do you think this was like in the eighties? I was a government delegate...We hadn't met yet..."

"Things have changed a lot since then. The world was dirtier, but politics was cleaner."

A blast of naïveté, at last. "If only you knew, Patricia," he thought, and for a moment his wife's naïveté made him feel stronger than her. "You, with your amazing ability to stop hearts and lungs; you, with your well-supplied bank account, your love of theater. You, with your ability to speak in-depth, at length, about the plot in *La Traviata*, with your collection of Cecilia Bartoli albums, your Château Lafite, your Château Latour, your "it's a Pauillac," with your perfect French, you, my dear wife, not even you know everything. You know almost nothing about my world. About my previous life. If you knew you know nothing, would you live with me at all? Would you've ever opened the door to my petty-bourgeois humiliation? *We're going to stop the heart and lungs to be able to work more comfortably...* what would you say if I told you that I too know a thing or two about that?"

He thinks it, but he doesn't say it.

The world was dirtier then, but politics was cleaner.

Wasn't it the other way around? *We were all younger*, Fontecha tells himself, that was the only difference. The smell of putrefaction was different among the young and the old. Even though they were all corrupt, young and old putrefaction attracted different kinds of flies.

"What's on your mind, Javier?"

"Maybe you're right: I shouldn't put myself forward. I'm too old for this."

"You're too good to go on the first row. That's all I'm trying to tell you."

It was Pedro Vargas's idea to hand over the weapons in the reservoir. They bring the missing documentation too, as well as the car and its key. By the time they collect them from the bar Beti-Jai and bring them over, he and Hernández are waiting with the materials.

"Only one key?"

The man with a second eyebrow above the first says he wants a duplicate key.

"What for?"

"What happens if we lose it?"

Pedro Vargas doesn't even respond. It's not worth it. He hands over the documentation and the photographs, and introduces them to Hernández. The Portuguese don't object much to the documentation: they only pay attention to the photographs, like people who skim through the society and politics pages of newspapers until they reach the sports section, blatantly ignoring the reports with too much writing on them. Vargas opens the trunk of the car and shows them the weapons. The Portuguese stare at them like children contemplating a candy store. Initially, they are dazzled by the semiautomatics.

"Benelli?"

"Yes, Benelli."

They remove the safety locks and inspect the ammunition: everything is in order.

"And the Beretta guns?"

Pedro Vargas opens the second box.

"There are no Beretta guns: these are Star. Aren't they good enough for you?"

"We asked for Beretta guns." It's not the guy with the double eyebrow who speaks now, but the other. A thorough brute.

"There are no Berettas, I'm sorry."

"We won't do it without the Berettas."

Pedro Vargas starts to get nervous. He thought the boss had already negotiated all that. He takes one of the Star guns and loads it, furious. So much so, that the thorough Portuguese brute for a moment fears he might intend to kill them right there and then: he regrets the two brandies he had for breakfast; if he hadn't drunk them, maybe his reflexes would be quick enough to get the little Derringer gun out of his jacket pocket. Pedro Vargas's change of humor takes everyone by surprise. Not only the Portuguese. Also his colleague Hernández.

He places the silencer on the gun and rams it into his belt. He takes out the spare wheel, which is under the box of weapons, and rolls it all the way down to the birches that loom over the edge of the reservoir. He rests the wheel against a tree, and walks back to the spot where the Portuguese and his trusted men are standing.

He shoots the improvised target three times, from an approximate distance of twenty meters. One shot after another. Steady pulse. The first two bullets go through the tire. The third deflates the inner tube, but impacts near the aluminum rim.

Pedro Vargas stares at the Portuguese with ire, rubs his fingerprints off the butt of the gun with his sleeve and hands over the weapon to the man with a double eyebrow.

"Star. You won't find better guns. Can you do it then?"

The Portuguese stare at each other, they seem to be in doubt.

The man with the double eyebrow signs his agreement in a hoarse voice, grumbling:

"Okay. But we'll need another spare wheel, just in case."

Motherfucker, thinks Pedro Vargas to himself, but immediately feels for the medallion of the Holy Virgin of Vera Cruz inside his shirt, asks Her forgiveness, and decides to calm down.

He remembers Ivan Lendl, the Czech tennis player. He who knows how to control himself and never loses his temper. Slavic blood. He'd like some of that.

Ever since he made the decision of entering the primaries to become his party's candidate, Fontecha was up to his neck in work. Thankfully he could count on Belen, his secretary.

Belen was a rara avis. She had a sort of aura. Was it just the energy of youth, in the eyes of a mature man? That was very possible, yes, but Fontecha wanted to believe that Belen's aura was

– 234 –

something more than an ephemeral biological springtime that would eventually wither away. He had to believe in something, didn't he? She had just joined the party, spoke four languages fluently, and was at the top of her class at the University of Deusto. Her only defect was to have a degree in law, too ordinary a degree for such an outstanding person. Like the majority of people who studied in Deusto, she liked to specify that she'd studied "financial law," as if somehow hoping to simultaneously draw maximum mileage out of her years of study and distinguish herself from the mediocre hordes of usual shysters. An elitist side? Was she a classist, perhaps? Maybe. After graduating with one of the ten best academic records of her year, she did a masters degree in journalism and was immediately hired as an assistant to the chief of communications of the Basque Autonomous Region. Until the primaries were over, she would be his right hand. Having found such an absolute jewel, Fontecha harbored hopes of their walking the long road ahead together.

They were very relaxed, it was cease-fire time again, and, since they'd learned that those periods of peace didn't last forever, it was their duty to enjoy the interlude, to the point that they almost forgot the bodyguards that walked discreetly behind them at a distance of two hundred meters. A summer that lasts forever is no longer a summer.

"We have an interview. Local news, nothing much. The journalist's name is Idoia Erro. She worked for the leftist Basque press in her youth, but she's been in the Bilbao offices of *El Mundo* for a few years now."

Fontecha's memory wasn't good, but bitterness is a very good fixative and that name was branded into his memory. Idoia Erro. The article that journalist had written about him was very present in his mind, as it had provoked an argument with Patricia. After so many years together, he never managed to get Patricia to stop buying *El Mundo* and start reading *El País* instead.

"You'll have to clarify to the journalists that I am not exactly a cardiologist, but a *cardiovascular surgeon*... if this is how rigorous they are with all their news..."

"I assume that her idealization of the struggles of the past must have dissolved somewhat, but you'd better be careful, just in case."

Pedro Vargas was an old-school man. Not only because he believed in God and divine punishment. But also because he believed in loyalty and revenge.

It was the pull of an old bond of loyalty that put him on the road to Palencia, with the oxygen tank as copilot; even though he had to take the mask to his nose and mouth every now and then, he knew he would arrive there safe and sound. The Virgin of Vera Cruz would carry him. He had an important meeting there, the kind that reassures one that they'll reach their destination safe and sound. Before entering the freeway, he took a side road and stopped for a moment by the reservoir. The place had hardly changed. The birches were still standing there. Star bullet casings must still be buried somewhere there too. Without leaving the car, he moved over to the passenger seat and held the oxygen tank on his lap. He lowered the window, however, and breathed the air outside instead of resorting to the support of his oxygen tank. Contrary to his expectations, the clean air was not enough. He had to put the mask back on in a hurry, or risk asphyxiation.

What was that stop at the reservoir about? There was nothing there anymore. Calm waters, perturbing thoughts. And, despite everything, that place meant a lot to him. It brought him lots of memories. It soothed him and it made him nervous. Beretta and Benelli.

He arrived in Quintanaluengos before nightfall. He found his brother pulling weeds. They hugged. He would have gladly told him: "You're too old to be pulling weeds."

"Why didn't you warn me you were coming? How are you? Let me fix you something to eat ..."

He told him politely that he didn't have much of an appetite, but he wasn't able to refuse a beautiful slice of melon.

"My son-in-law brought it just yesterday from Murcia. It's perfectly ripe."

Fresh and sweet: it'd been a long time since Vargas had taken such pleasure eating anything.

"Why didn't you bring your son along? It's crazy to have

undertaken the journey on your own in your state. How long are you planning to stay?"

"In this world, do you mean?" Vargas was tempted to answer. But he didn't come to see his brother very often, he didn't want to be an asshole.

"You shouldn't be driving. I'm alone until tomorrow afternoon. If you want, Nuria can take you home..."

Pedro Vargas said no.

"More melon?"

"Maybe tonight..."

"No melon at night: *Por la mañana, oro; por la tarde, plata; y por la noche, mata.*" The old Spanish refrain says that melon is gold in the morn, silver at noon, and deadly at night. "Don't you remember our old man's sayings?"

Old sayings, of course, Pedro Vargas knows a lot of those: Only a selected few, the finest, like in a drugstore. *Como en botica.*

"I remember many things about the old man. For example, why he became a civil guard."

"So that everything is in its right place."

"Exactly. *So that everything is in the right place.*" Don Emilio here, Don Emilio there, everyone knew Emilio Vargas and held him in great esteem; everyone called their father by his first name.

"Ours is a small town."

"Small town, big hell."

"He never shot once. Not even into the air."

That was a stab in the back. They had never spoken about the matter face-to-face, but his brother knew something about the war in the North in the eighties. He didn't agree with the methods they used. His son didn't either; he was like his uncle in that regard. He felt an uneasy itch in realizing that no one in his family was ever able to put themselves in his shoes.

"I would say that our father...mistook being a civil guard with being a night watchman," Pedro Vargas scoffed.

"You didn't however."

"When you were a child, didn't you want to be like him? Never? When we were kids...what did it mean to you, to be a civil guard? They hadn't yet invented the 'northern syndrome' back then."

"But Franco died when you joined the corps, Pedro...you could have chosen a different life."

"One like yours, you mean?"

He's not able to say that. His brother was never enthused with Pedro's decision to become a civil guard. He was always involved in farming and farmers' unions, and never felt tempted to leave Palencia, not even when it looked like his whole family might die of hunger. His cooperative went bankrupt twice, and on both occasions Pedro lent him money. Not to mention his daughter Nuria's business studies.

"When I became a civil guard, do you think I was thinking of Franco?"

"You don't regret it, then?"

"We each live our lives. We do what we can."

They were both in agreement about those two last sentences. Either one of them could have been said by Pedro or his brother. But the lack of regret had different nuances for each of them.

Vargas went to pray to the Virgin of Vera Cruz three times. For a moment, he thought that her image looked like Ivan Lendl. That kind of thing happened to him every now and then, ever since he stopped taking medication for his mental illness. Fuck that. He was already stuffed to the gills with cancer drugs.

Don Gregorio received him with arms wide open. Pedro was generous back in the day, when the church bell fell and money was needed to buy a new one. That donation by Pedro Vargas had been *anonymous*. It was the money he'd had to spare after buying the house in Nerja. That was back in the eighties too, there wasn't as much control as there is now for money seized in the war against drugs. Or for church bills and donations either, apparently. The taxation of the church was still mysterious nowadays, however. Even though the affluence of parishioners had declined quite a lot, in the end, the business that had suffered the least in the past few years was Don Gregorio's. The priest didn't take long to notice the oxygen tank on wheels that Vargas dragged along everywhere.

"It's affected your lungs, am I right?"

Vargas had decided that he wouldn't have one more puncture, X-ray, or scan. His last visits to the doctors had only confirmed that new territories had been conquered by metastasis. He had lost the battle but, unfortunately, he couldn't, like a marshal, order the retreat of the men under his command and abandon the battlefield. The Star, the Beretta, the Benelli semiautomatics were of no use here. Because the battlefield was his own body. It was too easy to think that the expansion of that crab he carried in his organism was a consequence of all the bad deeds of his life: God's punishment, Soto and Zeberio rotting his entrails, two tiny young men, two skeletons spreading poison around his intestines and lungs. No, things weren't that simple, but the human mind sometimes operates in such simple ways...

Vargas was dumbstruck when, as he was asking the doctor to up his morphine dosage, he heard his wife's words:

"This is torture."

The truth always comes out, in the end.

Vargas told the priest about those days in October 1983, but not like he'd done before, the way someone tells himself "you did what you had to do," but in a completely different way. The way he remembered it, without forgetting any details, without taking the trouble to justify himself. In a way he had never told himself the story, surprised by the easy way in which words and sentences got together and came out of his mouth. He repeated Rodrigo Mesa's words to him too, without mentioning his name.

"They look pitiful, we can't leave them like that: make them disappear."

Every now and then he'd take the oxygen mask to his mouth and absorb one more gulp of air from the tank, which was truthfully a kind of storeroom of last gasps that offered no certainty as to when the last gasp might arrive. The countdown had started. The last gasp might be more than one. How far were the days when he used to be able to play five tennis sets without breaking a sweat. All that pretend McEnroe fury: the ball was in, close, very close.

The priest listened to his story, and both stayed silent for a while.

"These things you're telling me are terrible, Varguitas."

He took the mask to his face, although this time it wasn't because his lungs were begging for air. He took the mask to his face, not as a carrier of oxygen, but as a mask of disguise.

Telling terrible stories to compassionate priests. What was it that made that possible at the turn of the twenty-first century? The answer was very simple: consciously or not, whoever goes to confession knows that no institution has committed more atrocities than the church. It is much easier to narrate your barbaric deeds to those who've committed similar ones, safe in the knowledge that the institution you face is much more bloodthirsty than yours will ever be. Why hadn't people realized that yet? The savagery they indulged in, the Inquisition, the dictatorships; these aspects made up the church's largest chunk of moral capital: its way of functioning was cryptic and opaque, that's why it still attracted dubious, dark people and their testimonies. They made business out of secrets. It had the pull of dark holes. The moment the church became a transparent, democratic institution, its power would disappear.

Vargas was calm, at peace. He felt relieved, kneeling down in the wooden confessional. It was too hot outside, but there, in the coolness, his lungs didn't demand the oxygen mask as often. He could have stayed there all afternoon, in the half-light, awaiting his sentence. He was slightly curious, in truth: so many years had passed since his last confession, he hadn't "truthfully" confessed in the longest time – Beretta and Benelli – and he didn't know if the priest would tell him *ego te absolvo*, or if he would just bless him with his hand. He had no idea what sort of penitence the compassionate priest would think up for him; he didn't even know if he would take pity on him, seeing him in such a deplorable state.

Vargas remembered his honeymoon to Italy, how during the visit to Milan's Duomo they were astonished to see, inside the enormous cathedral, dozens of confessionals lined up next to one another, each one more elegant than the last. You could take your confession in dozens of different languages. That was a true multilingual secret processor. Next to all the small confessionals they saw a bigger one: *penitenza maggiore*. Vargas and his wife joked about what grave sin they'd need to commit in order to go in.

Now he knew it.

They say that, in the end, truth always comes out. But most of the times it happens too late, when there is no use to it. So it was like the melon: *por la mañana, oro; por la tarde, plata; y por la noche, mata.*

They say that truth always ends up coming out, and that, generally, it does so because the person who's been hiding it for years confesses; the secret is revealed because the person who's kept it wants to reveal it, and not because of the arduous research of the person who's been digging after it, but because the person in possession of the secret no longer wants to be its keeper. We give ourselves away, after all. Most detective novels are based on a falsehood, therefore. They are not credible at all. A spontaneous confession is always more important than rational inquiry.

"Their families should know where their bones are," the priest whispered to him, and Vargas understood he'd heard his penitence.

What drove Fontecha to start that relationship? Had he, though, started it? Did Belen? It wasn't easy to explain what'd happened.

The long work hours they'd spent together, the nights away

from home, in the same hotel but in different rooms...and also, especially, those intimate moments that occurred during the long hours in each other's company; long, boring hours, neutral and flavorless, devoid of any intention of slipping into a physical or sentimental relationship; moments that unexpectedly brought their professional relationship into the private sphere. One of the stories he told himself – a lie, therefore, in all likelihood – was about the time the special correspondent from The New York Times interviewed him. The interview was long, although when it came to writing the article the journalist only awarded him four lines; Belen was his translator. She didn't just translate his words; like interpreters do, she whispered the interviewer's juicy questions in his ear, as she sat next to him on the sofa. That closeness, the girl's thigh pressed hard against his, her lips in his ear, the murmur of her voice, that's what ended up hypnotizing him.

Fontecha thought he could spend all the hours in the world like that, like those horse whisperers, he as the horse and Belen as the whisperer. He was excited by having her so close, her perfume of white petals, the scent of the moisturizing lotion she put on her face. He was nervous before the interview, and surprised when Belen sat so close, not only their thighs and waists touching, but also their shoulders, without qualms. As the girl moved her hands while explaining the questions, Fontecha stared at her fingers intermittently, trying to avoid looking into her eyes all the time – as this made him even more nervous. He wanted to let her know that she had his attention, that he understood the questions, yes, but what Fontecha really wanted was to hold those hands, to caress them, to fuse into that fine skin, that soft fabric. Everything was very professional, just professional, pure professionalism, an impersonal exercise in simultaneous translation; they only spoke of politics, of Basque society, of the passion of Basque nationalists and Fontecha's critical perspective on that passion; and, despite that, Fontecha hoped the questioning would never end: "Ask me long questions, please, I want to keep hearing Belen translate into my ear."

Once the interview in the hotel lobby was over, they spoke about it in a room they were sharing at last; about how Fontecha's pulse quickened just by thinking that she could probably see his ear hair as she translated the questions, about how Belen was worried that her breath might be disagreeable to Fontecha, "as if ears were noses in disguise, capable of sensing smells..." Eventually, after the heterotopia of hotels, the day came to visit Belen's house, a huge step, of the vertigo-inducing kind; they went in through the garage, fearing someone might see them, very late at night; but no one saw them, and they felt safe in each other's arms, a clandestine hideout, a refuge. And her house was a simple house, very domestic, the house of someone who's just stopped being a student and doesn't have enough money yet to be entrapped by designer furniture – apparently, wages in the communications section of the party weren't very generous. Ikea furniture and mugs, nothing to do with financial law: here was normal, everyday Belen, echoing the clothes she wore, in a loft-like attic space, a bohemian space, even, it could be said, and the tenderness she inspired in him as he watched her apologize over and over, shyly, about her place being *quite tiny, not much* for Fontecha, "my place is very very normal," how many times she must have repeated that apology, not knowing that Fontecha probably felt more comfortable there than in his own home, that it helped him relive the intermittent memories of his student days, that her place rejuvenated him almost as much as the velvet of her skin, that he got goose bumps watching Belen ride him, hold his penis and caress it as if it were hers, transformed suddenly into an impossible transvestite, "It's been years since anyone masturbated me."

And later, things that are better avoided when occasional lovers want to continue being lovers: the risk of knowing the daily routines of the other, the habit of preparing simple meals together that freed up time for sex, the fact of helping her fold her clothes, of learning to open and close Belen's jars and zippers, whispering things that made her laugh into her ear, it's the New York Times's special correspondent's fault, of the words translated into his ear.

To know that risk, and to fall for it. The risk of the fall, and the certainty that you'll have the chance to fall again.

When he read that they'd identified the bones of Soto and Zeberio in Cartagena, Rodrigo Mesa called Vargas immediately. But he didn't pick up. Then, overwhelmed by impatience, he tried Fontecha directly.

Rodrigo Mesa's was the last voice Fontecha wanted to hear in this world.

"Have you seen the papers?"

"They bring dogs sometimes too."

"Dogs?"

"Yes, to train them."

"Well, they can't bring them anymore. No more dogs, no more motorbikes, no more tennis matches for a while. Is that clear?"

"Rodrigo…"

"Have you seen the papers?" he heard again.

Javier Fontecha didn't need to unfold the newspaper to know what it said, although he'd read the news soon enough, diagonally, like someone who knows everything, only to check how much it departed from the version he'd already written in his mind, and, especially and above all, to make sure that his first name and family name didn't appear anywhere.

They didn't, but – the pathways of the mind are inscrutable – that didn't make Javier Fontecha feel any calmer.

"I want a good attorney," Rodrigo Mesa told him threateningly, "not someone like the clown I got the last time."

"Not over the phone, Rodrigo…"

"Where should we meet then?"

As soon as he arrived home, Patricia noticed his pallor.

"Did something happen, Javier?"

Since they had declared the cease-fire over, Patricia paid more attention to her husband, his ins and outs, the unexpected things; she even paid more attention to the news on the radio. She always checked her clock when there was a TV nearby and turned the radio on every o'clock to listen to the first minute of the news, to make sure they hadn't killed her husband or anyone else: a tsunami in Malaysia, an earthquake in Haiti, the labor agreement threatened, avian flu rampaging through Asia. "It's okay, I'm sorry, but my body requires a sigh of relief." Certainly: the diameter of the catastrophes that affect us is very limited, and it shrinks further with the passing of time. *They haven't killed Javier today either*, or, at most, *another day without an attack*, she'd tell herself; and her heart – the functioning of which she knew so well, with its valves and its ischemias and rocky electrocardiograms – would return to its usual vital signs, her cell phone would no longer be a time bomb, it would stop feeling like a hand grenade in her pocket, ready to explode in her carrier's hands, to become, once again, the usual message-carrying implement: a fun object with which to send and receive frivolous messages.

She had a bad time every time she had to wait for Javier, especially when he attended public events, although deep down she knew that those occasions were really the safest; that they *obliterated* – "God, what kind of a verb is that?" – most of them early in the morning, when they expected it the least, because of some tiny error or some minimal relaxation of the security measures, bodyguards and all, with car bombs, "obliterate them like rats"; and she knew that little could be done, that all that would be left would be hearts torn to shreds, that it would be impossible to restart them afterward with a spark, that there was no replacement valve or special alloy metal that would revive them. Patricia was used to seeing blood in her job: transfusions, an unexpected spurt of blood, latex gloves, face masks and hospital coats that ended up in the garbage after the most complicated surgeries; only rarely patients would die in the operating room, hieratic masks impossible to revive, hard to detect aneurysms, miracles weren't always possible. It was part of their profession: certain smells, certain images and certain gestures, precise and unerring, quite mechanical, from having repeated them over and over again. The unbelievable technological advances of the past few years had forced her to continuously learn new practices and new gestures – witness to this, in their home library and next to the pile of novels Javier liked, were the thick surgery manuals that filled the shelves, together with the articles on research carried out in the United States and Australia – but blood will always be blood, and she was used to the scalpel's precise trace, to the predetermined cut, to feeling sternums with her fingertips. All that had nothing to do, however, with the possibility of finding her husband bleeding to death on the sidewalk. Although she had never confessed this to him, she thought about it often when Javier kissed her goodbye, his last kiss before leaving the house. They changed their schedules and daily routine, thanks to the fact that at least their children were in university or already married now – each had their own children from previous marriages, in another lifetime. They congratulated themselves on having had their children so soon, at least that way only they needed to swallow that bitter pill. A lesser evil. A lesser of a big, big evil, however.

"Did something happen, Javier?"

Loving someone means not throwing in their faces the sudden changes of direction and switching of vital coordinates we've undergone for them; how often have relationships been ruined by a blowout of reproaches: "If it weren't for you, I wouldn't mind, but you, you don't realize that if it weren't for you...I said no because of you, I stopped going because of you, I gave it up for you and the kids, don't you realize?" To love someone – Patricia often thinks – is never confessing to them that you gave up the after-work conversations you used to enjoy so much, that you have abandoned the beer you used to drink with neurologists and the chief plastic surgeon from the polyclinic. Why? To reach the car before seven, and not at seven fifteen, because you want to hear the seven o'clock news on the radio, sitting in your newly purchased car, surrounded by the smell of leather seats. And to love is also to pray when you are not a person of faith, while you stare at your cell phone as if it were an oracle, hoping not to hear your husband's name being mentioned in the news.

"Did something happen, Javier?"

"I love him; I loved him and I got into the habit of living with him; later the habit gained weight and the love lost it; but you can love a habit too, right?" So much literature, so much fiction, so much cheap psychoanalysis has been written as a result of that simple equation: how to coordinate habit and hormones, how to blend reason and passion into one without self-annihilation, how to accept the battles that are fought and lost within oneself, and keep walking down the street with dignity and your head held high, with a look and an attitude we might have found ridiculous in ourselves a few years ago.

"Did something happen, Javier?"

Habit has given her that, the ability to read Javier's face as if it were the palm of her own hand; it happens every year and it's the only thing that comes with the passing of time we are thankful for: there comes a point when all the types of people and faces we know, we've seen somewhere else before, in someone else's features. *Nothing seems new and, from a certain point onward, it's even relaxing that there is nothing new*, thought Patricia, *and that's why I know that my husband's pallor means something, and I'm worried and want to know what it means, because he's alive, here, and with me, and because the goodbye kiss he gave me this morning – I didn't know it then, but I do now – wasn't the last one.*

Javier told her that no, there was nothing to worry about, but Patricia knew that it wasn't true and that Javier would end up confessing.

"I've something to tell you, Patricia."

"She needed six stitches, but your wife is all right."

"Thank you so much, but…she's not my wife, actually, we work together."

The doctor stared at him from above the rim of his glasses, which seemed to be a low prescription for nearsightedness.

"How did she injure herself?"

"We were fucking like crazy, you should have heard her screams. This woman makes me feel twenty years younger."

"She slipped and fell backward, and hit the bedside table."
He realized then that he hadn't agreed on a version of events with Belen. That he didn't know what she'd told the doctor. He panicked. The hemorrhage was considerable, he'd made an ice pack and put it on the back of her neck and they ran to the ER without thinking of anything else.

The doctor didn't say anything and wrote something down on a notebook he was carrying.

"In these kinds of cases... we have to write a report, as you well know."

"As you well know."

Of course he knew. Javier Fontecha tried to ensure his voice wasn't trembling too much.

"I understand."

Fontecha would have never imagined, when they brought forward the law against domestic violence, that it would affect him like that one day.

"You can visit her if you want, we've given her painkillers. It doesn't look like she has any blood clots, but it's better that she spend the night here."

Poor Belen felt guilty, as guilty as if it'd been her who designed the sharp edge of her bedside table.

"Are you all right?"

"My skin feels very tight, but it's not painful. They had to cut quite a chunk of my hair to sew the stitches more easily. I... I don't know what to say, Javi. I'm so sorry..."

That face like a frightened squirrel. He wanted to approach the subject with tact, but Fontecha was too worried.

"The doctors... did they ask you what happened?"

"I told them the truth... in other words... that I was cleaning and hit my head on the wardrobe..."

"On the wardrobe?"

Suddenly he realized it was no joke; the damage that stupidity could cost Fontecha was greater than he'd anticipated.

"Did they ask you too? What did you tell them?"

Fontecha did a mental comparison of Belen's and his versions of events: "She slipped and fell backward"; "I was cleaning and hit my head…"; it wasn't the same, but they could be complementary versions. Although one of them had said "bedside table" and the other, "wardrobe."

"Don't worry about that."

"What were we thinking about, Javi? You shouldn't have come inside the hospital with me…if this causes you trouble, I'll never forgive myself."

"Rest up and let the wound heal, forget everything else."

Javier Fontecha didn't know how to say goodbye. He would have kissed her on the lips, but there were nurses around. The doctor could come in at any moment too. He squeezed her hand, caressing all her fingers with his thumb. Belen answered by gripping his thumb hard.

"They'll send you home tomorrow morning, it's nothing."

Belen took Fontecha's hand to her lips.

"I love you, Javier. Go home now, before things get even more complicated."

"*I love you, go home.*" His lover spoke the first three words; the last two, his secretary.

Fontecha gave her one last kiss on the forehead, and, like an arrow, the memory of that woman's naked body crossed his mind, how they'd embraced two hours before, the savage sex in her bed; he remembered how, because of his demented desire to hold her in his arms and watch her breasts bounce in front of him, he'd made Belen turn around so she'd ride on top of him, changing positions over and over again without it ever slipping out, and how Belen, in the last gasps of her orgasm, had thrown her head back and accidentally hit the corner of the bedside table. Fontecha got frightened. Belen lost consciousness for a few seconds.

He took the hospital elevator and headed to the street. He felt that everyone recognized him. But there was no reason why they should: he was just an ordinary citizen, things happened to him too. Maybe he was feeling paranoid, maybe people were surprised that a politician such as him could go around without a security detail. "She slipped and fell backward," "I was cleaning and hit my head..." Beyond the matter of guilt, Fontecha tries to evaluate the impact that hospital visit might have on his political career. He tries to persuade himself that it's not so bad, but is irritated by the tendency of events to go awry just when you think you've everything under control. Fortunately, no one had seen Fontecha enter Belen's house, or leave it; he was careful to take the elevator up straight from the garage.

And, despite that, one could never be completely sure.

His candidacy to the primaries hung by a thread: Fontecha had to declare in the Soto and Zeberio case. The party, however, publicly offered him unconditional support. Three days before news of his summons was made public, Patricia moved to her parents'. From one day to the next, the life he'd been living until then began to disintegrate.

What was it that Patricia couldn't forgive? That he'd taken part in the dirty war? That he hid this from her? That he confessed all of it too late? Did she expect him to deny everything, would that have been better? Fontecha had always considered Patricia the woman of his life, but in the past few months everything had become a little relative: he had Belen now, who, even though she didn't drink bottles of Pauillac that cost the monthly wages of a *mileurista*, was in possession of an impetuous aura and had a respect and a consideration for politics and politicians that Patricia lacked; and, what's more important, she believed in his innocence. He had intended to leave Patricia sooner rather than later, and the fact that she'd initiated the move only made things easier. Javier Fontecha opened a bottle that his wife kept for special occasions and decided to invite Belen to his home.

"My wife is away, you can sleep over."

Belen was reluctant at the beginning, but accepted in the end. "Patricia is on a work trip, in Bordeaux," the fact that she was far away made Belen feel safe.

Javier Fontecha had thought everything through: he'd let a

few weeks pass before confessing to Belen that he had spoken to Patricia about their relationship and that they'd both agreed to separate. She would see that he was a *gentleman* who was willing to leave everything for her.

Belen arrived at Fontecha's house exhausted, almost an hour late. She didn't apologize for her tardiness.

"I've just been with the party's attorneys."

Fontecha was surprised.

"I thought the meeting was tomorrow."

"We're trying to get ahead of the work."

"Is there anything new I should be aware of?"

"They want you to step out of the primaries."

"What? No way! That'd be an admission of guilt!"

"It isn't that: you'll deny everything during the trial, of course. You didn't know anything and they acted of their own volition. You'll have the best lawyers. The key to everything is Trota's funeral: you'll declare that you were the only one to speak to Rodrigo Mesa that day. Mesa has been told already..."

"And can't Rodrigo Mesa take care of everything? It was him and Vargas, after all, who..."

"That's what we tried at the beginning, but they have too much evidence that links you to Rodrigo Mesa... can't you see? Too many loose threads... They have recordings, Vargas's confession... And then there's that guy, Diego Lazkano..."

"He must have some weak spot... There must be more than one way to attack him."

"We're investigating him in depth... But he identified the palazzo, El Cerro, in the preliminary investigation... I'm sorry, Javier..."

"I don't believe it... I... Are they going to leave me on my own? You too? They want me to eat this whole thing up on my own? I'll go to jail!"

"Don't think the worst. And, if that came to be, you know that we'll all be with you..."

"If this comes to light, it's the end of everything, Belen! Don't you realize?"

"I will be with you, we'll prepare the trial down to the last detail. You won't go to jail. But you'll have to get out of the picture for a while."

"Why did the party publicly support me, then?"

"Because they are hoping that you'll make the decision to retire."

"And if I don't accept? And if I decide to tell the truth? That I was only following orders, that I felt coerced, that they alleged 'reasons of state,' that they blackmailed me? If they won't let me be candidate, I care very little for anything else... I complied with the years of banishment in Europe..."

"Javi..."

"What? They are asking too much of me…Forget the party for a moment, speak to me as a friend: don't you think I should tell the truth? If I have to go to jail, I won't go on my own! Let everything be known, so be it! If the higher-ups are involved too, they'll pardon us sooner!"

"There'll be no pardon for you, because there'll be no sentence."

"I'm not so sure."

"You owe loyalty to the people who chose you."

"I don't recognize you, Belen. Did you pass them information behind my back? Who are you with? With the party or with me?"

"We're together in this."

"No, we're not. This doesn't concern you. You weren't with me in those days. You've no idea about what kind of hell that was, Belen. And, you know what? I'm disgusted…I think it's time for people to know everything."

"Think about what you're saying, Fontecha…"

"You call me Fontecha now?"

Belen glanced at the expensive furniture in the room. How many households could be decorated with Ikea furniture by selling those pieces?

"They've got me too. They found out about our visit to the hospital. It wasn't a good idea to go together."

Javier Fontecha got even angrier:

"What do you mean, Belen? Would you be willing to testify against me?"

"Seriously, Javier, are you stupid? They don't need me to testify at all. They can just leak my medical report, your signature is in the ER registry. All they need to do is make two copies: one for your wife, and another to be sent to *El Mundo* newspaper, to that Julio Virado who loves you so much...Even if I don't testify, the result will be the same, maybe even worse, because my silence would corroborate their worst hypothesis: 'Socialist candidate beats up secretary,' in capital letters. And below: 'He was in a *relationship* with her.' That's a huge scandal. Even if you came out of the trial unscathed, you'd have to retire."

"But it isn't true..."

"What isn't true?"

"That I beat you up!"

"Oh really, that's news. Since when does truth matter? They wouldn't forgive you: not the truth in lowercase, nor the lie in capital letters."

"I thought we had something special."

"That's not going to change...but you know very well that I had no other choice."

Javier Fontecha goes silent.

"Because...you didn't tell your wife that you took me to the hospital, did you?"

Javier Fontecha stays silent.

"That's what I thought."

She forgave him everything, even the fact that he questioned whether she was more loyal to the party or to him. They continued to be lovers, despite all that. He had her by his side throughout the torment that was the trial, and that meant something.

On the other hand, how do you celebrate freedom? Is there a way of celebrating your freedom, when you've just eluded, *in extremis*, charges that you were guilty of, and you know that your trusted men, Rodrigo Mesa, Vargas – who's almost dead – and the others who collaborated with the Portuguese are going to have to spend some time in prison? Champagne was absurd, but sometimes one can only adhere to the cliché and follow the script. With the bottle of Taittinger spurting foam – which they'll even delay sex for – Fontecha pours out two glasses, brimming with joy.

"To us…"

Belen pushes a lock of hair behind her ear. She responds to the toast with a smile, a slightly forced one.

"I'll have to spend some time under the radar, I have two or three offers from the private sector. They asked me to join the foundation, but I don't know… It's too boring for those of us used to these levels of adrenaline, don't you think?"

"No doubt about it…"

"Wherever I go, I want you with me, of course. That's non-negotiable."

Fontecha grabs Belen's wrist. She leaves the champagne flute on top of the TV. She hasn't touched it.

"What's wrong, Belen?"

"Tell me one thing: have you celebrated with your wife already, or will you do that later? Do you have another bottle of Taittinger in the car? Did you buy them, or did you ask someone else to buy them? I'm curious, I'd like to know…"

"I don't understand…Do you want me to leave Patricia? I'm leaving her soon…As you must have noticed, she hasn't been with me during the trial."

"Look, I'm not going to beat around the bush: they've offered me a post in the president's ministry."

"In Madrid? Who?"

"Fuchs and his group."

"I don't understand…"

"Rumor has it that he'll be the socialist candidate in the next general election. With you out of the picture, chances are that Erviti and Subiol will step aside too."

"Fuchs has always been the man in the shadows…He was never entered into the draws."

"No, but the existing need to reach consensus for a candidate will spur him on."

Fontecha feels like he's inhabiting the skin of someone else, not himself, and saying words that aren't his own either.

"You are not thinking of accepting, are you?"

Belen stays silent. Fontecha should have guessed it from the start. Their insistence in asking him to put himself forward. The great generosity of the party in putting the best possible coordinator by his side. To *help him*? More like to make perfectly sure that he didn't step out of line. On someone's command. A request from Alberto Fuchs and his group. And Fontecha had believed it all.

He decides to pressure her a bit more, without waiting for her response.

"You're not ready."

"They told me they want new blood, Javier."

Fontecha can't repress a bitter smile. "They need someone who isn't tainted by corruption, Javier," that's what Belen meant to say. They need a *virgin* that can conjure up powerful enough mirages and hopes in the electorate. A young woman who can conquer voters by pushing a lock of hair behind her ear. Make room for the youth. New blood. The law of life. The party was nothing but a machine to win elections, what was Fontecha so surprised about?

He feels volcanoes of jealousy and ire inside him: Alberto Fuchs doesn't speak English. Fontecha can imagine who will be whispering translations into his ear.

"You're not ready and you know it."

"You never know if you're ready until you leap into the pool."

"So...you've decided."

"We're talking about Alberto Fuchs...surveys are against us, it'll be a challenge to join the campaign if he truly decides to put himself forward...It's a national campaign, Javier, I can't say no to this."

Her eyes are shining, he's never seen Belen like that. Ambition makes her spread her imperial eagle wings. Fontecha begins to resign himself.

"He's offered you something else, beyond working in the president's ministry, isn't that so?"

"He wants me to be in charge of the press bureau."

"And, if he wins, a ministry. A female minister, young and stylish...Bingo...The Ministry of Equality, perhaps?"

"Fuchs loved the work I did with you, I will always owe you that, Javier. Without you, I would have never..."

Every time she says his name, she hammers the nail in his heart some more.

"What do you know about Fuchs? You don't know him, Belen. He's always stayed out of the limelight. The same in the eighties. Do you know what that means? Have you looked into it?"

"We'll stay in touch, what's between us doesn't need to..."

He doesn't want to seem desperate but he thinks it's time to change attitude, because really, he is. Desperate and disappointed. He wants to inspire a bit of pity on her, although he knows it won't work, because, unlike Patricia, he was never any good at injecting the exact amount of compassion.

"I won't be able to dig myself out of this hole without you, Belen."

"This is my opportunity: who knows if I'll ever have another one like it. Some trains only stop once."

"You never used to talk like this... You've changed a lot since the party's Extraordinary Congress in Toledo."

"I wasn't sure about what I wanted before. Now my eyes have been opened, thanks to you..."

"I haven't paid you enough attention lately, I know. I've learned the lesson. I've understood. Things will change."

"I'm sorry, Javi."

Fontecha picks up the flute of Taittinger from the top of the TV, it's lost its bubbles. He pours it down the toilet.

"They are going to destroy you, don't you realize?"

Fontecha feels pathetic when he hears himself utter borrowed words, words that Patricia had pronounced before. The Minotaur wants a young woman, and that woman will be Belen. Or maybe not. They may not destroy her and she might get out of it safe and sound. The girl will have more options than Fontecha, she's right: she's young, she exudes freshness, which is what's most highly valued nowadays, maybe they'll forgive her

– 266 –

missteps. She will need a good manager, just that, an agent that will arrange easy matches for her, who'll help her reach the top bit by bit, without burning her. And that manager is Fuchs. Is Belen really the chosen one, the one the party barons pointed at with their fingers after evaluating a multitude of factors; press chief to the candidate today, minister tomorrow, first female candidate to the Spanish presidency the day after that? Is Belen really the chosen one for that journey of thorns? Maybe so. Undoubtedly, Patricia was right from the beginning, and Fontecha had made a gross mistake in thinking that they'd placed Belen next to him as an assistant: Fontecha was the *assistant*, and not the other way around. Without hardly realizing it, he had taught her everything he knew, the things he did well and, above all, the things he did badly and she'd better avoid. Javier Fontecha imagines a conversation between Fuchs and Belen many months ago: "Pay attention to this or that when you're with him, his weak points are this and that, keep an eye on all his contacts in that time. The most important thing is to have a good address book. If in doubt, it's better to remain silent. Don't say anything. It's better to regret silence than to have to retract your words. We'll have to go slowly with you."

Yes, they've used him from the beginning, and now that they've squeezed him completely, they push him to the side without even thanking him for the services provided.

The last shot is always the most desperate one.

"Fuchs belonged to the group...in the eighties they'd come to funerals from Madrid packing guns...In Trota's funeral... We received a message from him...'Guarantees.' Did he tell you that?"

There is no answer.

"Did he talk to you about that, Belen?"

"You had your chance to say all that during the trial, Javier. It's too late now."

Javier Fontecha feels humiliated. Destroyed.

And it's then that he sees Belen entering a hall filled with people, late, true, but in possession of a certain magic that makes the wait sweet, people accept it willingly; he sees her with the same clarity that we see what we know will happen tomorrow or the day after, he sees, clearly, Belen shaking hands with people, mechanically but effortlessly, a walking potential equation, repeating words that are not her own, slippery, an eel that flirts and slithers away avoiding all hooks, with a wide smile that reflects that the money her parents spent having her teeth corrected when she was a teenager was money well spent, "Wonderful to meet you, it's a pleasure, I've heard great things about you."

PAPER REQUIEM

FEDE EPELDE LAUGHS SPONTANEOUSLY and wholeheartedly when Lucio walks into his office.

"They just called from jail..."

Lucio doesn't think this is a laughing matter.

Fede continues to laugh. Like seldom before. Humor isn't his more marked characteristic. Lucio still doesn't understand what's triggered his laughter.

"The last package, the books for a prison..."

"Have they not arrived?"

For months they had stopped shredding and recycling surplus books, they sent them to prisons now. The stock in storage, but also books that piled up in their respective homes that they knew with absolute certainty they would never read again. From a certain age onward, an overabundance of books can be exasperating. After a mass email to authors in the publishing house and their respective friends, they too started to get rid of their *merchandise*. They managed to gather a considerable number of boxes at the end of every month.

"They have actually arrived, but they didn't like them. Can you believe it? They didn't like our books in Martutene

Prison! 'We appreciate the delivery, but please don't send us your detritus!'"

"I don't believe it…they've no shame."

"On the contrary! They are completely right: being in jail shouldn't deprive them from accessing the best literature in the world, we shouldn't torture them with that infantile pseudoliterature for adults our authors produce!"

"Are they going to return the package?"

"No, but henceforward they won't be accepting *just anything*. What do you think? They take reading very seriously in jail. Who would have thought? Maybe we were mistaken, maybe there's hope after all…"

"Should we notify our authors so that they don't send *just anything*?"

"No way. They'd be offended…Authors are like Chinese porcelain vases; worse, even, Lucio, if you add their tendency to feel affronted to their fragility…It's important to know how to look after them. Keep in mind, though, that the editor must also know how to provoke an author's jealousy when they are feeling too sure of themselves: by praising books by other authors every now and then, by suggesting that other writers with very different styles to theirs are more to your liking, even if it's a lie, so that they keep giving the best of themselves in the next book…"

"Don't you run the risk of losing them?"

"You have to know when to tighten and when to release the leash, Lucio: you have to do the opposite with authors who have low self-esteem, dismiss their colleagues so their morale stays up."

"I see, you're half editor... half psychologist."

The newspaper director Julio Virado called a meeting with Idoia, Victor, and Roger. They've seen him many times before, on TV and in photos too, in the multitudinous dinner parties the media group celebrates every year. This is the first time he's right in front of them, however. At least in the case of Idoia and Roger, who very quickly realize Victor must know him, since he patted his shoulder with familiarity. As is often the case on such occasions, Virado seems smaller than they'd imagined. The fact that he undertook the journey from Madrid to see them instead of asking them to travel to the capital doesn't bode well. Their suspicions are soon confirmed.

"Unfortunately, we have to restructure all our newsrooms. We need to adapt to the times and be very careful with expenses from now on... As you well know, we have a radio station, have purchased three digital terrestrial television licenses, and our hope is to keep expanding our empire. Which means that you'll have to become complete journalists; we'll be asking you for brief commentary on the news in our stations, at least for now..."

"Will we have to go to the studios?"

"This is not applicable to you, Roger, but to Victor and Idoia. And no, you won't have to go to the studios: you'll be able to make your contributions via phone. We have a good ISDN connection in the office, don't we?"

At this point, Julio Virado hesitates and with his eyes begs his secretary for a support she can't give him. As was to be expected, there is also an encyclical about *strategic business lines*. When they all get up from the table and Idoia thinks she's finally earned the right to breathe easily, Virado holds her by the elbow.

"I'd like to talk to you, Idoia."

As the conversation advances, the revulsion Idoia feels for Virado increases; for his clothes, which are expensive but tasteless, for his too-dry lips and too-wet gums, for his mane of dyed black hair, which he doesn't comb in excess – hoping but failing to appear youthful.

"I wanted to tell you this in private: you're the most indispensable element in this newsroom."

Even though she knew that it was all an act and nothing but an act, Idoia momentarily lowered her lines of defense, immediately berating herself for retreating her troops so joyfully. That's how weak we are: the most squalid bit of praise from someone we hate is enough to incomprehensibly undo our lack of appreciation for that person.

He'll ask me now, deduces Idoia, coming to the conclusion that she's got reason enough to begin to tremble.

"You have a great voice. Have you ever worked on the radio?"

"When I was an intern, but only for a few months, in Herri Irratia."

"Herri Irratia?"

"Radio Popular."

"Ah! The Cope channel! Our strategic allies…"

I should have stayed quiet, thinks Idoia, knowing that there was no point in her trying to explain the difference between Radio Popular and Herri Irratia, and it wasn't in her interest at all to do so.

"That's it then, it's clear: you're what we need. We'll release you from certain jobs in the newsroom and you can be in charge of the disconnections during news bulletins. You'll be working in the street… A bit of everything. For as long as you accept, of course. We'd raise your wages, of course."

She didn't dare ask how much her wages would increase. Why? She didn't want to disappoint the person who'd showered her with such fake praise. It was difficult to explain how much and in how many ways Idoia was annoyed by her evident low self-esteem. Whatever happened to her dialectic ability, her verbal ping-pong prowess? They shook hands; Idoia offered hers docilely, Julio Virado squeezed it with determination.

– 273 –

In the bar, Roger wanted to know what they had talked about.

"What did Virado say?"

"That I'll have to work more: newsroom, radio bulletins, 'working in the street…a bit of everything.' It's unbelievable. I didn't have the guts to say no."

"At least they'll increase your wages."

"A symbolic increase."

"How much?"

"He didn't say."

"And you didn't ask?"

"No…"

"Why not? Are you nuts?"

Roger moves his hands wildly, expressing his despair at his friend's hopelessness. For an American, it's impossible to envision not speaking frankly about financial terms; Idoia's inability to freely speak about money seems incomprehensible to him, an attitude that, he's noticed in these past few years, abounds among Basques, so much so he believes the tendency could be subject to a complete Freudian treatise: Be generous and don't worry about money, it's in bad taste. *From now on you'll have to become complete journalists,* Roger mumbles, imitating Virado's voice. He manages to get a smile out of Idoia.

"I have a New York Times journalist at home, would you like me to introduce you? He might offer you a job, *who knows…*

He's writing an article about the Basque Country. We could eat a burger together…"

"I'm sorry but Diego is waiting for me. I have to catch the bus."

"Your relationship with that guy is too absorbing, *you know*?"

Idoia has just left her husband, after many years together, to go and live with an ex from her youth. A writer. He knew that she'd had a really bad time while they were separating, but Roger estimated that the period of *quarantine* during which it was better not to joke about the subject was now over.

"Don't start, Roger. We live together."

"As I said, too absorbing."

Fede woke up at six o'clock in the morning every day. He always had breakfast in a café, the only place open at six thirty a.m. in the neighborhood: he liked to accompany the small Swiss roll with a black coffee, no sugar, and on the days when they didn't serve his coffee in a glass, he felt something bad would happen. By eight fifteen a.m., and after a half-hour swim in the swimming pool, he was sitting at his table at the publishing house.

That day, fortunately, no authors were due to visit. A quiet morning, for a change. Instead of that, he had an appointment with Lucio, the typesetter. For a while, he had been trying to persuade him to buy the new version of the Garamond font, he was going to show him the possibilities the typography had to offer, the different new options available for the typesetting of their collections: his hope was to narrow the box and slightly increase the space between lines and between letters. People in their sector spoke a lot about different typographies, but in the end they all used the same: the damn, overused Times Roman, or, at most, Garamond, illegally downloaded to make matters worse, they never paid for that license; those very same editors that complained about terrible financial losses and fervently defended copyright laws for writers were the first not to respect typographers' rights. What was to be expected from such a gang of daylight robbers? Lucinda, Bembo... Fede always felt stimulated by all those fonts with women's names. He'd go through the pages of volumes bought in France or Italy with jealousy; they were much better bound and typeset, they breathed the air of a better tradition and oozed a special kind of grace. Each country – each language – had its own characteristics and tastes when it came to font types and sizes, even when it came to the white spaces that should be left between them. Some liked the spaces between words to be more evident, and to narrow the distance between the letters that made up the words and keeping those tighter, to clearly delineate – too clearly, according to Fede – where each one of them started and finished. Such a disposition of the words and letters seemed to Fede to amount to an insult to the reader's intelligence; he much preferred the tendency that leaned toward keeping the white space between words without piling up the letters on top of one another, to afford them certain levity and harmony.

"The difference is almost imperceptible, but when lower case *f* and *l* follow one another there is more white space, a small void between the two letters. See? They make a beautiful shape: that curve at the top of the *f* stretches out and touches the tip of the *l*, but still leaves a lot of white space in between. Unaccustomed readers might feel there is a typo and the space is too wide. What do you think?"

Lucio observed the pages and the aforementioned spaces with true devotion, as if he were admiring a sculpture. For Fede, to receive his visit was like having a piano tuner at home. Someone who belonged to an old, charming profession that was at dire risk of extinction.

The lower case *l* and the capital *I* will be distinguishable at last, right?"

"This time there are no problems with that."

The common mortal wasn't aware of the vital importance of separating letters and words with the right amount of space. Added to that were the typographical battles, each font with its baggage, long history, and development: there was always an artisan behind it, whether it was Claude Garamond or Sir Aldus Manutius, guardians of good taste. The main battle was always about the roundness of the letters: on the one hand were the sans serif fonts, which tended to be more sticklike and rigid, and on the other, the ones that tended toward a curvier, more rounded style. In between both tendencies, infinite possibilities. There were even those who detected a battle of the sexes between those two groups. Both Fede and Lucio were firm supporters of the Bembo family of fonts, but they never dared use it in the books they published, fearing that stepping too far away from predominant currents could disconcert readers. Yes, even in that sense they were dependent on the mainstream.

With the same passion with which others argued about motorbikes' cylinder volume or car models, they spoke about font types and small typographic variants that were imperceptible to the untrained eye. Lucio thought it was strange that Fede had agreed with him on everything without hardly questioning him.

"Is everything all right, Fede?"

Fede nodded, although as soon as he did so he realized that Lucio had doubled up, that he had two Lucios in front of his eyes, and two doors, two telephones, and two right hands and two left ones. He was seeing everything in duplicate.

He realized that morning that something was wrong with his eyes, as he as usual fixed his eyes on the dark blue line at the bottom of the swimming pool to avoid slipping out of his lane: he had a sense that the glassy blue line was moving slightly and, while it took on the color of alabaster, just like it was happening now, it had doubled up in a curious aquiferous split that he hadn't paid special attention to and had even found slightly funny.

Lucio noticed that the secretary's table was empty.

"You lost your assistant again?"

"They say it's difficult to work with me. Can you believe it, Lucio? Difficult, me? What's hard is to fulfill people's work expectations: they want to fill up their pockets without breaking a sweat, that's what they all want. They don't understand that this is a *cultural enterprise*. That, usually, we lose money. That it's a miracle to survive.

"You should reconsider the option of digital publishing."

"No way. That's out of the question."

"It's getting more and more difficult to distinguish between offset and digital, Fede."

"The day they manage to make them indistinguishable, I might change my mind. Meanwhile..."

"I mentioned it because of the cost, it's quite a bit cheaper... Many publishing houses have switched already, and the readers haven't realized."

"They can go fuck themselves. I'm not in this business for the readers."

The first job she had to do on the radio was to read the submission guidelines for a competition the Spanish army organized on International Armed Forces Day. The Spanish army organized artistic competitions? Disconcerting, but true; and, of course, the subject wasn't completely free: "Particular value will be placed on pieces that highlight the values of the army." Idoia never identified herself in those chronicles, but the mere thought that one of her old colleagues from Egin might hear and recognize her voice gave her goose bumps. *This is worse than working on Radio Maria*, she'd tell herself.

That was only the beginning. She still hadn't had to confront the inexcusable coverage of the pro-virginity movement in the United States and the chronicle they asked her to prepare about the influence such a trend could hypothetically have in Spain.

Because of her sense of professional responsibility and, why not deny it, a certain degree of masochism, she began to develop an interest in the radio she worked in, something she'd never done before. She listened to it all the time. The degree of manipulation was so obvious and unsophisticated that she almost popped a vein every time there was a news bulletin. Soon she realized that given the state of the citizens' purses, the in-house editorial line of defense was focused on associating financial fraud with everything the shareholders ideologically disagreed with. They had thought of every last detail, nothing was left to fate: they were against abortion, and the first item of news they highlighted was the apparent multimillion swindle carried out by abortion clinics on the public purse. As if that weren't enough, it turned out not to be true that her segments could be carried out from the newspaper offices; the radio was on the outskirts of the city and she spent half her days traveling between the newspaper and the radio offices.

The day she reached rock bottom, however, arrived when they forced her to record commercials: one in praise of the Pope's visit, a short advertising break about the importance of ticking that box on the tax form that signals you agree to allocate a percentage of your taxes to the Catholic Church... After complaining that those sorts of jobs went beyond the scope of her job description, they accepted her request to assign the recordings to professional voice actors. It was Diego who reminded her of La Bella Ines, "she works in a tollbooth in Biriatou." When she called her, a man let her know that she was not at home. Finally, La Bella Ines agreed to record a commercial for a telephone company. After the recording session, they had a few beers and mentioned how things had changed since the days when they used to throw Molotov cocktails at the Telefónica headquarters. It's just the way of the world, they told each other to finish the conversation. It had rained a lot since then.

Idoia leaves the radio and returns to the newsroom without any break in continuity, from and to, through and for work and without the possibility that the dark rings under her eyes might lessen. She leaves her skin. She draws up a list of possible PSOE candidates for the general elections: in truth they've asked her for the profile of a single candidate, the Basque candidate, Fontecha, although she is certain that he doesn't stand the slightest chance. A Basque in the Moncloa presidential palace? The thought of it makes her laugh. Tanned and with thick hair, with a neat side parting, charisma and a poker face, Fontecha was photogenic in the eighties; he had the talent to avoid the anger and sudden irascibility that had proven to be the downfall of so many politicians, he had of the gift of gab, of a flexible waist and the sort of thick skin that allowed him to draw up gentlemen's pacts with his political adversaries that he had no intention of fulfilling. And no less important: he had an admirable ability to control his facial muscles. But, after a long banishment in the European Parliament, he had lost his ability to swim against the currents and surmount the pull of the eddy, qualities that were so prominent in him during the stormy days of the Ajuria Enea Pact. Fontecha, the candidate? Hard to believe. Even putting aside his often mentioned but never sufficiently proven association with the dirty war, Idoia sees weak spots in him.

Javier Fontecha Alberdi, born in Bilbao, divorced and remarried to a cardiologist from Getxo, fifty-eight years old, father to three children, all three from his first wife, born before he was thirty (*What wouldn't I give to interview his ex*). A law graduate. He worked at Fontecha and Company, his father's offices, for two years, before he was voted to Bilbao's municipal council. Later on he cut his teeth in Biscay's Provincial Council, and after that he was named delegate of the Spanish government in the convulsed eighties. Having fulfilled his years in exile, he took the mandatory rest, spa, and hydro-massage break in Strasbourg, and returned to the parliament of the Autonomous Community.

She's asked Pilar, the new intern, to look for a photograph: the most recent ones she finds archived are two weeks old, but not one of them is a close-up. The intern has to trawl through six months of news to hit on a portrait that doesn't lose much quality when magnified. Cut the head, copy the head. The photograph was taken during a press conference for the Human Rights Tribunal. Even though he still parts it the same way, his hair has turned almost completely white. Add to that a swollen countenance and the look of someone who's abused some legal or illegal substance – cortisone? Cocaine? Both? "That's not the face of a candidate, not by a stretch," agrees her intern.

Apparently it was going to be a matter of time. A sort of variant of retinitis pigmentosa. The sickness was related to pigments and the neuronal interpretation of images, reception problems, transmission, decoding, and who knows what else. He didn't pay as much attention to the details in the beginning as he did to those three adjectives: chronic, progressive, irreversible. Having heard those words, the rest was unnecessary for Fede. How quickly would he start to lose vision? They couldn't be specific. "Everyone is different." There was no cure or possible treatment, that much they said pretty clearly. Likewise with the bitter ending: almost complete blindness, able to perceive at most some isolated shadows here and there. But science keeps moving forward and someday there would be a way of stopping the progression of the illness, "look at what happened with AIDS," but for the moment all that they had to offer was some general advice regarding the health of his eye: plenty of vitamins, better to give up alcohol completely, a monthly checkup to control the illness's advance.

"What do you do for a living, Mr. Epelde?"

Fede remembered the years when he worked in that big publishing house: how energetically he opposed the launch of a collection of audiobooks. His reasoning: that they would end up becoming an unnecessary luxury for the blind, a whimsical purchase for the blind and the lazy that would never pay off; his opinion was that such inventions only worked in the United States because people often undertook long car or bus journeys. They didn't follow his advice, but time showed that he was right: the project failed and the collection was abruptly interrupted when the bosses decided that they'd wasted enough money on it. But it'd been a long time since he'd been under the umbrella of that big publishing house, and, what was worse, under their insurance coverage.

He took a slow, deliberate glance around the massive amounts of books piled up on the shelves over the decades. New, old, deteriorating. Inch by inch, those books revealed the true progression of his moods, the wide spectrum of his anxieties, year after year. It was the catalog of his worries and tendencies, the reason and the cure for his sleeplessness, his alibi for going out so little, the unrepentant reverse of his nonexistent social life, the symbol of his squandering, his deadly financial investment.

A whole life in books. So much deadweight moved from place to place to place, so many assaults on his wallet. So many missed meals he'd renounced when he was young and poor, back in the day when, forced to choose between a book or a meal, he chose the former. His soul cracked when he thought that soon that entire library would be absolutely no use to him. He switched the light off and put a Puccini opera on the record player. Would he manage to find a reason to go on living? Would he be able to renounce to his lifelong passion to become, for example, an expert in opera, which he always liked but never approached as anything other than a run-of-the-mill aficionado?

The ophthalmologist mentioned a word he didn't want to hear under any circumstances much sooner than he'd hoped: Braille. Of course he could learn that new language and keep reading and rereading multitudes of examples of universal literature with the tips of his fingers…but, what about the originals? Writers never sent manuscripts written in Braille to publishing houses! He would have to close down the publishing house. Or, alternatively, be victorious in the area where he'd been an abject failure so far: he would need to hire the best assistant ever, someone outstanding, whose virtues now would need to include the ability to read out loud every manuscript he ever received.

Idoia fought with Roger over the computer graphics. After a heated exchange, and just when they've come to an agreement at last – "not so colorful, it's easier to understand if it's more muted" – Victor arrives, the sports editor: he demands an additional page because a Basque cyclist has had a positive drug test during Le Tour. It's not like he's asking for an additional page, he's insisting on it. Apparently he's got priority. Idoia and Roger are dumbstruck, stumped for words in the face of the miraculous appearance of this superior dictator, someone capable of crushing the layout designer's small dictatorship: with or without the graphics, there is no room for Idoia's article.

So Victor stays behind, with the phone stuck to his ear; for once, he's going to close the newsroom. He seems to be enjoying it, however. The reason? They found a dose of Celesemine in the urine of a cyclist. We are all slaves to our emotions.

"C'mon, I'll buy you a beer." Roger's tone is conciliatory.

"Oh, now you want us to be friends? No, thanks."

"*Fuck*, please, I just want to bitch about Victor."

Idoia sighs: all right, she needs that too.

Roger is an American, that's why he can drink flavorless Budweiser beer, but he's been living in Bilbao for years. He came like many others, during the Sanfermines, met a girl in Pamplona and ended up living with her in Arrotxape. When Arrotxape and the Basque girl disappeared from his life, he found a job in Bilbao. He belonged to the first batch: he joined the newsroom at the same time as Idoia, when the newspaper pushed a more open and combative editorial line and the newsroom was still worthy of that name, but things had declined quite irritatingly. Image had gained importance in the past few years, while the written word had gradually lost it. Whether we like it or not, that's they way of the world now.

"*Fucking sports.*"

"You only say that because we don't have baseball here."

"*I hate baseball!* My father was obsessed. I was a good hitter, I just didn't like running."

"You were a sedentary child? You don't say...."

He must weigh around one hundred kilos, it's easy to imagine Roger as a child of a similar build. He still has a childish look about him, with his rounded face, his blue eyes that easily get red when he drinks too much Budweiser. Sandy hair from Wisconsin.

"Have you written the interview with the fat cat?"

"I'll finish tonight, at home. I want to read some articles first. I don't know how to approach it yet."

"You shouldn't take work home. It's a bad habit to keep working on the bus... You should learn to separate your life from your work. Another round? A Budweiser and a Voll-Damm, *please*."

"I don't know how you can drink that beer."

"A habit from my youth; it reawakens the memories of the States that are stuck to my palate, *bad habits die hard . . .* What was that thing . . . *about that bird?*"

"*Orhiko txoriak Orhira nahi.*"

"That's it. *The Orhi bird wants to return to Orhi.*"

"In any case, I don't know if you're right: we've always been a country of immigrants."

"Yeah, immigrants like the Chinese: thank God you're not a thousand million people . . . You build your own *Basquetown, wherever you go . . . the* txistu *goes with you.*"

"Not necessarily. We'd have to check who, where, and when."

"You say that because you're a Basque separatist . . ."

"And proud of it . . ."

"If only the bosses in Madrid knew . . . they'd give Pilar the intern your job."

"And how would they know? Will you tell them? I'm good at pretending, don't you think?"

After spending three days and three nights crying and listening to opera, Fede determined that the naked truth of what fate had in store for him was too horrible and led him straight to the abyss. *I've dedicated my life to books, I'm five years from retirement, this is how far I get, it's over for me.* Without a speck of drama and in a completely cerebral way, he decided to end his own life. He filled the bathtub with water and brought out one of those big flat razor blades, the kind he used to shave his beard when it was more than three days old, and to contour his sideburns, an old-school blade, double-edged, with an indentation in the middle, fit for double-edged razors. The hot water soon steamed up the bathroom mirror. Force of habit, he had poured bath gel into the water too and the bathtub was overflowing with bubbles. He closed the tap and carefully placed the razor on the side of the tub, mindful of not cutting himself up *too soon. Wait until the bubbles disappear, Fede*; as far as his memory allows, he can't recall anyone killing themselves in a bubble bath. At least not in the movies he's seen. Despair is not compatible with the rise of bubbles. Or maybe the truth is that they did do it, but the bubbles had disappeared completely by the time they found the corpses bled to death?

Be that as it may, in the end Fede fell asleep in the bathtub. Until he heard someone rapping her knuckles on the door: it was Yolanda, the Ecuadorian woman who came to clean his house once a week.

"Can I come in?"

"One second!"

You learn something new every day, Fede, but I had you for someone with a stronger will, he berated himself, and afterward he thought that *it was really the bubbles' fault*, while his mental press chose big capital letters for the headline: SAVED FROM SUICIDE BY HIS ECUADORIAN CLEANER.

It wasn't that easy to plan a suicide, and Fede thought for a moment that he should write some instructions for the purpose. In the list of contingencies to take into account, the first one would be: if you're going to kill yourself at home, make sure it's not on the day your cleaner comes to clean. If he hadn't considered that detail, how many other even more important ones may he have missed? Having made the decision to end his life with a well-executed suicide, he was embarrassed to see the razor on the edge of the tub. Before doing what he knew he had to do, it'd be advisable to leave everything well tied up; he didn't want to give too much work to his poor niece, and he didn't want to make orphans of his authors in the publishing house all of a sudden either, although many of them deserved to be left without an editor.

He was going to go blind, true. But he had a few months left before that happened. He had to make good use of those months. An absurd title for an absurd book in an absurd series that was already in existence came to his mind: *1000 Things You Should See Before You Go Blind*. Or, more dramatically: *1000 Things You Should See Before You Die*.

In his mind, being blind and being dead were the same thing.

He had to write that list. See those thousand things and then take his own life. Or maybe he'd develop such an enriched imaginarium after observing those thousand things that, thanks to those thousand icons branded into his memory, he would manage to renounce suicide and find reason to keep living. *Therein lies your challenge, Fede.*

Staring at Yolanda, he thought her shortness and chubbiness

seemed more vivid than ever: he excused her from all cleaning duties for the week, and, handing a book over, asked her to read it out loud instead. As was to be expected, Yolanda was puzzled by such a request, momentarily even a little frightened, and was close to saying no to her employer's potential perversion; her job had its limits, she thought, she wasn't willing to do *just anything*, and simultaneously pondered what other perfidious perversions people who ask to have books read out loud to them might request. Once she overcame her initial mistrust, however, Yolanda turned out to be a lively, gifted reader. *Pity she doesn't speak Basque*, thought Fede, because it was beautiful to hear her Ecuadorian intonation as she read Ernest Hemingway's short story "The Killers" in Spanish.

"One thousand things I must see before I go blind (I mustn't just see them, it'd be more accurate to say that I should see them and lock them into a corner of my brain, so I can resort to them and *see* them again once I'm blind, with absolute clarity, as if they were in front of my eyes)." He begins the list: "Dürer's etchings, Tiziano's *Pietà*, Vermeer's milkmaid, Goya's Black Paintings, the canvases from Rothko's darkest period.

"Rodin's *The Thinker* in the Rodin Museum. It's no good to look at reproductions, it's imperative that I travel to Paris. I want to see his chin and cheeks, I must memorize the nooks and shadows sculpted into the bronze, process the just pressure of the locked jaw, check the length of the fingers.

"The scene in *Body Heat* where Kathleen Turner and William Hurt have sex in a cabin by the river, a scene that excited me so much when I first watched it, I must try to see it again on the big screen, no matter what. I've never been too concerned with cinema, most of the films I love I could enjoy just as much by listening to the dialogues alone (any Marx Brothers, Wong Karwai's *In the Mood for Love*). There are exceptions, however: Fellini's films (especially *La Dolce Vita*), Dreyer's films (especially *Ordet*)." He must consider what to do with silent film movies: it might be enough to watch them again paying close attention to their soundtracks...

"One last hike up Mount Aralar, memorizing the texture of the blankets of leaves. The nervation of each fallen leaf. To observe the density of the smoke coming out of the sheds, to consider whether such density could be compared to something else.

"To focus special attention on the rusty stains that blossom on the skins of *reineta* apples.

"To focus special attention on women as they paint their nails, that hyperfocused gesture when they coat the surface of their nails with a little brush, with a steadfast stroke, never failing.

"Never forget to scrutinize the worry-free walk of adolescents who seem unaware of their beauty. How they take their high-heeled shoes off in the middle of the night as they board the elevator, returning home late from one of their first nights out in town.

"To glance at fashion magazines, at different kinds of haircuts. The texture of tweed.

"The sea in stormy days from Paseo Berria. Photographs I took in Buenos Aires and Hong Kong. Photos of my classmates and my ex-girlfriends. My ex-wife's photos. Photos that show my niece's every age. Photos of the child that I was.

"To memorize my home. To memorize my own face. To memorize every step from my house to work and from the swimming pool to my house, to try to walk those steps then wearing dark sunglasses, eyes shut. To learn to confront situations. To train for my life as a blind man."

To train for my life as a blind man.

He'd come up with a hazardous list, slightly nonsensical. It was frustrating. Was that really all he wanted to see and do? Wasn't there anything else? No, there wasn't. Maybe his blindness was just a means to stop being a tourist to himself. A means of leaving aside all the expendable bullshit and holding on to the essentials. Why not say it, this was an opportunity. That morning, on the way to the swimming pool, he took longer than usual standing in front of the fire station in Amara. Like a child, he visually gobbled up the trucks, their shiny red paint, their silver mudguards. *That's it, I got it all in my head*, or *I've memorized all of you*, he told himself after five minutes, as if he'd stamped an image into his retina with a burning iron. Afterward, when he arrived at work, he closed his eyes to make sure he hadn't forgotten any details. No, he hadn't forgotten anything. It was all there. The firemen's truck, with all its accessories. In his retina. In the black box in his head.

To memorize every single thing you will *never* see again. To learn by heart every piece, so that you can effect infinite combinations of them afterward. The way we learn the letters in the alphabet, a Letraset set in Garamond. But with eyes always shut.

Idoia found a message from a friend in her inbox congratulating her on her recent radio program about the European elections.

She couldn't believe it. Her friends never wrote to her about work, even less so to congratulate her about anything. Astounding. Finally, when someone did, she wrote to congratulate her on a job she didn't do: Idoia didn't cover election night, her intern Pilar did. She hated her friend and was convinced it was a deliberate mistake, as if she'd congratulated her on purpose, to harm her self-esteem.

She turned the radio on with curiosity, to check if her voice was really that similar to her intern's. She listened for a whole hour, while she ran around the house doing this and that, with the radio on at full volume. And she had to confess that yes, coming from the radio, the two voices were more similar than she'd like to admit. It wasn't as much a matter of timbre – Pilar's was softer – as a matter of tone. More than her way of speaking, it was her way of pausing between words, her way of staying silent to gather impetus, the cadence of her sentences, her way of laughing, her pet phrases – "we're telling it like we're hearing it," "so that our audience understands," "Okay, let's wrap it up" – even her welcome and goodbye formulas were exactly the same. None of those turns of phrase were terribly specific, but together they were identifiably Idoia's. What that girl was doing required cold blood: nothing was her own, not even the smallest trace of her own personality, she had borrowed everything from her. It didn't seem something that could have happened unintentionally, she could have only done it consciously, premeditatedly. This was someone who had listened to her attentively for weeks, someone who had rehearsed for many hours before becoming her shadow clone. Or was that not the case? Was she becoming too suspicious? In Idoia's opinion Pilar's attitude didn't demonstrate admiration or a desire to learn at all, what she saw in it was a clear intention to erase her from the scene. Her twin voice started to feel like a very disagreeable threat. It turned her stomach and suddenly she felt exhausted, as if a leech had been sucking her blood.

They've stolen my voice, she told herself.

What to do when someone who is as similar to you as your own self – even more so – tries to supplant you, when they copy your way of doing things to the letter and they do it well, even better than you? Who can you talk to about this kind of thing? It's embarrassing; you have to be careful, people might accuse you of having an obsessive ego bursting with vanity. "Do you think yourself that different, that unique or inimitable? You're not the center of the world, that girl who you see as your *imitator* drinks from the same sources you used to drink, you both copy and supplant equally, it's not just her," someone could tell her. How to prove it? Who could she tell this to? Who could she talk to about these things without sounding ridiculous?

On her way to work, just before she entered the newsroom, she saw Victor walking ahead of her. He was distracted, reading the sports section, and for once Idoia thought she saw something attractive in her annoying colleague. When she decided to walk faster to catch up with him, she noticed that Victor had done the same after taking his eyes off the newspaper. It looked like he was trying to catch up with someone ahead of him.

She heard him shout the name of the person he was chasing after:

"Idoia!"

His call-out paralyzed her. "I am Idoia and I am behind you, you cretin, not in front of you." The girl walking three or four steps ahead of Victor turned around, puzzled. It was Pilar, Victor had confused her with Idoia. "*I* am Idoia," she wanted to scream... She realized that the haircut and clothes the girl had been sporting lately weren't very different from hers. She perceived Victor's momentary embarrassment when Pilar turned around, but Idoia decided to save him from further discomfort, from the humiliation of showing him she'd witnessed his mistake. Instead of approaching Victor, Idoia hid behind the door to the cafeteria.

But, what was she afraid of, really, wasn't she the *original* one after all?

Picking or trashing the manuscripts as they were read to him was the easiest thing. To tell the truth, when manuscripts were read out loud Fede could clearly *see* – more clearly than ever – which ones were unpublishable. Mediocre texts were intolerable to read out loud. If only he'd known, he would have set that system in motion much earlier. Many pseudowriters deserved to receive a recording of someone reading a couple of pages from their novels with a note attached: "Listen to this, do you really think this shit can be published? It's embarrassing." His main problem was with the manuscripts that survived the cull, once he started to perfect them: although he was able to immediately detect convoluted or obscure sentences, Fede found it hard to propose syntactical and word order changes by ear. It wasn't enough to have a reader by his side for that; he needed someone who could not only read, but who could also write.

After losing four secretaries before their trial week was out – three left of their own volition, only one was fired – he decided to call Diego Lazkano, in hopes that he might find the woman of his dreams.

"Does it absolutely have to be a girl?"

"You know full well that the number of men with whom I can work side by side is limited to zero. It's bad enough that I have to deal with myself, that's hard enough..."

"Let me think about it, I'll call if anyone comes to mind."

"I would pay her well."

"That'd be a new development."

"It's either that or I close the business. By the way, forget the *offset* in your next book."

"Are you finally taking the step?"

"I didn't have a choice."

"Don't worry: you can't see a difference."

"I can't at least... I promised myself that if the day arrived when I couldn't spot the difference I would leave the *offset* behind and switch to digital. What I didn't expect was for that day to arrive so soon."

When he hung up, Lazkano thought of La Bella Ines. She

wasn't exactly a great writer, but the job as a reader fitted her like a glove. She had a great voice. When he called her, just as he feared, she mistakenly believed that his call wasn't strictly professional.

"I'm calling you about a work matter."

"You're coming for dinner, right?"

Lazkano felt cornered and had to say yes.

During dinner he tried to quickly shift the conversation toward Fede, apologizing about a prior commitment that would force him to leave very soon, but it was in vain. Before he realized it and not knowing very well how it'd happened, he found his cheeks between Ines's thighs and two hungry hands were feeling for his belt buckle. He couldn't deny that their reciprocal licking was more pleasant than making love, although Lazkano's septum required a few days to return to its usual position.

"Are you interested in the job, then?"

"I would have to meet the famous Fede, right? And you say he's almost blind?"

Lazkano didn't know what to say. Was he almost blind? Fede behaved as if that wasn't going to happen; he liked to tell everyone that he had *limited vision*, but Diego was convinced that he was on his way to becoming a full-blown blind man, if he wasn't already on the threshold of that bitter moment.

"He still sees a bit, but it's getting harder and harder."

"And you say he used to be an incorrigible womanizer?"

"I hope that's not a problem...it was a very long time ago, he's pretty old now."

Ines started putting her work uniform on.

"If you don't mind, I have to go to work..."

Lazkano felt offended. "No one is more ready to leave than I am." But the truth was that Ines got ahead of him when she said she was due at her evening shift in half an hour. And Diego, half naked still, felt more comfortable than he'd like to admit in that damp bed that smelled of lilacs.

Said and done. Ines and Fede's story was love at first sight – puns aside. The man who hated social engagements so much started turning up everywhere with Ines on his arm.

Lazkano visualized Ines's soft butt perched on top of Fede's nose, and he felt pity for his septum.

Not that any of it softened the editor's grumpy disposition; not a chance.

Whether it was Cupid's fault or not, Ines and Fede didn't click well at work. Fortunately they realized it soon, before it shattered what they had into a thousand pieces. Astonishingly, instead of thanking him, Fede rang Lazkano to accuse him of being incapable of finding anyone suitable for the job. He had hit on something much more difficult than a secretary, something almost miraculous – someone who'd put up with him at home – but, despite that, the editor could only grumble and complain.

"I need a reader…as soon as possible!"

It was absurd to expect stubborn Fede to change at this point in his life. And anyway, Lazkano was aware that the editor had him by the short and curlies. He had to suck it up and take the rain of insults and scorn.

"I'll try to find someone else, but I'm not promising anything."

"Have you seen any tennis players? They told me that Rafa Nadal turned up last year," asked Victor, scanning the room with his beaten-down ox eyes. Roger, on the other hand, was keeping one eye on the canapés and another on the slutty *Madrileñas*. Idoia, on the other hand, was trapped in a bubble she couldn't quite burst, feeling uncomfortable in front of the intern Pilar, who would go quiet when she came by her side.

"All I see here are Catholic fundamentalists from the Opus Dei. The sort who don't play tennis."

"No, they tend to prefer *paddle tennis*," Roger interjected.

Idoia felt ridiculous in her dress. She didn't want to dance. Pilar, however, was going from hand to hand, cheerfully dancing with some and chatting with others. It was obvious: they were the same person, but with different degrees of existential tiredness.

The newspaper laid out a New Year's Eve party for their workers every year. It was the first time that Pilar, Roger, Idoia, and Victor attended the event, at the insistence of the latter. Idoia immediately regretted accepting the invitation, but things weren't good with Diego and any excuse that kept her from spending the holidays with him seemed good. Swallowing your boss's grapes on New Year's Eve was maybe taking it too far though, she had to admit.

The newspaper's headquarters, which had been remodeled that very year to add a large glass balcony, was in the very center of Madrid, an expensive whim in times of crisis. They had organized everything carefully in that grand American style, down to the speech from the director.

"You must remember that last year we celebrated this party in the lobby... This year we are in the penthouse. You are free to draw your own conclusions, but know that the change is not due to our director suddenly becoming suicidal..."

There were bursts of laughter from the crowd, some clapped, the alcohol was beginning to have an effect. The cava cocktails and maraschino cherries in them were setting Idoia's teeth on edge.

The dance music came back on after Julio Virado's speech. Idoia saw Victor and Pilar talking animatedly with the director, and Roger in the company of two young pretty things that smiled nonstop. Her instinct told her that a conga was not far coming. Cool, they were all where they needed to be. All but her. It was time for a prudent retreat. She boarded the elevator, heading to the hotel. She was carrying the company's present, a fountain pen without ink cartridges. Another significant detail. Everywhere you looked, fountain pens that you couldn't write with, a sign of the times.

Impossible not to notice the geometry of her nipples. Ines has generous breasts, if slightly droopy. Her nipples, however, what miraculous nipples. Fede had never seen pointier ones, and he knows that, quite likely, they are the last ones he'll ever see: pointy and pointing right and left, each facing one direction, as if they were cross-eyed breasts creating two separate and distant vanishing points; impossible to focus on his bedroom duties while contemplating those two points. He raises his head slightly with the intention of checking how far those two vanishing points might reach; the left nipple points toward the window like an arrow's head, toward the window and beyond, toward the horizon, passing through precisely the third street lamp on the road; he calculates that, if Ines's nipple's imagined vanishing point had a laser pointer, it would easily reach the police station on the other side of the road. And what about the right one? The right nipple's vanishing point points exactly and irremissibly in the opposite direction, toward his own library. But, which book exactly does that vector point at? Fede guesses that it must be on the third shelf, although his eyes see only a blurry library these days; his illness started wreaking havoc quite a while ago: his field of vision and pigmentation are noticeably affected.

It's getting harder and harder to move because of the thrusts from Ines's waist; the girl's impetus has put a lock on his own, it looks like his Adam's apple is about to tear up his neck and break it; the same thing is happening with the curved axis of his backbone, it could crumble any minute, and the girl's right nipple, still pointing at the third shelf in his library, like an index finger, Christopher Columbus's finger pointing to the Americas...there you have it, considers Fede, *I was never able to separate pleasure and literature*; would it be too adventurous to assert that the diagonal line drawn by that right nipple reaches perhaps the very corner inhabited by his valuable collection of Gallimard editions?

Think of your Gallimard books to hold off ejaculating, hold it there, Fede...Vive la France! *A French nipple, no doubt, of course!* Gallimard, hourra! While he licks the breast with the tip of his tongue his mind fills with the rounded curve of the Claude Garamond font, unable to pinpoint what type of font exactly might that nipple resemble, what font and what typography, and immediately after he lets his head fall back while Ines rides him even harder, the black hole of the girl's enormous open mouth a reminder of the dark future ahead of him. Awarding a certain French *je ne sais quoi* to Ines's nipples only made him more excited. Two nipples and two contrasting vanishing points, comme il faut! One leads him diagonally to the police station, the other to his library, two opposing geometries leading to promiscuity; he feels that the woman riding him is being unfaithful to him with those unbridled breasts, such pleasure, a pleasure that allows Fede to be unfaithful in return. But it's all in vain, being as he is in the thrusting grip of her pubis, and he comes inside her.

Will she, later on, when he's recovered his strength, let him rub his member against her breasts? As it turns out, she does, and Fede feverishly desires for one of those nipples to enter his penis, for that little tail end of a Frenchie breast to penetrate the cleft of his shaft, to push in and out, in and out, that's what he really wants. But he doesn't dare ask so much.

Ines's cross-eyed breasts simultaneously point to the police station and the corner of his library where his Gallimard collection sits, and to ask more than that at this incipient stage of their relationship would've been to ask too much.

Lately the journalistic endeavor had evolved into the role of the anniversary collector. A hundred years since the birth of such and such a painter, fifty since this other one died, twenty-five since that scandal exploded... To observe the present with one eye while keeping the other on the past, that's how Idoia understood her work. It'd been a long time since the sort of journalism that wasn't about anniversaries and automatism existed beyond the realms of press conferences. Anniversaries were a good excuse for more or less meaty reportages, but when you'd been doing your work for more than twenty years and kept an infinity of folders filled to the rim with your own and others' articles on Alfred

Hitchcock, it became increasingly arduous to add something new, or even moderately sensible, to the existing narrative about the Master of Suspense. You could feel lazy, get a complex about being nothing but a rewriter. Like you were handling secondhand goods, recycling remnants, warming up previously frozen ready-meals in the microwave. Some anniversaries were celebrated yearly, with their attendant and tedious round of opinions voiced by the currently fashionable lowlifes; the remembrance of some events filled pages and pages. But, every year that passed, the names of characters shrank, the passing of time is implacable and those important events were remembered only in the important anniversaries. Only the gold and diamond anniversaries of events and the dead were remembered. After a century, what anniversaries would we remember? The French Revolution? The liberation of Auschwitz? The attack on the twin towers? Which of the three would have more media repercussion among us? Which of those three events would be the first not to be celebrated?

Press conferences were a whole other story, an invitation to the stables and to burying your snout in the trough, swallow whatever was thrown in there without asking what it was, digest all the bullshitty information however best you could to then spew it on the mock-up. That's what's come to be known as journalism.

Idoia was about to ask for a leave of absence, but when the newspaper requested a "flexible" special envoy, she decided to take a chance. It was after her mother died, right after she'd convinced herself that after her affair with Txema Santamaria, the photographer, it was going to be impossible to fix things with Diego. It would be a way of unmooring herself.

Special envoys were a special breed. They experienced journalism in a completely different way, they felt their profession viscerally, they suffered and enjoyed the fragility and discomfort of reality and the precariousness of their schedules, and in exchange they relished a freedom they could never dream of while working in the newsroom. The special envoy abroad was someone who, in the end, took the responsibility of interpreting a whole country upon her shoulders; she chose the focus – be it liberal or conservative, neutral or colorful, for or against. The special envoy *reconstructed* and *invented* whole cities, even whole states…That's where some war correspondents' tendency to fantasize, to retell nonexistent battles, their conscious or unconscious literary leanings, came from, it was a direct consequence of belonging to that special breed they belonged to. Hence too, the paradox of left-leaning special envoys working in conservative media: some had requested the transfer voluntarily, others had been exiled to foreign countries.

Idoia was sent to Paris. Soon she discovered that the political intrigues of the French country weren't of much interest to her newspaper. They expected other kinds of news from her: movies being filmed, literary novelties, public spats between intellectuals. Nothing could make her happier. The new job she was supposed to carry out was a return to her origins, to the culture section, her natural terrain; soon she was harboring hopes, imagining how wonderful it would be to interview Houellebecq and Beigbeder and to attend the latest concerts, exhibitions, and fashion shows.

She soon realizes, however, that the proposals she sends her boss in the culture section don't interest him either. He accepts only one or two every week. This means that her wages – she's paid per piece – do not meet the agreed minimum and she can hardly afford to pay her rent. Idoia is losing money in Paris. She tries to speak with the director, but Julio Virado never picks up the phone.

Fede Epelde was alone in the office, without his assistant. This happened quite a bit before his problems with retinitis pigmentosa started, when he was still able to manage on his own. The face of the red-haired man who crossed the threshold seemed familiar to him. Had he seen him in the papers? On TV? He couldn't be sure. He wasn't a writer, no doubt about that. He had the face of a Viking. The familiarity he sensed may have had something to do with the rarity of his type, the flame-red hair, clipped short and showing a few gray hairs; such bristly hair, cut short like a rookie soldier's, you couldn't help but want to touch it. And, even though it'd been some time since he'd been the age of a rookie soldier, the man still exuded a perturbing military air.

He wouldn't be the first aspiring writer of a certain age to come to personally submit a manuscript to him, but he lacked the profile of an *amateur* writer. A frustrated writer who undertakes to write his memoirs halfway through his life? No, the red-haired man didn't fit that profile.

As well as his ruddy appearance, it was impossible not to notice the folder he carried under his arm. It was a very old folder by all accounts, a shade of salmon pink that the merciless passing of time or prolonged exposure to natural light had muted visibly. Maybe it was someone else's manuscript, Fede wondered, one of those unexpectedly "found manuscripts" that fall into the hands of someone incapable of evaluating it who naïvely believes it may spark the interest of some publishing house or other. Rarely did a masterpiece appear in a forgotten drawer, but you never knew. Fede was a professional, above all.

"Sit down, please."

The red-haired man sits, but when he does so he turns the chair slightly to face the wall so that he can keep watch on the door from his seat. Fede soon realizes what the gesture implies: sitting in front of him is someone who once belonged to an armed group. Old habits die hard.

He leaves the salmon-pink folder on the table. He slides it across, pushing it toward Fede, as if intending to make him understand that the folder belongs to him and he doesn't want it back.

"Xabier Soto. Ring any bells?"

"Xabier Soto...the same Xabier Soto as the one in the Soto and Zeberio case?"

"The very same."

"This folder contains his writing?"

"Indeed."

"I've heard he used to write theater plays..."

"Mostly theater plays, among other things."

"We...we don't publish theater plays."

"Are you sure? It turns out that you have published this...Is it possible, Epelde *jauna*, to publish someone involuntarily?"

"I don't understand."

"Read these texts, you'll find them very, very familiar. What you do afterward is up to you."

"I'm sorry but...you...where did you find these papers, this folder?"

"These are carbon copies. Back then everything was made in duplicate. Diego Lazkano has the originals. You publish his books, right, if I'm not mistaken..."

Julio Virado is overconfident and the way he speaks reflects this, always.

"So you want to return home. Your adventure hasn't lasted

very long, has it? You haven't even allowed yourself a period of adaptation... why don't you stick with it for a bit longer?"

"I'm not comfortable, I haven't found my place here, the milieu... I don't know."

"You must realize that your post is covered by someone else. We gave a six-month contract to... what was your intern's name?"

"Pilar."

"You wouldn't want us to fire her, would you?"

"Of course not."

"We'll find a solution: and chin up, woman, I can hear through the phone how low you are. I've good news for you: Victor is relocating to Madrid."

"Victor Irigoien?"

"The best sports journalist of the Cantabrian coastline."

The words *cornisa Cantábrica* make her want to puke. Cantabrian coastline. Asshole.

"We'll need to fill his post."

"Sports?"

"It is what it is, time to cinch our belts... you know this better than I do."

"Don't I know it, you've cinched my belt for sure, you bastards, but around my neck!" She thinks it, but she doesn't say it.

"Female sports commentators are all the rage. Before, sports were a man's world, but things have changed and it's all much more fun now. Do you like sports?"

"I don't like soccer that much, to be honest."

"It's not all soccer, though, is it, Idoia: there's cycling, track and field, tennis... There must be something you like... Victor will be here in fifteen days, you've two weeks to bring yourself up to date."

"And the radio?"

"You'll keep collaborating: we need a commentator there too."

Idoia swallows some saliva. She tries to detect traces of cruelty among the slight crackling sounds that distort the phone line, a click of the tongue, some indication that Virado is sadistically twisting the receiver's cable. It feels like the director is acting, like he isn't alone in his office and the guest audience is laughing behind her back.

"Will I have to broadcast the matches?"

"No, we have that covered for now... Would you like to, though?"

"No, not especially."

"That's okay. Take the rest of the week off; we'll be waiting for you in Bilbao on Monday."

The rest of the week is not much. It's Friday evening. Even though it's more expensive, she takes the high-speed that goes to Hendaia on Saturday morning.

Diego Lazkano would like to be a salmon. To swim against the current, stop the arrow of time, take a step back and, why not, regret things. To take that folder and leave it where it was. To never have picked it up. To never have opened it up. How could he not have considered that Xabier Soto made duplicates of everything?

"To live his life ... You had no right to do that."

"Why not? I haven't lived his life, that's not true; as a matter of fact I've used his notations, his drafts, his dreams, nothing more than that, Fede ..."

"Nothing more? *No less!* Do you think that's not much?"

"I took those sketches as a starting point to create my own works, I've transformed his ..."

"*Transformed? Sketches?* You've taken a theater play and turned it into a novel, call that transforming a sketch?"

"That was an exception, most of his ideas were just notations, they were lacking development ..."

"You've padded out his short stories and turned them into novels ... You owe him your success! You owe it to Soto! All of it!"

"It's not exactly like that and you know it."

"I've read every sheet, every page, one by one, and there are whole paragraphs you've copied from beginning to end, verbatim ... but what am I saying ... whole paragraphs? Pages and pages! Only the weakest parts are attributable to you ... or did you copy them from someone else? No, those passages seem yours: they're useless! I can't say I haven't enjoyed comparing the manuscripts page by page...Given the care I've taken to go through it all, I could be an expert witness should a judge call upon me."

"I've written thousands of pages in these past twenty years... in Soto's folder there were hardly two hundred pages. You're being unfair with me. There isn't...I don't really have...anything to hide."

"That's why you won't mind if the newspapers find out your real *source of inspiration*..."

"I haven't said that, Fede...I took it...I took it as a starting point..."

"Of course, now you'll explain to me what cocreation is... Picasso said it: mediocre artists copy, real ones steal. Or what good old Foster Wallace said: that modern artists are kleptomaniacs with good taste, all of that bullshit; Google, hypertext..."

"Fede..."

"Perhaps it's because of my obsolete humanist education, Lazkano, but I have to confess that this is very difficult to understand for me. Soto is a martyr for your people, and what you've done, what you've done is the worst thing you can do to a martyr: you've desecrated his tomb, you've taken his relics, and as if that weren't enough, you've used them for your own personal interest, you've made money off of them, without ever acknowledging that you were using relics... you've made money at his expense! I can't get my head around what you've done, to be honest..."

"You've made money too, indirectly, thanks to me."

"They'll take us to court!"

"I was tortured too, I too know what it's like..."

"You all say that."

"But it's true. It's pointless to try to explain hell to someone who's never been there..."

"What is that thing they say...? Oh yeah: *an eye for an eye...*"

"They tortured me, that's the truth. And the people who tortured me continue to exist with impunity, God knows where."

"Are you trying to convince me that your actual sin was atoned for before you committed it? Is that what you're saying? That the fact that you were tortured excuses you from any and all subsequent desecrations? Please! Are you trying to make me feel sorry for you?"

"I've worked hard. I...I know very well what it means to suffer."

"And you think you deserve a compensation for that suffering: to appropriate someone else's life. We are exactly where we were; I understood your point of view from the word go."

"I never stole someone's..."

"You are a plagiarist, a usurper, a parasite: not only did you appropriate his writing, you tore the skin off his back when he didn't even have it."

"What was I supposed to do? What would you have done in my place, Fede?"

"Are you asking me as your editor? As your friend? As your confessor? Tell me... what am I supposed to do now? Go on as if nothing had happened? Do you realize the position you put me in?"

"How could you... ?"

"It's not like I ever had much faith in humankind; not in humankind and not in people... As a general rule I only ever believe in *exceptions*, but... I just can't believe this, that's all. After everything you've done, tell me at least that you don't have the gall to say that you've done it as an *homage* to your friend..."

"If you've thought it, it can't be so completely absurd..."

"To have the head to think something doesn't mean that such thoughts aren't absurd when we speak them. Diego, I know you well, I'm very capable of entering your moronic head. And, believe me, it's a terrifying place."

"I'm going to ask you again: what was I supposed to do?"

"Easy: you could have polished his works and published them in his name, for example, allocating five minutes of glory for yourself in the prologue... That's what Max Brod did!"

"Soto wasn't Kafka, and I'm not Max Brod."

"And neither am I Gaston Gallimard, needless to say..."

"The way I see it, I did something to rekindle his embers. I improved on his works..."

"Your modesty knows no limits, Lazkano."

"Publishing everything the way it was would have been a mere archaeological exercise. Don't you realize? I didn't want that."

"No, you wanted to live at his expense."

"Not at his expense, it's been a way of living *next to him*! We were thick as thieves, so close, we had a special bond... You can't imagine. He and I. We've walked this path together. All these years."

"You haven't published anything in five years. Let me guess: has your imagination dried up... or have you reached the end of the contents of the folder?"

"You're right in that there may not be any more novels coming from Diego Lazkano's pen. But I'm going to write a chronicle, the chronicle of the Soto-Zeberio court case... it's going to start soon... I'm going to declare, as a witness."

"You've plundered his tomb down to the last bone. Pity that there was only one folder..."

"Are you going to give me up? Are you going to hand the folder over to the press?"

"Tell me: what else can I do?"

"Don't do it. I beg you. They'll sink us both."

"Wake up once and for all! Whatever I do, my hands are tied...that guy...the red-haired guy...he may well have copies of everything."

She was going to earn her right to eternal life by working as a sports journalist, it seemed to Idoia: working hours were never ending, every day lasted a century. Basque handball pelota players' press conferences, item selection, soccer training sessions... Seen one, seen them all. Did Victor hate culture as much as she hated soccer? Probably. Sports and culture journalists had to exercise different parts of the brain, there was no other explanation. The cross she had to bear wasn't as much the fact of her syncopated pilgrimages between the radio station and the newsroom. The worst part started when she had to write the chronicles or transcribe the interviews. Each word was more tiresome than the previous one, she needed twice as much time as she'd need to write up a cultural chronicle to produce a sports commentary half its size, and she always ended feeling profoundly ridiculous, like what she had written was worthless hogwash.

Idoia had never followed Victor's work – she'd never followed the work of any sports journalist, as a matter of fact – and she secretly looked down on him, the vain editor who always did what he wanted and whose assistant she had the misfortune of being for the next two weeks.

"I never understood you guys: your adherence to certain colors, to a nation... Can one be a sports journalist without being ultranationalist?"

Victor stared at her in puzzlement.

"It's all pretense, Idoia... you need to create some tension to narrate a soccer match, I thought you knew that. They are just cheap tricks; to create morbid excitement, to feed the idea of the rise and fall of the hero... Shakespeare in its purest form."

Shakespeare! What? Victor was giving her lessons on drama, talking about playing a part? Was she really supposed to believe that Victor had the smallest idea about Shakespeare's plays?

"Come on, Idoia. Readers always want the same roughage; the names change but everything else is the same. Who will survive the lions today? Who will be crowned emperor? All you need to do is listen to what our competition says on the radio every morning."

"As I understand it, then, your advice to me is not to overcomplicate things."

"You guys in the culture section add a comma in the morning and remove it in the afternoon. This is a newspaper, for God's sake! Diagonal reading, a couple of spicy headlines for the reader to consume with his coffee and that's it, that's all!"

Roger hadn't been any luckier than Idoia, they'd burdened him with a segment for English-language lessons, a learn-over-the-airwaves language-learning method. The fact that he was North-American sufficed, pedagogy wasn't really the point. Idoia often asked herself what would her life be like if she'd continued working for *Egin*. Would she be happier? Probably not. These days, what put food on her table were people and ideas diametrically opposed to her ideology and her lifestyle. It was painful to admit it, but it was true. How long had she been deluding herself? What next? Would she start to sympathize with her newspaper and radio station's editorial line?

The exact opposite happened. And it happened on the first day she had to take over the news reports on the radio to cover for Pilar during her holiday – life lessons: she was her substitute's substitute now. She was reading, on air, a news item about of a group of Somali militias who, after stealing uniforms from the Blue Helmets, had pretended to be UN soldiers, taken over a village, shot every single member of its community, and then set everything on fire. She froze in front of the microphone, went mute. It was a long, suspenseful silence that lasted half a minute, one of those silences that are explosive during live retransmissions, and that lasted up until the technician made use of his quick reflexes and put on a song.

She requested a leave of absence for depression and when they refused to extend it any longer, asked for voluntary unpaid leave. She spent weeks without leaving the house, without reading the papers, desolate, broken, living in a small attic that a friend who was away from the city had lent to her. She cried all the time. She carried a bottomless well of sorrow inside. Roger called her often at the start, but when he realized she wouldn't pick up the phone, his calls gradually came less often, and eventually he gave up.

One morning, she found an old newspaper on a paper pile her friend hadn't bothered to take down to the recycling point.

It was a newspaper from the competition, that's what she told herself, "from the competition," and she was annoyed to have thought that, to realize that she still considered that newspaper she'd worked for her own. She was struck by one of the headlines, and felt a bit sad that hardly ever had she seen a headline like that one in her newspaper.

PORNOGRAPHY AS THERAPY.

She remembered Txema Santamaria then – "a true photographer in this world of fake artists" – and that project he had for a series of pornographic portraits. Did he carry it out in the end? She thought the article was a major piece of bullshit at the start, a cheap trick from some second-rate hack who thought that the only thing that sold papers was sex. Pure bait. But she'd taken it.

This article explained how some psychologists prescribed pornography to overcome affective problems and traumatic breakups. It was true that the world of porn had changed a lot. The impossible curves and perfect bodies of yore had been pushed aside in favor of realism and the verisimilitude of "real" bodies and faces, thanks to the *amateur* and the *gonzo* genres, which had made available to users online an infinity of gigabytes of domestic and naturalistic sex. Systemically classified, sophisticated menus grouping the most bizarre variants of sexual proclivities down to the smallest detail. If the thing that really excited you was to watch a couple of smokers masturbating on a roller coaster, you only needed to type in your request, *et voilà!*

"The problem with pornography is that if you develop a habit, it can become addictive, and it's necessary to know to reduce its consumption in time so that this way of experiencing sex in a univocal and a virtual way doesn't completely take over your human relationships. A habitual consumer of pornography is used to holding all the power and it can become difficult for them later on to get used to satisfying their partner's sexual needs; in other words, to remember the fact that we are not alone in bed." Apparently not all psychologists agreed on this type of therapy. "Although it can be effective in some cases, it is not treatment that can be generally applied. It might be useful perhaps for people who identify love with sex too much, so that they realize that once their desire has been satisfied with pornography they don't miss the person who rejected them so much, although that's not generally the case. Using pornography in some measure is healthy, the danger is in excessive use, in believing there's nothing beyond that."

She went online and tried her luck on different pages, with curiosity, amazed at people's lack of prudishness, at the fellatios recorded on cell phones in public transport, at the women of all ages and colors who blindly milked anonymous cocks that protruded from tantalizing holes in dark walls, at the wild adolescents who seemed to rock as if they were bouncing on elastic beds, swaying their breasts and making it look like they were riding the person on the other side of the screen, at so, so many videos that studiously aligned the camera with the eyes of the Internet user being ridden. As was the case in the pornographic magazines she had occasionally glanced at in her youth, at the beginning it seemed to her that the point of view of the domineering macho prevailed on the Internet too, that she would never find anything remotely exciting for her in there, that there was nothing there beyond an enormous quantity of stimuli for horndogs that did nothing but jerk off all day. But, as she navigated from one site to another, she hit on a couple of girls savagely licking each other's sex, gone from this world, at the mercy of pleasure. The attractiveness of their small naked bodies, beyond their flat, delicious breasts, resided on the glow of their cheeks and in their inability to control their expressions. There was no fakery there, just pure enjoyment. Before she realized it, Idoia's eyes were glued to the monitor and she'd pressed full screen. She wanted to lick every pink pixel on the cheeks of those girls. She felt like kissing those open mouths. But something was missing; she noticed the audio was off. After she put the volume up, it didn't take much for her to undo the buttons of her jeans and start caressing herself softly. When the image started to seem too repetitive, she closed her eyes and turned the chair around: the girls' burning sighs, their screams and accelerated breathing were enough to bring her to climax.

With time she learned to introduce more specific words into the search engine, and although she found it difficult to accept that she was on the brink of porn addiction ("I can stop whenever I want"), she stopped switching the TV on after dinner and started to spend evenings in front of the computer, alternating lovers, one after the other. She didn't need to meet these ones in hotels ("I'm at the Hotel Orly, call me"; "don't even dream of hurting me, okay?"). These ones didn't upset her.

According to what she had read, "mirror neurons" were to blame when it came to experiencing analogous emotions to someone whose enjoyment or suffering we're watching, even if the actions that provoke such enjoyment or suffering are not affecting us directly. Many researchers believe that the fact that some people enjoy pornography more than others is related to their more abundant proportion of "mirror neurons." Idoia thought she belonged to that group. For once, she felt rich. She should update her profile: ex-journalist, O negative blood type, forty-something, divorced, without children, allergic to house mites, overabundance of mirror neurons, enough to become a donor.

She wanted to talk to somebody. Finally, she decided to phone the newspaper. An automatic message let her know that the number no longer existed.

Later on she found out that they had closed the newsroom in Bilbao and that all her colleagues had been fired.

Lucio finds Fede bent over an Albrecht Dürer catalog. It looks like he's inhaling it, sniffing it, even, bringing the image of the painting closer to his eyes with a gigantic magnifying glass.

"Look at this, it's astonishing…"

Fede shows him an etching from the book *Melencolia I*, from 1514, which some experts say marks the start of the Renaissance. Melancholy is represented by a sitting angel who looks tormented. Behind them, an unfinished house; in front of them, a multitude of objects: an hourglass, a feather, an empty scale, an inkwell, a ladder… objects that speak of a half-finished job. He says:

"Back then melancholia was not what we understand it to be today: it was the least appreciated of the four temperaments…"

"Indeed. It was related to madness, to the color of the earth, to the fall, to the north wind, to cold weather and drought, to

Saturn, which seems to influence creative types so much… it was also related with the time in life when men turn sixty years old…"

"With our time in life, therefore."

"Melancholia was always associated with laziness…but that's not the case in Dürer's etching. Look: it's true that melancholy has abandoned its work, but it's not doing it because of laziness, but because it's realized that it makes no sense to continue."

"The strangest thing is that we don't have a Melencolia II or Melencolia III…"

"Lost works of art…"

"I am not so sure…I have always believed that the I is not a number, but an invocation."

"An invocation?"

"Yes: *Go away, Melancholia!* in Latin…Out of here! It's the desire to say goodbye to the dark Middle Ages and embrace the light of the Renaissance…"

"It was around that time that our beloved Aldus Manutius showed the world his first book using the Bembo font…."

"Garamond also emerged around the same time. Do you know what, Lucio, I've just realized why I prefer the Bembo font to Garamond: the Garamond font has smaller eyes, as if the eyes of the letters *a* and *e* were half closed…"

"As if they'd just woken up from a long sleep…"

"The Bembo font, however, has wide-open eyes…the Bembo

font is the first font that remains alert, attentive and vigilant. The Garamond font suits the sleepy, those who haven't quite woken up yet, who are still dormant...It's a bleary-eyed font...After looking at this painting by Dürer, I believe my conscience is clear and I am ready to go blind."

It only takes a small step to go from consumer to creator. It was a much smaller step than it seemed. She activated the webcam and placed it so that her body could only be seen from the neck down – she wanted to make sure her body was in full view, but she didn't want her face to be seen. In contrast to most of the female masturbatory exercises she'd seen online – they all wore jeans, swimsuits, or simple miniskirts, when they weren't just naked from the word go – she decided to wear a dress, white and light, and diaphanous enough to allow her dark nipples to show through. She started to touch herself, imagining she had an audience, as if she were in a private theater, in a *peep show*. She squeezed her breasts hard, crushing the thin fabric, she showed and hid her navel, flouncing her shoulders and hips while keeping her feet in place. She inserted her middle finger between her breasts, caressed her areolas, pressed her breasts together, inviting her imaginary audience to bite them, almost touching the webcam with her lower lip. She started to sigh, issuing exaggerated moans that weren't a response to pleasure but that, bit by bit, and by virtue of listening to her own sighs, started to excite her: soon other sighs followed, not fake ones this time, but resulting from true pleasure. Was it possible, therefore, to become one's own conductor? Mirror neurons worked too when the observed actor was oneself. Self-suggestion? Maybe, but there was more than that. She lowered the top part of her dress and brought her breasts closer to the camera again.

"Come," she whispered. It was the first word she'd pronounced in weeks.

A word that emerged from a sigh.

Shame stopped her from watching the video she'd recorded for three or four days. When she did, however, instead of being ashamed, she felt excited again. She was persuaded by the authenticity of her fake sighs, those fake sighs that were followed by others that were brought on by true pleasure. She couldn't stop pleasuring herself. What was the sexual drive if not the search for a continuous repetition of familiar pleasures containing surprising variations? Was it maybe the lack of such surprising variations that spoiled the passion of many couples and drove them to idiotically fall into the arms of others? As she started to imitate what she saw on the screen, her real moans began to overlap her recorded ones. She started to depart from the recording then, to mumble words in search of her own variations: "Take your clothes off for me, take it out, pump it for me, faster, faster, here, on my belly."

She watched the video over and over before taking the step, to make sure that when she kissed the camera and the lens steamed up her face was still out of view. No one would recognize her. After checking that, she uploaded her onanistic exercise to one of the web pages with free menus. Each video had a clicker: a scoreboard that showed the number of visitors. She was amazed to see that by midnight, her video had already had fifteen hundred cybervisitors from all over the world, giving it an overall score of four stars.

As if her porn addiction wasn't enough, she was overwhelmed by a pathological and egotistical curiosity and kept eagerly and frequently checking how many people were watching her masturbatory performance, incapable of holding back her need for popularity. Since she'd uploaded the images online, only in the first twenty-four hours, twenty thousand people had downloaded or streamed the video. After a week, the numbers went up to one hundred thousand. The score was still four out of five.

How many young and adult women with their eyes on her all over the world. How many adolescent boys pumping it nonstop. She imagined Roger, Julio Virado, Diego, or even her ex, Mikel, doing it. Men and women, desperate and not-so-desperate beings, sighing over a moment of peace and oblivion – the *petit mort* – from their work.

She had achieved what she never had in her almost thirty

years working in newspapers: to capture people's attention. *Audience*, some called it, and hers was enormous. Before, no one read what she wrote; now, so many were trying to read her skin.

But Idoia was aware that she needed to get out of the hole, leave behind her winter refuge, get out into the world and find a job.

She remembered the conversation she had with Diego before breaking up the relationship:

"Fede always needs readers at the publisher's house..."

It had been months since then, but you never know. She decided to call him. She knew it was demented, but there was nothing to lose, she could talk to the grumpy old man. She needed money.

To say that Fede had vision problems was to be overly optimistic. He took a taxi from his home to the publishing house and, once there, he felt his way around with difficulty, barely able to find the way to his office, following an automated sense he'd developed through force of habit. The first time Idoia visited the publishing house she was astounded: the corridor was filled to the brim with shopping carts stuffed with envelopes piled up without rhyme or reason, no one bothered to classify them as they came through the post. At the bottom of some of those carts were some increasingly colorless, postmarked A4 envelopes that no one would ever open.

"That would be your job," Fede explained. "Let instinct be your guide, choose one, open it, and read the first page. Most times one page is enough. I would ask you to do that for half the day, after midday it becomes irritating…I would discard *Ulysses* itself. I know it's not a very thankful task, but if you could stay to put things in order in the afternoons, I would be able to offer you a fulltime contract for six months. Fifteen hundred euro per month.

It was only a little bit less than what she'd earned at the newspaper.

"Since I'm half blind, I'd pay you cash in hand."

Idoia didn't understand his comment.

"It's a blind man's joke, don't listen to me."

"Don't you want to hear me read?"

"You'll do. I heard you on the radio."

On Radio Maria? Idoia blushed so deeply even Fede noticed it, despite his growing blindness. At least it seemed so to her. She had always held on to the hope that no one was listening to her radio utterances.

Idoia walked through the corridor filled with shopping carts.

Fede had rolled up his sleeves, as if he were about to introduce his arm into a lobster tank. He remained sitting on his chair, however. It was Idoia who was about to go fishing.

Idoia didn't know where to start: after two weeks of intense work, she had managed to classify the manuscripts by order of arrival, but new envelopes arrived every day, which inevitably created new tectonic layers of potential literature in the shopping carts. It was amazing how much people wrote, as amazing as their eagerness to see what they had written published. Should she start from the oldest envelopes, following a strict chronological order? That didn't make much sense: some manuscripts had been submitted three or four years ago, their authors must have given up, they could hardly still be waiting, cross-armed, for an answer from the editor. Either those aspiring writers had found another publishing house to call home, or they had changed their calling. At any rate, what was a logical and reasonable waiting period for an editor's response? Was it fair to make an author wait a whole year? Idoia estimated that six months was more than enough and, with the wisdom of Solomon, decided to start there. She was very sorry for those who had sent their manuscripts before that.

She chose half a dozen manuscripts at random and started reading them out loud, one by one.

Fede discarded the first three after hearing the titles.

"What? No way! What did you say? Forget about it!"

The fourth was cast aside because of the author's quote the book started with.

"There's no way he can write well when he's not even capable of stealing a quote properly."

The remaining two were sent to the pyre before Idoia finished the first page. He shouted like a quack dispensing snake oil:

"Next!"

Or otherwise:

"Where are all the true writers hiding, good God!"

Or otherwise:

"Plagiarize Cheever, that's right!"

Or otherwise:

"Oedipus? Again?!"

Or otherwise:

"Please send her a copy of Virginia Woolf's *A Room of One's Own.*"

Or otherwise:

"Why don't they read something before they start writing?"

Or otherwise:

"Why don't they spend some time living before they start writing?"

Or otherwise:

"That's not literature, it's karaoke! A pure copy! He's just whistling over a melody someone else composed; if at least he did it well..."

Or otherwise:

"Garbage!"

Or otherwise:

"Bring me a bucket, please, I beg you! I'm going to puke!"

After two weeks of hard work, Idoia read Fede a short novel by a young, unknown author from beginning to end. She had heard that there was such a thing as professional readers in Cuba; in cigar factories, a woman would read whole novels to the other women as they rolled cigars. She identified with that professional Cuban reader as she read herself. The novel's title was *The Bodyguard Who Read Moby-Dick*.

"Did you like it?" Fede asked her.

Idoia felt it was a trap. She'd loved the novel, but she was afraid to say that yes, she'd liked it. She decided to answer indirectly, leaving room to backpedal from her statement if necessary.

"I was hooked from the start..."

"Ring the author, then. What did you say his name was?"

They were in luck: the author hadn't contracted his manuscript to any publishing house. He was ecstatic about their call.

In the following six weeks they weren't as lucky. In a heartbreaking way, with insults and wild gesticulations, Fede rejected dozens of works after hardly ever getting beyond the first chapter. The initial reservations Idoia had turned into sympathy: that editor, Fede, was like a character out of a book.

The joke was too easy: editorial faith. Blind faith. A faith he didn't place on anything apart from literature.

"Would you walk me to the entrance? Call a taxi, Ines can't pick me up today...they changed her shift in the tollbooth."

"Of course."

She took his arm to guide him outside.

Fede was silent for a while. He adjusted the lapels of his raincoat and straightened up before the Dürer etching tacked to the wall as if it were a mirror. *Melencolia*. It happens sometimes: a sudden sadness overwhelms us at completely unexpected moments.

"Tell me the truth, Idoia, do you feel pity for me? I don't want to be working with anyone who feels pity for me."

"Pity? None at all. I'm very happy here."

"I'm glad to hear that, because I don't feel pity for myself at all. Do you know what? Vision is overrated, it's much worse to go deaf."

Idoia found the comment strange, coming as it did from a man of letters who had practically scorched his eyebrows between books and documents.

It was cold outside, they both buttoned up their coats and raised the lapels to their noses. Idoia felt comfortable in the company of her boss. They waited.

"Your taxi is here, Fede."

Idoia felt Fede's hand rest tenderly on her shoulder.

"You have eased things for me so much, the year has ended very well."

He handed over an envelope. *The Bodyguard Who Read Moby-Dick* had saved their year. Not only this one. Part of the next one too.

"We're going to have to look after this young lad. Let's hope he doesn't send his next book to a big publishing house, like they all do."

Idoia opened the envelope. There were only a few bills, but she wasn't used to seeing any of that color.

"There's a lot of money here..."

"You have managed what no one else does: to stay in the company after six months."

Company seemed too pretentious a word for that dump of an office, but she wasn't about to correct him.

"I can see you smiling from here, you know?" he said jokingly, with his back to her, from inside the taxi, as if he truly was capable of such witchcraft.

Maybe he was.

The envelopes she'd taken so long classifying all over the floor, books taken from bookshelves and stomped on everywhere, unplugged lamps strewn over tables, Klimt and Dürer's reproductions torn off the walls... Idoia found their office in a mess. At first sight it didn't look like anything was missing, if it was money they were after, they had come to the wrong place. Did they hope to find any in a publishing house? Professional thieves would have known that such a thing was impossible. And they hadn't even touched the computers. She was in doubt as to whether she should call Fede before attempting to bring some order to the mess. She didn't want to upset him more than was necessary. It occurred to her that maybe it made more sense to leave things as they were and file a report with the police. Fede should make the decision, what the hell. After all, the publishing house was his.

"Don't get upset, Fede, but we've had visitors in the office. Some vandals I think. It doesn't look like they've taken anything."

She decided to play it humorously, so that Fede wouldn't get angry.

"I wonder if they were looking for a manuscript. Do you think it might have been our competitors?"

Fede was still silent. Idoia could hear him breathe rapidly.

"Are you okay, Fede?"

"Listen: I want you to open the first drawer in my desk."

That was the only drawer he locked with a key. He never opened it in front of her. Idoia was familiar with this type of paranoid behavior: Diego did the same.

"You know that I don't have a key."

"Go and check all the same, try to open it."

Although it resisted initially and it looked like the drawer was closed, when she pulled the handle it opened softly: it was empty. Someone had forced the lock and emptied the drawer.

"There's nothing here. It's empty."

"Isn't there a salmon-pink folder in there? An old folder?"

"There's nothing here, Fede. What was in that folder? Was it important?"

READY-MADE

"EIGHTY GRANDMOTHERS SEPARATE US from the Neolithic. We are eighty grandmothers removed from the cave. To say it differently: there are only eighty grandmothers between us and the cave. Eighty grandmothers, eighty pairs of legs, eighty laps, eighty births. Eighty, that's what the artist-philosopher Jorge Oteiza used to say. Does that seem like a lot? How many live relatives do you have? Not many more than that, isn't that true? Fewer, perhaps? Could you count them with the fingers of one hand? Six, eight, only three? So, think of your family differently, think of your dead ancestors, of the close and the not so close ones, think of a lineage made only of grandmothers. They could easily fit under one roof, they would fill the first four rows of a small theater, can you imagine? Only four rows of seats, odd and even numbers, a ball for retirees in the sports center; see, they're no more than that. Think of those eighty grandmothers of yours, imagine their features, so similar to yours and yet, progressively further from you – truly, we've mistakenly adjudicated an origin here, it is you who is departing from them and not the other way around: you are a worn-out photocopy, more of a caricature, you're simpler, increasingly at the mercy of unknown bacteria; forget Darwin, evolution, and continuous improvement, you are but the blueprint of a faraway hunter, a black mold, something that could be painted with an aerosol can on the wall of any village's fronton court. Eighty grandmothers, and then this; eighty grandmothers and then you, can you remember eighty names? Really? Seriously? How many women's names are there in your address book? How many women have you come across along the way? How many have you fantasized of starting a new life with? Many fewer than eighty, although if you were Don Juan, maybe there'd be more. Eighty women's names? Could we remember them one by one? Let's make the effort to put a face on each of those grandmothers: Katherine, Ohiana, Elisabeth, Lurdes, Viviana, Tatiana, Begoña, Lide, Laura, Tannia, Larraitz, Karmele, Margarita, Miren, Olaia, Irene, Dolores, Leire, Kattalin, Ursula, Martine, Teresa, Neus, Vanessa, Eneida, Tarsila, Paula, Elena, Lucia, Suzanne, Jennifer, Juana, Aizpea, Julene, Alejandra, Nora, Marilar, Cristina, Maria del Mar, Agurtzane, Lierni, Goizargi, Myriam, Ainara, Koro, Gabriela, Maria, Esther and Maria Esther, Isabel and Maria Isabel, Yolanda, Joana, Visitación, who was Visi to her friends, Ruth, Monica or Monique, Maialen, Reyes, Arantxa, Maite, Ingrid, Rosa, Esperanza, who as a child was Esperancita, Ainhoa, Olga, Monse, Izaskun, Blanca, Zuriñe, Ihintza, Nerea, Amaia, Nagore, Eulali, Lola, Frida, Brigida, Alfonsina, Paz and Mari Paz, Marijo and Marijose, Idoia, Maribel, Luisa, Eva, Asun, Iratxe, Mercedes, Irati, Alaitz, Itziar, Eider, Naroa, Angelines, Olatz, Marta, Marie Ann, Clementina, Anna and Ana and Ane and Anne...and enough. There are more than eighty there, without repeating a single name, and we haven't even mentioned Marina yet...

While Gloria told the story of her eighty grandmothers, she and Lazkano reached a photo of one of Marina Abramović's performances. It was a portrait of the piece *Rest Energy*. Truth be told, that photograph was the only thing Lazkano remembered about the exhibition: Marina Abramović and her companion Ulay, the taut arch between them, both of them holding the arch and the arrow, a frozen moment of their most renowned piece; Abramović and Ulay dressed in white and black, both of them slightly inclined backward, as if about to fall, Ulay holds the arrow on the taut string and Abramović holds the arch's frame. They are in front of one another. It is not a game, the arrow's tip is very sharp and points directly at Marina Abramović's heart. All it would take would be for Ulay to release the string and the arrow would pierce the artist's heart and she would die immediately. They stare at one another, both dressed in white shirts; she wears a long black skirt, he, dark pants. The photograph is astonishing. Ulay held the arrow for two hours – they held each other for two hours – and all that tension, the whole avalanche of chained reflections and the insufferable, sustained suspense the exercise demanded. The artists placed microphones under their clothes too, to capture the beating of their hearts and hear how their heartbeats increased as the performance advanced. Unlike with other live artistic events, in this case the photograph perfectly reflected the power and the intention of the performance. It was an image capable of reconciling anyone with contemporary and conceptual art: what's art for, why write, the answer is there. The question is to keep the arch taut and the arrow ready, to have an objective in sight, to risk death and, despite that, show passion and a desire to live; intelligence and generosity, humility and pride. The arrow, ready, and the target, oneself, with the motto of a Zen archer in memory: May hunter and hunted be one. It'd been years since Lazkano had seen that photo for the first time, and on that occasion Gloria was there too: it was on her fridge, a flimsy newspaper cutout glued to the fridge door with adhesive tape in the apartment Gloria shared with other students. It was during the years of cords and bushy sideburns, the years when bad poems and letters to the editor were duplicated through black tracing paper, and after sending one to the newspaper, the other one was kept in a cardboard folder, to store at home. The years when the first few punks arrived from London with their mohawks and their tight jeans, veritable atomic bombs against uniforms.

Gloria had some gray hair now and she wore it short. She never married, she didn't have children; during the first few years he visited her in Barcelona she used to tell him about her occasional adventures. It'd been years, however, since Gloria had updated him on her amorous escapades, as if she didn't have the age for it anymore, or as if she believed that Diego didn't care about that aspect of her life anymore. He didn't know whether Gloria had completely lost all interest in men, or if, simply, and given that she enjoyed touching upon other subjects with him, she did it to make better use of the little time they had together; Diego wasn't very keen on talking about his sentimental life around that time either.

It's funny what some relationships are based on: on which subjects and premises, on which tones and unwritten rules. With Gloria, especially, he talked about art, about the last films they'd seen and the latest books they'd read. "What are you translating?" she would ask him in those early visits, and Diego told her what he was immersed in, what he'd translated the previous year and what plans he had for the following: the books he translated made up Diego's biography, that was the truth. Nineteen eighty-seven was the year of Tolstoy; 1988, the year of Gogol; 1989 was the year in which he fell in love with Anna Akhmatova's writings... Later on, when Diego Lazkano started to publish his own novels, they started to talk about the books he would never write.

Although in the past they'd had heated political arguments, these days they hardly touched the subject, except to mention people's general meekness in the face of the incommensurable ability of neoliberal politics to poke fingers in our eyes, or to invent package bombs virtually placed in electricity and phone companies. They were childishly passionate in those areas – incendiary, even, some would say – but it never occurred to them that their passion might travel if they got emotionally involved. Or maybe it was so long ago since it had crossed their minds that they didn't remember it anymore. Diego's distant approaches toward her had been so timorous, Gloria could scarcely have interpreted them as approaches. Gloria didn't know that Diego had joined the theater group because he found her attractive when he saw her putting posters up in search of new members. He feels vertigo now when he thinks how young they had been, as if more than eighty of Oteiza's grandmothers stood between them. It was Diego's juvenile hesitation that made him behave with excessive caution. Hesitation? Maybe it was only the simple, plain naïveté of his candid youthfulness that drove him to understand that a friendship like that was worth preserving, or maybe it was just the classic fear of outright rejection. Passionate conversations and carnal attraction can be compatible, but back then he thought that their relationship couldn't reach such heights of compatibility; and now their ability to share bodies and intimacy had become lazy, or maybe they found it somewhat passé; Diego didn't feel that taut arch he used to feel when he visited Gloria in Barcelona. He didn't feel like Ulay anymore, holding the arrow pointing straight into Marina Abramović's heart. From a certain perspective, it was actually kind of relaxing.

Although she came from a well-off family, Gloria never kept much of a relationship with her parents after she left home immediately after her eighteenth birthday. Not at least to ask them for money. The word Gloria used most often to refer to her family was *facha* – fascists. She led quite the Spartan life since she cast aside her theater experience to escape to Barcelona and become an artist. Although she had shown a great talent for leading groups back in the days when they worked together, she always worked alone now. She grew tired of hanging out with people; apparently, she wasn't willing to put up with any *egomaniacs* (a word she used often). "I've enough with my own inner orchestra, thanks," she used to say. She was now a visual artist – Lazkano had attended a couple of her very popular openings – though Diego suspected she hadn't advanced very far in the jungle that was the art world: although her work was exhibited in several galleries, it hardly sold, and – at least as far as Diego knew – no museums or big corporations had ever purchased any of her works for their collections. Diego couldn't help but notice that, lately, Gloria was losing friends: unlike in previous years, during this visit her phone had hardly made a noise. His friend was isolating herself in Barcelona.

"Another bottle?"

"Not for me, I've been drinking less lately."

She had a loft in the foothills of Montjuic: a place to live and work; life and art all in one, in the Marina Abramović sense.

Even after cooking, the smells of acrylic paints, emanating from abstract paintings finished long ago, imposed themselves over the grilled eggplant. Despite that, Lazkano liked dining there, especially in the summer, as they contemplated the enormous orange-scented marijuana plants that they'd sample with coffee, the distant cars and the city lights down there, both nothing but murmurs; auditory murmurs and luminary murmurs dulled by the distance.

That day they spoke about forgiveness. About shame and guilt. About the copilot of the *Enola Gay*, who decided to become a clumsy sculptor.

But dropping the Hiroshima bomb required something more than a feeling of guilt.

"So, according to you, what should he have done? Kill himself?"

"Some people have done just that."

"One thing is to feel guilty, but, was he really guilty? Guilty of what? Of having chosen a profession? Of having become a soldier? It was his luck to be on a plane with a specific mission: he didn't know they were dropping an atomic bomb. He was the copilot of *Enola Gay*, that's all...what was he guilty of? Of having chosen to become a soldier instead of a whisky brewer in Kentucky?"

"Now you're adding flowers from your own harvest, Gloria:

I don't think he was from Kentucky, precisely. It says here that Robert Lewis was from New Jersey... and a soldier."

"I don't fucking care if he was a soldier or if he worked at a gas station..."

"I do: that's the difference between you and me."

"It's a choice to be a soldier, an option that can be the consequence of a certain kind of education or very limited life expectations, an option that can be hard, unavoidable, or innocent, or can well be free, intentional, and vocational... Who knows what his case was... On ninety percent of occasions, it's a lack of consciousness that drives us to do things. They must have had their reasons, but you're mistaken if you put all soldiers in the same bag."

"In the same duffel bag, you mean..."

"Yes, he took part in dropping the bomb on Hiroshima, so what? He didn't know what it was, exactly, he couldn't have guessed the effect an atomic bomb would have. In a sense, he just did his job..."

"Following your logic, the Nazis did the same..."

"The Nazis did the same, true: the idea of the chain of command is very well thought. We all carry inside an obedient being, willing to work for the Devil."

"I believe in individual freedom, I fought so that things would change..."

"And did they change?"

"Maybe they didn't... or at least not in the sense and in the direction we hoped. Things... things seemed possible back then. But if we hadn't fought the present situation would not be what it is, and I doubt that if we'd been more docile..."

Lazkano could see ants in his mind. *"Dale una* pasara *con esto.* Wipe with this. "We're going to let him go, right?" "Let's submerge ourselves in subjectivity." Differently, perhaps, but he also felt guilty. Had he ever crossed paths, unknowingly, with some relative, some friend of the engineer?

"You've Soto and Zeberio in mind, don't you?"

"They never even had the chance to fight... They held up a bank... with toy guns..."

"I think about them too... I warned you, I told you you'd end up badly..."

Diego Lazkano was uncomfortable. He didn't want to go down that path.

"We're detouring. We were talking about the atomic bomb."

"About Robert Lewis: twenty-five years after dropping the bomb, he started sculpting a piece of marble, a statue, in his garage..."

"Do you call that art? It's a crude image."

"What matters is that he found a means of escape from his anguish... and the title he gave the piece, *God's Wind at Hiroshima?* With that question mark and all, because he hesitated between calling it *God's Wind* or *Devil's Wind*... because Robert Lewis didn't know, couldn't tell if God or the Devil were responsible for it. It's good to remember what he wrote in his diary too: "My God, what have we done?"

"And do you think he redeemed himself with that? That the soldier was healed by the months he spent sculpting a block of marble? That it was good therapy for him? Please! He killed a hundred thousand people..."

"He at least had that gesture. He realized he had to somehow fill the black hole of bitterness he had inside..."

"Cheap semiotics, don't talk to me about symbolism now..."

"... that he needed a symbolic stone, it couldn't just be any stone, and he came to believe that one that was sculpted by his own hands..."

"...a ridiculous atomic mushroom..."

"He turned himself into a sculptor to be able to do that work, don't you understand? It was a complete transformation!"

"But in the end he was an American soldier through and through."

"We don't know that. As for the nuclear matter, you know that the first few tests were carried out on the Bikini Atoll... Nuclear energy has always had a sexy, playful side, as well as its deadly side... That positive understanding of nuclear bombs led to the two-piece swimming suit being named for the atoll where the first nuclear tests were carried out, because the expectation was that this swimsuit would have the same effects as a nuclear explosion on women at the time...Wait...Look at this..."

Lazkano looked at the photograph Gloria had uploaded onto her screen.

Admiral William H. P. Blandy and his wife appear in it, and next to them an older, red-faced military man. They are cutting up a spectacular cake in the shape of the atomic mushroom. It's not just any cake, it looks like a wedding cake without a bride and groom. The photo dates back to 1946, so it was taken after the massacres in Hiroshima and Nagasaki. Admiral Blandy looks very elegant, just like his wife, who wears a hat mirroring the atomic mushroom shape of the cream and meringue cake next to them. The astonishing similarity between the hat and the cake is what's made that photograph so famous, that brutal contrast between frivolity and sacredness, not to mention the cold-bloodedness of the crass gastronomic reinterpretation of the iconic symbol of a massacre. Crime repurposed as aesthetics; the mushroom, embraced by fashion, turned into a chic pastry. Bikinis, cakes. The "newly married" joyfully hold the knife with which they're about to cut up that cake in the shape of an atomic mushroom, holding hands, although doubtlessly the person who's having the most fun in there is the third military character with his moonshine drinker's face.

"Apparently, Blandy was an old-school Admiral: he took part in the first bombing of Iwo Jima, and was well known because, before firing the cannons, he liked to place his ships as close to the coast as possible, to the point of putting his own ships at risk. "I want to see the white of my enemy's eyes," they say he said once... Imagine, Diego, the white of his enemy's eyes! When the war ended he took part in the nuclear tests in the Bikini Atoll, where, apparently, he pronounced the sentence that would make him famous: "I am not an atomic playboy.""

Gloria showed him a Wikipedia entry on her laptop.

"The bomb will not start a chain-reaction in the water, converting it all to gas and letting all the ships on all the oceans drop down to the bottom. It will not blow out the bottom of the sea and let all the water run down the hole. It will not destroy gravity. I am not an atomic playboy – as one of my critics labeled me – exploding these bombs to satisfy my personal whim."

"I am not an atomic playboy," that's what Blandy had said, but the photograph completely contradicts his words.

"Apart from meringue or cream cakes that look like atomic mushrooms and ladies' hats in the shape of atomic mushrooms... they also made pop songs about it... and the people cutting up cake ever so joyfully, like it was a party... There is a very thin thread between the frivolous and the sacred, and whoever manages to swing on it without falling, wins."

Muslims had often stated that Western societies had lost all shame: the tendency to feel guilty had spread in the West, but shame, not a speck of it. In the East, however, they didn't feel guilty, but they had clearly interiorized the feeling of shame, and it was a shame that surpassed guilt by far when they acted in morally reprehensible ways according to their own parameters.

It had all started as a result of a new *performance* that Gloria had in mind. Lately, she'd been analyzing the works of Esther Ferrer, and she would call Diego, very often way after midnight, under the euphoric effect of marijuana, to tell him about an idea she'd thought up that evening that was as *genius* as it was fleeting, and would be *useless* come the following morning.

"This, for example: twenty-four hours praying the Our Father in an art gallery... Completely still, unmovable, praying hieratically... I'd have to prepare myself physically, though, for sure. In this way I'd be making a critique of Christian redemption... All I need is to come up with a good title, *Redemption for Six Murders* or something like that. What do you think? Hang on, no, something more provocative: *Christian Redemption of the Atocha Murders*... I might be able to do a whole series, changing the title and the length of my prayers on each occasion, purging a different crime and portraying the issuers of prayers as executioners... Fuck! I could spend a year going from gallery to gallery, crisscrossing the whole of Europe, at least Christian Europe, to then write about my experience! You could help me write the book...what do you think, Diego?"

She said everything, and at that point there was not much that anyone could add to what Gloria said; Lazkano couldn't do more than, as that Mexican writer once said after visiting Borges, intersperse the conversation with "wise silences" here and there.

It was three a.m. when the phone rang in Lazkano's house.

"Were you asleep?"

"What do you think?"

"I have bad news, Diego, very bad news..."

"What happened? Has there been an accident?"

"Rauschenberg died."

Gloria appeared to be drunk.

"Rauschenberg...the artist?"

"Who else?"

The man who built art and humor with garbage, taxidermied animals, car tires, old radios, and other objects that he'd picked up in gas stations, ditches, and scrap yards had died.

"*Souvenirs without nostalgia*, that's what he used to call his pieces."

"And you're a receptacle filled to the brim with nostalgia, Gloria..."

"That's not true...he was a rescuer...Rauschenberg! A true artist! My favorite artist of all time!"

That wasn't completely true, but she always took refuge in hyperbole when she got sentimental. Diego tried to shoo away her sorrows, telling her that they'd talk in the morning, that it wasn't so bad, that Rauschenberg was eighty years old already... but he didn't have many friends like Gloria and when she got sentimental it was better to proceed with caution, he didn't want the depressive tendencies of her youth to resurface.

"Are you all right, Diego?"

"Hanging in there, thanks for asking. What about *you*?"

"I've been drinking..."

"I can see that: nonstop since dinner, am I wrong?"

"You aren't completely right: I didn't eat dinner. What for? I want to dissolve, like Joseph Beuys."

"You have to go to bed and, when you wake up tomorrow, have *pan tomaca*, toast with tomatoes and olive oil, in full sun on your terrace."

"It's raining, Lazkano: will you please banish, once and for all, your idyllic perception of the Mediterranean? It's all a bunch of junk."

"Rauschenberg would do something with it, don't you think?"

"I'd need his talent for that."

"I'll call you tomorrow morning."

"I won't be picking up the phone."

"At midday, then."

"No, don't call me. I wanted to tell you something else, Lazkano... You know I love you lots, don't you?"

"Me too."

"You're just saying that, but I really love you. And one more thing, as for Miró..."

"Miró?"

"Joan Miró, you know who... That argument we had the last time: you said that he was an escapist of color, and I rejected that repeatedly..."

Lazkano didn't remember having that particular discussion. They had so many that it was difficult to keep track.

"Yes, I remember," he lied.

"I found something he said when they asked him what had he done to counter Franco in one of his catalogs. Wait... I'll tell you the guy's name now: Georges, Georges Raillard. It was him who asked Miró what had he done to fight Francoism. Do you know what he said?"

"I haven't the slightest."

"*Free and violent things.* Did you hear me? It says so in the catalog, Lazkano, those exact words."

"I'm exhausted, Gloria..."

"And one more thing I wanted to tell you: do you know the *Bodegó amb sabata vella*? *The Still Life with Old Shoe*? It's a painting by Miró, from 1937, they called it "Miró's Guernica"... he made a great mural for the Spanish Republic's Pavilion at the Paris International Exhibition that same year – *El Segador, The Reaper*, which is considered a lost work now... What do you think about that?"

"I think you're right."

"He might have drawn the logo for the Caixa Bank, but Miró wasn't a sellout like you said."

"I never said anything of the sort."

"Yes, you did."

"I was mistaken then."

"That's what I'm saying."

"Good night, Gloria..."

"Wait, wait... and what about the seventies? When Franco condemned Puig Antich to death by garrotte? Miró answered with *L'esperança del condemnat a mort. The Hope of a Condemned Man.* And do you know something else? Miró was a savage, he knew how to draw like a savage..."

"You've persuaded me, Gloria..."

"What time is it? It's late, isn't it?"

"It finally dawned on you?"

"What do you expect? It's not my fault! Rauschenberg... he died!"

"I know, you told me already. *Your favorite artist of all time.*"

"Honor and reverence to Rauschenberg!"

She downed what sounded like her last drink. That's what Lazkano thought: he heard the sound of muted swallowing at the other end of the line.

"You'd laugh if you saw me, Lazkano…"

"Maybe I'd cry," he thought. He thought it, but he didn't say it.

"You'd laugh. My living room floor is covered with open books, catalogs… opening these books is like spreading a woman's thighs, isn't that true? This is a bacchanal! What an orgy! *Partouze*! I'm going to sleep right here, nestled between the books… what do you think?"

"I think that you're going to wake up with a terrible backache. Promise me that you'll try to sleep a little."

"Yes: having come this far there isn't much else left to do, is there?"

"Not much, truth be said."

"Besides, poor Rauschenberg… I emptied the last bottle…"

"Listen to me, Gloria, for once: go to bed."

"It was a reserve. A *federal reserve* bottle, Lazkano."

"More the reason to go to bed."

"I could, like Miró did, lock myself up in a fortress in Normandy and draw stars and colors… *free and violent things*… plant staircases on the ground so that we climb them and reach the sky… Lazkano, have I told you how much I love you? I have Miró's

La masía in front of my eyes: don't ask me why, but I can see two dogs and you and I fucking at the same time..."

When he called her the following day she claimed she didn't remember a thing.

"A phone call? From me? Are you sure it wasn't some other girl?"

"Listen, Lazkano: Roman Ondák, in Venice, made an exact copy of the gardens outside *inside* the Slovakian Pavilion; he did it in such a way that the inside of the pavilion was also a replica of the outside... You see gardens outside, you go in, and you see the same gardens inside. More gardens and floral arrangements! Inside and outside! What did we come here for? To see art? What did we actually expect? What if we erased the differences between the inside and the outside of the museum, but not by turning the outside into art, but by turning the interior into something common? What if everything was garden, or everything was art, or museum, or city center, what if everything was everything at the same time? Why compartmentalize everything? It'd be a game of mirrors, an homage to empty spaces..."

"Repetition ad infinitum..."

"I'm thinking of doing something like that. Imitation is not new. Serialization, appropriation, is all the rage in art right now. Should we order some food? The grilled fish is fantastic here."

"How about we share a bream?"

"For the fish…what do you think, a Sumarroca?"

"That sounds better than an orange juice…"

"*Orange*…funny you should mention that. It was the color of modernity at one point. Remember the late sixties and the whole seventies: furniture, big round lamps, patterned dresses and wallpaper. Orange was very present, but it got old, so to speak…For a while it was a color that spoke about the future, remember the uniforms in *Star Trek*… The color of the future has evolved: gold, silver, titanium, then white, green became popular with *The Matrix*, but it's passé again…The key is to pay attention to the décor inside Hollywood spaceships, the colors of the letters and graphics that appear on the computers that are represented in fiction."

"You seem very up-to-date on all matters pertaining to color. Are you going to paint again?"

"No, please. No one wants paintings here. That's a thing of the past. If you don't mind, later on, when you're drinking your coffee, I have an errand to run…"

"I'll come with you."

"As you please. I have to pick up a parcel from the post office."

After sucking the bones and the head of the bream and drinking two grappas each, they removed themselves from the lovely afternoon in the port of Barcelona and headed toward the central post office building. Gloria had to pick up a parcel sent from Germany for her father, apparently.

Lazkano couldn't help remembering his own missing father, "I came to the wrong place, Diego," that time he went to the post office to return his library books, the bitter beginning of his mental confusion.

"He always uses my address to buy things abroad, I don't know why."

"He must want to give you a reason to visit him whenever you go back home."

"Maybe."

"What a strange parcel."

"My father is an incorrigible collector. Don't even ask me what he collects, I don't want to know. All I know is that he spends a fortune."

"You've never been tempted to open a parcel?"

"I'm not a writer, I don't derive as much pleasure as you do from sticking my nose everywhere."

Later that evening, Lazkano accompanied Gloria to the Mutt Art Gallery in Barcelona; when she'd mentioned it to Diego the previous night he thought she was pulling his leg.

"What? A painter who's a horse?"

"You'll see it with your own eyes."

At the entrance of the exhibition there was a photograph of the horse, whose name was Napoleon. There was also an explanatory video: his "trainer" – *his agent?* – would place a paintbrush between his teeth and the horse would paint the canvas with impetuous brushstrokes, until he completed a colorful, abstract sketch. His paintings were lined up next to his photograph: there were more than a dozen pieces by *Napoleon*, none of which cost less than three thousand euro.

"And people buy this?"

"Don't start, Diego. A brilliant idea that the media find funny or compelling: that's, whether we like it or not, modern art."

"Maybe we have just bored ourselves now, and there's nothing left to do but delegate: to machines, to computers, and lacking that, to animals..."

"Vargas Llosa wrote an article about that not long ago."

"I don't understand anything...The story of the Spanish painter who burned the pieces he didn't sell in the yearly San Juan summer solstice bonfires made some sense, but this...It'd be a very appropriate subject for an equine psychologist, should such a person exist."

"They've carried out similar tests before; for example, teaching monkeys in zoos to use cameras...it's true that the results won't make it to the annals of the history of art, but..."

"I suddenly feel an overwhelming desire to get drunk."

"Wait: one must earn alcohol's oblivion. First, I'll take you to see an exhibition that writers always like very much. If it displeases you, dinner is on me."

"You have no pity, Gloria."

It was a contemporary Portuguese art show, exclusively

about Portuguese writers and artists. Thinking that the occasion merited it, Lazkano tried to impress Gloria with a quote in Portuguese:

"Cheguei a Lisboa, mas não a uma conclusão."

I arrived in Lisboa, but not to a conclusion.

"Fernando Pessoa: herewith your favorite author."

Gloria pointed out a game of foosball, an installation by the artist José João Brito. Two opposing teams. For one of them the goalie was João Gaspar Simões, and the team was made up of ten other Portuguese writers from across the ages. On the opposing team, the eleven wooden figurines were copies of just one, Fernando Pessoa. He remembered Soto and Zeberio, and of the match they played against some guys from Bordeaux at the beach in Bidart.

"Pessoa against Portugal, I love it. Someone who was capable of creating so many heteronyms can certainly fight the whole world on his own."

"I knew you'd like it."

"You've been lucky. We can split the cost of dinner."

"Wasn't the deal that if you enjoyed it, you'd pay for it?"

Gloria was in Donostia after a long absence. Lazkano had made plans to have lunch with her, but using the excuse that she could bring the parcel she'd received in Barcelona to him and her father, had invited them both to lunch at his home.

"You have to promise me that you won't laugh."

"Laugh? Why would I laugh?"

"This has to stay between us: my father is a fascist, don't say I didn't warn you."

"I never laugh at fascists, you've nothing to worry about."

"I don't trust you."

The living room was filled with expensive hardwood furniture, and the walls, with still lifes and hunting scenes; but, against all expectations, it wasn't a dark space: thanks to the wide-open, high, south-facing windows, there was no lack of light in that room. A lawn of olive-green carpet provided an unhurried tranquility to the whole room, it even reached the ceiling, which was easily ten meters high. The ambience was cozy, nothing like the typically impractical, inherited aristocratic surroundings, so clumsy and in bad taste; this was a natural aristocracy, refined from generation to generation, layered with skill for the owner's pleasure, following old tastes and motivations. Lazkano started to understand those parents who despair at their children when they reject their aristocratic privileges; to reject the scent of that ancient distillation was, in a way, a failure of respect. *We judge the aristocracy too easily*, Diego told himself.

So that was the *facha*'s office. Come on in. Diego was particularly disturbed by an immense tapestry, about three meters wide and just as many high, behind the desk: whose were those unnaturally large eyes, those eyes staring at him with the stern look that dictators often exude in stamps, street statues and official portraits? Whose if not Generalísimo Franco's? Gloria let out a sigh.

"Okay, you've seen it now. Do you believe me?"

Diego didn't feel repugnance; in fact he felt the very opposite, such was the shock of the sudden apparition of the dictator on the tapestry, so out of context, so out of season. He decided that, undoubtedly, the man who kept such an obvious image of Franco in his private office surely harbored an inoffensive, almost tender kind of nostalgia for the dictator. He'd been curious to meet Gloria's father before, but that detail increased his curiosity.

"Do you mind if we wait by the entrance?"

"Objects will survive us. We will be gone, but objects will remain. I'll confess: I am an incorrigible collector."

"I noticed the tapestry in your office," Lazkano told himself, but he was careful not to mention it. He remembered his visit to Kafka's home in Prague, how moved he was when he saw himself reflected in the same mirror in which Kafka had looked at himself, and how for a moment he believed the impossible fantasy that he'd seen the writer's semblance inside the mirror.

"I like these old things: these little lead soldiers, for example, represent the battle of Verdun. I haven't finished painting them all yet."

"My father likes reenacting famous battles."

"I don't just like it, darling, it's the joy of my life."

Theater once again, thought Lazkano, little toys, marionettes, lead soldiers, representations. But maybe it was only a symptom of the regression of old people: they substitute some toys for others. Gloria's father stood straight as a rod, and although his hair had been black once, he kept all of it, white and wiry; he must have been seventy-five years old at least.

"Gloria tells me you're a writer."

"I try to write, when they let me."

"Don't be so modest, Lazkano, I've looked you up online and I can see you do well with your writing."

"I'm not complaining, Señor Furmica."

"You even speak Russian."

"I've forgotten it somewhat, but yes, I do."

"Tell me, do you like Chekhov?"

"I love Chekhov."

"I think I'm going to get on well with this friend of yours, Gloria..."

Señor Furmica opened the parcel that Gloria had brought him from Barcelona. He brought an impeccably bound old book to his nose with obvious delight. It was a big, gorgeous volume, from 1923, written in Cyrillic characters.

"His complete dramatic works, a whim."

"It must be worth a fortune."

"Money, of course. Money is important. In Chekhov's works

too: characters continuously going through dire straits, borrowing money from usurers, always on the brink of losing their mortgaged homes...Plus there is bribery, libertines who marry in exchange for supposedly juicy dowries...Very current subjects, come to think of it...

"In any case, it's not his theater that interests me the most. I much prefer his short stories."

"We've something to disagree on...You prefer his short narratives? The *short stories, racconti brevi?*"

"I'd say so."

"Think for a moment, do you know where Anton Chekhov's short stories come from? Any idea?"

"He was a doctor, he must have seen and experienced many of those stories while visiting patients..."

"Yes and no...Theater was one of Chekhov's interests when he was a teenager: he and his brother would stage brief comic plays at home, for the family. The characters of those little improvised theater plays later became the heroes of his better-known short stories. What do you reckon? There are many theater plays at the root of those short stories..."

Diego choked on the sweet wine they'd been served as an aperitif.

"I'm so sorry."

"You don't like it? We'll serve another one...Gisele, please..."

"No, no, not at all, please...the wine is delicious."

"It's true that when they premiered *The Seagull* people didn't understand it...But he had a second chance, which is something we should all enjoy in life; and then, yes, his success was extraordinary...He even married Olga Knipper, an actress in the Moscow Art Theater...Nothing happens by chance..."

"I'm liking your skeptical sense of humor."

"Actors and directors never knew if they were performing humorous tragedies or tragic comedies. They didn't know whether to laugh or cry."

"Both at the same time, probably."

"Both at the same time, that's the way it is in life, usually. I've always thought that Gloria should direct a Chekhov play, like she used to back in the day."

"*Papá*, don't start with that again..."

"No, no, let me finish: I'm completely serious. You were good, you had a very good sense of staging...I'd finance you myself."

"Theater is artifice..."

"Not if the actors are not *too theatrical*, darling. Chekhov used to keep pretty quiet during rehearsals, but he would offer his opinion when they asked for it: 'It'd be better if you were less theatrical...Keep it simpler...like life itself,' he would say."

"That's not the tendency of theater plays around here, as far as I know. But I am not the best person to judge, I haven't set foot in a theater for more than twenty years."

"You too, Diego? Why is that?"

"It traumatized me in my youth, who knows."

"In any case...If Gloria were to direct a Chekhov play... you'd be forced to break your theatrical fast, *n'est-ce pas?*"

"In that case..."

"When are you going to do it, Gloria?"

"Some day, *papá.*"

"Lunch is ready," Gisele pointed out.

A schnapps to start. Afterward, hake with almonds, paired with a harmonious white wine from the Rhine Valley. The food was good in that house. The cook, the servant...it seemed to Lazkano that everything was from a different era, even after he'd banished the Franco tapestry and the chandeliers from his mind. He felt like he was in Victorian London. Diego had harbored hopes of having fun with the old man, but the experience was proving to be a torment. Gloria wasn't comfortable either. It was obvious that in the past few years she had lost the habit of eating in her father's company and, above all, of having servers constantly around.

"Change the music, please, Gisele. This aria doesn't suit the hake at all."

"I'll change it, *papá*; you can leave, Gisele, don't worry."

If Gloria's father's manners hadn't been so staid, Diego would have found the situation comical. Gloria had warned him again and again: "You know that my father is a *facha*, he's going to try to provoke you, just go along with him. It's easier that way."

A fascist? He really was one. He thought himself intelligent, but he lacked the tiniest speck of charm. And what was worse: he didn't bother to hide his leanings.

"It's always Germany and France who pull Europe's cart. Isn't that shameful? It's such a pity that we weren't born a bit farther north."

You seem to be managing well, thought Diego to himself: wine from the Rhin, German opera, schnapps. We can chose where we are from despite the accident of our birth, even without leaving the comfort of our home. Diego remembered his time in Lille, where he used to sell canonical volumes of world literature for a pittance in order to buy alcohol. *The Book of Disquiet*, by Pessoa, in exchange for a bottle of port...

"The Basque nationalist EAJ-PNV party missed a great opportunity when they ruined the chance of an agreement with the Nazis."

"But they lost the war..."

"The EAJ-PNV? Yes, you're right."

"The Nazis too..."

"Hmmm, you could say that. But how much money does the US film industry spend, still today, producing films about the Nazis? Isn't that true? One might be forgiven for thinking that winning the war wasn't enough, that their victory left a bitter taste in their mouths, or that they couldn't quite believe they had won. They're still fighting an enemy who, having disappeared a long time ago, remains more present than ever."

"Perhaps the objective is to make sure that Leviathan does not rise again," Lazkano suggested, and Gloria, knocking her glass back in one, gestured for him to drop the subject. But Lazkano was on a roll already: "The first battalion to enter Paris was the Gernika Battalion, the Basques…"

"You're mistaken, young man, I'd say that parade took place in Bordeaux: 'Let the Basques through, they've had to suffer that horrible painting Picasso painted for them, maybe this can be some sort of consolation'… who knows…"

"More wine, *papá*?"

"Gisele, more wine."

Gloria released Gisele: "Don't worry, I'll take care of it." Lazkano had noticed that the servant was tense, that he and Gloria got in the way of her usual routine, that she would have preferred to do things her way without having Gloria and Lazkano touch her bottles of wine. Their intentions were good, but they were just annoying the servants.

"This wine from the Rhin… It's really fruity; I like it, *papá*."

It irritated Lazkano to see Gloria continuously try to change the subject, so completely at the mercy of her father's words. Now he understood why she had decided to leave the parental home so young, and why her mother's death had cemented her decision to remain in Barcelona indefinitely. But all Gloria's comments about the wines from the Rhin weren't enough to change the course of the conversation.

"The Nazis were disciplined people, it's not fashionable to say anything in their favor, they throw you to the dogs as soon as you do, but the fact that so few people die on German roads nowadays, isn't that thanks to the Nazis? The best roads and the best cars, no speed limits on the autobahn...How many people die here, by contrast? They took some of their ideas to the extreme, I agree; but shouldn't we subtract all the people who *haven't* died on Hitler's roads in the past seventy years from the number of those who died in the camps? The fact that roads here are deadly traps is another form of terror, and who is responsible? The mediocre rise through the ranks and we accuse truth tellers of being cruel; it's sad, but that's the way of the world. Have you ever thought about any of this, Lazkano? About the fact that certain people are demonized, and not others?"

They took a little bit longer than they would have liked to arrive at the chilled *panna cotta* and the coffee that common courtesy demanded.

"There's a lack of discipline, Señor Lazkano. Authority. The work they used to do in the German Gymnasium with the young, with Hitler's youth...Günter Grass's case must be familiar to you."

Diego was beginning to feel weak. It was him who was holding on to the bottle of white wine like a shipwreck now, hurriedly filling up the glasses. He drank in order not to talk. How many shy people, how many cowards, must have become alcoholics in this way?

"Wouldn't you like a digestif? An herb liqueur? A grappa? It's not my favorite but we also have homemade *patxaran. Etxekoa.*"

"No, thanks."

Etxekoa was the first Basque word he'd issued since their arrival. *From our home.*

"It's been a pleasure, Diego. Come back whenever you want. It's difficult to find people to properly converse with in these tumultuous times."

Diego lowered his head docilely, lacking the stamina to add anything else, as if the authoritarian hand of Gloria's father were forcing him to curtsy.

Gloria led him to the door.

"He has a certain charm, your father."

"You mean when he's not saying something hair-raisingly horrible? He's old now, but imagine him forty years ago, when I was a child."

"We always clash with our parents: or do you think you would have had a good relationship with him if he hadn't been such an enormous fascist?"

"You don't need to pretend, I'd like to shoot him myself sometimes."

"We don't choose our parents, you're not responsible for them."

"But parents are responsible for their children? Do you think it's easy to live with that? I'm sorry, Diego. I should have told you. My father was a friend of Melitón Manzanas."

Gloria sighed.

"Okay, I've said it. I was going to explode if I didn't."

Some names can freeze your blood. For many people, Melitón Manzanas's is one of them. The first policeman the ETA had killed deliberately. A dark legend hung over that man. Apparently his enjoyment of torture wasn't enough for him, he had a habit of making wives and sisters *pay* for the favors he carried out for the men he detained. Not even his work colleagues at the police department wanted anything to do with him. He belonged to a class of exceptional sadists.

Lazkano had heard that he'd even been accused of collaborating with the Nazis in his twenties: they said that he handed Jews over to occupied France in exchange for people of interest to the Spanish government.

Lazkano wondered if Gloria had heard about that. He hoped, for her own sake, that she hadn't. It must have been hard enough for his friend to digest her father's relationship with Francoists and torturers. But Señor Furmica's philo-Nazi rhetoric was easier to understand now. Wouldn't it be something to listen to the postwar anecdotes that good old Melitón and her father must have told each other over schnapps. Definitely, it was better that she didn't know anything. He decided not to let her know how that friendship of her father's warped and waved itself around the greatest massacre of the twentieth century. Without our knowledge, the loose-end-thread of a plot linking us to the cruelty of the world can be so close to home – much closer than we think.

Start pulling at the loose thread of a simple tapestry and you'll arrive at unsuspected places. "Objects will survive us."

The atmosphere turned to ice, and it didn't look like there was anything to be done about it.

Gloria hugged Lazkano in a way she hadn't hugged anyone in a long time. Maybe it was just an illusion, but he felt that if Gisele hadn't interrupted them at that precise moment with Diego's jacket, he might have even kissed her lips.

That day Gloria didn't come to pick him up at Sants Station. Lazkano was surprised, but he didn't think anything of it: she must have just been late. He bought a couple of newspapers and sat down in the cafeteria to wait for her. Seeing that she wasn't turning up, he called her. The call went straight to voicemail. She must have been immersed in one of those impossible conceptual works, oblivious not only to her appointment with the visitor she was supposed to pick up, but also, quite likely, to the time of year and the world outside.

Thinking that Gloria must have gotten confused about the time or the day, Lazkano decided to hop in a taxi and go to his friend's house. He rang the doorbell. There was no response. He ate a light dinner in a neighborhood pizzeria and returned to knock on her door at dusk. It didn't look like there was anyone there.

He left a third message on her voicemail, letting her know he was staying in a boardinghouse in her neighborhood. The following morning, after breakfast, seeing that he hadn't received any calls from her and that she still wasn't picking up the phone or coming to answer the intercom, he decided to call Gloria's father. He didn't keep his phone number in his address book, but he found it easily in a Pakistani cybercafé, in the white pages. There weren't many people with the Furmica family name in Donostia. Although it was Gisele who picked up the phone, he heard Gloria's father's voice soon enough.

"You didn't know?"

Lazkano should have suspected something when he saw all the plants on Gloria's balcony. There were too many to be all for her own consumption. But who knows, she might have been sharing the herb with her friends . . . Although it was obvious that Gloria didn't earn much with her works of art, Diego hadn't realized that her financial circumstances were so dire.

He couldn't help remembering what Gloria used to tell them when they were late for rehearsal, all the reprimands that made Soto so angry:

"You're going to end badly," "Don't expect me to come to get you out of jail," "Like we've money to pay an attorney."

Her father had already paid her bail, but they still needed to send a registered fax with the bank transfer's receipt and complete some paperwork. She was being held in the Eixample police station.

"I didn't know you were in Barcelona, Lazkano . . . Gloria will be glad to have a familiar face waiting for her. I'd be very grateful if you called me when they release her."

"Of course."

Diego Lazkano spent the morning in the police station's waiting room. Rubber stamps, the toxic smells of ink and fluorescent lights that buzz and buzz but never quite burn out, posters of the most wanted criminals. Vestiges of the eighties: he still felt nervous in places like these.

When midday arrived, as soon as the policeman in reception abandoned his post, he had to explain Gloria's case all over again to the officer who took over the afternoon shift. They released her shortly before five p.m. She didn't look too bad.

"I'm sorry, Diego, they only let me make one phone call and it's not like I was going to ask *you* for the money. Where did you spend the night?"

"Are you all right?"

"I shared a cell with two Bulgarian prostitutes . . . They looked like two of Oteiza's grandmothers . . . Would you believe that I couldn't remember the capital of Bulgaria? Do you know that they don't use ink to take your fingerprints anymore? Even that's over."

Gloria didn't want to expand on her job as a dealer. She confessed to him that she'd only been doing it for a short while, dealing to "friends of friends," and that she'd bumped into a cop in civilian clothes during one of her deliveries. Bad luck. According to her public defender, she was going to be all right, because it was her first time and because they found only a small amount on her. But she couldn't forgive herself for having to ask her father to bail her out.

"My entire life I've always managed on my own...And now I owe him one. He's going to claim this one; of course he will, the old fucker."

"If you're in dire straights...you know you only need to ask, Gloria...Do you need money?"

"No, but if you want, I'll let you pay for a round of martinis in Boadas."

Professor Heiner Stachelhaus sat in the main auditorium of the MACBA. Given the small turnout, the organizers were shamelessly collecting the wooden folding chairs they'd added, envisioning a larger number of attendees. Gloria's pupils were dilated.

"You'd think it was David Bowie..."

"He knows more than anybody about him..."

Josep Ramoneda officiated the introduction and did it effortlessly, with his deep, woodwormy voice. Lazkano enjoyed his radio programs, although he had never seen him in person. Professor Heiner Stachelhaus drank Vichy Water, welcomed the audience's presence in Catalan, and proceeded to speak in German. His interpreter was very good, although it was too obvious that he was someone who read and that he wasn't a professional simultaneous interpreter.

"Beuys was half gangster, half clown. Hat, raincoat, fragile appearance, insatiable need for action. There are people like that, people who never rest and who calm down by working to exhaustion, who turn tiredness into fuel. 'The very outpouring of power is my energy,' Joseph Beuys used to say."

Lazkano remembered Soto. That's what his friend was like. It was almost like he was describing him.

"Beuys was born on May 12, 1921, in a town called Krefeld, near Düsseldorf. He had a nomadic year before finishing high school, working as an assistant in a circus: he worked in construction, as a sandwich man, and as an animal keeper. He was at peace with his years of service in the Hitler Youth, it was normal, his obligation to be a soldier in the war. He believed in destiny..."

"We should have invited your father, Gloria."

"Will you shut up please?"

"After studying to become a radiotelegraph operator in Posen, they trained him to be a war pilot, first in Erfurt and later in Königgrätz. A crash in Crimea in the winter of 1943 would determine his future. Having bombed a battery of Russian antiaircraft cannons, before he was able to regain height in his ascent maneuver, the JU 87 plane he was piloting was shot down. Against all expectations, Beuys and his copilot were able to fly the plane across enemy lines. However, an altimeter malfunction caused the plane to crash in the middle of a snowstorm. In the crash, Beuys was thrown from the plane. His copilot was dead. From there on the story gets murky, but for years Beuys claimed that a tribe of nomad Tartars found the remains of the plane and took him in, gravely injured: they took care of him in their camp for eight long days. They rubbed his wounds with animal fats, they wrapped him in felt to keep his body warm. They fed him milk, cheese, and curds. When the Germans rescued him they sent him back to the front, in revenge, because some thought he had never sufficiently embraced military discipline. He was wounded in combat four more times, and showered in medals as a result. They also demoted him, twice, for indiscipline. When the British captured him in 1945 his body was covered in scars."

"David Bowie, what a hero..." whispered Lazkano into Gloria's ear.

"I don't want to hear another word, Diego."

"In the happenings he carried out with the Fluxus group he provoked emotions that frustrated many people: pianos filled with detergent that he then destroyed with an electric saw, tearing the hearts out of dead animals live, fat, flickering TVs, primal screams, loud noises...all sorts of madness. Most times people didn't understand what Joseph Beuys was doing, but he didn't care a damn. He carried on as in a trance.

"In 1945, his fiancé, much younger than him and an employee

of the Düsseldorf post office, returned her engagement ring. Joseph Beuys sank into a depression; his friends had to climb into his house through a window to rescue him, and when they found him he was sitting in the dark: 'I want to dissolve,' he told them in a weak, barely audible whisper. On the ground, broken drawings. He ordered a box from a carpenter of Krefeld, intending to coat it in tar and 'bury' himself in it. Finally, he understood his depression as a process of purification and moved on.

"Even before his famous intervention with the coyote, he always had a special relationship with animals. Proof of this was his piece *Honey Pump in the Workplace*. Like Rudolph Steiner, he admired bees, because they were ancient sacred animals: 'Sacred, because the destiny of bees reveals the destiny of human beings... When we pick up a bit of beeswax, what is it, really, this thing in our hands? A mix of blood, muscles and bones.'"

"Gloria..."

"What now?"

"You know that bees have been disappearing lately, don't you? They don't know why, but they're disappearing..."

"Will you shut up already?"

"But if there's one animal that Beuys had a close relationship with, that's the hare. 'I am not a human being at all, I'm a hare,' he said once. Consequently, he carried out the performance *How to Explain Pictures to a Dead Hare* in the Schmela Gallery in

Düsseldorf: he walked around the exhibition space with a dead hare in his arms, explaining the pictures on the walls to it with great tenderness and detail.

"When Beuys proclaimed that all humans are artists, he wasn't saying that there's a painter or a sculptor inside every person, but that all human beings have artistic abilities, and that we need to take those abilities into account, and try to improve them. For him, creativity is the science of freedom.

"Although the shamanic character of his performances has been particularly highlighted, Beuys didn't intend to use his ideas and happenings to return to scenes of the past, but to look for clues with which to face the future. It's undeniable, on the other hand, that there was something of the shaman about him, even in his external appearance: Beuys always wore a fisherman's waistcoat, a felt hat and white shirt, in addition to his jeans.

"What is a shaman, after all? The shaman is not just a sick person: shamans are sick people with the ability to heal themselves.

"On June 2, 1967, during a demonstration against the state visit from the Shah of Iran, the police killed the student Benno Ohnesorg in West Berlin. Twenty days later Joseph Beuys founded the Deutsche Studentenpartei, the German Student Party. His provocateur's soul had no limits: 'My party is the biggest on in the world, most of its members are animals,' he stated. In 1971 he organized a successful protest against some tennis courts they were intending to build on a forest near Düsseldorf: they *cleaned* the forest with gigantic brooms.

"Joseph Beuys's work is closely linked to the Documenta festival that takes place in Kassel: in Documenta 1982, he proposed planting seven thousand trees in the following five years, probably the most transformative artistic intervention ever carried out in a city."

Lazkano listened up: his mind unconsciously went to the eighties. While Joseph Beuys planted trees, things happened to him: he met Soto and Zeberio, Idoia left him, he moved in with Ana soon after, they arrested and tortured him, he ran away, met Lena in Lille...

"The social change Beuys advocates is a change without violence: 'Without violence, not because violence, for particular reasons, doesn't stand a chance to be successful or effective, but because of human spiritual morality and because of political and societal norms. Partly, because the dignity of the human is linked to the inviolability of the person, and because those who forget it abandon the realm of the human. And partly, because the systems that we wish to transform are structured around violence expressed in every imaginable form. That's why all violent expressions echo the behavior of the system and, rather than weakening it, reinforce that which they wish to destroy.'"

"Is he going to go on for much longer, Gloria?"

"Leave if you want, I'm staying."

"Years earlier, in 1964, Beuys, as a provocation, recommended that they elevate the Berlin Wall by five centimeters, arguing that in this way it would be better proportioned.

"In 1969 he shared the stage with a white horse that was eating grass..."

"Wow, is he talking about Napoleon?"

"That's enough, Lazkano."

"'The artist and the criminal,' Beuys said, 'are traveling companions, they are both in possession of a crazy creativity, a creativity without morals fired only by the energy of freedom.' But of course, Beuys' words shouldn't be understood literally. Provocation was a part of it.

"But, as was made evident in the happening he performed in 1974 at the René Block Gallery in New York, Beuys was no mere provocateur. The title of the performance was *I Like America and America Likes Me*, and it had a second protagonist as well as Beuys: the coyote Little John. It's the most widely renowned and debated work by the German artist. Beuys arrived in JFK airport wrapped in a felt rug. He asked to be placed on a stretcher and taken to the art gallery in an ambulance, without him ever touching the ground of the United States. The coyote Little John waited for him in the gallery in a bed of hay. There were also piles of copies of the *Wall Street Journal* and several pieces of felt. He carried a walking stick and wore his perennial felt hat. He sat on the ground and spoke with the coyote. Beuys then hid under the felt, leaving only the tip of his walking stick outside it. The coyote then pulled the felt and ripped the fabric. As the days progressed, Beuys ended up surrounded by hay, and the coyote, resting among the felt and the newspapers. Every now and then, Beuys made music with a triangle that hung from his neck. After three days they got used to living together. Beuys gave the coyote Little John a big hug before saying goodbye to him. He spread handfuls of hay all over the place they had shared. He returned to JFK in the same way he had arrived: they lifted him into an ambulance on a stretcher, wrapped in felt, without him ever touching the ground with his feet, and he left New York and the United States without seeing anything in the city other than the space he had shared with the coyote.

"He accepted an invitation from the Solomon R. Guggenheim Museum and to the surprise of his nearest friends and acquaintances, he started to enjoy caviar, Cadillacs, and other luxuries. Thomas Messer, the director of the Guggenheim Museum at the time, reported on Beuys's change of attitude with the following words: 'I was afraid that Joseph Beuys had decided that, from his point of view, destroying and wrecking a museum might be a formidable work of art... Happily, his attitude changed from one day to the next, as if he had suddenly realized that he was done with the theatrics...'"

"Eva, his wife, used to say that Beuys had always been dead. She called her husband Beuys, and his children, Wenzel and Jessyka, didn't call him dad or father either, but Beuys, always. 'He was dead his entire life,' Eva Beuys used to say, 'but at the same time he was always very alive. Beuys never complained about the weather, he always said: no matter what the weather is like, it's always good.'

"He created his last installation in the Museo di Capodimonte in Naples, on December 23, 1985. He died a month later.

"It's strange that Beuys's ghost doesn't manifest more often. Maybe the words I saw this afternoon graffitied on a wall in El Raval, words that Beuys himself said, are right: 'I think, therefore I am redundant.' Maybe we are the dead hare in Beuys's arms, we just haven't realized it yet.

"I thank all of you for being here."

"Aren't you going to ask him for an autograph? He's the great Heiner Stachelhaus!"

"Go fuck yourself, Diego . . . this is the last time you come with me to a conference."

It was a balmy night in Barcelona and it would have been nice to have dinner on an outdoor terrace, but Gloria chose a place indoors, quiet and with white linen tablecloths.

"Are you sure you want to have dinner? You look thoroughly satiated . . . "

"I used to admire Beuys a lot back in the day, he was always one of my idols, but I've neglected him a bit in the past few years to be honest. This was wonderful, even though he forgot to mention the story about the lightbulb..."

"Have the lady and gentleman decided what they're going to have?"

Escalivada, the Catalan salt cod salad, to start, and a sea bream to share. To drink, white wine: they asked the server to choose it, their only condition being that it be a Penedès wine. By the time the server came out with the fish they needed a second bottle.

"Apparently the heating vent was blocked, so he climbed on a chair to try to unblock it: he lost his balance and had a tremendous fall. It was such a bad fall that they had to take him to a hospital in Düsseldorf. When he returned home, he put a red bulb with this sentence on it in the dining room: 'Always stay awake.'"

"You could have told that anecdote in the Q & A session."

"I am not an exhibitionist like you."

"It would have been a way of earning the support of Heiner Stachelhaus... That anecdote could have led you to have dinner with Ramoneda and Stachelhaus! You could have spent the evening with two big fishes, making contacts that could help you exhibit your work in Berlin, instead of sharing your table with two dumb fishes, like you're doing now!"

"Go fuck yourself."

"*Go fuck yourself, go fuck yourself...* Don't you have anything else to say? You're repeating yourself, and that's not a creative way of living, Beuys wouldn't approve!"

"You're mistaken: shamans, as a matter of fact, tend to be quite repetitive. Repetition is the key to trance: *Go fuck yourself, go fuck yourself!*"

"I much prefer *Always stay awake*. Or even: *Heiner Stachelhaus, Heinerstachelhaus, Heinerstachelhaus*... Isn't that a great name? What a great advantage, to have a name like that! Don't you think that being in possession of a name like that and making people's jaws pronounce those words must definitely cause astonishingly complex neuronal connections to happen?"

"We shouldn't have ordered that second bottle of wine, Lazkano. You're delirious."

Lazkano was dead tired. The sea bream, however, pushed against the current of the white wine, and removed gravity and weight from the tiredness of the night. The next day's hangover was going to be lethal, but thinking that the memory of Beuys deserved that and more, they kept squandering their energy conversing and drinking one Trentino grappa after another, until they ran out of strength and money.

They zigzag back to the house. Lazkano lies down on the sofa without taking his shoes off.

"Would you like to sleep in my bed?"

Diego Lazkano gets up and gets into Gloria's bed.

"Who gave you permission to get into my bed with your shoes on?"

She takes his shoes and socks off. Shortly after Gloria is in her underwear: she's tanned; having sunbathed on the terrace, her swimsuit has left some sexy pale areas here and there. They've slept together before, sexless bed companions, but that was many years ago. Although this woman of prominent curves is very far from his usual standard of skinny fragile girls, Lazkano realizes that his preferences are changing slightly. It's funny how our carnal tastes evolve with the years.

Gloria pushes her ass against Diego's package and feels his penis's reaction through the two layers of fabric.

"It breathes, still," Gloria lets him know, in a tone that's anything but lustful.

"When he's got reason to," Lazkano answers, and falls immediately asleep with his arms around Gloria's waist. When they wake up in the morning, they both have the soothing impression of having fallen asleep at the same time.

"Have you ever wondered why we never slept together?"

"Because we're good friends?"

"More the reason..."

"I come to Barcelona because I can't get it right with the women back in the homeland, and you want me to sleep with you? Who will I run to, then, to tell them that you're obsessed with me and I can't get rid of you?" Lazkano says jokingly.

"You're so vain...someone might think you're a writer. A fuck without alcohol...you're not tempted?"

"To overcome the hangover?"

Gloria touches Lazkano's package with her fingers.

"It breathes, still..."

How can he say no to that friendly smile, to those caresses. It seems unbelievable that they're on a terrace in a big metropolis, they can't hear the slightest sound from that house in the foothills of the Montjuic, except the occasional trill of birds. Lazkano places his hand on the inner side of Gloria's thigh, searching with the tips of his fingers. Gloria undoes the buttons of his shirt and caresses his ribs with her fingertips and with her lips. Her first bite on his neck drives Lazkano completely and unexpectedly wild. They're both sitting on folding chairs, and Gloria abandons hers to remove her panties and, without bothering to lower Diego's pants to his ankles, releases his penis from behind his briefs. When she sits on top of him, Diego takes her breasts out of her blouse and buries his head in them, surprised by the fact that the folding wooden chair hasn't collapsed under them and sent them to the floor. Gloria takes her time caressing his shaft and rubbing it against her pubis. Their mouths meet, unable to hold back. Gloria presses harder against Diego when he grabs her ass, pushing her cheeks aside. A middle finger slides in search of a center, a thumb feels for a crack, a penetrating smell, not at all cosmetic, Gloria's own, mixed with the spiral of his own excitement. As she rides him, Diego feels a profound wellness, something completely unlike an orgasm, as the sun's rays tickle the hairs on his naked thighs. He stays like this for three or four minutes, inside her, and only reacts when he realizes that Gloria is getting ahead of him, and then he starts to grind her too.

Gloria's moans and sighs are not that different from her laughter, and even though ecstasy and laughter have always seemed essential but contradictory and independent pleasures that should never get mixed to him, he is pleased to see that they can happen simultaneously. Those breathless moans excite him more than all the obscene words in the world. Is it the unexpected novelty of it that's making everything so pleasurable?

"Nothing is stopping us from repeating this..."

"And if I fall in love with you?"

"Would you look at that, here I was thinking that my falling in love with you was the risk here."

"I'm human too."

"You're mistaken: you're a writer, the Devil. You're going to miss the train. Have a good trip back home, and *don't* call me when you arrive."

They smile. Their skins hold one another's scent, and they like it.

He has a gut feeling when Gloria doesn't open the door. This time he calls the Eixample police station directly.

He guessed right. Bingo.

"She's given evidence in front of the judge and spent the night in jail."

"In the police station?"

"No: *in jail.*"

"They sent her to jail? For selling marijuana?"

The policeman sighs, and asks who might he be speaking to.

"Are you her legal representative? A relative?"

"No…a friend."

"In that case I can't tell you anything else. I'm sorry."

Lazkano makes a quick decision:

"Look, I'm her boyfriend…more or less…she doesn't have anyone else."

"Go the courthouse, with an attorney. She's going to need one."

He has to give his name, family names, and national ID number to the courthouse secretary before he'll agree to let him in.

"Yago Machado?"

"No, Lazkano. Diego Lazkano."

A cold sweat runs down his back. These places, these people.

"When is she going to be…when will they let her go?"

"She's a *defcondos*…"

"Excuse me?"

Lazkano is not very familiar with police slang.

"*Defcondos*…it means this is not her first arrest."

"But it's only herb, it's not such a big deal."

"They seized fifty doses of ecstasy from her home. And she's got priors."

"You're going to end badly."

"Don't expect me to come to get you out of jail."

"Like we've money to pay an attorney."

He manages to see Gloria alone before dinnertime.

"What have you done, Gloria?"

"New business models... Someone has to pay the electricity bills."

"Didn't you learn your lesson the last time?"

"They say I have *priors*. Because of the marijuana... But it wasn't weed this time, right? It's something else. Besides, isn't there a statute of limitations for priors?"

"Not in three months, Gloria."

"Oh..."

"Where did you get the ecstasy from?"

"People introduce you to people, and those people to other people. It's not so difficult. Why? Are you interested?"

"This is not a joke, Gloria. Have you called your father?"

"That *facha*? No, he doesn't know anything."

"They've set bail at ten thousand euro this time."

"Ten thousand! Fuck..."

"I could lend you half of that now... but I'd need a couple of days to get the full ten thousand."

Gloria is despondent. She didn't expect such a heavy fine.

She is going to have to talk again with that person she doesn't want to talk with. The favor she owes him grows bigger. And she knows perfectly well that he'll charge her interest.

"The Roma exhibition didn't come through."

"I'm sorry."

"Maybe it's better that way, I'm not sure the space would actually work."

"Couldn't you do it somewhere else?"

"No, I don't think so. To compensate, I have other news...I'm embarrassed to tell you...They've asked me to direct a Chekhov play."

"You're kidding..."

"Like in the good old days. And with the same sort of wages."

"I thought *we hated* the theater."

"Chekhov is Chekhov, no? Besides, the play they want to put on is *Platonov*, it's too tempting."

"*Platonov*? I haven't heard of it."

"It's his first theater play. Some anthologies don't include it, they say that Chekhov disowned it. Truth be told, some even argue that it is not quite finished."

"Do you have complete freedom to direct it however you want?"

"Yes and no. I have to turn the four acts of the original into one. The company wants to do something new... I'll have a space for rehearsals, an apartment on Aldamar Street... They'll give me everything I need. The only obstacle is my father."

"Your father? Is he the money man?"

"He contributes the money and the director's name. Would you believe it? Trapped in the spiderweb again. He also wants me to include an old friend of his from his stamp collectors' club in the cast... Ever since he's been sick, I submit to all his blackmail."

"It doesn't seem such a high price to pay. We'd see each other more often. Why would you let an opportunity like that pass?"

"I thought you'd be more disappointed by my failure. Look at Gloria, the anarchist, the alternative artist, eating out of her Francoist father's hand, directing little projects for the Victoria Eugenia Theater, on commission..."

"Don't punish yourself so much: you always do that. You're your own judge and executioner."

"Aren't we all?"

"Maybe so."

"If I decide to accept... The translation is really bad... I would be so happy if you wrote a new one."

"Don't ask me that, Gloria."

"Please... where else am I going to find someone who speaks Russian?"

"I've lost the habit, it's been years since..."

"Tell me you'll take a couple of days to think about it. Read the play at least…I brought a copy for you…"

"Okay, but don't get your hopes up."

"You'll have to come to the premiere, to make sure I don't hang myself from the ropes of the fly system."

"I hate theater auditoriums."

"But you love me. You'll sacrifice your feelings for me, won't you?"

"Diego Lazkano?"

"Who is this?"

"I have something that might interest you."

"Who am I talking to?"

"Let's say that I'm calling for Javier Fontecha?"

"Fontecha?"

"He wants to meet up with you."

"I'm sorry, but I'm in Barcelona."

"As chance would have it, so is he."

A shiver went up Diego Lazkano's back: they were shadowing him.

"Make a note of the address."

It's a hotel lobby. Noisy and full of tourists. They have to speak into each other's ears. Maybe it's because they want to avoid microphones.

"It's very simple: don't declare in the court case and the folder is yours."

Lots of things come into his mind at the same time: the Toad, his daughter Cristina, Idoia, Ana . . . It's strange, but this time Soto and Zeberio are not as prominent.

"You engaged in state terrorism."

Fontecha stays silent. Diego has never heard a louder "yes." He doesn't feel any pleasure, however. Only pity and disgust. He doesn't feel compassion, but almost.

"Let's be done with this once and for all."

"You admitted it. You're guilty."

"And what if I did admit it? The present absolves us. Sometimes we do things, things that the future makes you guilty of. It's not always fair, if you think about it."

"You don't have to excuse yourself with me. The courts will have their say, unless you've bought them off in advance, of course."

"Do you mean to say that you won't agree to the deal? You're no angel, Lazkano . . . You passed as your own works that belonged to someone else . . . Do you think that you can redeem your guilt by making us the guilty party?"

"Did you bring it?"

"The folder? Only when the court case is over."

"You're irrelevant, Fontecha. You're pathetic. Don't you

realize? You've nothing left to do...Your own party has abandoned you...I don't know what I'm doing here with you. Nothing can bring back the dead. You can't give back my friends that you killed."

"Not your friends, no."

"What then?"

"What, or who...?"

"I've nothing to say to you."

"Are you familiar with the name Santos Herguera?"

Diego Lazkano reacts defensively. A stage and a set of actors he didn't expect to see emerge before his eyes.

"Your father's friend. His trusted doctor."

"What does Herguera have to do with any of this?"

Little by little, Fontecha ceases to be a cardboard cutout. He speaks very slowly, as if he were giving the most important press conference of his life.

"There are people like this in all professions, Lazkano. People who are dark and perverse, good at going through the garbage, always ready to carry out all sorts of favors. That friend of your father's, that Herguera, is one of the witnesses who'll testify in Rodrigo Mesa's defense."

Lazkano is speechless.

"What a strange world, don't you think? He will declare that the state the bones were in when they were found precludes anyone from establishing whether they were tortured or not; warn your attorney so that he takes it into account. They are flying Herguera in from Dallas, a researcher brought in from abroad always looks good...He owes favors to the party, apparently; don't ask me, I don't know why. Something to do with the children who disappeared during Franco's dictatorship, who knows, maybe they're only rumors. Fake death certificates, I don't know what, exactly..."

"What are you trying to tell me, that I'm one of those stolen children?"

"No, that's not it, Lazkano. Think for a moment. It wasn't you who was stolen. Rather, they stole someone from you. How long has it been since you last saw your father?"

"My father died as a consequence of dementia."

"Are you sure?"

Fontecha hands him an envelope.

"I'm not going to negotiate this, Lazkano. The case must continue, it's all in the hands of God now...I'm tired of hiding things too. I want to know what it feels like to remove the mask, even though I know perfectly well that what's underneath is just more masks."

Diego opens the envelope. There's a report about Gabriel Lazkano. Some black-and-white photos, quite overexposed, of a man watering a garden: he wears a hat in all of them, and sweats as if he'd never fully acclimatized to the place. If this man was really his father, Diego would end up looking like him in twenty-five years' time.

"We have done a lot of research, as you can see. We've researched you and everyone around you."

"It's impossible..."

"He hasn't changed very much, has he?"

"Who's...? Where did you get these photos?"

"He's in Mexico."

"That's not true..."

"Go for a visit, if you want: everything is there in the report. I know that I am not paying any debts off with this, but at least it'll show you that things aren't always what they seem. If you want the folder back, you know what you must *not* do."

SUBMERGED WORLDS

PUBLIC TRANSPORT DOESN'T REACH THERE, at least not at this time of year. Maybe during the summer season, but that's still a long way away. "Are you sure you wouldn't like to rent a car?" For the umpteenth time: no. Instead, he boards a bus at the airport in Puerto Vallarta, and then another to continue on his route. Having completely lost all sense of time, he sleeps in Mismaloya, unable to separate the hours he spends in dreams from the hours he spends awake; his periods of sleep mix with his periods of wakefulness, turning into one viscous, febrile paste. He blames the weather. They tell him that it's six kilometers away, although he'd swear that they left Banderas Bay behind more than forty kilometers ago, if what the taximeter says is anything to go by. John Huston made a film there. "Are you here because of *The Night of the Iguana*?" they ask. He asks the taxi driver to drop him off at a circle, "the closest circle to the beach," he specifies, although in the end he drops him off in one of the circles above the beach. He has to walk all the way down to the sand, and can't help thinking how sweaty he's going to be climbing up that steep hill on the way back. It looks like they hollowed out part of the rock some time ago so that the road could reach all the way down, the carved wall is flat and almost red, like sliced beef. There are steps that lead to the beach too. It's the first time he's going to see the Pacific Ocean properly, and for a moment it seems to him that he's gone down the wrong path, because the steps are not exactly steps: they're more like small stands that no one uses, covered in weeds and stubble. People probably reached the beach by car or motorbike. Or maybe they just don't go there at all, there must be thousands of spots like that one all through the coastline. He thinks he sees a miniature replica of an Aztec tomb covered in brambles in a corner of the stands. Aztecs, here? An amphitheater? He must admit that he has no idea. But later on he sees a small hole and the penny drops: nothing to do with the Aztecs, the place is an abandoned minigolf course, with its little ramps and tiny arches, a minigolf course made out of minilabyrinths that the golf ball can easily negotiate. A failed tourist resort, he guesses, built who knows when or why. "The closest house to the beach," they told him, and he's chosen two or three intuitively.

"Güero Juan? Señor Bicho lives right over there as you come into the beach."

Señor Bicho. Mr. Bug. The Bug Outer. The Bug Offer. Sir Insect. Mr. Infect. It's surprising how appropriate some nicknames can be, Lazkano thinks, amazed. He scrutinizes the cute little gardens made of cacti and pebbles, as if rocks and vegetation could give away the clues that revealed the hideout of evil Mr. Bug.

A green lawn tended to with care, with more dedication than

the others surrounding it. Reeds in front of windows to shield the house from the world outside. A perfect refuge that doesn't look like a fortress. A man wearing a straw hat, shorts, and flip-flops waters a rosebush. As he focuses on the whitewashed wall, Diego notices a gigantic fly stuck to it, red eyed and with parallel blue and black stripes running down its back, the same colors as the jersey of Turin's Juventus team. *Even flies are more elegant here,* he thinks.

A visual ability test: Would you be able to recognize your father from the back and from his way of tending the garden? Although many years have passed since he last saw him, it doesn't take Diego long to recognize him, because of the mechanical way in which he shakes the hose, as if he were a human sprinkler. He used to spread weed killer on the vegetable patch like that, when he was still just a kid.

He takes his time observing his father. There are several chairs upside down on a table on the patio: he's about to sand them down. The scratching sound of sandpaper on wood is almost hypnotic. Diego is moved when he notices that his father has kept his old ability for DIY intact. As if he'd forgotten to water something, he puts aside the sandpaper and returns to the hose.

Diego Lazkano is suddenly overwhelmed by an irrational impulse to turn around and flee.

But to disappear, that would be unexcusable. He wouldn't be able to forgive himself. *No, I am not like my father.*

Lazkano thinks of the people they disappeared. He held those disappeared in his memory for many long years: every dawn, every dusk, when he slept with a woman, when he wrote, when he dreamed, they were always there; it was the disappeared who interrupted his working days, his days off, his Sunday rest; they appeared unannounced as he reached peak orgasm, during his masturbatory sessions, in any corner, everywhere, whenever he debated with himself while trying to pick a bottle from the supermarket shelves. He couldn't afford to disappear like that, of his own volition, just because. How could he do something like that? Soto and Zeberio, his two disappeared, tormented him enough as it was, and his father later on, him too, after he left without a trace, not an inevitable disappearance as he now knows, not because of senile dementia as he made them all believe, but in spite of his family and without a speck of a care for the hurt and abandonment he would be inflicting on them, breaking all ties to evaporate, to vanish from their lives and start again. It was monstrous behavior.

What should he call his father? Should he approach with a plain "Good afternoon, *aita*", as if nothing had happened? Which name or nickname, which polite form of address should he use?

Mr. Bug? Güero Juan?

No, nothing like that.

The green hose's flow is interrupted, although at no point does Diego notice his father closing the water tap.

Up until the last moment, he doesn't know what words will be coming out of his mouth.

"It's true, then."

His father takes a moment before turning around. The time he needs to compose his face into an expression of fake surprise? Maybe he's been waiting for that visit since day one. More than waiting for it, secretly wishing for it. There is no greater fear for a fugitive than the fear of never being looked for, the fear of never ever being chased after, or found.

"Diego...!"

Diego wants to appear inexpressive, indifferent, reproach him coldly, severely, and although it takes a superhuman effort to overcome his fury, he does it. His father doesn't make a gesture to approach. He's still holding the hose in his hand, five or six meters of lawn separate them. Diego is surprised not to see a dog.

"I should finish you right here, in your paradisiacal lawn."

"I would deserve that, I don't deny it."

"How could you do what you did?"

"Sit down, please, I beg you, let me look at you... You still look so young... Would you like something to drink? How is Josune?"

Diego hadn't noticed the name of the house until that moment: Casa Morel.

"Do you know why I chose this house? Because of Bioy Casares's book, *La invención de Morel*."

"Do you honestly think I've come here to talk to you about literature?"

"*What else is there in life?* I read you said that in an interview I saw online a long time ago... It was something like that, more or less."

"Is this some sort of joke?"

"Life is an infinite joke."

"I'm not in the mood for jokes."

"Whatever you say..."

"Couldn't you've gone about it some other way?"

"I thought my way of going about it was quite... original."

"Original? Is that really the best way of describing what you did?"

"You tell me, you're the writer."

"*Ama*, Josune, me... Do you think we're characters in some cheap novel?"

"I'll give the novel mention a pass, because I know how important fiction is for you. But I can't forgive that cheap comment. Where do you think your vocation to write comes from?"

"Not from you. You're clearly more of an actor. You're an impostor, a fraud. And a son of a bitch."

"Hold it there, Diego: I'm still your father, I didn't raise you to speak like that. The key here is that we both carry storytelling in the blood."

"How could you...? You..."

"I felt miserable, I led a bland life, an insubstantial life, I wanted to start over, and for your mother to have a new life too."

"So it was an act of generosity? Is that it?"

"Depending on how you look at it, yes, you could say that. Being selfish is a way of being generous with oneself. And I want to think that in this case I wasn't just generous with myself, but with others too."

"There's such a thing as divorce!"

"Paperwork, courthouses, drama, vaudeville...Divorce is a sticky thing, Diego: it looks like you're starting over, but the stickiness of the issue follows you around. I wanted something more drastic."

"Drama and vaudeville? Paperwork? Courthouses? You didn't save us from any of that! Do you want to hear stories about paperwork? How many petitions do you think we filled in? How many visits do you think we made to the morgue, to hospitals? Do you know you're legally dead...?"

"That was my intention."

"Have you ever considered how much you made our mother suffer?"

"She might have suffered, but she also felt relief, admit it. I'm certain that she is happier now. I made sure to follow up on her, my conscience wouldn't leave me in peace otherwise. Her relief is also my own."

"Relief? She's got cancer…Not to mention the years she's been high on Valium…"

"I'm sorry to hear that."

"You've thoroughly lost your mind if you really think that dementia is a lesser drama than divorce."

"You won't deny that it's more definite: believe me, it's possible to start anew. I've done it."

"That woman Angeles, from Eivissa, was she real? Was any of that true?"

"Think like a true writer, Diego: her name was Angeles but she wasn't from Eivissa, but from Formentera. That story only lasted so long, afterward I came to Mexico on my own. We depart from the truth, but only so much. If we departed too much, we'd be found out, and if we didn't depart enough, the same. We must find the right, the perfect, measure. Poe's 'The Purloined Letter' is a good example."

"*No me jodas,* you fucker; what, you do creative writing workshops now?"

"I imagine they must have told you everything in town: I still work as an exterminator. But yes, you'd be surprised to see what a voracious reader I have become…By the way, you haven't published anything in a long time…"

"Is that what concerns you? Must I believe that you keep a library back there, one that includes my books? You're pathetic: all we need now is for you to ask me to sign your copies."

"I was going to."

"And to whom should I address the dedication, according to you?"

"What do you think of 'to my old friend?'"

"'To my old motherfucker' would be closer to the truth."

"Whatever you say, I have no intention of arguing. I'll agree with you on everything and afterward you'll leave me alone."

"Do you really think you're in a position to impose your deal and your conditions?"

"It was only a proposal. I'm willing to hear yours."

"And your wife, where is she?"

"What makes you think I have one?"

Gabriel Lazkano noticed quickly. Some women's clothes were hanging out to dry next to a rosebush. A minuscule bikini, brightly colored. It'd look ridiculous on anyone beyond their forties.

"Do you really want to meet her?"

"Is she the one in the photograph?"

"The woman in the photograph was a flight attendant I met in Amsterdam. Angeles, I told you about her... Tight skirt, beautiful legs. A one-night whim. She stayed in Formentera... You're losing the plot, my son, it's understandable, not everyone can withstand this heat."

"I should strangle you with my own hands. Asphyxiate you. It would be easy."

"Why would you do that? Think about it: you can kill me

or reveal the truth. Will that make your mother suffer less? Will Josune suffer less? You? Will you suffer less? Who wants to know the truth, Diego? Truth is ugly... Live your life and relish the fact that you have fewer chances than you thought of developing dementia thirty years hence..."

"Dr. Herguera...?"

"He owed me a favor. It's always good to have friends who owe you things. Be honest with me: aren't you happy for your old man? Margaritas and tequila, torrents of sunshine... Even though I still do things that aren't common for a man my age, time moves very slowly here. People will call anything retirement: I wanted a true and thorough retirement."

"'I came to the wrong place, Diego; I was *convinced* that the books were parcels that I needed to post... that pantomime in the post office, looking like a beaten-down dog... you lied to me.'"

"I played the part."

"All those things you said to our mother, how could you be so vile?"

"Admit it: deep down you liked my being so sincere, so uninhibited, so horny, a perfect satyr... I've even read some of my lines in your books: 'When will you let me come all over your tits, Angelines?'"

Diego Lazkano clenches his fist and, after regressing many years to gather momentum, punches his father on the nose. His father falls like a sack, landing on the garden table, which breaks under his weight. His nose starts to bleed.

"Damn it! You broke my nose…"

"What are you complaining about? That way no one will be able to identify you."

"All right, little fellow, I probably deserved that… Now, go. That's the deal."

"I'm going to report you."

"You won't do that…"

"I'm going to the police."

"You won't dare."

"Really? I'm going to go to the police, to the courthouse if necessary, I won't stop until you're destroyed."

"You won't do that: you've never been keen on the police. Are you going to change your dealings with them now? Isn't it a bit… late? That would be a radical change indeed, son, way beyond starting anew. Besides, what police are you talking about, Diego? If the Mexican police is what you have in mind, you're crazier than I thought…"

Diego feels dizzy. He leans on and then sits on the only varnished chair, before his father is able to warn him. He's literally stuck to it.

"I've discovered scuba diving here in Mexico. You should try it sometime. It's a relief to know that no one is going to ask me to exterminate any of the creatures down there… I experience things with another temperament under the water, son, I have found another life. It helps to be in a place where no one owes you anything. A place where you owe no one nothing."

Diego Lazkano remembers the reservoir. How they went through it inch by inch, in vain. How they weren't able to find Soto and Zeberio's bodies there, or his father's. And then he remembers the Toad, the attorney, his daughter, Cristina. "Let's submerge ourselves in subjectivity, let's dive into it."

"Things look different under the surface, even your own reflection. You have no idea how calming it is to be able to dive among the corals, to marvel at the undulating glide of the manta ray; everything is more harmonious under the water, there's hardly any speed, it's life in slow motion, a means of stretching life out...I used to close my eyes whenever I went swimming, I used to prefer not knowing what was down there. Until I opened my eyes and discovered a new world. You should try it."

"You've told me that before. You're repeating yourself...Are you sure you don't suffer dementia after all?"

Gabriel Lazkano doesn't take that comment well at all. Diego tries to take advantage of that moment of weakness in his father to move the conversation in a direction of his choosing, but the old man is faster than him.

"It would be ironic, wouldn't it? First you interpret the role, and after years it becomes your reality. It happens sometimes, in this life."

He is not mistaken, but Diego is unwilling to acknowledge that his father is right about anything.

"When that day comes I'll go into the sea and never come out. It's much more agreeable to contemplate the void in the sandbanks at the bottom of the sea than to look at anything outside the water. Marine vegetation...those gigantic ladybushes that break through the sand...with the years we end up finding sex where there isn't any, in food, in drink; sights and smells become substitutes to action...there is a lot of that under the water, believe me."

The Toad and his theory about cold showers come to Lazkano's mind. They would get on well, his father and the Toad, for as long as Mr. Bug didn't exterminate him, of course: toads can be pests, and not marine pests, precisely.

Mr. Bug. The Bug Outer. The Bug Offer. Sir Insect. Mr. Infect.

"Your new life. Should I admire you for what you have achieved?"

"I've worked hard, son. New beginnings have their disadvantages: I haven't been able to cash my pension. I've had to continue with the business: all sorts of plagues, the owners of these homes don't like to wake up with ants. They don't know that they're fighting them in vain, those poor fools don't realize that ants aren't the intruders in our homes: we are the intruders in theirs. These cliffs belonged to the seagulls and the albatross, until speculators came to cash in. And despite everything, that unease toward all living things has been tremendously beneficial for me. The Danes, the Germans, the Dutch...they are most generous with their tips. The Americans, which is what you usually find here, not so much."

"You've continued killing bugs, following your true vocation."

"I wouldn't call it a vocation, it's not the same as yours. But it's true, when you are competent in a field, whether it's due to vocation or not, you end up being fond of your routine: rodents, insects, microorganisms, *Psychoda alternata*, mold, *Mus musculus*, *Blatta orientali*s, *Hofmannophilia pseudosprettella*...Brown mice *Rattus rattus* or *Rattus norvegicus*...the cockroach *Blattella germanica*, *Ctenocephalides canis*...Latin always adds a little something, it looks good on the leaflets...*Periplaneta americana*, *Musca domestica*, *Lasius niger*...I sound like an Oxford professor when I say them all in a row, don't you think?"

Non bis in idem. Diego fucking hates Latin. They could definitely be good friends, his father and the Toad.

"What does this or that name matter, you may say, they're only bugs after all...But the truth is that to read them all in a row really soothes my clients, especially if next to each Latin name of the species you tick the little boxes that mark whether the infestation is severe or mild, that, of the whole list of potential threats

to their homesteads, only one or two need to be combated...
that the incidence is two on a scale of one to five, that they are
relatively safe..."

"That's how you made a living, that's how you were able to
buy this house."

"I had to start from nothing, kill lots of bugs to build it. How
many dispatched bugs for each of these bricks..."

"Us among them."

"Don't be so melodramatic."

"It's the truth."

"I always kept track of you, I read your books, I bought them
over the Internet, they were posted to me. I bet that the trail that
left through the post office has something to do with you having
located me. It's ironic, given that all of this started in a post office,
with a bunch of books..."

"I came to the wrong place, Diego; I was *convinced* that the
books were parcels that I needed to post." Diego's face is expres-
sionless. "Let's submerge ourselves in subjectivity, let's dive
into it."

"My son's trajectory never ceased to surprise me, your chosen path; your mother and I would have never imagined that...I
don't know...I would have liked to show you mine too: explain
things to you that I've never been able to tell you all these years,
our relationship with the Institute of Toxicology, for example,
how methods of extermination have changed, the way in which

we approach preventive inspections, how we combat infestations through chemical, biological, mechanical, or passive measures, how the first step consists of differentiating the inside of a house from the outside ... Ants, for example, are very stubborn ..."

Why the sudden insistence on ants? Did his father remember that strange phone call of his all those years ago, perhaps?

One of the bad holes. Best to fumigate. Your friend's house. Quite a big nest.

No, no way, it was impossible. But Diego stood on guard, as if his father really knew how much and why he hated ants so much. But no, it was just his paranoia, his father couldn't know anything. The ants, the engineer. How he was in charge of the *zulo*, how all his work guarding that place ended up being completely useless. Or maybe not. Maybe not completely.

There's something disconcerting, a kind of sadness that open chasms in the rock causes him to feel, the resin of the varnish that's stuck to his clothes, something that stops him from leaving that place. He had found his father and his father was safe and sound, but he was incapable of forgiving him. Should he? Was he being too mean to him? No, what his father had done to them was unspeakable. To escape to start over was in itself unforgivable, but to feign a degenerative illness showed an unmatched degree of cruelty. His mother, his sister, and he were not fictional characters, but they had been treated as such.

"Would you like me to walk you to the village?"

His father makes one last attempt, in vain. Diego Lazkano walks without saying a word, and only takes out his cell phone to order a taxi when he's certain to be out of his father's field of vision.

That was the last time he saw his father. He exterminated him from his life, in the same way his father had exterminated them.

Ghosts should be left alone, even when they are living ghosts; he knew that, year after year, the more he resembled his father physically, the more he would try to guess what he might look like and where he might be, that he'd be curious to know what that portrait of a submarine Dorian Gray hidden in a wardrobe might look like, precisely because he was deprived of the mirror that could provide him with an advance view of his own decline.

Lazkano was trapped. His hands were tied. Either he accepted Fontecha's deal, or he allowed the matter of the folder to come to light, sacrificing his whole career in exchange for one last attempt at justice in a case in which the chances of implicating Fontecha and his superiors were, let's face it, rather slim. He'd been held in El Cerro, true. He had been tortured, true. Soto and Zeberio's murderers had been there, true. But he didn't really have any specific proof against Fontecha. Even though he had threatened his father with the courts, old man Lazkano was right, he would never do it; as a matter of fact, he never did declare in the Soto and Zeberio case. He left Agirre Sesma and his daughter in the lurch, forced to embarrassingly remove one of the witnesses for the prosecution at the last minute. Fontecha came out of the process unscathed, by the skin of his teeth: his subordinates, not so much. The Toad did a great job, he got far, even without him. Would the result have been any different if Diego had testified? He would never know. Cowardice is stronger than us: we choose to maintain our miserly plot of land, even when the price to pay is the betrayal of an incorruptible attorney like Agirre Sesma and his beautiful daughter, Cristina. We are guardians of repetition, we push for everything to remain the same, even when we switch homes for a while, even when we spend a few days in a hotel, we transplant our habits, our ways, our patterns of territorial distribution, reconstructing our *original* bedside table with little mementos – accessories, little jars, watches. And just like we replicate and reconstruct with objects, so we reconstruct our essential misery. We are all crazy, and the omniscient narrator that looms over our craziness, that narrator who inhabits our minds, knows that very well. We almost always make the myopic choice that preserves a reasonable degree of misery, that covers up our shame and sustains the nonsense of our daily doings. Diego remembered Faulkner's quote: "But I ain't so sho that ere a man has the right to say what is crazy and what ain't. It's like there was a fellow in every man that's done a-past the sanity or the insanity, that watches the sane and the insane doings of that man with the same horror and the same astonishment."

Lazkano felt his world crumble, he remembered his father, that man he hated so much, that fraudster, the enormous dimension of his cruelty, and the way he'd punched him on the nose in Casa Morel, where do you think your vocation to write comes from? How could he not have noticed it before? How could he have been so blind? Why did he replicate his father's behavior in his own way, appropriating what was someone else's, turning into a usurper, perpetuating the same mindset he reproached his father for, if not something even worse? A terrible shiver ran down his spine as he imagined the satisfied cackle with which his father would rejoice if he found out his real story. What better reproach to indulge in than that salmon-pink-colored folder that rose and swam against the current? "You are like me, I can be proud of you," he would say, raising his margarita to the heavens, like a transparent hot-air balloon, among noisy seagulls, Peruvian boobies and albatross, in his inscrutable refuge among the rocks, in his hideout under the sun.

Lazkano felt his world collapse, felt such impotence and anger at the realization that his DNA knew more about him than he did. That's what it was all about then. There was nothing else: to live, consciously or unconsciously, a life that was a carbon copy of someone else's sketch, a true or a false life, whatever you want to call it; we are but borrowed skins, everything was in vain, we thought we fooled everyone when in truth we only managed to fool ourselves.

When all that was over – although it looked like all that would never end – Diego would only have one path left: to start writing, once and for all, from his own skin, to tell the story of how he met Soto and Zeberio, to write everything that happened in the time they shared together and everything that happened in the time they *weren't able* to share. Exhume their bodies with a fountain pen. Sculpt their profiles. Try to go deep into the dark jungle. Recompose the thread of his mental jungle. Reconstruct all that on paper. Leave his skin in the endeavor. Every inch of his skin. Tell all. Get malodorously naked. Gobble himself up and leave nothing but a snake's shed skin behind. Don't hide any infamies. Write that book and heal. Some people call that redemption, as if using one word or another mattered.

You are right: it matters.

Lazkano wanted to tell the truth, he was eager to start finding his own skin. To write, as soon as possible, the first few lines of a story only he could tell; as soon as possible, that very night preferably. But, having arrived at this point, he could well wait one more night: the truth is he was going to have to wait a little, given that the theater play Gloria was directing premiered that night, and he couldn't miss that, even if he could only turn up in a precarious, borrowed skin.

Lazkano didn't know *Platonov*, but the play hooked him from the start. Although it wasn't as famous as *The Seagull*, *Uncle*

– 419 –

Vanya, *Three Sisters*, or *The Cherry Orchard*, Diego liked it better than all of them, more so when he found out that Anton Chekhov was barely twenty years old when he wrote it. Just twenty years old, and all the obsessions and concerns of the great Russian writer were already there: his bitter humor, indebted families forced to leave their lands and mansions, passionate, thrilling characters led to perdition by fate and alcohol, lucid dialogues that would drive any wretched fellow human being to self-destruct, a heartless dissection of the human condition... Pathetic gentlemen who would challenge each other to a duel only to cry like children immediately afterward, promises to lovers to run away together that never ended well, criminals scorned by feudal lords who end up becoming customers of their criminal handymen...he was a great master, Chekhov. A huge crook, Chekhov. A damned bastard, Anton. A monstrous genius like him made any writer feel tiny in comparison to him. He was only twenty years old when he wrote that, a similar age to Soto and Zeberio when they made them disappear. Some similarities can kill: Chekhov died of tuberculosis at the age of forty-four, an age Lazkano had already surpassed. *Platonov* was a very long play, were it to be performed in its totality, it would last five or six hours, he was sure that Gloria was going to shorten it a lot, not even the most fervent theater fan would be willing to suffer in silence through such a lengthy theatrical tour de force.

The main character in the play was the schoolmaster Mikhail Vasilievich Platonov. It was clearly a version of *Don Juan*. Charmed by his attentive words, each and every one of the women who appear on the stage, be them married, teenagers, or widowed, eat out of his hand. Platonov doesn't hide his seductive character, and he warns the women at his feet that they will be unhappy by his side, that he is a married man, that he will use them and then abandon them, but they care little for any of this, they love the schoolmaster all the same. Platonov describes another one of the characters in the play like this: "The hero of the most contemporary of novels. Unfortunately, that novel hasn't been written yet."

There was another detail that made Diego feel close to the play. When he wrote it – Anton Chekhov didn't even bother to give it a title – the brother of the great Russian playwright sent the play to Maria Yrmolova, the famous actress. She, as was to be expected, didn't even take it into consideration. And Chekhov destroyed the manuscript with great sorrow. They found a hand-written first draft after his death. This was, precisely, the original he used to develop the copy that he then destroyed…Once again, salmon-pink folders, salmon that swam against currents, manuscripts that came to the surface. The blessed damned copies. It was like his own story, one hundred years ago.

The phone rang. It was Gloria.

"What did you think?"

"You didn't tell me that it was a version of *Don Juan*."

"Why do you say that? Did you identify with Platonov, or what?"

"Not at all, but I must admit that every now and then I gave your face to the female protagonist Anna Petrovna: 'In this world one mustn't trust one's enemies, and apparently one's friends either...'"

"I prefer this line from Anna: 'As long as there are intelligent people who want to grow increasingly intelligent, the rest will come on its own.'"

"You should play Anna yourself."

"Not in a million years: Sara Fernandez said yes to playing the part. All I need is for you to tell me that you'll do the translation... will you?"

"I can try."

"Diego! It makes me so happy to hear that!"

The translation wasn't too complicated. Oral register, but with the marked reflective tone of speech typical of the turn of the twentieth century. Chekhov's writing wasn't at all rhetorical. There was little overflow in his texts. Lazkano had to admit that he was enjoying that occupation, for the first time in a long time he felt a certain lightness in abandoning creation to undertake translation, in the process of searching for a voice. What he'd told Gloria wasn't completely true: he did identify with Platonov every now and then, and not exactly because of his Don Juanism, but because of his fatalistic approach to life. Platonov wasn't the only tormented character in the play, not at all, the play was brimming with them. As a matter of fact, the script oozed fatalism through every pore, why deny it. He underlined a lot of passages as he undertook their translation:

GLAGOLIEV: *We loved women like the most faithful gentlemen, we had faith in them, we adored them, because in them we saw the best of human nature…Because women are a better kind of human, Sergei Pavlovich! We also had friends… In my day, friendship didn't seem as naïve or useless. In my day, we had salons, meetings…Back then we would jump into the fire for our friends.*

VOINITZEV *(yawning): Those were the good old days!*

GLAGOLIEV: *In our time, we weren't ashamed of tears and no one laughed at them…We were happier than you are now. In our time, people who understood music would never leave the theater, they would stay until the end…*

Lazkano is particularly struck by the way in which Platonov self-flagellates, his absolute lack of self-pity, his profound awareness of his own process of self-destruction, and his lack of willpower to do anything about it. He perceives himself as a harmful person, but never displays the tiniest attempt to straighten up his toxic personality: "Gentlemen, I am afraid that my friendship is certain to bring you tears too. Let us drink to the happy resolution of all friendships, ours included! May its ending be as pleasant and deliberate as its beginning."

Almost nothing is hidden. The husbands of the women Platonov has taken as lovers are all aware of the facts. The criminal Ossip is presented to us without reservations too: "Known to anyone and everyone as Ossip, horse thief, parasite and murderer and assailant." Platonov's perception of Russia and the Russians is pretty priceless too: "To be a pig and not want to acknowledge such a thing is an awful peculiarity of the Russian crook," he maintains.

Lazkano gets up to make some coffee. Afterward he irons a couple of shirts and leaves the translation for the following day. Typical, that morose postponement of work for the following day. This is what Platonov declared to the young Sofia Egorovna, the lover who at the end of the play shoots him with a revolver and ends up killing him.

> PLATONOV: *Don't you recognize me, Sofia Egorovna? I'm not surprised. Four and a half years have passed, almost five, and not even rats would have been able to gnaw at a human figure more thoroughly than the past five years of my life have gnawed at me...*
>
> SOFIA EGOROVNA: *It's too old and too banal a story for us to waste any time talking about it so much, or award it an importance it doesn't deserve... Besides, it's not about that... But when you speak of the past, sir... you speak as if you*

were asking for something, as if before, in the past, you hadn't
received what you deserved and you wanted to receive it now…

Lazkano thinks of the women in his life: Idoia, Ana, Lena, Gloria herself… How passion drove them to embrace. How tiredness drove them to embrace each other's tiredness in order to be able to remain standing.

Those kinds of books exist. Books that arrive at the perfect time, grab us by the scruff of the neck and shake us hard. We go waist deep into their lines, they swallow us. That was exactly what happened to Lazkano with *Platonov*. He felt that all those characters spoke about his life, something that hadn't happened to him in years.

> *TRILETZKI: If only you could see the article I whipped up for the Russian Messenger, gentlemen! Have you read it? Did you read it, Abram Abramich?*
>
> *VENGEROVICH: Yes, I read it. Only, you didn't write that article yourself, Doctor, but Porfiri Seminovich.*
>
> *GLAGOLIEV: How do you know that?*
>
> *VENGEROVICH: I know it.*
>
> *GLAGOLIEV: How curious. I did write it, it's true. But how did you know?*
>
> *VENGEROVICH: Everything can be known, it's a matter of finding out things.*

"It is sometimes the case, my friend, that one feels the need to hate somebody, to bury one's teeth in somebody, that one seeks someone to take revenge on for some bastardly thing that's happened..."

It was all there, the turbid issue of his plagiarism, his middle-age crisis, the evidence that such crises offer no other consolation but the option to become contemplative beings.

> *PLATONOV: Is it possible that it's time for me to be content to just contemplate memories? Memories are good but...is it possible that this is the end for me? My God! My God! It'd be better to die... We must live... We must keep living...I'm still young...*

As Lazkano translated Platonov's tragic monologues, he couldn't help putting Chekhov's face on the schoolmaster's character, only to, given that it was all about getting under the skin of another fellow human, replace Chekhov's face with his own as he advanced in the translation. When did narrators manifest with their own voice, and when with the voice of the author? Authors were at their best when they managed to get under the Devil's skin, to be abducted by Him – or, even better, to abduct Him themselves. Lazkano knew this well, but interferences were inevitable, and as the days passed and he travailed over the translated paragraphs, the sensation that he'd been magnetized by Platonov settled in him, the feeling that he'd totally fallen under the spell of his influence, also because he kept hearing Gloria's own voice in his head every time he translated Anna Petrovna's speeches.

> PLATONOV: *Because I feel a deep appreciation for you. And I appreciate that appreciation for you in me, to the point that I would rather be under the earth than deprive myself of it. My dear friend, I am a free man, I have nothing against an agreeable pastime, I am not an enemy of relationships, not even an enemy of noble beds, but . . . to have a little adventure with you, to transform you into the object of my idle digressions, you, such a marvelous, intelligent, free woman. No! That's too much. I'd rather you'd vanquish me to the antipodes. To be together for a month or two and then . . . depart, ashamed? Let's forget this conversation . . . Let's be friends, but let's not play with one another: we're worth a lot more than that!*

Those words that Platonov said to Anna Petrovna, those half-truths, cheap excuses disguised as principles, but also as cowardice and lack of courage, how often had such words been repeated on the face of the earth, before and after Chekhov's death, in the past hundred years?

Lazkano spent weeks absorbed by *Platonov*, without the strength or the disposition for anything other than that theater play, disheveled, unshaven, sleep-deprived, lacking the impetus to even change the sheets. When the acrid smell of sweat that had taken over his bed became unbearable, he started to rest on the sofa. It wasn't only Platonov, all the characters in that play had entered his home, including the villain Ossip and his evil deeds; such irony, the living room of the man who never set foot in a theater was now filled with undesirable guests; Diego had become some sort of Pirandello; perhaps it wasn't the stench of sweat that made his bed unbearable, but the fact that it was Platonov who slept there.

PLATONOV: *When people remind us even a little of our impure past, how disgusting those people seem!*

ANNA PETROVNA: *I want to have my life already, and not in the future...*

PLATONOV: *How beautiful you are! But I wouldn't bring you happiness. I would do with you what I've done with every woman who throws herself at my feet... make you miserable!*

ANNA PETROVNA: *You have an exaggerated sense of yourself. Are you really so terrible, Don Juan?*

PLATONOV: *I know myself. The novels in which I appear never end well...*

ANNA PETROVNA: *What else do you want? Smoke me like a cigarette, squeeze me like a lemon, break me into bits... Be a man! Something about you is so off!*

The Bug Outer. The Bug Offer. Sir Insect. Mr. Infect.

And later on, through Ossip's mouth: "I'll strangle him... don't be afraid."

For a time in his life, in Lille, Diego Lazkano sank into drinking. He wanted to forget Soto and Zeberio, forget his confession, the torture he suffered, the folder he contemplated from the corner of his eye like a "souvenir without nostalgia," feeling its elastic bands and caressing them without daring to open it, like a man afraid to get his lover naked. He wanted to banish his dreams and ambitions from his mind, he lived like a zombie. In secondhand bookshops, he'd sell the books he'd lovingly collected over the years in exchange for a pittance, and then he drank his own books, each day he drank one, some days as many as two. *I'm drinking* The Odyssey, *the small change they gave me for it is disappearing down my throat*, he'd tell himself, *look how little I got for the paperback edition of Martin Amis's* Money. He exchanged literature for alcohol, *Robinson Crusoe* became a bottle of Baileys, *The Brothers Karamazov* a bottle of Smirnoff vodka, the three gin and tonics he'd just ingested were *The Life and Adventures of Lazarillo de Tormes*. He got his hands on an expensive bottle of Lagavulin whisky in exchange for the leather-bound copy of James Joyce's *Ulysses* that Ana had given him as a gift; if, on a given day, he sold Montaigne's essays for next to nothing, he would buy himself a Bordeaux red, trying to be coherent with what he drank; if he got rid of Madame

Bovary, he had to try to find a potion similar to something Flaubert might have ingested, to be able to emulate him; in exchange for Italo Calvino's *Our Ancestors* he'd get a Chianti or a bottle of *pelaverga* from Saluzzo, maybe. *Who ever said that literature doesn't feed us, that it doesn't comfort our spirit or our soul?* Diego Lazkano hardly ate around that time. His companion, Lena, the girl from Kursk, got frightened when she saw him on the verge of delirium tremens, and Diego had to confess to her that he saw news bulletins inside his head incessantly, news bulletins that had beginnings but no endings; he saw wars among guerrillas, Kennedy and Nixon, Margaret Thatcher and Mitterrand, not necessarily in their corresponding roles. He might see Mitterrand with a kamikaze bandanna wrapped around his forehead, holding an AK-47 in the middle of the jungle, and then more news; he couldn't hold back that flow, switch off that news bulletin, it was like being alone and defenseless in a gigantic cinema, in the middle of an atrocious scene, an item of news linked to the next one uninterruptedly and, suddenly, the flow would end and Diego Lazkano would find himself, at dawn, in an industrial area on the outskirts of Lille he'd never been to before, without his wallet, with his shirt ripped to shreds, incapable of recalling where he'd lost his jacket, feeling horribly nauseous.

Back then alcohol used to stimulate his desire to have sex. The shy pupil Lazkano, the dedicated student and occasional translator from Russian, met many girls who liked him, to his surprise. And he took advantage: he would have sex, phone them, stop phoning them, make excuses or not, hurt them in ways they didn't deserve and be hurt in turn, and fool himself into thinking that he enjoyed the pain.

One day, not having the remotest idea where he was, he puked everything he had inside in an empty gas station, next to the air-compressor pump, he poured it all out, completely, and felt himself touch rock bottom, the deepest bottom, when he surprised himself scrutinizing his own vomit attentively, *reading it*, trying to hopelessly find some clue about where he might have eaten dinner the previous night, judging by the bits of food he'd just expelled. But he couldn't remember a thing, he had forgotten everything, there was a big black hole in the place where his whereabouts of the past twenty-four hours should have registered.

He stopped selling his books then and started going to the cinema compulsively, almost every day, in an attempt to substitute the fast-flowing stream of terrifying news from his conscience with fictional stories.

He poured all the bottles down the sink (*Gulliver's Travels, The Belly of Paris, Wide Sargasso Sea*) and promised Lena to become a new man. But it was too late: the girl from Kursk decided that she'd already had enough.

Diego Lazkano kept only one bottle of Irish whisky, as a trophy. A bottle he never opened, and which survived every move since Lille, quite a few of them. He kept it intact, seal and all, that bottle he'd bought with the peanuts they'd given him in return for James Joyce's *Dubliners*. He'd decided to become a social drinker a long time ago, not to drink unless he was in company. But this time he's going to make a little exception. The occasion deserves it.

If there is a knife in the house, that knife will be used sooner or later. The same goes for a bottle of whisky. "I'll strangle him… don't be afraid."

By the time he realized, he was already halfway through the bottle. He was dying to speak with Gloria. He dialed her number, going against the old order of things, which determined that it was always her who called him in the middle of the night.

"The chapter I sent you the other day… I'm not completely sure I'd inserted the last revisions. Would you mind going through the passage in which Platonov and Anna get drunk together?"

"Of course, Diego. Hang on a sec, I'll switch on the computer."

"PLATONOV: I'm never drinking again…"

"That's good, let's start there."

"We might meet again in a few decades, and then we will both be old and senile and able to laugh and cry about these days we lived through, but for now… Sshh! Silence!"

"It's the same up to that, keep going a bit further, from the point where it reads: "I am an immoral woman.""

– 432 –

"I am an immoral woman, Platonov... am I not? And I love you perhaps because I am immoral...I am headed for perdition...Women like me always end up there. Do they match?"

"Yes, Gloria. They *match*. To the letter."

"We've already started dramatized readings with the material you sent us. And if I asked you to come to the rehearsal tomorrow...?"

"In your dreams, Gloria."

"Okay, I had to at least try..."

As soon as he's hung up the phone, Ossip appears before Lazkano, performing acrobatic leaps like a jester: "And the general's wife, why did she come after the other? And where is his woman? Which one of the three is the real one? And aren't you a villain after this?"

Diego tries to knock Ossip down with a punch, as if he were really there. He doesn't land the punch. It is he who ends up falling, and he rolls the carpet up then to try to asphyxiate Ossip. Afterward, when he's convinced there's no one there but him, he lies under it and goes to sleep.

A thermos filled with a liter of coffee to his right, a liter-and-a-half bottle of water to his left, and the computer in front of him. Next to the mouse, a cup.

Lazkano was determined to finish the job that very night. He would start by translating every passage he'd put aside because he couldn't be bothered or because his talent didn't stretch that far. After that, he would fix his clumsy sentences and correct all the fragments that were underlined in red, the parts he wasn't completely convinced by. He wanted to put a full stop to his long night. That translation, that appropriation he'd initially undertaken with such gusto, had become a torment. He wanted to stop looking at the world with Platonov's perspective and through Chekhov's eyes.

Toward the end of the play, Platonov's wife, Sasha, attempts suicide by ingesting matches. But the doctor finds her in time, she doesn't die. Will Platonov use the opportunity to redeem himself?

He places the butt of the revolver on his temple.

"Finita la commedia! One intelligent animal less!"

But Platonov is not capable of killing himself.

The girl Grekova is still tangled in his web. She stops him from doing it.

PLATONOV: *Thank you, clever girl . . . A cigarette, water, and a bed! Is it raining outside?*

GREKOVA: *Yes, it's raining.*

PLATONOV: *Sophie, Zizi, Mimi, Masha . . . You are legion . . . I love you all . . .*

Lazkano remembers Oteiza's eighty grandmothers.

GREKOVA: *What ails you?*

PLATONOV: Platonov ails me! You love me, don't you? To be frank...I don't expect anything...Just tell me that you love me...

GREKOVA: Yes...

PLATONOV: They all love me. When I am healed, I'll corrupt you...Before, I used to redeem, and now I corrupt...

GREKOVA: I don't care...I don't expect anything...Only you are...a human being.

Finally, it's Sofia Egorovna who fires the revolver. Platonov lies on the ground, gravely wounded.

Lazkano reads Triletzki's reaction to his friend's death for the umpteenth time, and is moved once again: "If you are the deceased...who will I drink with at the funeral?"

Dawn breaks. The bottle of water is empty. Just a finger of coffee in the thermos. He closes the lid of the laptop. It's finished. It's all over. He stands up to open all the windows in the house, unmake the bed, and throw the sheets in the washing machine.

Ossip watches him, sitting on the washing machine, dangling his legs playfully. "A dog deserves a dog's death."

"Go," Diego commands. "Get out, don't ever come back. Leave me alone."

Ossip leaves. Head hanging low, tail between his legs.

The house is silent, all he can hear is the sound of the washing machine's spinning cycle.

Lazkano should shave and he does so.

"If you're the deceased . . . who will I drink with at the funeral?"

Diego had constructed a coherent narrative to answer the question of why he hated the theater so much, one of those narratives that skirt around the truth, a comfortable narrative that you end up believing from saying it so much: he dislikes the modulated whispers and resonant screams actors are forced to deliver to make themselves heard, and even more so the social ritual going to the theater involves, entering corridors and passageways, going through balconies and stalls, shaking hands or dispensing – yes, *dispensing* is the right word – a couple of kisses every time he bumps into an acquaintance that requires a courteous stop; fake courtesy, always. There is no way to reach your seat without coming across some acquaintance along the way, because the city is small, and because there's always a chance you'll bump into some neighbor, a friend from school, an ex-colleague, some undesirable from the same association or union you revoked your membership from years ago, or any other scattered member of the populace of lowlifes you yourself used to belong to. The better the ticket, the better and more central the location of your row and seat, the greater the chances that you'd bump into the pseudolordsandladies of the manor and other members of the glove-wearing bourgeoisie. And let's not forget that in that city practically *everyone* belonged *by default* in this category of gloved bourgeoisie; even if they didn't actually wear them anymore, they still gave themselves the same airs. He hated the whole process of reaching his seat from the bottom of his soul. But if there was one thing that he hated above everything else about the theater, it was premieres. On such days, as if the discomfort of the crowds and unwanted encounters weren't enough, actors were in greater need of adulation than ever after the final ovation, and not happy with returning to the stage two, three, four, and even five times after the last curtain drop, they forced the extension of the applause from behind the scenes, demanding the audience's continued clapping from the wings, coming out again and again, loitering around and crisscrossing the stage as soon as they detected – what sharp ears they have, it must be said – the slightest sign that the applause might be about to cease, giving the impression that it wasn't the audience's gratefulness or opinion that they wanted to receive, but lavish and never-enough attention for their swollen, ravenous egos.

But, of course, the ordeal could be even more exhausting when actors and directors were old friends: the mandatory pilgrimage to the dressing room to cover them with kisses and hugs and regale their ears with praise and compliments, adulation and congratulations, flattery and reverence. "Rubbing down the horses," that's what Gloria sarcastically called the need to adulate at regular intervals insecure creative types who thought themselves stars.

But on occasion it was impossible to avoid those hateful premieres: the people who sent you the invite could get offended if you dared decline it; they didn't understand your not coming, they took your rejection as an insult and as a clear lack of interest. That day, for example. When Gloria was about to show her creature to the public, Diego had no option but to attend the premiere, even though he knew she would take refuge in the Boulevard's cocktail lounge for the length of the play, knocking back the gin and tonics, reliving an ancient ritual.

He hadn't been able to escape the occasion, especially since he had translated the script himself and had systematically rejected every single one of Gloria's requests to attend rehearsals.

He tried to appear as late as possible, pushing time to the limit. He regretted not having left his coat in the coat check. Although it was cold outside, he felt slightly overheated inside the theater, he had no other alternative but to rest the folded, thick item of clothing on his knees.

He diverts his eyes toward that proscenium to avoid acknowledging the president of the Basque Writers' Association, and it is then that he spots Gloria smoking a cigarette in the semidarkness, exactly where smoking is strictly prohibited, ready to head to the cocktail lounge: she greets him, waving the smoke with her hand, and Lazkano raises his, imitating a gesture that looks a lot like the raised fists that populated the demonstrations of their youth. *"Forza*, Gloria, I believe in you"; or "be brave, Gloria, soul sister, dearest, crazy friend."

There are only two empty seats on his row, the two to his left. While he is sitting there, with his coat on his lap, before he is even able to take a glance at the program at hand, the last bell rings and the lights start gradually dimming. In that precise moment, as if to prove to Diego that other people cut things even thinner than him, a couple join the fifth row. The couple come to sit on the only two free seats next to him. Lazkano smells the woman's sweetish perfume, hears her apologetic whispers to the others in their row. Without raising his eyes from the program in his hands, he steals a glance toward the woman's lap, but he can't confirm his intuition, he only catches a glimpse of her white hands.

When the woman addresses a few words to the person who must be her husband, sitting in the next seat, Diego finds the voice familiar. He almost stops breathing when he thinks he's recognized her. He foresees what is about to happen: the woman he hasn't seen in more than twenty years will break his stupor with "Diego, it's been so long," her perfect teeth, the shiny puddles of her green eyes, her raven hair framing the tunnel of her pale face, Ana's face; they will kiss, awkwardly, *giving* each other kisses rather than dispensing them, and, revealing a certain surprise whose agreeableness or disagreeableness is hard to ascertain, she will introduce him to her husband, "this is Fernando," or "Fidel," who the hell knows what's the absurd name of that hateful husband who's most certainly not good enough and certainly too common for a woman of her category. She will ask him if he's there alone, and Diego, in a slightly pathetic way, will answer that he is, he'll have no other option but to say that "yes, I'm here alone," highlighting not his solitary autonomy, not his entrenched and interesting bohemian life, but each and every fold of his painful, grim loneliness; "more than twenty years have passed and I have no one to bring to the theater, there you have the heartbreaking breakdown of the two long decades we've spent without seeing each other," a synopsis that could be offered without a need to resort to the program at hand. "You were the vanishing point I turned my back to, my only choice, I've spent ten years thinking you were the woman of my life, and another ten thinking that I spent ten years thinking you were the woman of my life, and I no longer know what to think, what conclusion to derive from all this." He won't tell her any of that, of course, but he hopes that she will be able to read it in his eyes. In the brief lapse of lightening that illuminated nothing, Lazkano had the chance to rewind his memories up to that point, to get ahead of what might happen but hasn't happened in the end, because no lightening is good enough and all the theater lights are switched off now and, since there isn't an orchestra in the pit either, the bloodred curtain has risen not to the clash of cymbals, but to the speedy drum of his own heartbeat.

His cardiac rhythm hasn't settled yet, and much as he tries to focus on what's happening on stage, his thoughts meander to the woman sitting next to him over and over again; to keep his neck straight and look ahead to avoid the shiny green puddles of Ana's eyes requires a superhuman effort from him. *Has she seen me?* he asks himself repeatedly, *Did she see me in that moment when the lights went off and the curtain started to rise? Did she notice, could she have realized that it's me? And, if that's the case, could she have recognized me after so many years? And, if she did, could she have really recognized me, without the shadow of a doubt, or only half recognized me, like when we think we detect someone's resemblance in someone but are not able to specify who it is that they remind us of, and doubtfully wonder is-it-or-is-it-not? She has plenty of reasons to hate me, but, does she still hate me from the bottom of her heart, because I left without saying a word, because I disappeared from her life from one day to the next?* He guesses and neurotically second-guesses that she must have recognized him, that she's doubtlessly aware of his current looks through seeing his photographs in newspapers, that she must have decided to ignore him to avoid the awkwardness of the situation, because women are good at detecting such things, women know when to leave a party in time, they are absolute masters of the art of the disappearing act. But, on the other hand, he thinks it's ugly to behave like that, they are so close, they could hold hands if they wanted, they could smell each other; maybe that's what it is, it's about the awkwardness and about the fact that she loves him and hates him still; otherwise she would greet him openly, introducing him to her husband, "this is Fernando" or "Fidel", whatever the absurd name of that undeserving and hateful husband of hers was. Could he put his hand on the fire? Is he absolutely certain of the identity of the woman sitting next to him? Is it all a cruel joke of fate? Could it all be a perverse mirage? It could well be that the woman next to him wasn't who he thought she was, maybe the combination of his deranged desires and deepest anxiety had betrayed him, maybe his prejudices and his fears of meeting someone unexpectedly in the theater had fooled his subconscious mind and were teasing him mercilessly. But no, he's completely certain: she is Ana.

Under the bluish and almost watery light of the stage, a man and a woman – La Bella Ines herself – open and close windows in silence, and change the sheets of an unmade bed, and although Diego keeps his eyes locked on the stage, his mind is very far from there, the shifts he hardly distinguishes on the boards are clearly displaced by another play, an old performance, from his youth, which overlaps and gets confused with what he's seeing. Who would have told him that he was going to encounter the great love of his life sitting in the seat next to his on the precise day in which his translation of Gloria's damned play was being premiered?

Those happy, those fragrant days, thanks to Ana: touching each other and trying to make things different each time, one caresses the other's face, for example, after peeling an orange with his fingers, it doesn't matter if his fingers are cold between her legs, and later against his nose, cold and smelling of orange. It's all Diego needs. They are one of those couples people envy when they see them walk down the street; so attuned to each other they even smile in the same way: they're like loving siblings, and should disguise their happiness to dampen the disgust they induce in jealous pedestrians. They've infected each other not only with their gestures, but also with each other's reasons to be happy. Impossible not to remember how, when they started living together, they used to compete to see who could do the dishes first, who could make the bed first, to surprise the other and see their smile when they realized that the job they were about to do had been completed by the other; and to make love then, tearing the sheets from the bed, unmaking the bed that had just been made.

Those moments seemed condemned to become an eternal loop; however, they're abruptly interrupted. Or perhaps not completely, nothing has been interrupted in that regard: everything is a helpless, repeating loop, but his attention turns completely from the disconcerting unease he breathes in that seat toward, now for sure, what is taking place on the stage. One of the actors who's joined the scene is to blame, his face, the first few words he pronounces when he sits at the piano and plays a few notes, the broken timbre of that voice when he says: "It's hot!"

It's Vengerovich. The actor who plays Vengerovich, the member of Gloria's father's stamp collectors' club. "This heat, like the Jew that I am, reminds me of Palestine. They tell me that it's very hot there." Vengerovich tries to describe hell, and Diego Lazkano's heart freezes.

Old Vengerovich, vengeful Vengerovich, Abram Abramich Vengerovich the detector of plagiarisms. "Only, you didn't write that article yourself, Doctor, but Porfiri Seminovich...Everything can be known, it's a matter of finding out things."

Lazkano swallows saliva and his stomach takes a leap, a double somersault.

There he was. It was him.

"He's so into theater, you know. He used to love the stage, but had to give it up because he wasn't making enough to live on. Now he doles out the parts. *Se encarga del reparto.*"

"Get it? Do you know what he means when he says I dole out the parts? *Soy yo quien reparte.*"

That voice hadn't aged one bit. Although he'd never seen his face at any point, he knew it was him: his hunched walk had become more marked with the years, and the chisel of two decades had made his husky voice even huskier. But, what was that man doing in that theater ensemble? How could that be? He started pulling at the thread, trying to unravel the ball of yarn in his head. Gloria, her conflictive relationship with her father, "you know that my father is a *facha*, he's going to try to provoke you, just go along with him. It's easier that way"; what she had to agree to in exchange for his making her bail, because nothing is for free and there are some things one cannot say no to: "He also wants me to include an old friend of his from his stamp collectors' club in the cast... Ever since he's been sick, I submit to all his blackmail."

Fabian and Fabian.

Fabian is Vengerovich.

As the minutes pass, Lazkano feels he's levitating. Even though every now and then a loose sentence from some other character, like Petrin, manages to get through his ears and get into his brain ("When they're born, humans choose one of three paths in life, there's nothing else: if you go right, the wolves will eat you; if you go left, you eat the wolves; if you go straight ahead, you eat yourself"), but Platonov and Vengerovich prevail over all the others, sucking his attention:

VENGEROVICH: I need you... To a certain degree... Let's walk a bit farther... Keep a distance, as if we weren't talking... Lower your voice... Do you know Platonov?

OSSIP: The schoolmaster? Of course.

Diego Lazkano knows very well what comes next. How could he not, when he's translated it himself? How could he not know it, when he's been Platonov's very reincarnation during the past few weeks? The villain Ossip and the schoolmaster Platonov have been his bedfellows, they've dirtied his sheets by transpiring their gargantuan alcoholic intake into them, they've pushed him to the edge of the precipice. He knows very well what comes next, because he *wrote* it. And because he wrote it, he's suffered it in his own flesh.

VENGEROVICH: Yes, the schoolmaster. The schoolmaster who teaches how to insult the world and nothing else. How much would it cost me to injure the schoolmaster?

OSSIP: What do you mean by injure?

"What do you mean by injure, Fabian? What do you mean by injure, Vengerovich? Tell me, please, tell me what you mean."

VENGEROVICH: I don't mean to kill him, just injure him . . . Thou shalt not kill . . . Why kill? Murder is so . . . Injure him, hit him and beat him up enough so he'll remember for the rest of his life.

"Nothing more than that, Fabian? Only that? What happened with Soto and Zeberio then? Did you do the same to them? Or were you not among them?"

OSSIP: All right, that's within my scope . . .

VENGEROVICH: Break something, disfigure him . . . How much will that cost me? Shh . . . Someone's coming . . . Let's walk a bit farther . . .

Nailed to his seat, Diego holds tight to its arms, although what he would really like to do is hold on to the hand of the woman sitting next to him – to have to hold on to an object rather than a person, what a sad turn. How to forget that hand that rests on the arm of the adjacent seat, that hand with the very well kept nails, which ran across his body, caressing it, which took his erect penis when it unexpectedly slipped out and slipped it back in to keep riding it, which turned sticky with his sperm, and sticky too the spaces between her fingers, her eyelashes once, a drop of sperm on her forehead, by her hairline, the arch of her back naked on the mirror, how to forget that, how to forget so many promises they'd made each other, that chimera of a future they built with words, how many castles in the air, names for their children that were never born, precarious constructions that came down like a house of cards, the scent of orange and coffee, naïve dreams from the age when naïveté is like a bunker and doesn't inspire compassion but tenderness, but yes, he had to forget all that, he had no option but to do that: the woman sitting next to him has been erased from his mind in hearing "Fabian" Vengerovich's voice on the stage.

He feels a cold sweat on the back of his neck, the folded coat resting on his lap is suffocating him, he would like to leave, but how, he can't, he could leave the stalls discreetly through a corner, but what would he tell Gloria afterward? "You hired one of the men who tortured me as an actor in your play, well done!" Here is an opportunity if there ever was one to stand up silently in the darkness of the theater, to rise up and make a scandal proclaiming, on the very day of the play's premiere: "This man tortured me, this man is a beast, how can he be walking the streets, how come he's not hiding in a sewer forever, why isn't he ashamed to show his face to the world?" Doesn't he contemplate the possibility that someone in the audience might be one of his victims? How can this be happening to me, just as I find the woman of my life sitting next to me, a woman I lost more than twenty years ago, a woman I spent ten years thinking was the woman of my life, and another ten thinking that I spent ten years thinking she was the woman of my life; maybe I could hold her hand without her husband noticing and ask her: "Have you forgotten about me, really? I can't believe you forgot me so easily."

Diego knows very well what he must do, of course he knows it, and that's what he'll do: he will climb onto the stage and grab Vengerovich by the throat until he stops breathing; after screaming that he's a torturer, he'll squeeze his neck until he dies of asphyxia, that's what he'll do, and he won't miss a heartbeat doing it.

But, what are you thinking, Diego? You are not capable of doing that, not in a million years, any time actors requested a volunteer from the audience you were the guy sinking into his seat; when they turned the lights off on stage and turned them on in the stalls, you were always afraid they would pick you, the idea of standing up and climbing onto the stage was terrifying to you, how far are the days when you'd walk into a scene to say your four lines, you'd be incapable of doing that today, and, even if you were, do you really think they'd let you strangle one of the actors with your own hands? If at least you had a weapon at hand, then yes, everything would be easier, how many assassinations have taken place in theaters, Lincoln's own for example, wasn't he killed in a theater?

But Diego is paralyzed, he doesn't move, he's not capable of moving.

He can't help it: his five senses are on that stage, what's taking place there subjugates him, body and soul. He unfolds the program on his lap trying to hit on the actor's name, *so many years without being able to even mention the Devil*, Fabian, *but I'll be able to do it now*, he tells himself, but he can't see anything in such darkness; even though his eyes have grown accustomed to the dark, he can't distinguish any names, not with the tenuous blue light that emanates from the stage; such is life, the stage is right there, the truth of the facts, everything happens right in front of your nose, but what little light spreads over events, we're not the actors who propel them, making the story move forward, it is not us who move on the stage, we're not lit by stage lights, and, despite that, and besides, only a glimpse of that light reaches us, an insignificant ray, a speck, almost nothing.

Platonov is dead on the ground.

"Who will I drink with at the funeral? Tell me: who with?"

"Kepa, Xabier, tell me: who with? Who will I drink with at your funeral?"

And a sentence he didn't remember reading in the original: "You've all seen it, it was a suicide."

When the play comes to an end, the theater bursts into enthusiastic applause. It's been a long time since Diego came to see a play, and he doesn't know if the applause is sincere or bought, spontaneous or fake, or if it's simply the audience's attempt at persuading themselves that the past two and a half hours of their lives have not been completely wasted, and that the price they paid for their tickets was money well spent. The play seems to be a success, at any rate. A bunch of flowers for Gloria, another round of effusive applause, most of the audience on their feet, Lazkano included. And although Lazkano wants to look to his side, although what he really wants is to confirm that the woman next to him is who he thought she was, he doesn't turn toward her; instead, he looks for Vengerovich on the stage, and there he is, grateful for the audience's response, holding on to Gloria's hand no less. And Lazkano is terrified now, because people have started to leave the theater, because the couple sitting next to him have been swallowed by the crowd, and because, now that everyone is done with their performance, he is about to start his own, as soon as he meets Gloria in the dressing rooms and she asks him the hateful question:

"Be good to me and tell me the truth, Lazkano: what did you think about the play?"

As usual, Gloria's call catches Lazkano profoundly asleep. But this time she's not calling from Barcelona, but from Donostia.

"I need your help."

"Are you on Aldamar Street?"

"No, come to my father's house."

Gloria is quite flustered since her father's death. The subterfuge the old man had concocted had exasperated her, so obvious was his strategy: far from attracting his daughter from Barcelona to have her direct a theater play, he did it so that she would look after her much shrunken father, knowing that the leukemia he'd been diagnosed with would only let him live a few more months. Gloria's anger was quickly substituted – just like her father had calculated – by pity and compassion, and they ended up sharing the five months he took to die. He didn't make it to the premiere alive, but the actors did a rehearsal in full dress and performed exclusively for him.

When Lazkano arrives, Gloria is very pale.

In seeing that she's emptying the house (a huge chaos, boxes and objects wrapped in brown paper everywhere), he thinks he can guess why she called him: Franco's tapestry. Gloria wouldn't have known what to do with that gigantic portrait, how to get rid of it, who to give it to without feeling ashamed. A three-meter-long and as many wide tapestry of a dictator wasn't something that one could just discreetly dump by a garbage container around dusk.

But Lazkano was mistaken.

There's no trace of Franco's tapestry – so glaring, the void it leaves on the wall. Dodging through boxes, Gloria takes Diego to her father's office. Once there, she leads him to a little chest resting on top of the open strongbox. The velvet lining of the chest denotes that its contents were valuable to its owner.

"It was inside the strongbox."

Lazkano lifts the chest's padded lid.

The order of its contents follows a rigorous logic of alignment. Fetishes. Little objects that were billed to his name and sent to Gloria in Barcelona, little collector's whims that his daughter had diligently brought home to her father for years without ever daring to even imagine what it was she was carrying. Nazi swastikas, medals from the SS, original, dated photographs of Franco and Mussolini. Fascist memorabilia. A black market of terror. Why not? Weren't there magnificently organized networks for the exchange of pedophile materials? As a matter of fact, no one could actually say that the private, intimate use of such sinister objects could really hurt anyone, it only used a hurt that had ceased long ago to incite or to calm the unspeakable inclinations of sick minds. "Objects will survive us," old Furmica had affirmed once.

"What am I supposed to do with all this?"

Gloria is paralyzed, which was quite hard to believe. Her father was a Franco supporter, he had never hidden it, Lazkano even thought it logical that his sickly fetishism would lead him to invest his savings in nostalgic Nazi trinkets, given that, as far as he was aware, he hadn't bothered to hide his sympathy toward them during their after-dinner conversations. Wasn't something like that to be expected? Why the shock? Why did Gloria find it so strange? He was a friend of Melitón Manzanas, for Christ's sake!

"Tell me: what am I supposed to do?"

"What do I know... donate it to a museum... dump it in the garbage..."

Lazkano, despite his sleepiness, notices that Gloria's every last hair, her eyelashes even, stand up in horror. She's terrified.

"And the soap too?"

Diego hadn't noticed that soap. It's a very somber-looking bar of soap, discreetly hidden under medals and photographs. It's Lazkano who acts surprised now, who takes a moment to understand what's happening. He takes it in his hands.

"Soap?"

"Jesus, can't you see it?"

It dawns on him suddenly: it's one of those bars with the acronym RIF printed on its wrapping, one of the bars of soap that Rudolf Spanner allegedly made from the corpses of Jewish prisoners, a numbered bar, *a limited edition*, as if it were a book.

According to what Lazkano had read, it was never completely proven that they used the corpses of people in concentration camps systematically for that purpose, for the mass production of human soap, but the traces left by Spanner were the most verifiable.

"My father...he was a monster!"

It was pointless to try to console her. Lazkano remains silent, he has no words, he can't quite comprehend until he begins to understand...everything. That out there – on the Web, on the Internet – there are all sorts, there are people willing to grow rich out of the most ominous objects in the history of humanity, people who have decided to exploit the macabre reverse of whimsical *souvenirs*. Above the horror and the disgust, another, frivolous question rises: how much did Gloria's father pay for that despicable bar of soap?

Lazkano buys a small sack of rapid concrete, adds water, pours the mix on top of the Nazi memorabilia, the photographs, and the bar of soap. He waits a day then, until the block of cement is dry and compact. For the first time in his life, Lazkano damns the fact that he doesn't own a car. He places the block of cement in a sports bag and a taxi takes him to the reservoir. He asks where he can hire a kayak. He's afraid that the weight of what's inside the sports bag might be excessive. He changes clothes and starts to row, departing from the shore bit by bit. It's a bit misty and he can't see anyone around. The reservoir is sufficiently big, but he doesn't want any surprises: he wants to row to the very center, as if being in the center of something might help.

There's hardly any wind and the kayak barely rocks. He stays like that for a moment, still, with the oar on his lap and his eyes closed. Afterward, without any kind of gesture or ceremony, he unzips the sports bag and takes the block of cement out, just that. He throws it in the water without giving it a second thought. The block sinks rapidly and immediately disappears from sight.

How many people like him must have done something similar? Throw something uncomfortable into the water, hoping that it will never surface again.

It occurs to him that the water that comes out of the taps in our houses is filled with spectra: he remembers his mother's lock of white hair, how she deliberately blocked the sink once, just so she could ask for Diego's help. Our ghosts and the ghosts we must inherit. Those who make us guilty and those who make us be born guilty.

The water that comes out of the taps in our houses is filled with spectra and we drink those spectra and introduce them inside ourselves. How many like this one. Impossible to know. Spectra that we swallow and that turns us into spectra in turn. Transparent souls. Intermittent beings.

"Can torture be sublimated through art? Can terror be overcome through art? And, if the answer is yes, who has the legitimacy to do so? The tortured? Or can the torturer redeem himself? The artist Gloria Furmica wanted to address these and other questions through *Rats*, her latest installation, which is guaranteed to be controversial."

"You've really raised dust now..."

"Seeing as how it's a carpet it makes perfect sense, don't you think?"

Having paid off her debt to Chekhov, Gloria decided to pause her career as a theater director for a while to return to the visual arts. Lazkano never dared ask her what had became of the enormous Franco tapestry, and he never knew where it'd ended up until the day her exhibition opened in the Koldo Mitxelena Cultural Center. Astonishingly, in the KM, next door to the post office, so close to the place where his father's fraud had started so many years ago – "I came to the wrong place, Diego; I was *convinced* that the books were parcels that I needed to post." The tapestry was inside a huge horizontal glass case, not hanging like a tapestry, but on the floor, like a carpet. An *objet trouvé*, Lazkano wasn't sure what artists called those found objects that only needed to be recontextualized for their meaning to change and for them to become "works of art" in their own right. Franco's portrait lay on the floor, fully spread, and on it, a dozen little mice joyfully gamboling and playing around. The glass case had a few holes with small tubes on the sides, which allowed visitors to give food and water to the rodents running around Franco's face. The little transparent receptacles could be filled to taste, the trapdoors out of which the food flowed were strategically placed on different areas of the face and extremities of the dictator so that the visitor could lead the litter of mice toward whichever part of Franco's anatomy they wanted, playing with the location where the trapdoors opened and where the wonders of mechanical engineering made the food fall. The interactivity was impressive.

"What do you think?"

"Isn't it a bit sadistic?"

"That was the intention."

"Did you talk to Animal Protection?"

"Don't be such a party pooper. I treat them like royalty."

"You treat them to dictators, more like..."

"Only the best for my rats."

"Truth be told, Gloria, they are mice, not rats."

"What's the difference?"

"My father was an exterminator, don't forget. There is a difference, a big one: one thing is *Rattus rattus* and another..."

"You're always such a fusspot... What was I supposed to do? Start looking for rats in garbage cans?"

"You didn't... *buy them*, did you?"

"Of course I did."

Diego Lazkano smiles. *These artists, there's no hope for them.* He raises his glass of cava then.

"We're here to celebrate. The truth is, your installation is magnificent. Congratulations."

"You gave me the idea, actually: 'donate it to a museum, dump it in the garbage,' remember? And I told myself: why not both? My first idea was to leave the tapestry in the street, next to a dumpster and record people's reactions with a hidden camera, show how it's brought to the landfill, film the whole process of decomposition of the tapestry... But then I thought that it would be much more stimulating to do it live, in front of people."

"But the title, however, I think it could have been improved: why not *The Mousetrap* instead of *Rats*? It would have been a subtle homage to Agatha Christie."

"I didn't want La Bella Ines to be offended."

"We all need to pay a toll."

They both laughed at the same time and clinked their glasses to take another sip, until an admirer took Gloria by the arm and dragged her to another area of the exhibition intending to introduce her to someone. She was in great demand. It was her big day.

Rats wasn't the only piece in the exhibition to generate controversy. Another piece, which she'd built from a front cover of a Penthouse magazine, got everyone talking too. There was a vintage porn actress on it, naked from the waist down, with her legs wide open, a kind of version of Gustave Courbet's *The Origin of the World*, only that, in this case, the model was contemplating her very bushy bush with curiosity. All that Gloria had done was to Photoshop a menstrual stain onto the original *Penthouse* model's thighs, a stain in the shape of the seven Basque provinces. The title of the piece was *Blood Loss*.

Without saying anything to Gloria and for the length of the exhibition, Diego visited every single week, spending time, mostly, contemplating *Rats*. In this way he was able to see that the little mice got chubbier, and that one of them had had a litter in the third week. As the days passed, Franco's face became more and more diffuse and threadbare. Although the glass case was isolated, it inevitably stank a little, as a consequence of the abundant mouse poop and the decomposing bits of food spreading everywhere.

Once he was able to rescue Gloria from the claws of her many admirers, he interrogated her about the future of that installation once the exhibition was over.

"The Artium Museum has bought it . . . do you want to know how much they paid?"

"Tell me that it's more at least than the going price for those paintings Napoleon the horse did."

"A fair bit more. What would you say if I told you that I'd be able to finance my next theatrical production with what they're going to pay me?"

"I'd say you've become a star?"

But Diego couldn't help but think of more questions. Diego

always had more questions. Were the mice included in the price of the installation? Would the museum be in charge of substituting them when they died? Or was she just selling the idea, the concept itself? Was all that specified in the contract? What would happen to the original carpet?

"Look, I want to introduce you to a friend of my father's: Roberto, Diego...Diego, Roberto..."

The color suddenly drains from Diego's face.

"Maybe his face is familiar to you? He took part in the Chekhov play."

Vengerovich.

"I don't mean to kill him, just injure him...Thou shalt not kill...Why kill? Murder is so...Injure him, hit him and beat him up enough so he'll remember for the rest of his life."

Life offers him a second opportunity. *There you have it, it's now or never.*

They shake hands. *He hasn't recognized me,* Lazkano tells himself. How can he trust fate so blindly? Did he feel so safe, so untouchable, so immune, just because he'd covered his face with a hood? Hadn't it occurred to him that someone might recognize his voice?

"Break something, disfigure him...How much will that cost me? Shh...Someone's coming...Let's walk a bit farther..."

"How do you do," are the first words his torturer addresses to him when they are introduced.

How do you do. You've no fucking idea.

Yellowing gums due to nicotine abuse, porcelain implants in his mouth. Groomed and straight-backed all the same. Lazkano feels a mad need to take his shirt off, as if the word *chibato*, snitch, were still on his shoulder. *Why did you let your colleague make that spelling mistake, Fabian?*

But Lazkano doesn't move an inch; instead, he starts to take little sips from one of the two glasses of wine his torturer has dexterously fished from the tray a server was carrying and charmingly offered to him.

He decides to ask him about the exhibition.

"What did you think about *Rats?*"

Roberto doesn't feel uncomfortable at all.

"Oh, you know, modern art and I... I'm just too old to understand such things."

"But, did you like it? Some people found it excessive."

"I'm not objective enough in this. This must stay between us" – he says lowering his voice – "but I just know too much about that tapestry."

Lazkano decides to play along. He doesn't need to feign surprise. More than what he is confessing, he's surprised by the act of confession itself.

"Really?"

"Her father, rest in peace, was a fervent admirer of the Generalísimo Franco... didn't you know?"

"I had no idea."

"Times were different, it's pointless to try to raise hell about it now."

"Do you mean to say that Gloria tried to carry out a kind of... exorcism with this, maybe?"

"It's possible. But, without the financial help of her Franquista father she would have never made inroads in the world of art. That's the paradox of most great artists: almost all of them come from wealthy families."

He's not wrong about that, Lazkano agrees.

"These provocative works of art may have their point, although I personally don't see it. Given a choice, I prefer Tiziano."

This Roberto guy seemed quite sensible. *My torturer*, he forced himself to rectify. He couldn't let the occasion pass. Not this time. Not again. Things couldn't end like this. He had to say something.

"You... you've never felt that temptation?"

"What temptation? To carry out an exorcism?"

"Yes... I mean, I don't know, there may be something from your past you may be ashamed of, something you did or you were a part of, something that circumstances forced you to do and that you now regret..."

"Nothing like that, thank God."

"You are lucky."

Diego's voice trembles for an instant, and he wonders whether he'll have the strength to keep going. He does.

"And, tell me, do you wonder if *Fabian* ever regretted what he did?"

Roberto's face changes completely. He's on the defensive now, expectant, but not afraid. The policeman he carries inside rises to the surface.

"You don't recognize me, do you?" Lazkano places his left hand on the man's right shoulder while still holding the glass of wine in the other.

The trembling shifts: it now settles into Roberto's throat.

"No...I'm sorry, I don't recall..."

Maybe what he said was true. It only made it worse. It showed how many had gone through his hands.

"And if I mentioned the Boger swing? Would that help your memory?"

Roberto-Fabian-Vengerovich swallowed saliva.

"I think...I think you mistake me for someone else..."

Diego raises his glass, a toast that is not a toast. He stares into his eyes, until Roberto can't sustain his look anymore. Afterward he says goodbye to Gloria and leaves the exhibition, in conflict with his lungs, at peace with himself. His chest is a sewing machine now, all heartbeat, but Diego knows well that there are no wounds this sewing machine can possibly stitch.

THE THREE FRIENDS

DIEGO LAZKANO'S MOST PAINFUL MEMORY, by far, is one that he kept hidden in the remotest corner of his mind under the following epigraph: "Let's play a game, let's imagine where we might be and what we might be doing in twenty-five years."

In the candlelight, Xabier Soto is combing and left-parting his hair over and over again with a nacreous close-toothed comb.

"Whatever happened to the light, Zeberio?"

"A blown fuse, probably: what do you want me to do? What's wrong anyway, is your toupee at risk, Elvis? I don't think she'll leave you just because your hair is crazy today, my man..."

They pull each other's leg constantly, they always do. And Kepa Zeberio is particularly talkative and clownish today.

Lazkano goes out into the hallway too, just in case there's anything he can do. He presses down the switch twice: the landing's light switch clicks snappily, in vain. The lights are out in the whole building. Back then blackouts and strikes tended to be general.

"Check the electric panel, you're the specialist."

Soto is losing patience. The girl is about to arrive – "you don't know her," he told them – and he still hasn't been able to tame the curl that falls on his forehead, such is the wildness of his mane.

"So the electric panels are all for me, isn't that so, comrade?

Of course! You only understand other kinds of panels, Byzantine or... German expressionist ones, and that other dude... what was his name? Dunlop or something...?"

"Duchamp, Zeberio, Marcel Duchamp..."

Concrete thought and abstract thought. The eternal chasm between action and reflection.

On the front cover of *Egin*, the Basque newspaper, there's a photograph of the Minister for Home Affairs, José Barrionuevo, who'd visited the Intxaurrondo barracks the day before. Soto defaced the photograph with a marker, turning his face into an owl and translated his name into "Ol' Owl Newhood."

Lazkano holds a copy of George Orwell's *1984*, and although the blackout still hasn't been fixed, his eyes gradually adapt to the semidarkness and he manages to read to the glow of indirect light coming from the street. Soto sits next to him, still combing his hair fastidiously. He is a torrent of overflowing energy, a born activist; a tireless volcano and a free spirit. His excess of inner strength can be annoying sometimes, insulting even, if his conversational partner doesn't have the energy for it.

"Eighty-four... we're only one year away. Who knows where we'll be next year... and in twenty-five? Can you imagine? Where do you see yourself in twenty-five years, *primo*?"

Lazkano's answers tend to be brief. This is no exception. Soto and Zeberio's presence intimidates him.

"I'd rather not think about that."

"Well, I think about it, and a lot: nothing to do with what Orwell suggests. We'll have a free country and two or three wives each very probably... Such quackery about the divorce laws... Wives is not the right word either, I'm talking about squadrons of women willing to sleep... They'll demand their share, it goes without saying. And we'll give it to them: nothing is more beautiful than licking them with their legs wide open, especially if you can keep it hard and tight between their breasts... Your spunk reaches their navel while your lips sink into their juices... Are you embarrassed by my words, *primo*?"

Lazkano has indeed turned a deep shade of red.

"What kind of a leftie are you? You glow like a peach every time we talk about sex! Yes, I know... you don't need to look at us that way: our lady comrades will refute our theses, there'll be intellectual women with whom to share our concerns.... How fucking awesome would it be if intellectual fucks and the other kind merged into one... But, ah, to learn to detect the udders from which intellectuality flows, eh?... You read too much, *primo*..."

That's the kettle calling the pot black... It's a bit rich having Soto throw that in his face; the man with the thickest glasses, the great white hope of the new Basque theater, the man who spends hours reading compulsively, night and day, whenever he isn't, of course, bashing a typewriter or trying to tame his mane of curls in front of a mirror.

"Is that bad?"

"It's not good or bad, *primo*. But I think that lots of people boast about the books they read, like others boast about the yachts they keep in Marbella...I personally think they're both bourgeois habits, what can I say. Not the act of reading itself, but boasting about reading...You're not reading to look cool, are you, to big yourself up? Tell me the truth..."

Lazkano doesn't dare offer an answer, and there's no need, because Soto soon changes the subject.

"That bloody light! Did you fix it, Zeberio? Yes or no?"

"I'm fucking trying..."

Lazkano tries to go back to the conversation.

"In twenty-five years...By then our sons will have grown up."

"In my case, please, let them be daughters if at all possible, *primo*. Only daughters. After a certain age sons lose their looks and can get quite ugly.

When it comes to Soto, it's not easy to distinguish when he's serious and when he's joking. Lazkano finds his confession strange, however. Does he think of the future every now and then too? His arrogant, provocative stance, his way of talking, so irreverent and grandiose, are, deep down, just a façade. Diego decides to head to the kitchen before the conversation turns to lascivious terrains again. He finds Zeberio there: he's just activated the inner patio's fuses from the window and brought the electricity to their whole building.

"We've teased him enough for today, Lazkano," Zeberio whispers. "Besides, all we need now is for the partridges I hunted yesterday to go to waste in the fridge."

They're still students. The only money that comes into their house are the wages Zeberio gets from the little jobs he does with his father. They run in demonstrations and throw pamphlets in the air. They shout slogans. They feel they're at the threshold of so many things.

They feel so because it's true.

By the time they return home, Zeberio has already plucked the partridges. Under the tap in the kitchen sink, two buckets, one filled with cold water and the other in the process of being filled with hot water.

"Come here a moment."

Zeberio asks Soto to close his eyes. He takes his hand and submerges it in the bucked filled with almost-boiling water.

"Fuck!"

"Calm down, this is beneficial for your toupee! Hold it."

"Are you fucking crazy? I'm burning! It burns!"

He takes his other hand and submerges it in the cold-water bucket.

"For Christ's sake, Kepa! What the hell is wrong with you?"

"It's just an experiment…One hand in hot water and the other in cold water, isn't that so, Soto? Can you distinguish between the two? You know for sure which is the hot one and which one is the cold, right?"

"Kinda hard to miss!"

"But if we repeated this exercise over and over again, your nervous system would go crazy, you'd be incapable of detecting it. You'd feel your skin burn, but you wouldn't be able to tell if it was because of the heat or because of the cold. So that you know, this is how they torture people in Chile."

"Fuck, Zebe, this isn't Chile!"

"That's what you like to think."

Diego could hardly remember those days without Soto's incessant theatrics, his uninterrupted flow of jokes, and his playful personality. He was particularly good at imitating people, he'd quickly take on people's tics, pet words, and gestures – he could just as accurately imitate their dining companions, their old professors, or the politicians du jour who appeared on TV, anyone from Solchaga and Carrillo to Manuel Fraga or Felipe González, without forgetting the Basques, Arzalluz and Idigoras. He would liven up any and all after-dinner conversations with surrealist reinterpretations of some news bulletin. "Clown," Zeberio always said, "you're completely nuts," although he laughed like crazy and enjoyed Soto's slapstick as much as Lazkano, and couldn't hide it.

Soto's eyesight was as disastrous as his ear was sharp. Although he didn't have the first clue about Italian, and because his mother was a passionate fan of opera, he liked to sing bits of arias he'd learnt by heart, loose sentences, sometimes he'd sing them and sometimes he'd declaim them with exaggerated solemnity, leaving his companions astounded. He'd memorized about a dozen lines – much later, Lazkano would discover that most were just the titles of famous arias – and he always found the perfect moment to let them out: *Nessum dorma, Che gelida manina, A lui devo obbedir, Lasciate ogni speranza, E lucevan le stelle...* If his French was any good, it was also due to the acuity of his ear more than to his actual knowledge of the language. As a matter of fact, he spoke French not just with his mouth and face, but with his whole body, to the extent that even the way he held himself changed, he almost metamorphosed into another person.

Lazkano remembered, for example, the day that, using summer tourists as a decoy and camouflaging among them, they fulfilled their long-delayed desire to go to Biarritz to eat a delicious roast duck for lunch. Menu in hand, Soto mock-pretended cosmopolitan intonation and manners and requested several dishes in a fake Parisian accent, without moving his lips much; he loved theater, yes, and not just writing it. Lazkano would never forget the way he puffed his chest when the young server asked him if he came from the capital. That joy, that moment when they confuse us with someone we're not but we'd like to be, that moment can make us proud as much as being taken for someone we'd hate to be associated with can destroy us.

Lazkano remembered also the time when a friend going on holiday left his dog in Soto's care for a week, which coincided with the crucial last few days of his finalizing one of his plays. The dog wouldn't give him peace while he banged furiously on the typewriter. The doggy's head and ears bobbed up and down to the rhythm of the old Hispano Olivetti, submerged in a kind of tribal-dance-induced trance.

"Turns out Mr. Barker here loves literature, look at him," Soto said to Lazkano.

"I'd say he loves music. Your typewriter's percussive rhythms." "I put a Bob Marley album on earlier and he went half crazy. You'll have to ask Gloria if she needs a dog for her new play."

Later on he asked Lazkano, genuinely: "Oi, *primo*, do you know what these creatures eat?"

He meant the question. Being a child of asphalt, he'd been sharing steak he'd bought for himself with the dog, and he'd quite likely would have fried him a couple of eggs too, and given him bread to dip into the yolks, any sort of madness, a napkin around his neck, some cutlery; where Soto was involved, anything was possible.

Before he crossed over to Iparralde, the French Basque side, oblivious to his fate, he would avidly read Lazkano's sociology notes – for pleasure, he'd say; he would gobble down the notes of all his friends who were studying for degrees different from the one he'd chosen; his wasn't enough, his philosophy classes, which he passed with high marks without barely ever turning up to a class, were too thin a gruel for Soto's voracious curiosity and intellect.

One day that week, Lazkano accompanied Soto to renew his ID card. Still today, Lazkano finds the offices where they issue ID cards and passports unnerving, but back in 1983 they were worse than unnerving, they were scary. There were many reasons why the two of them could be thought to be suspect, they were at risk of being detained; they'd taken part in demonstrations against the Lemóniz nuclear station, in demonstrations in favor of the amnesty for Basque prisoners, and they weren't just screaming in those demonstrations. That's why it was a terrible ordeal to have to renew the ID card, to have to go there, voluntarily, and sub-missively hand over a photograph to complete your own file. A disagreeable calvary that one had to go through, rubber stamps, toxic smells of ink, fluorescent lights that buzzed and buzzed but never quite burned out; the mere fact of having to breathe that air pregnant with static electricity was hateful, although Soto was very capable at being oblivious to it all, thanks to the constant syncopated pulsation of typewriters, which made him feel at home. Lazkano's hair stood on end, however, in seeing the posters of the most wanted criminals (members of the ETA

– 472 –

most of them), in smelling the old coffee, the stench of Ducados cigarette butts squeezed in heavy ashtrays, in facing the screech of the stainless steel filing cabinets, the stink of old sweat that coalesced with new sweat.

"But, are we really taking the dog?"

"Aren't we going to the doghouse, *primo*? One more dog, I doubt they'll notice."

The endless mockery, the infinite jest; Lazkano appreciated Soto's hunger to fuel the fires of everything every day of his life, with every step, in every exchange, no matter how banal and boring it was. There weren't many like him. It wasn't that he was always happy, it wasn't that exactly, it was that even on the days when he woke up in the dumps, he was sufficiently clearheaded to make the most of his darkened mood: inaction was something he wouldn't allow himself and, for Soto, the most direct action was to talk and to write, to never stay silent and to bash endless words out of his typewriter. Soto was a walking novel, a man whose daily life, the twenty-four hours of it, was an act of *performance art*, years before the word *performance* started to gain currency among us; maybe he didn't do it consciously, maybe he only did it because he was like that, because he oozed life out of every pore of his skin.

"They're not going to let us in with a dog, Soto."

"And you boast about reading Orwell, *primo*? Don't forget that it is us who comply, with our tails between our legs, with their demand to get ID cards so that they can better control us; it is us who do them a favor and not the other way around."

Lazkano offered to wait outside with the dog, but Soto, "fuck that for a game of soldiers," wanted to have fun, have a laugh "at the expense of the repressive apparatus the state's got going for us."

Besides the uniformed policeman at the entrance – not long before, an attack from one of the anticapitalist commandos had taken the lives of two agents in that very same office – there was a notice at the door. Soto didn't need much more to get going. That was enough, a little notice at the door.

"Están prohibidos los perros, joven," dogs are forbidden, young man, the policeman at the entrance warned him.

Soto then pointed at the little notice on the door with fake naïveté, and an apparently submissive stance:

"Están prohibidos los perros, excepto en el caso de perros lazarillos." No dogs, except guide dogs.

"Él es un perro lazarillo." He's a guide dog, he indicated to the policeman, as if he were doing him the courtesy of giving him the chance to read, again, a notice he must have read a million times.

Lazkano, meanwhile, was feeling increasingly alarmed, and kept his eyes fixed on the weapon the policeman carried on his belt.

The policeman's answer was to be expected:

"Pero usted no está ciego." But you are not blind.

If he hadn't been so frightened, *"pero usted no está ciego,"* Lazkano would have laughed hard, it was impossible not to notice Soto's extremely thick glasses, minus seven diopters in each eye, no less. Soto was shit-scared too, but, resisting the temptation to crack a joke about his accelerating farsightedness, he answered by opening another salve with a line that one may think he'd rehearsed at home.

"No veo que en el cartel diga nada sobre estar ciego." Where in the notice does it say anything about blind people?

Soto was like that, and even though the policeman gave him the brush off with a *"no me vacile,"* don't waste my time, and the dog had to stay outside with Lazkano in the end, he entered the government office proud of his *deed*, smiling and victorious, an uncommon human being who knew how to draw mileage out of the obligations he was forced to comply with, *"pero usted no está ciego,"* "but you are not blind, *"pero usted sí,"* but you are, so many outbursts, imagined but never pronounced, so many words and sentences, thought and said, for once.

"No dogs, except guide dogs."

"Where in the notice does it say anything about blind people?"

Although Soto and Zeberio's names have been linked forever (never Zeberio and Soto, always Soto and Zeberio), and although we are so used to seeing them together it's almost unthinkable to separate them, truth must be honored, we must acknowledge that they were two very different people. They would probably lead separate lives and be engaged in different professions and different environments, had they been born in any other part of the world or lived at a time that wasn't the tumultuous eighties. And, had they coincided by chance, say, sitting in adjoining seats on a plane – they never boarded a plane, their murder robbed them of that experience too – they would have probably found it hard to find a subject of conversation in common after those two initial minutes of courteous exchange. Among different groups too, and against all prognoses, sections cross over and shared areas emerge; some couples are sufficiently stubborn to perpetuate a youthful summer love – and end up regretting it, or not – and on occasions we start off using each other only to end up loving each other, or start off tolerating each other and end up believing that to tolerate is to love; maybe it's just a matter of aptitude, of attempting to attract someone completely removed from it into our magnetic field, making that field attractive to them, or the other way around, abandoning ourselves into the arms of someone or something – how wonderful it is to abandon ourselves, don't anyone dare deny it, to abandon ourselves into the arms of someone or something – to abandon ourselves into the arms of someone who might initially seem a bit dull because they're so far removed from us, until little by little we enter their sphere, we get to know their hobbies and pastimes, we assimilate their tastes and begin to think *they're not so bad, it's not such a big deal, why not?*, we give in, and let him or her – friend, lover, spouse – shape our conversations, our plans, our schedules, who hasn't done that sometime? Soto and Zeberio, had circumstances been different, may have been able to create a deep, long-lasting bond.

Maybe they would have, but it wouldn't have been as deep and long lasting as death.

When he regaled them with his theories like the one he had about "heat and revolution" (according to him, most revolutions took place in the summer), Soto displayed what a good orator he was, while, simultaneously, Zeberio proved what a great listener he was. Lazkano had borrowed bits of both of them. Soto's conspiratorial soul was insatiable, his hunger to try to understand how humanity worked and its tendency to do harm too. "Mussolini; I'd love to have a cup of coffee with him," he used to say, with the same passion with which he said "Silvana Mangano; I'd love to have a cup of coffee with her." He loved dialectics, fiery discussion, shocking his friends: "Oh we are dark inside, but may old age not catch up with us without us having done at least one crazy thing," he used to say, so many perfectly rounded sentences that seemed to spontaneously bloom from his head, and which years later Diego kicked himself for not having written down verbatim in some notebook, back in those days when he was still naïve enough to believe that Soto would be his closest dearest friend forever, how many hard-hitting sentences thrown about like they were nothing; Diego remembered some, like that one, that one he hadn't forgotten: "oh we are dark inside, but may old age not catch up with us without having done at least one crazy thing," events that won't ever take place, things that were impossible now, words that became painful because they were a testament to everything that could no longer happen, words like those are not forgotten.

Lazkano had no doubt about it: Soto was destined to be a great writer. And, whereas Soto's passion was human relationships and their dark core, Zeberio's passion, on the other hand, was focused on electrical structures: cables, simple and complex installations, dynamos, alternating currents and direct currents, plugs, switches, transformers, electrical boxes, outlets, peeled copper cables put back together again. If you wanted to know something about the weakness of the human spirit and its few moments of lucidity, Soto was the man to ask. If you needed to know why a blackout had taken place or the way in which light flew and forked through buildings and series of rooms, all you had to do was ask Zeberio.

Soto and Zeberio's duties were split according to their abilities, of course, you didn't need to think too hard to realize what kind of occupation they would have been destined to if their years in hiding had stretched a bit longer. The allocation of duties would have been quite obvious. However, they didn't have the chance to put their predictable abilities into practice within the organization: they didn't have time to regret it, they didn't even have the time to do anything they might regret. While Soto developed his theory about "heat and revolution," Zeberio would feel the urge to talk about thermodynamics, give them a brief lecture on the renewable energies of the future (back then they didn't even have that name), about the possibilities and benefits of wind power versus nuclear power.

"Do you intend to turn the four winds into electricity, Kepa? Really, tell me, how does that happen?"

"It's very easy, Xabier: with windmills."

"Windmills? You're not going to turn into the Knight of the Sorrowful Countenance now, are you? The fields of Castile are filled with windmills . . . we won't live to see that."

"We won't live to see that." "Oh we are dark inside, but may old age not catch up with us without us having done at least one crazy thing." "Where in the notice does it say anything about blind people?" Sentences that had been carbon-copied into Lazkano's head, as if he'd typewritten them into his brain with burning brands.

Soto and Zeberio always. The sentences of one, the silences of the other. The memory of Zeberio was constant in Lazkano too, to the point that his eyes filled with tears every time he saw one of those windmills that had proliferated so much in the past few years on the hills on the sides of highways. "We won't live to see that." How right you were, Soto.

On occasion Lazkano forced himself to think about the presumed advantages of dying young. Coldly. When he watched, say, a documentary about James Dean's death on TV, about the way in which his early disappearance fed the mythology of his persona; he would speculate then about whether that could be applicable to Soto and Zeberio's deaths. Nothing to do, of course, although the actor also died young, truncating the promising future ahead of him: the driver coming toward him never saw the silver Porsche James Dean was driving, the actor's gray car disappeared in the gray asphalt, it dissolved, the sun diffused and melted the Porsche in the eyes of the driver who crashed against him, making it impossible for him to see it, blinding him. Had James Dean been driving a red car, a car in a more vivid color that was easier to distinguish for the person driving the car in front of him, the deadly outcome probably wouldn't have taken place. If Diego Lazkano had had the ability to drive a red car or a vehicle of any other color, the events would also have been very different. It didn't take much to imagine James Dean living on a ranch in Texas, aged eighty; a Republican, having undergone some cosmetic surgery, grumpy, alcoholic, an inveterate cocaine addict. "If I were handsomer, I'd be dead," whose line was that? Perhaps that wasn't the exact quote: "Thank God I'm not too tall: being as handsome as I am, were I six feet tall, I'd be dead." Who said it? It didn't really matter. The truth is that, in Diego's fantasies,

James Dean's death overlapped with Paul Newman's splendid old age; some people knew how to age, he told himself, some people, even if they didn't know how to, they learned; a lot of talent was needed for it, or, in talent's absence, the right amount of luck and enough money to buy a sailing boat, plus the benefits of good health. He could draw up a long list with the aches and discomforts that came with the passing of time, with the disagreeable humiliations we had to suffer, with the bloopers that made us wish the earth would swallow us, with the mean simian feelings we all carry, hidden deep in some recess of the brain, which come out at the worst possible moment, "Oh we are dark inside, but may old age not catch up with us without us having done at least one crazy thing." Who wished for disloyalty, for the aging of parents, for the face's vocation to turn into orange peel, for thinning or graying hair, for the loud presence of viscera, for the body that stops obeying, little by little or suddenly? Did a natural vocation to tiredly instruct our children – those tiny paralytics with promising futures – really exist? Despite the fact that they would end up fundamentally enacting our same mistakes, if not some other worse ones? Who needed all that? The betrayal of our vital organs, the crunching vindication of a set of bones that, back in the day, were silent and discreet, the cancer in our dearest ones or in ourselves, "let's do some tests just in case"; in other words, who wished for decadence? Who would want that? Who didn't find that they could do without one half or three quarters of life? Not to mention appearances, the extensive, never-ending list of undesirable things that day by day, week by week, month by month, and year by year we did against our will. Even the good things in life, Lazkano knew this well, became repetitive from a certain point onward, even the good things in life could drive you mad: to fuck once or a thousand times, to get drunk once or a thousand times, it's obvious after a certain age that the best bender and the best fuck, the most spine-tingling adrenaline high, is already in the past. Why go on, then? To reach the wisdom that could be the recipe for tranquility, or the tranquility that could be the recipe for wisdom? To try heroically to become Paul Newman without being in possession of his genes?

All the writers' festivals were the same, Lazkano told himself, every new person he met resounded with the exact echo of someone he'd met many years ago who looked suspiciously a lot like them. The repertoire of men and women, psychologists knew this well, didn't extend beyond around twenty personality types, and Lazkano already knew about twenty examples of each of those twenty typologies; repeat patterns, enough people and more to satiate even Soto's unquenchable thirst for knowledge. Or maybe Lazkano lied to himself about that. Maybe life would never satiate Soto. Maybe it was a matter of having the talent to live – Soto had oodles of it, Lazkano lacked it. Maybe that was why it was so boring for him to meet new editors, writers, and readers lately. Would Soto have been able to keep that dynamic spirit intact, "where in the notice does it say anything about blind people," if he'd lived for another twenty years? It was hard to ascertain, but he probably wouldn't have.

And, despite that, on occasion Lazkano forced himself to think about the presumed advantages of dying young, and although one thing couldn't be compared to the other, although a car crash or a suicide had nothing to do with torture, he never tired of seeking similitudes, parallelisms, the comfort of likeness. In the case of suicides, there was always the consolation that those who take their own lives are exercising a right that belongs to them, even though some studies establish that people who've failed at their attempted suicides and survived them are said to regret them: Hopefully they thought it through, hopefully they put all the pros and cons on the scale, why doubt their opinion was reasoned, generous, measured, the wise decision of someone who's decided to say enough to eternal repetition and stand their ground. The suicide has the chance to say goodbye, to write their last few words or not, to chose the moment and time, to leave everything in order (or not), to be conscious as to whether they have left everything in order or not. To know that is to know a lot, those who didn't choose to come into life, choose the moment of their death, and they have the right to do that, even if it causes pain or if it leaves more than one with a feeling of guilt: they'll say their decision was selfish but . . . let's repeat it even if it isn't true, is being generous with oneself maybe another way of being generous?

Soto and Zeberio's case was very different: a sudden death – not one but two, and not so sudden after all: they probably saw centuries buried in every second while they tortured them, pinnacles and abysses that the living rarely face; a sheet of paper still inside the typewriter, an interrupted sentence on it, so many expectations reduced to rubble. And, despite that, Lazkano forced himself on occasion to think about the presumed advantages of dying young, when he found himself in a predicament or when he felt too overwhelmed by everything to carry on, when he thought that it was absurd to celebrate life as if it were the greatest, because life wasn't all that after all.

But it was: life was all that, even the most despicable and miserable one was all that, "where in the notice does it say anything about blind people," there was always the possibility of a sharp joke, the invigorating racket of children and their moments of eternal innocence – the centuries buried in seconds, maybe we've forgotten them, but the child we were still remembers those buried abysses. The promise of love and sex – just the promise is often enough, it's enough, even, to be a witness to that promise, sometimes it's even enough for others to make that promise to each other and for one to see it from the crack of an open door; like an old fox or a tired god who needs his eyes washed, sometimes it's enough to be a witness to that promise.

Life was nothing and it was everything, life was a vanishing point, the only possible one, "oh we are dark inside, but may old age not catch up with us without us having done at least one crazy thing," let's forget for an instant that we represent a role that someone wrote for someone who isn't us, let's forget our inescapable personalities of mediocre second-class actors, let's absorb those rays of light, let's drink up the escape, even if it's intermittent and fleeting. Everything, intermittent. Everything, fleeting.

The pinewoods reach all the way down to the beach. On the sand closest to the pines, dry leaves shaped like needles pile into reddish heaps that look like they've been there for years. The beat of the drums emanating from the squalid speakers sounds like it could be anything but a percussive instrument: a gas can being hit with a stick. "Come on, let's twist again, like we did last summer; yeah, let's twist again, like we did last year…" The voices and chorus – "uh, uh; wah, wah" – save the song. Soto and Lazkano, lying down on the sand, can see Zeberio from their spot; he's bent over, taking the punctured tire off the axle of a Volkswagen van, keeling over slightly because of the jack. Soto smiles, half closing his eyes impishly.

"*Consumatum est, primo…*"

"What?"

"He's got her in the sack, man…"

"Shouldn't we help them?"

"Ménage à quatre? No way! Let him be ... It looks like he's getting on very well with that Dutch girl. Besides, for once he hasn't asked the girl to change the music."

"...and round and round and up and down we go again! Oh, baby, make me know you love me so..." The melodies of the empire. Lazkano remembers the arguments they used to have in the apartment: Victor Jara, the Doors. Afterward he remembers Ana: Echo & the Bunnymen and Errobi. Mikel Laboa and Patti LaBelle. The lanky girl standing next to Zeberio wears a semi-transparent orange dress and smokes a cigarette while wearing a straw hat; it's almost as if the wind were smoking the cigarette for her: it burns quickly, as if the quick lapse in which tobacco became ash were trying to warn them of something. The girl blatantly stares at Zeberio, looking him up and down, with her hands on her hips, while the wind makes the ribbon in her hat flutter, an accessory made out of a remnant from her dress. In contrast to her dress and the ribbon, the wind doesn't blow the pine needles heaped at the feet of the trees. It's curious how some things find their place in the world, having retreated and in silence. Among pine needles, for example.

The radio on the VW van is on and they can still hear Chubby Checker's playful tune, parodying the voice-over in the old Superman series: "Who's that flyin' up there? Is it a bird? No! Is it a plane? No! Is it the twister? Yeah!"

When the saxophone solo starts, the girl offers Zeberio her cigarette.

Soto and Lazkano stop looking in that direction and lie down belly up. Looking at the sky.

"Do you remember when things were really hummin'?"

When they turn around to look in that direction again, the tire still hasn't been changed, and two sets of ankles can be seen behind the screen created by the small van: two naked ankles and two covered ones. For a moment that seems eternal, they see how the bare feet stand on tiptoe. Some reddish pine needles are stuck to the dirty soles of the girl's feet.

It was easy to imagine: Soto had woken Zeberio from a siesta, or not, he hadn't woken him exactly, Zeberio was the lightest sleeper, he slept like hares do, with one eye open, he'd wake up with a leap, fearing an emergency and ready to defend himself, leaping from the bed was his way of drawing his weapon; he was the weapon, and the sheets, his holster; since he didn't have a weapon he drew himself, "here I am, I am the weapon, what's going on?" Zeberio liked to have siestas, but he always remained alert, he was the only early riser of the three – he had a hunter's habits – although seeing as it was usual for Soto to spend the night awake, writing, it was possible for him not to have even gone to bed at all, so disorderly were his sleeping habits; "enough with your siesta, let's go to the festival in Ustaritz right now, let's go and live a little"; something like that, maybe Soto had been reading and Zeberio was bored – "you read too much, *primo*" – or, simply, he felt like going on a bender. He had abandoned the book he was reading on page 215, *As I Lay Dying*; Zeberio had noticed the title, "what on earth are you reading, my man, it sounds super joyful, what is it, a collection of obituaries? It's quite the tome . . . doesn't it go on a bit too long to be about someone who's dying? And that Faulkner dude with his mustache, who the fuck is that Faulkner, he looks like a self-satisfied member of the bourgeoisie . . . Is that the kind of writer you dream of becoming, Soto? Why don't you write a version of Mao's red book, translate it into Basque, and hand it over for free in factories?"

Those were too many words for Zeberio but, who knows, even shy guys have their exuberant days.

It was easy to imagine, and it was difficult to imagine. Lazkano tried once and again. Because that day he should have been there with them. Because he could have been there instead of them. And because he wasn't there with them, or instead of them. Because he was locked up in El Cerro, and had just confessed his friends' whereabouts.

Soto had been singing that silly song about uncensored clothes and uncensored feelings from one of Madrid's new wave *movida* pop groups for days: "*No controles mis vestidos, no controles mis sentidos . . . ,*" swinging his hips; he loved dancing more than anyone, he wasn't your archetypal Basque of fused hips, Zeberio was much clumsier and prudish in that sense; even though they were both full of life, they exteriorized their vitality in very different ways: through dance, through hunt. *"No controles mi forma de bailar,"* don't censor the way I dance, Soto sang, he didn't know much more than that, he could only repeat the chorus of the song that had become all the rage in the past few months: *"No controles, ¡no!"* moving his hands in one direction and his head in the other, an almost hydraulic swing, crouching a little, looking slightly like a dancer from the days of the *swing*, "sing with me, Zebe," he said; "you're a clown," Zeberio would reply, "you're nuts, you don't make any sense."

"Nutcase," Zeberio would call Soto, nutcase, as if he were saying *brother*, but uttering *nutcase*, words aren't really important when they are said with the biggest smile. And Soto would take a piece of paper then, a train ticket perhaps, and place it inside the book, leaving it on page 215, to recommence his reading there *tomorrow*... That book, *As I Lay Dying*, "what the hell, just this once, it's just one day, we're still young and we won't be forever," and he decided to go out with his friend: "But I ain't so sho that ere a man has the right to say what is crazy and what ain't. It's like there was a fellow in every man that's done a-past the sanity or the insanity, that watches the sane and the insane doings of that man with the same horror and the same astonishment." We are many inside, we are many in the depths of our heads, it's paramount to understand that. But there are many outside too, and not all are looking after our best interest. And there was someone observing them, someone watching them, were they so important, really? They waited for them in the street, stalking them, hiding where they least expected it, they didn't let them get into their car, they caught them unawares, maybe they put dark hoods on them, whispered some threat into their ears, true, words aren't really important when they are uttered with the coldest of hatreds, something soft and terrible, "get in the car," a foreign accent they detected from under their hoods – don't all accents sound foreign when you hear them from under a hood? *Clown, fool, you don't make any sense, nutcase...* it was so tender, the way in which Zeberio pronounced those words, and now Soto can hardly breathe inside a dusty hood, what just happened, what dark hole have they fallen into, who pushed them there, and fear surfaces, "silence, don't say anything," they're both the same, they never had the smallest chance to defend themselves, they've been hunted down like rats, they were waiting for them, "are we so important, really?" "enough with your siesta, let's go to the festival in Ustaritz right now, let's go and live a little," for once, they're headed to a party they will never reach, an interrupted book "for tomorrow," for the following day, *As I Lay Dying*, "No controles," page 215, *clown, nutcase, brother*, "this isn't Chile."

"Where are you taking us?"

"Shut your fucking mouth."

"We don't know anything, we..."

"Shut your fucking mouth, I said," and this time they put a piece of metal between their teeth, so there'll be no doubt.

Better to think before they speak now, better to say nothing, to say it only to themselves, listen to what that other personality who is over there, who is us but isn't us, that strong and brave personality, stronger and braver than us, stronger than our madness and our sanity, capable still of speaking: *Where are they taking us?*

Had they known it – but they didn't know it – they would have looked at their room differently, they would have hugged the friends who had lent them the house, they would have left a beautiful note, *nutcase, brother, nutcase: I should have stayed, writing, God, why would I leave home? Home is the best! Whose stupid idea was it to go to the festival in Ustaritz? But we have to live a little too, right? We have to die too, right? But not yet, it's too soon for me, I still have a lot left to write, please*.

Soto hears Zeberio panting next to him, "calm down," he'd like to tell him, but he doesn't say anything, and even though they know that this thing has only started, they don't know exactly, *nutcase, brother*, what this thing that has only just started is.

They don't know and they don't want to know. To go on living. That's the only thing they want.

And maybe they're evaluating the possibilities they may have for remaining alive. To begin with, they haven't seen the faces of their kidnappers, the kidnappers don't want them to know where they're going... Could that mean that they'll let them free once they know what they want to know? What's the point, otherwise, of taking so many precautions to hide their identities and the place where they're headed? As for what they want to know, too... what do they know? Hardly anything. If they intended to kill them, they wouldn't have cared about being identified by them, about their seeing the place where they were headed. Or maybe it wasn't exactly like that? Maybe covering their faces was a way of suppressing all vestiges of humanity, so that they could do whatever they had to do without much of a problem of conscience? Maybe they've started to elaborate a list of motives and possibilities that reveal that they shall remain alive, but maybe they can't think of any. The inside of the car stinks of dark tobacco, dark tobacco they've smoked before and they'll smoke after, but that right now no one is smoking. They both sweat under their hoods. "*Vire à esquerda*," says one in Portuguese: turn left. "*Lado direito*," on the right, says the other. They breathe with difficulty inside their hoods, they try to guess the road they may have taken, they calculate they've been on the road for twenty minutes, although it's difficult to be sure, everything feels longer in circumstances like those, and the kidnappers' words sound strange, "slowly, up there, stop here, turn here, careful." They made them bend their heads down twice, as if they were afraid someone might see them from the outside, a sign that perhaps they're driving through some urban area. *"Vire à esquerda," "Lado direito."* Portuguese? They don't seem like policemen, although maybe they are, Soto and Zeberio haven't crossed paths with enough policemen in their lives to be able to ascertain that. It's time to learn a lesson, to observe and to learn; thugs or policemen, the smell of Ducados cigarettes, by association they imagine them all dark skinned, with mustaches, "where are you taking us, where are you taking us," pain in the joints, pain in the wrists, they're not wearing handcuffs, they've tied their hands with ropes, therefore they are not, they must not be, real policemen, or maybe they are, Soto and Zeberio want to go on living, they aren't the first ones to disappear and they know it, they've carried out attacks with Benelli submachine guns on Basque refugees before, they won't be the last ones, "park there, next to the tennis court, we'll bring the car in later," an unreal voice said, a new voice, a voice that seems to come from outside the car, this one, yes, this one has a Basque accent, he pronounced *park* with the same inflection with which Zeberio pronounces *Faulkner*, stressing the *r* and the *k*, and ironically, that type of linguistic inflection was enough for Soto to feel a speck of optimism, they have so little to go on, that was enough. *We'll be able to understand each other among Basques – he tells himself – there's still hope.*

Even the words *tennis court* seem soothing to him, very far away from death, words that foretell some semblance of civilization not too far away, despite the fact that, according to Soto, "*vire à esquerda*," "tennis court," "*lado dereito*," give away too many details about their location. Because, let's not forget, this is 1983, and there aren't that many tennis courts in this area, even if you pinned a compass on Angelu and amplified the radius of the search zone to a fifty-minute drive stretching in any direction.

"Are you all right, Kepa?"

"Yes, Xabier. And you?"

The situation is dire. They call each other by their first names.

"Yes, say how very much you love each other now, because we've prepared separate rooms for you."

Diego added one more to the list of advantages of dying young, and when he did he lost, once and for all, the fear of flying he'd experienced every time he'd had to attend the launch of one of his books abroad: to die young is a sure way of sidestepping dementia.

How many people like me must there be on this flight? he asked himself, *people who wouldn't be too sorry to die in a plane crash? Am I so strange? Am I not climbing into a plane like someone playing a very passive, bourgeois, comfortable, and improbable game of Russian roulette?*

It sent shivers up Lazkano's spine to think that when Soto and Zeberio disappeared, his friend was reading Faulkner's *As I Lay Dying*. When they released him and he returned to the house in

Moulinaou Street, he found that unfinished book among Soto's things: his toothbrush, a thick, hand-knitted winter cardigan, so common in Basque families – Ariadne's thread, Penelope's continuation – and a salmon-pink-colored folder. Soto had paused his reading of Faulkner's novel on page 215, never suspecting the interruption could be final; they didn't let him read beyond that. Whereas the pages read up until then were plagued with effusive underscores, there wasn't a single mark on the book from there on. The way Lazkano had of perceiving existence changed completely after that finding, and he told himself that every human life is just that, a book left unfinished; without forewarning, we are deprived of the privilege of knowing the ending, and are made aware of the fact that perhaps that privilege is not always beneficial: it could be the case that the ending of the book that corresponds to us is not actually to our liking. Since then Lazkano has developed an almost pathological tendency to never leave a book half read, no matter how much he dislikes it. Be that as it may, he thought it a joke of destiny – a macabre one, in very bad taste – that it was precisely *As I Lay Dying* and not another book that happened to be Soto's final read; his stomach still turned when he thought about it. Lazkano was never able to read that book or any other by William Faulkner, as a matter of fact, he couldn't even stand the sight of a photograph of the great American writer. Poor William, it wasn't the old man's fault.

But, despite that, when he collected his belongings and glanced at the book, the last paragraph Soto had underscored with his pencil was branded into his memory forever: "But I ain't so sho that ere a man has the right to say what is crazy and what ain't. It's like there was a fellow in every man that's done a-past the sanity or the insanity, that watches the sane and the insane doings of that man with the same horror and the same astonishment."

After he had collected the salmon-pink folder and his few belongings, when he was abandoning the house on Rue Moulinaou, he saw the red-haired man in the café across the street, watching his steps with his freckle-covered pale face, his impassive stare. The red-haired man followed his steps down two streets. Lazkano feared for a moment that he might catch up with him and grab his arm.

But he did nothing of the sort.

But, if Diego had to choose one moment among all the moments he'd shared with Soto and Zeberio, if he had to choose one that stood out, he would choose, without hesitation, the day when they played a soccer game with some French tourists in the beach in Bidart. For once, and without establishing a precedent, their usual arguments put aside – so stimulating sometimes, so bittersweet others – the three of them formed a solid team to confront four young men from Bordeaux.

Three against four on an open beach. Zeberio took control of establishing the imaginary goals with mounds of sand and like children in a hurry they pounced on that leather ball, barefoot, bare ribbed – their skin too pale to identify them as tourists, who did they expect to fool – their jeans rolled up to their knees, as if they'd spent the evening crabbing and had just cast their scoop nets aside. They played until they collapsed with exhaustion, for the pure pleasure of the game, the still-fresh memory of the childhood times when nutmegging and dribbling a ball through the legs of your opponent brought as much pleasure or more as scoring a goal, and the long passes and the short passes, and the runs and the kickoffs, feeling the harsh rub of that insufficiently pumped ball that was starting to lose patches of leather on their insteps – the soccer balls of childhood were always partially deflated – with that natural tendency of children to get together and make teams spontaneously. To honor the truth, Soto, Zeberio, and Lazkano weren't so far away from adolescence, that inflection point in which leather balls are abandoned because other kinds of skins and rubs start to become more interesting – even though Diego found his two friends much more mature than he was, a thousand leagues ahead of him, two upright, upstanding men, anything but adolescents. Soto was in the third year of his philosophy degree, Diego in the first one of his sociology degree. Back then two years were an eternity. Lazkano remembers specially that pass from Zeberio, when the ball flew just above their opponent's head, how the ball fell like a stone on the sand, making a dry sound, and how before the ball could even bounce Soto had caught it, turned around and faced the goal, and executing one of those moves that even professional soccer players are rarely successful with, galloped unstoppable toward the opposing goal, leaving behind one of the Bordeaux guys who was blind to the turn of Soto's hips, easily fooling the second one, who slipped and fell, and then stopping dead in his tracks and straightening his back for a moment to look straight into the third one's eyes before tunneling the ball between his legs, and leaving the fourth one behind after a parabolic self-pass aided by the irregularity of the terrain and blind luck.

He was in front of the goal, he had arrived, and he'd done everything alone, the goal was wide open to him, and he decided to enjoy it, not to shoot just yet. The sound of the waves was every bit as good as the roar of the Bombonera, the Argentine stadium of the Boca Juniors; Soto was narrating his play like an apoplectic sports presenter about to have a heart attack halfway through a retransmission, in an Argentine accent, as if running weren't enough, nothing was enough for Soto, nothing sufficed, he wanted to add a layer of excitement to the beach in Bidart and to his nonexistent, shocked audience – *"vibrante,"* he said – and he did it all in a Spanish that the Bordeaux guys would be able to understand, linking sentences together *"chévere pibe*, amazing kid, Soto advances, in-credible, leaves him behind, mag-nificent, Soto

– 498 –

gets rid of one, he allows himself a smile, he's in control of the game, *bárbaro*, the way he dribbles that ball," and yes, it looks like the more he speaks, the more confident he gets, the stronger he gets, the fact that he's speaking, rather than leaving him gasping for air, seems to give him *more* air, speaking nonstop motivates him, it could be said that words don't tire him – he could never tire of words – but that, instead, they feed him, they are his gas; and when he reaches the oblique line drawn in the sand by someone's heel, he holds the ball with the top of his foot and, looking back, takes his time observing the four paralyzed guys from Bordeaux who are waiting for him to score once and for all, and looks at Zeberio, and farther behind, looks at Lazkano too, who's keeping watch over their goal – Lazkano is the most conservative of the three, he always was, the most conscientious and straight-laced, the one who'd rather be goalie and not leave his designated area; would those roles they each kept have remained the same over the years had Soto and Zeberio's fate been different? It was impossible to know.

Yes. Back then the world could still stop. They could stop the world. It was possible to stop a soccer ball with the top of one's foot in front of a goal's line. And together with the ball, the hands of clocks would stop, and so would the axis upon which the world turned. Soccer in that moment wasn't the opium of crowded stadiums, but a full-bodied game that satisfied the spirit. It was possible to place the ball on that border, on that dividing line, on that boundary, on that forbidden frontier, "no trespassing," "do not enter," and renounce an easy goal like that, to kneel down on the ground like the Pope used to do at airports, prostrate, to kiss the wet sand and give the ball a soft header toward the netless goal, like Soto did that time, "mag-nificent, vi-brante, did you see that, *bárbaro*, the way he dribbled that ball," making the soccer ball and the world cross that line very slowly, aided, slightly, by the frame of his very thick glasses.

Lazkano would like to remember Soto like that forever. With the strength he had when he scored that goal, full of impetus, in the zenith of an energetic display that could bother those who tire too easily, bringing together words and actions, the spoken with the executed, narrating his doings nonstop and letting you know what he was about to do too, that's who he was.

If Lazkano could choose one moment among all the moments he had shared with Xabier Soto and Kepa Zeberio, if he had to choose one that stood out, he would chose that one without a doubt, because it was a moment of solid happiness, pure joy without a speck of shadow, the pinnacle of childish enjoyment multiplied and highlighted by the fact that it was never filtered by the reasoning of adulthood, underscored by the certainty that you are tasting, from a time and a territory that have become yours, another time and another territory, an older one, that used to belong to you and you weren't able to appreciate sufficiently when it happened. It's still possible to jump across to the other side. And if jumping across to the other side is possible, then everything is possible.

They celebrated that goal like someone who returns from the beyond. Like intruders who return to infancy from grown-up land. And that's how Lazkano relives it each time, bringing Soto back to the world of the living, although for the longest time and until his father, Gabriel Lazkano, reemerged, fully alive, one of his greatest fears was that the defective DNA traveling down his poisonous genealogical tree would erase and betray everything, even that memory, the last one of all his memories he'd want to lose; he was tormented by the mere thought that that precious day in Bidart might be suppressed from his mind by the illness that had theoretically taken his father.

How would that memory come to be suppressed, should Lazkano succumb to that illness, so fashionable, so in-with-the-times, so destructive with everything that came its way? Would he forget everything at the same time? Or would he forget its main characters first, remembering the soccer game in an abstract way, without any specific emotion attached to it? Would everything become blurred and mixed up? Would he turn himself into the goal scorer? *"Chévere pibe,* amazing kid, Lazkano advances, in-credible, leaves him behind, mag-nificent, Lazkano gets rid of one, he allows himself a smile, he's in control of the game, *bárbaro.*" Would he forget Soto, or Zeberio? Would the place where it all happened, the beach in Bidart, be the first thing to disappear? First the setting and then the events? Or, on the contrary, would the setting be what his traitorous memory kept? A deserted, empty beach without characters, without soccer, without ball, and without guys from Bordeaux? What life impulse would be the last in the wasteland of his mind, when his brain cells were torn from the root by that deranged harvester that lays waste to everything? Would some smells remain? The smell of rotting algae? The wet touch of flat sand? Would the last thing to remain be that John Paul II habit of kneeling down to kiss the ground? Would they find him in that position in the corridor of the old folk's home when he tried to escape at night and the nurses guided him back to his room holding him by the arm? "We found a true Christian," his minders might say, amused by seeing old Diego kiss the ground, without realizing that what he was kissing was something very different, and he was doing it while inhabiting someone else's skin, on a beach in Bidart, and in honor of Soto, his friend. Perhaps Lazkano should leave it in writing; maybe we should all do it: "Bring me to the beach in Bidart when I start losing my memory, give me a half-deflated leather ball, a ball that has started to lose its patches, make me a goal with two mounds of sand, re-create my most sacred memory, armor-plate the scene, even if it's nothing but theater, force me to be a part of that play, even if I don't know which part I'm playing or why, let something mechanical or physical remain even when there's no mental or neuronal trace of it."

The last memories he had of Soto all had to do with his type-writer: the carbon paper Lazkano brought him, which he used to make copies. Copies made in tracing paper. How could Diego not have guessed that Soto would zealously keep those copies in a second salmon-pink-colored folder? One for the originals, one for the copies. Soto wanted to be a writer – his attitude was already that of a writer, precociously, ever since he was nine-teen years old – but even though he wrote innumerable outlines, he hardly saw any of his works published while he was alive; the play Gloria directed and produced was perhaps his most renowned work.

The books Soto never got to write filled Lazkano's mind. When Lazkano wrote his stories, he tried to do so as he imag-ined Soto would have done, although it was impossible. He tried to remember his tone of voice, but he'd almost forgotten it. Although Soto's image was very present in his mind, he'd forgot-ten his voice. With the passing of time he'd made up a new voice, but he knew it wasn't the real one. When Lazkano asked himself why he decided to become a writer, he harbored no doubt: it was because of Soto's influence. Because he decided, consciously or unconsciously, to take charge of the work Soto had left undone. He hated theater though, that was true. He chose some of Soto's tendencies while discarding others. Sometimes we live instead of the dead, doing things they would have done in their honor. Won't that entity that's beyond sanity and madness laugh at us, knowing that most of the things we do, we do them for someone that isn't us? Are we the original or the copy in the transfer paper under the carbon paper? One and the other, in turns? Or maybe we are the most thorough confusion, the black carbon paper used over and over and over again, an unintelligible chaos? Do we at least know when we are truly the original and when the copy of that person we admired? Are we really conscious that as the typewriter's ribbon gets spent and increasingly faint, the original becomes grayer, more diffuse, while the copy underneath – if the carbon paper is new – looks sharper than the original?

If there was one thing that Soto was, he was a fun guy, a volcano of exciting ideas, although it's true that, often, sentences someone might say in jest might later gain weight and significance if they die a tragic death.

"What does a rational dictator do before he's about to be gunned down by a firing squad?"

"You don't know that joke, Lazkano? It's a revolutionary's joke…"

"A rational dictator, *primo*, gives an order before being gunned down: shoot me!"

Making a special effort, making an especially painful effort, Lazkano could almost imagine Soto's future, from the day they disappeared them until today. He could imagine Soto getting deeper into the organization, needing to go farther and farther from home, hiding in a farmstead in the French countryside, in a too-quiet environment for him, ready to leap into action at any given moment, or escaping to stare at the sea for a while, thinking that the first kidnap victims of an armed group are its own militants, that it's in fact a self-kidnapping, one that never ends, until they die or they're caught or they defect. Lazkano could imagine Soto reading spy novels or anything that fell into his hands, newspapers from beginning to end, complaining always that there was never enough reading material, the members of his commando complaining too because his voracious need to read put the whole group at risk when he made them all detour from the established route to stop the car and buy books, or carbon papers, the bloody carbon papers, "there's a bookshop here, come on, it's just a small detour," "vire à esquerda," turn left, "lado direito," on the right. He could imagine Soto moving into action, and returning after a device had failed, or being detained and miraculously escaping the gendarmerie by the skin of his teeth, or mentally sharing with his companions the aliquot responsibility that corresponded to each for the dead caused in an explosion, or leaving the organization, or planning for his future in jail, or reaching a top-level post just as he was about to leave it all behind, "it has to be you, this is an emergency, we wouldn't ask you in normal circumstances, but we don't have anyone else," and listening to the radio while in hiding, almost always the news, but also some music channel every now and then, Italian opera and France Culture, or, the very opposite, he could imagine Soto claiming that the only viable and legitimate way was the political way, or removed from the public arena, teaching literature at a university, or doing his doctoral thesis on Gabriel Aresti, pro- claiming, for example, let's say, that Gabriel Aresti was a virus sent from outer space, or writing a comparative analysis between the poems of Gabriel Aresti and David Bowie's songs, passionately and with huge doses of imagination.

Making a big effort, making an enormous effort and at risk of putting his mental health at risk, he could imagine Zeberio working in his parents' lighting showroom, zealously drawing up the store inventory, whether it was the inventory of a light- ing store or a store filled with accumulated explosive materials; carrying small messages to Iparralde, the French side, or bring- ing small messages across from Iparralde, always working on his own, until he was detained, until they took him out of his house in the middle of the night, in handcuffs and with a black sweater over his head; or creating his own business, something to do with solar panels perhaps, and climbing roofs on the mountains and valleys of the Basque Country to install them, working always in the open air and feeling that his work had a point, that those solar panels contributed to creating a freer nation; he could imagine him as a counselor in his hometown, as a representative of an illegalized party, or angry with his neighbors because he didn't want them to organize an homage to him after spending thirteen years in jail. He could imagine Zeberio visiting his friend Soto in the prison in La Santé, laughing or crying or arguing enthusiastically, "the armed struggle doesn't make sense anymore," or "of course it does," or "the things I have to hear," or "so many people are getting killed or caught lately," or "maybe what's happening is that Spain's Minister of Home Affairs is now ruling our viscera," "no way, think CIA, more like it," "fuck off, please, don't tell me now that you too believe that they insert microchips in our molars," and "how can you be so sure they don't?" "the days of Ol' Owl Newhood are over," "Ol' Owl Barrionuevo is a special zone," "we're throwing rocks at our own roof," "you have no perspective, you can't have it, history will absolve us," "that's what Fidel used to say and look at him," "look at him what," "well, look at how he's doing," "tell me how he's doing," "he's about to snuff it, on his last legs," "coming to the point of snuffing it is one of the laws of life," "maybe it is," "do you feel strong, at least, Soto?" "I feel strong, Zeberio," "that's a lot," "courage, my friend."

As if meaning to say: "nutcase, brother, let's go, there's a festival in Ustaritz."

"We'll follow on foot from here."

They warn them that it's important they all know the surrounding mountains. Soto is not happy, he's not exactly fond of mountain hiking, but once he accepted, Lazkano followed, of course. Who is he to question his two friends?

The weather is spectacular: the first few rays of sunshine always so welcome come the spring, a moderate breeze, blue skies. They take off carrying small backpacks and enough food to last the day. They each carry an aluminum canteen filled with water, some cookies, *reineta* apples, sandwiches. On top of that, Soto surreptitiously grabs a bottle of wine at the last moment, without saying anything to the others. It's a weekday and there are hardly any people on the mountain tracks. They engage in animated conversation under the generous shade of the beeches, inhaling tiny traces of moss in the air, before they undertake the steepest slope. Pope John Paul II was in Loyola last winter, and there was nothing else to talk about on the TV and radio news and in newspapers, "how tiresome they were," Soto points out. But Zeberio is not completely against that visit, thinking that the Pope might have carried over a message that could bring peace.

"The Vatican is going to conspire in our favor, is that so? Thanks to them we will achieve our own independent little state, like theirs, ain't that a joke. That dude didn't come here for anything other than to criticize the divorce laws and to delay abortion laws..."

Soto is always very belligerent about the church, he doesn't let them get away with anything.

"Not all priests are the same, Soto. The Basque church fulfilled an important role as an intermediary; the survival of the Basque language, who do you think we owe it to?"

"Fuck our mother tongue if it needs the baptismal font to survive! I'd rather be a Frenchie if that's the case... *Cherchez la femme*, and fuck them all!"

"Even at the inception of ETA, the church had..."

"Yes, of course, and they were there when Adam and Eve fucked for the first time, I know the story."

As the conversation grows increasingly heated, Zeberio points at little caves, huts and cabins peppered along their route: "There, there and there." There. "And there too."

That's all he says: there. Or maybe he specifies something else: "too humid there," or maybe "there, don't even think about it." With that, he makes it clear what each of those hiding places are good for.

As the vegetation becomes sparser and the shelter of trees diminishes, the conversation shrinks too. They begin to run out of strength, and they need everything they've got to face the steep slope. Despite being the biggest and hairiest one of the three, with his big beard, Zeberio is also sweating the least. Every now and then, when he sees Soto gasping for air, barely able to make it, Zeberio increases his pace, forcing his companions to walk faster and feeling superior to them for an instant, silently mocking his friends' suffering. One-upmanship is a curious beast, the way we inadvertently use it when we suddenly experience it, even if it's a squalid and ridiculous kind of power, we use it as a whip in the most innocent of ways sometimes, and other times we pitilessly harass and subjugate our friends with it. And if we enjoy it, it's not necessarily because we're sadistic and don't love our equals, but because we love ourselves a little more and won't disdain an opportunity to show our ability to have one over them. Perhaps it's not exactly like that. But there are moments and moments. And sometimes it was like that. In that moment, it was like that.

"Some water?"

"Keep your holy water for whenever you need it, Zeberio. I have my own."

Zeberio decides to be a bit evil. "Look, the peak is over there," he tells them.

His friends use the last remainder of their reserves to get there, as well as the last of the water they carry.

But when they reach the peak, as soon as Soto and Lazkano put their backpacks down, Zeberio continues walking on, whistling.

"It's right over there: just one more hill."

"There's another hill?"

Another hill, and another. Zeberio pulls their leg over and

over. And he keeps telling them: "There and there;" or maybe: "there, don't even think about it;" "too humid there."

Maybe that's the lesson: *there's always another hill.*

By the time they realize, the fog is over them. A tiny trace of moss takes over the air and stays there. A slight scent that, against all logic, seems to come from the sky this time.

"*Maite ditut maite, gure bazterrak, lanbrak ezkutatzen dizkida- nean,*" Zeberio sings.

Lazkano accompanies him, whistling shyly along to Mikel Laboa's song about his love of Basque landscapes half-hidden in the mist; he's the extra there, a distant second voice there to support Zeberio's, he always was, next to his two friends – "uh, uh, wah, wah."

"Let's hope it doesn't rain."

"No, it's gonna hold."

But it doesn't hold.

A thunderclap booms as if ready to destroy heaven and earth. As the rumble still echoes in their auditory chambers, the down- pour catches them, unprotected, in a completely exposed area without a single pathetic tree to shelter under. Their footwear and summer clothes are immediately soaked, and hard as Soto tries to push his dripping mane from his face, it keeps steaming up his glasses; his "toupee," needless to say, has seen better days. They are wearing shorts, Zeberio is the only one wearing long woolen socks. Soto's and Lazkano's ankles are covered in little cuts and scrapes caused by the brambles and the nettles. Having slipped in the mud, Soto hits the ground twice: reckless man of asphalt that he is, he's not even wearing hiking boots, but his usual sports shoes. Zeberio and Lazkano have to help him stand up. Every time he falls on the ground he swears loudly and feels his backpack to make sure that the bottle of wine he grabbed without saying anything to his friends hasn't broken. Lazkano had never seen Soto so annoyed.

"Who said it would hold? It didn't motherfucking hold, you fuckers."

Zeberio can't confess this to them now, but he's taken them down a shortcut he doesn't usually take, thinking they would reach their destination quicker that way. But he's lost now.

It's almost as if he's deliberately choosing the most zigzagging paths, and although he did hike up to the peak some time ago, it was actually quite a long time ago. Zeberio's clumsiness is a hundred-percent down to his unfamiliarity with the route. The mist, however – not everything is bad news – hides Zeberio's slips and his worried face from Soto's and Lazkano's eyes. It's not only Soto and Lazkano who are stumbling along now.

"Don't lose sight of whoever is in front of you, okay?"
He noticed the nervousness in his voice when he issued the warning. Did the other two notice their guide's unease?

Zeberio slips again and hits the ground face-first.

"Kissing the ground now? You're developing some very

Vatican-y habits lately, my friend," Soto jokes, without the strength to smile. His sarcasm can't smooth out the rough edges this time.

When he gets up from the ground, Zeberio doesn't feel the muddy, gravelly path he expected under his palms, but hard rock instead. And on the other side, he realizes, a slope. And something worse than a slope: a precipice. "That's the best part. The risk of the fall, and the certainty that you'll have the chance to fall again."

They should stop and seek refuge somewhere. But where?

Soto is still grumbling. He would beat Zeberio up something good if he knew they were lost.

"You're going to get us killed by pneumonia, Wojtyla."

"Calm down: we're going to take shelter over there."

"There? Where is *there*, Zeberio? There's always another hill."

There's always another hill. We won't live long enough to see it.

Saved by the bell. Zeberio breathes again. At last, a safe place where they can wait things out. The unease is over. This *there* is familiar to him; a hut made out of dark rock, guarded by a barrier. Nothing is more comforting than the feeling of knowing that you have been lost, when you no longer are. They walk into the shepherd's hut. An owl has its nest there, in one of the gaps that doubles as a window. It doesn't even flinch when the three young men come in. It scrutinizes the three friends with its eyes wide open, without fear, with curiosity, paternalistically, even.

"Shit!"

Soto's heart is about to leap out of his chest.

"This... won't this dude bring us bad luck?"

Having regained his strength, Zeberio is all jokes now.

"It's an owl, Soto, a beautiful, wise bird if there ever was one."

The owl's neck does an almost 360 degree turn. It's an extraordinary sight.

"I'd say it looks like Ol' Owl Newhood... You don't think it's been sent by Orwell's Big Brother?"

Nineteen eighty-four is still a few months away.

"Take your footwear off and leave the clothes by the door, try not to dampen the hay too much."

It's raining nonstop outside.

"It doesn't look like it's going to stop raining," Lazkano dares to offer, limiting himself, like he almost always does, to corroborating some small informative aspect.

It's getting dark. The rain won't stop. They'll have to spend the night there.

"There are a couple of blankets there."

"I'm not about to sleep under horse blankets, Zebe. I don't need any more bugs than you tonight."

"I brought them myself the other day," Zeberio counters, extracting a couple of woolen coverings from a hidden box quite proudly, like someone offering clean sheets in a hotel. "Surprised?"

In the hideout, according to what Lazkano can see, there are also some iron bars and dry matches. As if he didn't admire him enough before, witnessing Zeberio's planning abilities makes him rise even higher in his estimation.

Soto is suddenly animated. The Scottish woolen blankets are to blame.

"Unbelievable, Zeberio. Really? What is this, your love nest? Is this where you bring your little nuns? You like sex in the wilderness, hey?"

"Do you have anything to eat left?"

Soto's face brightens up.

"Diego, get the bottle of wine out of my backpack!"

"You brought a bottle of wine?" Zeberio asks, dumbfounded.

"We need everything we can get to survive the night."

"Do you have anything to open the bottle with?"

Soto's color drains from his face. Zeberio can't help laughing.

"No ... you don't have a corkscrew in your love hideout? You didn't bring your Swiss Army knife, Wojtyla?"

"I would have brought it, had I known you would be bringing a bottle of wine, commander ... "

"Fuck, Zebe, I wanted to surprise you ... "

"And you did, Soto, you did, big time ... but bring a wineskin next time!"

After discarding the possibility of opening the bottle by hitting its neck against the rock to avoid risks and cuts to their hands, they decide to reserve the wine for a better occasion. They bring wet cookie crumbs to their mouths. They eat one *reineta* apple each. Zeberio improvises a fire and digs out a pack of spaghetti from his Aladdin cave. Since they don't have a pot in which to boil water, they start eating the spaghetti uncooked, anything to stop the groans from their stomachs. It occurs to Lazkano that they could heat up the spaghetti in the fire, as if they were skewers. With an effort of the imagination, they can pretend they're eating tiny bread sticks.

Lazkano is proud to have been the one to think they could heat up the uncooked spaghetti in the fire. For once, he feels useful to his two leaders.

A wet but rainless dawn has risen.

"Look!"

Zeberio says *Look!* in the same way he's been saying *there. There: look!*

The owl is asleep.

"I'll bet my bottom dollar you've never seen a sleeping owl."

No one answers him. It's proving hard enough to stretch out their limbs and remove bits of straw from their mouths and the backs of their necks.

They shake the Scottish blankets and fold them up to put back in their hiding place while still yawning. Soto's eyes look tiny before he puts on his very thick glasses. Barely awake, he and

Lazkano look like old men. Zeberio, however, looks just as alert as he always does, which would seem to suggest he's been up for a while.

"Bring a couple of sleeping bags to your love nest next time. Otherwise none of your nuns is ever going to want a repeat session," Soto suggests.

"Sleeping bags and a couple of glasses, to serve the champagne you'll remember to bring without saying anything to anyone."

Despite not having even rubbed the sleep dust out of his eyes, Soto finds the strength to say goodbye to the owl.

"Look after yourself, Ol' Owl Newhood. Until we meet again."

They stop at the guard's house to have breakfast. Fried eggs with enormous yolks, a piece of stewed meat, fried bacon and broth, all of it accompanied by crusty dark homemade bread that's just come out of the oven. All three eat their breakfast without sharing a word, like castaways who have just been rescued, to the delight of the lady of the house, who is overjoyed to see how healthy *her boys* are. When they finish the first round, with a mischievous look, Soto orders a second round of breakfasts by drawing a circle around their three empty plates with his index finger. Afterward he opens his backpack to take out the bottle of wine, he'd almost forgotten it.

"Would you open the *wojtyl* of wine for us, madam of the house?"

The woman, it goes without saying, doesn't understand their private joke about the Pope, but when the three young men start laughing raucously she joins them too, they all end up laughing at the same time, and afterward they echo their own laughter, drunk in the laughter, celebrating the laughter with more laughter; shaking their heads right and left, *clown, what's wrong with your brain, nutcase, brother*, the three men continue eating, *fool, nutcase*, as if the theater of the world was limited to the circumference of those white porcelain plates, following the bacon with broth and the broth with egg, trying to stem the runaway free flow of volcanic egg yolk with the bread while they chew on the egg white, trying to turn that overflow of orange lava into invisible straight paths before taking that piece of bread into their mouths.

"There's your open bottle."

"There?"

"There, there and there."

The three friends laugh again, without apparent reason.

There's always another hill.

Adding up the ages of the three of them, they're not even as old as the sixty-five-year-old lady of the house. The cheap wine smells like paradise.

Only two of the three windows of the guard's house are open. The windows don't have curtains. The rays of sun soak the unvarnished floor with optimism, casting vivid puddles of rectangular light, reaching, bit by bit, the faces and the eyes of the three young men.

The light blinds them, and doesn't let them see anything that could take them from such happiness.